GUARDIAN
OF THE
FLAME

A SEVEN WONDERS NOVEL

GUARDIAN
OF THE
FLAME

A SEVEN WONDERS NOVEL

T.L. HIGLEY

B&H
PUBLISHING GROUP
Nashville, Tennessee

978-0-8054-4732-3

Published by B&H Publishing Group,
Nashville, Tennessee

Dewey Decimal Classification: F
Subject Heading: SEVEN WONDERS OF THE WORLD—
FICTION \ LOVE STORIES \ HISTORICAL FICTION

1 2 3 4 5 6 7 8 • 13 12 11 10 09

To my dear friends
Kelly Shennett
Michelle King
Connie Taylor
Amie Shumski
Dawn Hill
and
Joan Savoy

Through our many years of friendship,
you have taught me so much about what it means
to truly be a woman of beauty. I love you all.

Acknowledgments

Writing the Seven Wonders Novels continues to be a wonderful mix of research, writing, and travel. I am grateful to many for making this adventure possible.

Thank you to all the folks at B&H who work together to get the manuscript from my hands to bookstore shelves, with special thanks to Julie Gwinn for all you do to promote B&H fiction.

Karen Ball, it had been a long-time dream of mine to have you for an editor. Thanks for all you did to improve this book!

Thank you to my agent, Steve Laube. It's great fun to have a supportive and talented agent who also loves history!

Once again, my family and friends have offered encouragement, the occasional kick-in-the-pants, and most of all support. Ron, thank you for partnering with me in all I do in life, including the writing. I couldn't do it without you. Rachel, Sarah, Jake, and Noah, thank you for not complaining when you hear that "Mom's writing" and for making sacrifices yourselves. Life with the five of you is my best adventure ever!

Word List

abbas—*(Egyptian)* lion

agora—the marketplace

centuria—originally one hundred, but later eighty Roman soldiers organized into ten *contubernium*

chitôn—a form of clothing; square of linen draped and held in place at the shoulder by several small pins.

contubernium—the smallest organized unit of soldiers in the Roman army, comprised of eight legionaries

cornicen—officer in the Roman army, whose job was to signal salutes to officers and sound orders to the legions

corona vallaris—a gold crown awarded to a Roman soldier for achievement in battle

desino—*(Latin)* stop

gladius—*(Latin)* sword

heptastadion—causeway connecting Pharos Island to the coast of Alexandria, seven stadia long (about one mile)

himation—clothing usually worn over a chitôn, but made of heavier drape; a cloak

incedo dextro—*(Latin)*, march right

incedo sinistro—*(Latin)*, march left

kylix—*(Greek)*, drinking cup

the Legion—the entire Roman army; more common usage: the heavy infantry, a military unit, of the Roman army

legionary—professional soldier of the Roman army

milites—Roman foot soldiers

mina—unit of weight equal to 60 shekels

obol—a silver coin or unit of weight equal to one sixth of a drachma

optio—second-in-command of a Roman centuria

parados—the corridors in the front of the stage in a Greek theater

pilum—javelin (pl., pila)

Proginosko—*(Greek)* to foreknow

pugio—a dagger

signifer—standard bearer of the Roman legion

sporran—studded apron on the Roman sword belt

stadia—a unit of length; one stadium is equal to approximately 600 feet

testudo—Roman military formation, in which shields were held so that the soldiers resembled a tortoise

uraeus—the rearing golden cobra used as a symbol of Egyptian royalty and diety

vitis—the grapevine staff that signaled a Roman soldier's authority; a centurion's staff

In a lofty tower set high above a teeming city,
There lived a solitary woman
Whose guilt and pain had long ago turned to ugliness.
And when the ugliness became its own prison,
And the pain of rejection too much to bear,
Loneliness seemed the only answer.

ONE

Alexandria, Egypt
48 BC

S ophia pressed her forehead against the chilled window glass
of her private chamber and tried to capture a glimpse of life,
far below and out of reach.

The harbor, more than one hundred cubits down, churned
with boats whose sails flapped in the dying sun like the scales
of white fish, and with ant-sized servants who scurried to deliver
supplies to her lighthouse before its Keeper punished them for
their delay.

On a white-cushioned couch behind her, one of Euripides's
plays called for her return to its lines of tragedy. She resisted. The
words had already bled into her heart with remembrances she
wished to avoid.

Enough foolishness. Shoulders back and eyes unblinking, she
crossed the room to a cedarwood desk. Her astronomy charts
covered the wall above, but it was a more practical papyrus that
she spread on its surface. She weighted the top corners with
two small statuettes of Isis and Osiris with a muttered apology

to the gods, and let the bottom corners curl upon themselves. The late afternoon sun burned through the window, setting dust particles afire in the air and touching the lighthouse's fuel consumption chart and the scrawled labor requirements. Sophia retrieved her sharpened reed and ink and added notations to the latest entry.

Work first. Then she could spend the evening brooding over Euripides's plays, and even the past.

Behind her, sharp knuckles attacked the outside of her door. Only one person knocked like that, and only one person would bother to make the climb halfway up the lighthouse's three hundred cubits.

The door flew open before she invited entrance. Her personal servant stumbled in, eyes wide.

Sophia jumped to her feet. "Romans?"

Ares leaned against a marble stand that held the sculpted bust of Plato, winded. The heavy-footed Roman legion had marched into Alexandria several weeks earlier. Sophia had been waiting for war, as one waits for a ship returning from far-off trade. *Knowing it will come, never certain when.*

But Ares was shaking his head. "She is here! She climbed over the—"

Ares was shoved aside and another figure slid into the room. Sophia's heart danced over a few beats, then settled into a staccato. The young woman before her smiled, the languid look of a woman who knows her own power. "Sophia"—she extended both her jeweled hands—"how I have missed you!"

Sophia let out her breath with one quiet word. "Cleopatra!" She waved to her servant. "Leave us, Ares."

The boy backed out of the room.

"And not a word of this!" Sophia called after him.

When he had closed the door, she took a hesitant step toward the younger woman. "How? Have you made peace at last with your brother?"

Cleopatra flung the question aside with a wave of her hand. "The little brat knows nothing of monarchy. It is those three leeches that hiss in his ears that are the problem." She spotted the black and gold *kylix* of wine and brightened. "I am parched." She crossed to the table and ladled wine into an alabaster cup. "The sea, you know." She filled another cup and handed it to Sophia.

Sophia studied her, speechless. Her magnetic power seemed undimmed by her recent exile. Her white robe, trimmed in gold and purple, hung a bit more loosely on her frame.

"You are thinner."

Cleopatra sipped the wine and grimaced. No doubt it had been left too long in the bowl. "Will you never cease to fret over me, Sophia?"

Sophia's breathing had returned to normal, and she found a place on the couch. "Sit. Tell me."

Cleopatra came to her, dropped a knee to the couch, then curled herself next to Sophia like a leopard settling to rest. She lifted the skull of a panther from the low table before them and turned it around with her long fingers.

"Did you get in unseen?" Sophia asked.

"Apollodorus rowed me into the harbor in a small boat. We docked in the Eunostos Harbor, away from the crowds. I climbed ashore at the base of the lighthouse and circled to the door. I am safe here, Sophia."

Sophia swallowed. "Why take such a risk?"

"It has been an eventful few days." Cleopatra set the skull back on the table with a *thunk*.

"I thought you were in Syria."

"I was. My little brother Ptolemy and his three sycophants are camped at Pelusium, with their armies ready to attack my troops. But I believe the gods have other plans." She smiled again, the scheming grin Sophia had known and loved since Cleopatra's childhood.

"What have you done?" Sophia closed tight fingers around the girl's wrist, as fear clamped itself around her heart.

Cleopatra inclined her head and laughed, then stroked Sophia's arm with her fingertips. "An opportunity has come to me on the heels of Ptolemy's foolishness."

"So what has your brother done?"

"The Roman Pompey fled to my brother, hoping for Ptolemy's support against Julius Caesar. But Ptolemy's three advisors decided they would rather gain the favor of Caesar. They greeted Pompey with a knife point."

"He is dead?"

Cleopatra nodded. "And now Caesar has arrived here in the city." She crossed one leg over the other and bounced her foot. "My brother's men sent him Pompey's head as a gift. Caesar was furious at his adversary's ignoble death."

Sophia slapped her thigh. "These barbaric Romans. Impossible to comprehend. They stomp all over the world with their insatiable lust to conquer, but when someone kills their enemy, they are angered."

Cleopatra's eyes glittered. "Yes, he sounds fascinating, doesn't he?"

Sophia's apprehension returned. "What are you going to do?"

"Take advantage of the opportunity."

"It is not safe for you in the city, Cleopatra. You must return to Syria, under the protection of your troops."

Cleopatra removed her hand from Sophia's arm and unfolded herself from the couch. "You would have me remain a child forever! I am no longer your student."

Sophia stood as well, matching the fire in Cleopatra's eyes with her own. "You are twenty-one!"

Cleopatra flung her hair over her shoulder. Her face was a mere handspan from Sophia's. Her voice was low. "And I am Queen of Egypt."

Sophia shifted away, but Cleopatra clutched at her, spun her back to herself. "Do not be angry with me, my Sophia. Tell me you love me still."

Sophia sighed. *I could never control her.* "Would I have spent all those painful hours teaching you the languages of Egypt if I did not love you?"

Cleopatra lips formed a pout, reinforcing her youth. "You were well paid by my father."

Sophia touched Cleopatra's cheek. "And I would have done it for nothing."

The younger woman's expression cleared. "There, now you have made me happy. Next you must tell me how beautiful I look in spite of my thinness, and then I will be satisfied."

Sophia looked over the queen's long reddish-brown curls, her regal features, the fine fabric of her robe, and the twinkling jewels stitched to her headpiece and wrapped around her arms and fingers. "Cleopatra, as always, you are stunning."

The girl fluttered her eyelashes playfully. "You have them all fooled, Sophia. But not me." She pointed to Sophia's masculine tunic, carelessly belted. "I know the real woman beneath all your manly clothes and your harsh manner. I know there is something good buried."

Sophia's inner restlessness stilled, as though she had grown cold. She nodded once, unable to answer, and then retreated to the couch. *Let us speak of something else.*

Cleopatra dropped beside her and leaned her head against Sophia's shoulder with a sigh. The sun's last rays splashed through the west window and lit up the gold trim that edged her robe.

"What will you do?" Sophia whispered, knowing she would not like the answer.

Cleopatra did not lift her head. "Caesar is ill-disposed toward my brother and his advisors tonight. I will cause his favor to fall on me."

"And how will you accomplish this?"

Cleopatra laughed. "I know it has been a long time, Sophia. But do not tell me you have forgotten how a woman can gain the favor of a man."

Sophia pulled away from her. "No, Cleo. No."

Cleopatra tossed her hair over her shoulder. "I have only this brief moment to gain his favor. My brother will surely arrive by tomorrow. It must be tonight."

Sophia's stomach clenched. "You are young, inexperienced. And he is a Roman!"

"The world is changing."

Sophia exhaled heavily. "For more than two hundred years your family has ruled Egypt. The Egyptians have come to accept that. And you understand their ways. You respect their love of knowledge, you share their desire to decipher the world. You have even embraced their gods. But these Romans, Cleo, they are crude savages, interested only in blood and victory and power!"

Cleopatra looked away, to the darkening window. "I think you forget how interested in power I am myself, Sophia."

She traced Cleo's strong jawline. "Born to rule. Raised to rule. Queen at eighteen." *And exile in the face of your brother's treachery has done nothing to dull the hunger.* "Can I not talk you out of this foolishness?"

Cleopatra's lips twitched in amusement. "There we are. I knew you would come around." She pulled Sophia toward her and once more leaned against her shoulder. "Just let me stay until the darkness has fully fallen." She sighed deeply. "I am so tired."

Sophia relaxed into the cushions and took the weight of Cleopatra's exhaustion. The girl was asleep in moments, leaving Sophia to her own thoughts. She let Cleo sleep as the evening wasted.

Her hair hung over Sophia's shoulder, where Sophia own hair would have lain if she had not cropped it close to her head. She stroked Cleopatra's robe with one finger, then draped the fabric over her own thigh.

She is everything I am not.

And yet despite their differences, Sophia always found herself more whole in Cleo's presence. The girl was like pressed oil, filling in the cracks and brittle places of Sophia's soul with something warm and smooth. When they were together, all the tension and anger that seemed to define Sophia ran out of her, leaving her feeling almost human.

Sophia had begun to doze as well when Ares's knuckle-bruising knock again sounded at the door. She glanced down to Cleopatra, but the girl's gentle breathing continued. She shifted her to the cushions, then slipped away to open the door.

"For the love of Isis, Ares, what is it now?"

He stepped in, one hand still on the door. "A message for you, *Abbas.*" He held a scrap of papyrus. She pushed him into the hall and half-closed the door behind them.

Ares had called her *abbas* since he was a young boy. Whether the Egyptian word for "lion" was a compliment or a slight depended on each of their moods.

Ares peered over her shoulder, into her chamber.

"Well, give the thing to me, Ares! Don't simply stand there!"

Ares sighed and held it up to her. "Brought by one of the Library's slaves." He stepped close and held the message to her eyes.

Sophia moved back a pace. "You don't need to breathe all over me!" She snatched the scrap and read it, her pulse quickening at the request inked there.

"Will you go?"

She scowled at Ares. "Reading my messages now?"

The young man, though half her age, stood much taller than Sophia. He gave her one of his crooked half grins. "It is a long climb."

She shoved the papyrus back into his hand and turned away. "There is nothing in the Library that cannot be brought here to me. Send a message to Sosigenes that he may visit me here in the lighthouse if he wishes."

"The message sounded urgent."

She whirled on him. "Then I suppose he should run!" Ares pursed his lips, and Sophia exhaled. This boy knew her well by now. He had long ceased to be offended or intimidated by her moods. "Why can Sosigenes not send a report as usual?" she asked herself aloud.

"Perhaps he thinks it is time for you to emerge from hiding."

"I am not hiding!" Sophia put a hand out to the door. "I rarely need to leave the lighthouse. Why should today be different?"

"Because today someone has asked."

The door blurred before her. It was true, no one had requested her presence in the city for a great while. "They fear me."

Ares's laugh was soft. "Yes, the mighty Artemis, commanding the world from her high tower."

Sophia's lips curled into a sneer and she faced the boy again. "Which am I, Ares, a lion or a goddess?"

He lowered his eyes. "Both need sometimes to emerge from solitude."

"Well, not today. Send the message to Sosigenes. And send ten drachma with it, to remind him under whose patronage he spends his hours."

Ares bowed his head and turned to the ramp, his silence seeming to condemn her.

Sophia closed her eyes and pressed her fingers into the bridge of her nose. She disliked leaving the lighthouse, and it annoyed her that the old scholar would summon her. She pushed back the thought that Ares's comments were the true source of her irritation, then reentered her private rooms and lit several lamps. The flames played on the deep reds and blacks of the room's furnishings, on which she had spared no expense. The luxury of her chamber rivaled any in the palace. The money that flowed continually to the lighthouse enabled her to live as she wished.

She retrieved the wine Cleo had poured. At the window she lifted the cup to the harbor in a silent salute, then sipped the wine, ignoring its bitter finish. *Yes, I live as I wish.*

And every day the ever-present sea breezes whispered in her ear like a spiteful friend who would never let her forget.

She spent an hour over the charts, fine-tuning the plans for the coming month, searching for the slightest opportunity to increase efficiency. When the first noises shot up the cylindrical core of the lighthouse, Sophia barely noticed.

Moments later she dropped her reed on the desk, startling Cleopatra. The girl gasped, then heard the shouts. She turned wide eyes to Sophia. "Who is it?"

Sophia tilted her head to the noise again. Her fingers tightened on her chair.

"Soldiers."

TWO

Sophia placed herself between the door and Cleopatra. Cleo's servant, Apollodorus, was the first through the door. He burst in without knocking and scanned the dark room, his swarthy features tense.

"I am here," Cleopatra said, standing.

"Soldiers, my queen."

"Ptolemy's?"

He shook his head. "Romans."

Sophia crossed to the door. "Do they know she is here?"

"I know nothing more." The servant circled Sophia to stand near Cleopatra.

"Stay here," Sophia said. "I will get rid of them."

Cleopatra bit her lip. "Be cautious."

Sophia nodded, then left the room and began the descent down the spiral ramp, her chest pounding. Cleopatra should not have come, should not have risked capture. *And I should have sent her away to safety.* A sheen of perspiration broke over her forehead. She would keep her word and get rid of the Romans.

Sophia's quarters were in the first of the three tiers of the mighty lighthouse, also the tallest. If she tilted her head backward while descending the interior ramp, she could see straight up through the octagonal second tier and cylindrical third, to the final platform, where the light guided ships into the harbor.

The first tier held nearly fifty rooms, positioned around the spiraling ramp that led to the massive Base. Sophia ran lightly down the ramp, accustomed to the incline's pull on her legs. Over the rail she could see the torch-lit bottom floor filling with the clanking ranks of barbarians.

"They've all gone to bed," Ares was saying to one of them. "You will have to come back another time."

"We have orders, boy," a strident voice answered. Sophia could see the speaker advance on Ares. He did not look into the gloom above him to see her descent.

She reached the bottom of the spiral and pushed into the ranks that crowded the center hall. "What is this?" She raised her voice above the shuffle of studded sandals on the stone floor.

The group turned as one. A soldier stepped forward, the air of command about him.

"Are you master of the lighthouse, sir?" He spoke in Latin.

Sophia raised her head, let the torchlight play on her face. The soldier stepped back. "I ask your pardon, mistress. I did not realize—"

"Yes, I am Keeper of the lighthouse. What is the meaning of—of this?" She extended her hand to the sweating mass of leather and metal packed into the chamber. The torches rammed into wall sockets reflected from a thousand metal discs.

"We are here at Caesar's request, mistress. He wishes to meet with Cleopatra Philopator and her brother Ptolemy XIII and has summoned them to the royal palace."

Sophia shoved aside the soldiers to face the one who addressed her. His uniform differed from the others, with a crest of horsehair across his helmet. A red cloak of fine material hung from his left shoulder, and he wore waist-length chain mail armor and an ornate belt. Sophia did not miss the sword and dagger strapped to his body.

"Summoned them to the palace?" she repeated. "Do you mean to their *own* palace?" She looked him up and down, not even trying to hide her disdain. Two soldiers lowered long *pila* across the commander, the spears forming an *X* across his chest.

"Julius Caesar has taken up residence there, yes."

She laughed. "You say 'taken up residence' as though you are civilized men and not a plague of insects that has crawled out of the harbor to gorge on the wealth of Egypt."

The soldier removed his helmet and glared at her. "I am Lucius Aurelius Bellus, Pilus Prior of the First Centuria of the Sixth Cohort." He took a step toward her. "Men have been killed for words less offensive than yours."

"Perhaps I should use a language other than your own then to tell you what I think of you and your Sixth Cohort. What shall it be? Greek? Egyptian?"

Bellus straightened and pierced her with his hard gaze. "The choice is yours, mistress," he said in Greek, and then switched to Egyptian. "I would be happy to debate you in any language."

A learned Roman soldier? She fought to keep the momentary admiration from her expression and instead lifted her chin. "I was not aware that Caesar trained his soldiers in anything more than separating men from their heads." Inwardly she cursed the note of respect that had crept into her voice.

Bellus grinned. He pushed aside the crossed *pila* and stepped from the ranks to speak to her quietly. "He does not. But we have some moments of leisure to pursue other interests."

Sophia looked away from his smile and smoothed a hand over her tunic. Learned in languages or not, the man was a Roman, and he had brought his beasts into her lighthouse.

"The queen, mistress." Bellus murmured, too near her ear. "Is she present?"

Sophia put a hand to the back of her neck, to the hair she kept trimmed too short. "Of course not. She would not be so foolish. Take your cohort and leave at once!"

"Oh, this is not the cohort, mistress. This is only the first *centuria* of the sixth cohort. A cohort—"

"I care nothing for your military organization! You do not belong in my lighthouse or my Egypt, and I would see you all drowned in the harbor!"

Bellus's pleasantry faded and his hand drifted to his sword. "Take care, mistress. Or I may forget again that you are a woman."

Sophia blinked once then crossed her arms. "You are not welcome here," she said in a low voice.

Bellus tilted his head to look up the ramp, and Sophia's shoulders tensed. She stilled herself, purposing that he should not see her concern. But then he gave her another piercing stare, replaced his helmet, and commanded his men to exit the lighthouse. They filed through the courtyard to the south entrance in pairs, with Bellus at the rear. Before he disappeared through the doorway, he turned. Sophia could see his glare burning past the cheek plates of his helmet. "If you should see the queen—"

"If I should see the queen, I should tell her that Egypt is in grave danger and she must find a way to secure her from foreigners who would take the best of her and feed it to blood-thirsty soldiers."

Bellus's eyes hardened, and his right hand crossed to his left side, where his *pugio* hung from his belt. He turned back to his men without a word, and they slipped into the Egyptian night to cross the lengthy causeway that separated her island from the city.

Sophia expelled a nervous breath and leaned back against the wall. She braced her fingers against the cool stone behind her and slowed her breathing and her heart. The image of Bellus's intriguing smile rippled through her memory and she brushed it aside. Better to remember his insults.

"Interesting Roman."

Sophia spun to find Ares at the base of the ramp, arms folded and a sly look in his eyes. Sophia straightened and lifted her chin. "He may know languages, but he does not know Egypt. And he does not know Cleopatra."

She crossed the hall, pushed past Ares, and began the ascent to her private quarters.

Several more lamps had been lit since she had run down to deal with the intrusion. Apollodorus stood in the center of her room.

Sophia searched the chamber. "Where is she? What has she done?"

Muted laughter came from the side of the room where one of her tapestry carpets had been partially rolled. Apollodorus shrugged, went to the rug, and lifted it from the queen. She looked up from where she lay on her belly, then propped herself on her elbows with a cunning wink. "It is time, Sophia."

Sophia jabbed a thumb over her shoulder. "Caesar's troops are prowling for you. Ptolemy's spies are everywhere. And you expect to walk out of here?"

Cleopatra jumped to her feet and embraced Sophia. "Not walk, no. Quickly, find Apollodorus some clothes, something to make him appear a merchant."

"A merchant?" Sophia looked to the servant, who again had nothing more than a shrug for her.

Cleopatra's eyes flashed. "A merchant with a special gift for Caesar the conqueror. For his eyes only. An expensive carpet."

"This is madness, Cleo. You will never reach Caesar without being spotted. And who knows but his summoning of you is only a ruse to bring you out, where he can make an end of you?"

Cleopatra was tying up her hair. "The clothes, Sophia! Quickly!"

Sophia exhaled her frustration, went to her door, and called down the shaft of the lighthouse to Ares, directing him to bring the appropriate clothing.

Minutes later they were all assembled in the South Wing of the Base, with Cleopatra stretched upon the carpet and Apollodorus in a tasseled cap and wide belt. Apollodorus rolled the queen into the rug. Ares helped him heave it upon his shoulder. The carpet balanced there, bent slightly at both ends, and Cleo grunted. "Make quick work of this, Apollodorus," she said.

Sophia rested her forehead on the rough underside of the carpet. "Promise me, Cleo," she whispered. "Promise me you will be safe."

The wriggling of the carpet ceased, and Sophia strained to hear Cleopatra's muffled response. "No one has taught me better how to be a woman of great strength, Sophia. Now it is time for you to see what I can accomplish."

Sophia nodded to Apollodorus. "Go," she said. And then called after him as he moved through the doorway, "And I want my carpet back!"

She followed them out, watched the rolled carpet bounce on the servant's shoulder as he climbed down the steps from the Base, its massive red granite blocks joined with molten lead and looming over them. He scrambled down the steep path, slid once and used a hand for balance. Their small boat was moored on the western side of the lighthouse island. Apollodorus would row around the tip of the island that separated the two harbors, then across the Great Harbor to the other side, where the royal palace boasted its own private quay. It would be the middle of the night before they arrived. Strange time for such a gift.

The Roman has no idea what a gift he will receive.

To her left, a lone figure with a small torch crossed the causeway to the lighthouse. Sophia reentered the lighthouse but did not return to her chamber, knowing that some message approached.

The servant that entered was from the Library, sent back by Sosigenes, perhaps.

"What is it?" she said.

The boy looked both surprised and frightened to be greeted by Sophia herself. His mouth dropped open, and his torch-hand lowered until the flames nearly licked his chin.

Sophia braced her hands on her hips. "Well? Do you have a message for me or not? Does Sosigenes refuse to come?" She had been sure a reminder of who paid for his lifestyle would have brought submission.

"He has fled, mistress. They all have."

Sophia's eyes narrowed. "Romans?"

His lower lip trembled. "Yes, mistress. Soldiers. In the Library."

"Not reading, I suppose?" She looked toward the eastern windows, across the Great Harbor, to where the Library and Museum stood near the palaces.

"No, mistress. They scatter the scrolls like kindling."

"Yes, of course they do. Looking for coins, no doubt." She looked through an eastern window, toward the royal quarter. "The addle-brained fools do not realize that they shove aside something far more valuable." She turned on the boy. "But you said that Sosigenes and the others have fled?"

He bobbed his head and blinked. "They are saying that Caesar wants to gather up all of them, to force scholars to give him their secrets."

Sophia rubbed at the tension in her forehead. "Perhaps one Roman *does* see more value in understanding the world than conquering it, then. Do you have any message for me?"

He seemed to remember his duty at last and pulled a rolled papyrus from his belt with shaky fingers.

She grabbed it from him. The note was from Sosigenes, short and dire: *"Sophia, All that we have worked for is in danger. Your husband's work, my own, and the others. I have news too important to write. Take care and trust no one. I will send word soon. Sosigenes."*

She waved the boy away then went to the nearby window, the scroll held loosely at her side.

Sosigenes had been friend and mentor to her husband many years ago. Since then, she had flooded the Library and the Museum with the support of her money, enabling dozens of mathematicians, astronomers, and inventors to pursue their theories without thought of earning their own bread. Kallias would have been proud of her efforts, pleased that in spite of everything, she still believed that the scholarship flowing from the Temple of the Muses would one day change the world.

The Great Harbor crawled with the lamps of a hundred ships at port, floating with fragrant Arabian myrrh and cinnamon from India, silk from the Far East and cedar from Lebanon. The ships would disgorge their luxuries into the insatiable city, then feast again on Egyptian emeralds and amethysts, on Nubian gold and ivory, even salt from the mines of Mali.

Alexandria, center of the world.

And yet, all of it now threatened by family betrayal and foreign intervention. The Museum, the Library, the scholars. These were Sophia's only reason to continue. If they fell, if they were trampled under the sandals of Roman soldiers, what would become of her?

She squinted into the night, her eyes roaming every craft in the water.

Somewhere out there, in one small boat, a young Greek woman rolled in a carpet had the power to change history.

Sophia spread her fingers against the glass.

Have you any idea of what is at stake, Cleopatra? You hold us all in your hands.

THREE

The little boat surged and dipped through the waters of the Great Harbor, until Cleopatra, in her flax cocoon, thought she might be sick. The idea amused her, actually. What would Sophia say about her precious carpet then?

Ah, Sophia. Cleopatra smiled and felt her tense muscles relax. She'd counted on her former tutor for reassurance and support, and Sophia had not failed. It had been good to spend the hours with her. Cleopatra felt strengthened for the task ahead.

"How much farther, Apollodorus?"

The servant shushed her. "We are too near other ships for conversation, my queen. It is not much farther. I can see the entrance to the royal harbor."

I have been gone too long.

She rubbed her cheek against the roughness of the fibers and sighed, remembering the lovely harbor built at the base of her palace, exclusively for royal use. Wrapped up as she was, she regretted that she would see none of the marble steps that led from the harbor to the palace entrance, the terra-cotta pots overflowing with yellow chrysanthemums, the jumping fountains in the center of the royal gardens.

Ah well, tomorrow all would be changed.

Cleopatra had no doubts regarding her plan, nor her ability to succeed. She had been trained for this moment by a family of ruthless politicians, a city obsessed with beauty, and a tutor who had filled her mind with enough knowledge and quick thinking to impress any man. Yes, she was well equipped to deal even with Julius Caesar, the Conqueror.

"Quiet now, my queen," Apollodorus warned, and then she heard the bumping of other small craft tied up to the dock and the lap of seawater against the stone pilings. She remained motionless, ears sharp to identify her servant's every movement as he climbed from the boat, pulled the rope, secured it to the cleat, then returned, steadying himself in the bottom. She felt his hands under her body and turned slightly to face downward as he lifted.

No doubt he is glad I have grown thinner in exile.

The boat pitched and rolled, and she felt certain they would both be in the chilly water in a moment, but then Apollodorus regained his balance.

A few steps across and one step up, and she felt they were on the solid marble of the palace quay. She exhaled her relief, and her breath came back to her, warm, and still perfumed with honey.

She smiled in her dark shroud. *I am coming, Caesar. And we shall see who is the conqueror.*

Her father, the late Ptolemy XII, had constructed his palace to appear as though it fronted both the harbor and the city. Cleopatra bounced inside the carpet, through what she knew were the gardens that spilled down to the edge of the harbor, along the colonnaded hall that bordered the harbor garden, and up the eight marble steps that led to the entrance. Even at night the marble would be gleaming white, the light of a dozen courtyard torches reflected from the polished stone.

She shifted inside her wrappings, trying to dislodge Apollodorus's bony shoulder from her ribs. She felt him slow and held still.

"State your business." The hard voice called through the night, and her heart seized. Ptolemy's men could be anywhere about, ready to run her through if she were spotted. But these two spoke Latin, not Egyptian.

"A gift for Caesar," Apollodorus replied.

Cleopatra heard the scrape of metal and the shuffle of boots. Two soldiers, perhaps.

"What kind of gift comes at this hour?"

"Only the finest," her servant answered. "Too precious to risk being seen."

The voice moved closer. "You speak like a Roman and dress like an Egyptian merchant. Which is it?"

Apollodorus rolled his shoulder under her. She tried to lift her weight from him in part.

"Born in Sicily, but long on the seas, finding my fortune."

The smooth scrape of metal again, as though a sword had been drawn. Cleopatra held her breath, half expecting to be run through with that sword, and tasting fear for the first time.

"You will find no fortune here, Sicilian. And Caesar is in no need of purchases."

"A gift, I told you. I ask nothing."

There was a pause, and Apollodorus took advantage of the moment. "Though if Caesar should wish to show appreciation . . ."

The soldiers laughed, and Cleopatra felt some of the tension in Apollodorus lessen.

"Who sends this gift for Caesar?"

"The queen."

She loved the way he said it with pride, even now with her in exile.

More laughter. "Not much of a queen, we hear. Running from—"

"She is Queen of Egypt. No squalling brother's claims, nor the claims of his power-lusting advisors, will change that."

Careful, Apollodorus. You're just a merchant from Sicily.

He continued, as though to soften his words. "And the rightful queen of Egypt sends a gift to Caesar."

"Give it over, then. We'll see that he gets it."

"I promised delivery. The queen wishes me to place the gift before Caesar myself."

Another pause.

"Fine. Take it to him then."

"Can you direct me to his chamber?"

"Oh, we'll do more than that."

They started with a lurch, and Cleopatra closed her eyes, relief sweeping her. She trained her ears on the sounds of their feet, and could hear that one soldier led them and the other followed.

It will not be long now.

The corridors of the palace, though web-like, were her childhood home, and it took little concentration to follow their route through the audience hall, under the lofty square-cut doorway into the corridor that housed a dozen apartments for officials and royal family members. Though Greek, the Ptolemies had built their succession of palaces with Egyptian architecture incorporated, to please those they ruled with uneasy peace. This corridor especially had been her favorite, with its carved reliefs of the history of Egypt and of the sun god Ra, with his great golden orb, bestowing favor on Ptolemy XII as they sailed the sky together in Ra's barque.

Which chambers would Caesar have appropriated for his own? There would be many vacant since her hasty departure. Those who also felt the danger of a knife between the bed coverings had fled when she escaped.

But they reached the end of the corridor and began ascending.

Apollodorus grunted with the effort of heaving her up the stairs. Neither soldier offered to help, thank the gods.

When they finally stopped, Cleopatra fought the anger that heated her blood. Her father's chambers? These were the rooms the Roman had chosen?

She forced the emotion down. Anger was not needed now. The moment called for something far more calculated.

One of the soldiers rapped on the door, was summoned forth, and they were inside the rooms. She inhaled, trying to fill herself with the courage of the great Ptolemaic line of rulers, of whom she was next.

A wry laugh rang out. "What is this? Deliveries in the night?"

"He says he has a gift for you, General Caesar. From the queen. He insisted on delivering it himself."

The air stilled, and she was certain she could feel Caesar's eyes on her.

"Make your delivery then, man," Caesar said. "It is late, and I am tired."

This is my moment. Everything changes now. A chill raised the hair on her arms.

Apollodorus lowered her carefully from his shoulder and laid the roll of carpet on the floor. She took her last stale breath, even as she felt her servant slice at the cord that bound the carpet.

And then he began to unroll her shroud.

She rolled with it, feeling her hair wrap around her, feeling the carpet spin faster with her momentum. Coolness rushed in, then light—and she was free.

She pulled herself to sitting, leaned her head back, and looked into the eyes of Gaius Julius Caesar, Master of the Mediterranean.

The shock in his eyes was worth the effort. She let her mouth curve into a slow smile and swept her hair behind her shoulders.

"What—what kind of goddess is this, delivered to my feet in the night?"

She remained at his feet a moment. He was fair and handsome, with a fastidiousness of appearance that pleased her. Cleopatra moved to her knees, then stood. She found that her height nearly matched his own, though he was tall. She stood before him, hands at her sides, palms damp. "I am Cleopatra, Queen of Egypt."

He said nothing, only studied her hair, her face, her lips . . . then all of her.

He was lighter of skin than she expected. But the eyes, oh, the eyes were dark as basalt. His hair was beginning to thin, and in his vanity he combed it forward. Even in soldier's dress he exuded a cultured elegance.

And then he laughed. Deep and rich. Not the nervous laugh of an interloper, nor the ingratiating laugh of a politician. The full and hearty laugh of a soldier, greatly amused by the woman who stood before him.

She said nothing, only lifted her chin and smiled into his eyes. He grew serious, and she felt something pass between them. Something heady. Dangerous.

"I requested audience with you and your brother tomorrow." He took a step backward and retreated to the cedarwood desk her father kept at the side of his sumptuous room. He leaned over an unrolled scroll, as if too busy to deal with her.

She narrowed her eyes, preparing for battle.

"I am not foolish enough to walk into the palace in the daylight with my enemy's soldiers and supporters lining the streets."

He looked up and nodded once. "Very well, you were perhaps wise to be cautious. And you are here now." He motioned to the soldiers. "Take her to a room and post a guard." To her he said, "In the morning we will conduct our business."

"In the morning my brother will fill your ears with lies and empty promises." She shrugged. "But perhaps you do not care for the truth. I have heard that Romans are not very intelligent."

Cleopatra thought she detected the hint of a smile, but then his brows furrowed as though she were a disrespectful child. *I am no child, Caesar.*

He propped his fists on the desk and leaned forward. "So you would try to fill my ears with your own lies first, I suppose. Before your brother has his chance?"

She licked her lips and eyed him through lowered lashes. "I seek only to help Caesar understand the situation. Egypt is a complicated land, and family squabbles can be difficult." She pointed to an amphorae and cups on a side table, beside a window where gold silk window coverings billowed with the breezes from the sea. "A shared cup of wine, some small conversation, and then I will leave you to your sleep."

Caesar straightened, then came from behind the desk to stand before her again. She could feel his breath on her and lifted her eyes to face him fully.

He did not take his eyes from hers but spoke to the guards. "Leave us. I will see to her myself."

"General? She might intend harm—"

"Leave us!"

She heard the clink of armor retreating and half-turned her head to Apollodorus. "That is all. You have served me well this night. I will call for you soon."

He bowed from the room and closed the door, and then they were alone.

Alone.

She turned back, unable to take her eyes from her jeweled sandals, her mouth suddenly dry.

He lifted her chin with his fingers, and her heart raced ahead of her, as though it knew that the battle had begun. She felt a flush begin at the base of her neck and sweep upward with a wave of heat. *Focus, Cleo. This is not part of the plan.*

"Now you are quiet? I send them away as you wished, and you have nothing more to say?"

"Wine," she whispered. Anything to break the connection between them.

He half-smiled as though he could read her thoughts. "Of course."

He moved away, and she exhaled and took a step backward, collecting herself.

Her father's quarters were unchanged since she had left, with his varied tastes in Greek and Egyptian furnishings sprawled through the large front room, and extending back to his bed chamber, only dimly lit now by a small oil lamp on a two-drawered table beside the bed, still richly laid with red and gold coverings and boasting fat wooden posts, a true luxury in this desert land.

Caesar's only change to the room seemed to be the addition of a large yet crude soldier's chest. The sight of it reminded her that he was not a Greek. Not a philosopher, nor a scholar. He was a Roman savage, come to take her land if he could.

She looked around and made the quick decision to seat herself on one of the four red-cushioned couches that formed a square in the center of the front room—her father's approximation of the Greek's andrôn, and his favorite place to host drinking parties.

She had only finished arranging herself and her robes upon the couch when Caesar was at her side, wine in hand. She accepted the cup. "Thank you."

He lowered himself to the couch on her left, then reclined as she did, so that their heads drew close together in the corner. In the heartbeat of silence between them, she heard the scrape of soldiers outside the door and knew that one shout from Caesar could mean her removal.

"Your men seem quite loyal," she said, and sipped at the wine.

"A problem you are not plagued with, I hear."

She smiled over the cup. "Only temporary. My brother's advisors have spread poison in the city. I will soon persuade the people of the truth."

"It is an astonishing city," Caesar said, turning to the window opening. "I have never seen the like."

"You have been here only two days. Wait until I have shown you all its wonders."

He turned back to her with a tilt of his head, his only acknowledgment of her implied hospitality.

"But you came to speak of other matters."

"I came to meet the man of whom I have heard great things."

Caesar drank deeply from his cup, all the while studying her eyes. She felt in that moment that they were like two desert lions, circling the same antelope. Each one calculating the strengths and weaknesses of the other, always with an eye on the prize.

"Your father incurred a great debt," Caesar said. "He received the support of Rome, recovered his kingdom. And still Rome has not seen repayment. *That* is why I am here. It is time for Egypt to pay her debts."

"And you think that my brother will pay?"

"I care little for the machinations of your murderous family."

She drew back. It was true, the Ptolemies had a long history of killing off siblings and children who were rivals for the throne. But it was not generally spoken of.

"I only want my grain," Caesar said.

"A strong Egypt will produce enough grain to feed herself and all of Rome. Our mother, the Nile, feeds us well. But Egypt will never be strong with my brother's three fools ruling from behind the boy's throne."

"How old is your brother?"

"Thirteen. And still crying in the night for his mother."

Caesar laughed. "And how old are you?"

She reached across and traced a line of gray at his temple. "Not as old as you."

He gripped her fingers and held them there. "How old?" The words came out low, husky.

She stilled. "Twenty-one."

He inhaled and looked away. "More than thirty years between us."

She pulled her hand along his jawline, until her open palm was beneath his lips. "I care not."

He lowered his lips to her hand, then pushed her away and stood. "I will not release Egypt's debt, even for a reward such as yourself."

She sat upright on the couch and steeled her voice. "And I would not sell myself for all the grain in Egypt!"

Caesar reached a hand down to her hair and touched it. "What do you want from me then, Queen of Egypt?"

Cleopatra leaned away from his hand and stood. She crossed the room, to the open window, aware that he watched her every movement.

Outside the window Egypt's capital sprawled beneath them, its royal quarter overflowing with the succession of connected palaces built by the Ptolemies before her, alongside the Great Library, the Museum, amphitheaters and *stadia*.

Capital of the world.

Caesar came to stand behind her, close enough that his shoulder brushed her own.

"Have you been to see his tomb yet?" she asked.

"I have had urgent matters to tend. But I hope to soon pay him honor."

"Alexander the Great," she whispered. "He has lain in his crystal sarcophagus here for nearly three hundred years. We Ptolemies have ruled our part of his kingdom as best we could." The breeze surged, wrapping the silk draperies around the two of them, secreting them away.

She turned within the silk to Caesar, their bodies nearly touching. The warmth in her face returned. "But I fear the time of the Ptolemies is ending, and the time of the Romans is coming."

"Coming? I would say that we are already here."

"Will you rule an empire such as Alexander's alone, Caesar?"

"There are many in Rome who will share the burden."

"Ah"—she let her lips lift in a knowing smile—"but what do they offer you? Money? Loyalty? I can give you all that, and Egypt, too."

Caesar looked over her head to the glittering lights of the city. "You are so willing to give away your jewel?"

"Give away? Neither of us would find benefit in that. But with me by your side, Caesar . . . We could unite two kingdoms and then move forward together, across the east and to the west, until our boundaries would push past even those of Alexander's." The light of conquest leaped into his eyes. She saw it, measured its intensity, and was pleased. "Caesar and Cleopatra." She pressed fingertips against the tunic that showed above his mail. "The world has never seen the like."

Caesar lifted her other hand to his chest and gripped both of them there, his black eyes invading her spirit. The triumph she felt a moment before gave way to something else—and fear pounded through her when she recognized it.

In her battle for control of Egypt, she had made the choice to use the only weapon that her brother did not have—her femininity.

But would that choice also be her downfall? *I had not counted on my heart interfering with my will.* He was an attractive man, it was true. But there was something more. All her life Cleopatra had been surrounded by power-grasping family and those that hung onto their robes. And her lust for power, she knew, was as great as any. But each was weak in his own way. Too weak to do whatever necessary to rule a wild and mysterious people such as the Egyptians. No Ptolemy before her had learned their languages, their religion, their customs the way she had. And still she filled her mind with Greek philosophy and mathematics, astronomy and medicine. All of it had distilled, she knew, into a formidable intelligence and a ruthless will. Never had she met another who matched her intellect, her warring spirit, her hunger to rule.

Until tonight.

He still looked down into her eyes, and she saw that he felt it too.

"You are not a child," he said, as if to convince himself.

"Not for a long time."

He drew her fingers to his lips. "Caesar and Cleopatra." He murmured the words against her hands. "The world has never seen the like."

Heady victory swept her. She had won. Obtained the support of the one man who could restore her kingdom. The tension in her shoulders eased. But as he bent his lips to her own and she gave herself willingly to him, a whisper of dread played about, warning her that this was a dangerous game.

In aligning herself with Caesar and Rome, she might lose everything.

FOUR

Sophia pulled herself from the window in the South Wing of the Base, one of four wings that formed a square of rooms around the lighthouse. She crossed the central courtyard and reentered the bottom level of the lighthouse. The night shift of servants worked to load the lift with fuel, then hoist it up to the top platform. Her mind still grasped for an idea of how to protect the Museum, its scholars, and her husband's legacy from the filthy hands of the marauders. She could not lose it all. Would not.

She eyed the four men who stacked the bundles of acacia wood and bricks of dried dung beside the lift, and then checked over the pile from which they drew their supplies. "Where is the rest of the fuel for tonight?"

One of the servants bowed low and wiped his dirty hands on his tunic. "Abbudin encountered p-problems—" His stutter annoyed her tonight.

"What problems?"

"The Romans, m-mistress. Since the general m-moved into the palace, they are c-controlling the royal supplies. But Abbudin is working to p-procure all we need—"

Sophia waved away the rest of his explanation. Romans. Everywhere she turned.

She looked up through the ramp to the signal fire so far above them that it blended with the stars in the Alexandrian sky. The mirror was constructed in such a way that a small fire could be magnified to a great light, one seen two hundred stadia away on the dark sea. But even a small fire required fuel.

The servants worked quickly in her presence. No wonder. But concern for Cleopatra eclipsed lighthouse trivia tonight.

One of the men glanced her way with wide eyes, and she checked his work to find his cause for fear. Nothing. Which could only mean one thing.

The cause was behind her. And again, it was Roman in origin.

He had returned. Lucius Aurelius Bellus. The pilus-whatever-he-called-himself.

She stepped in front of the servants and faced the soldier, this time without his ranks. "Did you not understand me previously? Perhaps your Egyptian is not as fluent as you would think."

Bellus wore no helmet now. He stood easily with his legs apart and crossed his arms over his wide chest. "You received a message?"

"Does Caesar force his soldiers to stand guard around the clock? I should think you would be quite fatigued by now, marching around with all that metal."

Bellus's face darkened and silence spread between them for a long moment. "The messenger. Did he bring word from Cleopatra?"

She pushed past him, into the courtyard where the night air had cooled.

Bellus followed, his sandals scratching at the sand. "Get back here, you infuriating woman, and answer me!"

Sophia reached the South Wing and whirled on him. "You do not belong here. This is my lighthouse, and my home. You will not intrude again!"

He stalked to her and grabbed her arms. Sophia lifted her face. Let him strike her, she would not show her fear. Her traitorous eyes blinked too rapidly. "Go ahead, barbarian. Show the peace-loving Greek the way you handle things in Rome!"

"Aahh!" He thrust her away from him and strode a few paces down the corridor before turning. "I am here at Caesar's orders! If you know where the queen—"

"Go and see your fearsome general. I think you will find he is no longer so concerned with searching out the queen."

Uncertainty flickered in Bellus's eyes. "What do you know?"

Sophia pointed to the doorway. "I know that you are in my lighthouse and you have no right to be here."

He said nothing. Did nothing. Just stood before her, staring her down as she pointed out the door, using that wicked silence. Eventually her arm tired and she dropped it. She licked her lips once, hated herself for looking away from his stare, and reached a hand back to grip her neck.

Only then, when it was somehow clear that he had won, did he meander in her direction, brush past her, and make his way out of the lighthouse.

By the gods, she hated this soldier.

Surely there was some way to get rid of them all!

She took to the ramp, circling up the lighthouse to escape to the blessed isolation of her private chambers. But the rooms felt hollow and cold without Cleopatra. The young queen's visit had been far too short. Sophia surveyed the room, trying to see it through Kallias's eyes. The piled scrolls were mute testimony to the knowledge she pursued. *Education is the best provision for the journey to old age.* But this was no time for Aristotle. She took the small lamp that the queen had lit, carried it to her desk, and pushed aside the papyrus she had been studying so long ago this afternoon. She pulled an unused roll from a small stack.

There was another man in Alexandria whom she hated. A man of power. A man who could get things done. Pothinus.

The boy-king Ptolemy's minister of finance had been a eunuch for many years. He had channeled his energies into a lust for pure power and nothing else. When Cleopatra's father breathed his last three years earlier, naming Cleopatra and Ptolemy as co-regents, the boy had been only ten years old. Pothinus had leaped in, along with Ptolemy's tutor Theodotus and the Egyptian Achillas, commander of the army.

Although Achillas had the military strength, in Greek society the real power belonged to those with intellect. And Pothinus was nothing if not a shrewd politician. Well then, it was to his intellect she would make her appeal.

She pulled reed and ink from a small ivory box on her desk and formed a letter to Pothinus in her mind. She scribbled the words, phrases scrambling through her mind in mad succession.

Roman invaders. Pay the debt of the father quickly. Secure the land for his children. Secure Alexandria's greatest assets. Philosophy, rhetoric, scholarship . . . I am being watched.

The rush of words slowed. She despised begging. She laid the reed aside to contemplate how to end her letter.

The cuttlefish's black ink had stained her fingers. She rubbed at the smudge, smearing it into her skin. Her eyes strayed to the engraved box she kept on her desk. Inside lay one of Kallias's last inventions. A gift on their first anniversary.

She took the device from its box, then lifted a tiny marble from its trough at the bottom and rolled the smooth ball between her fingers. They had been in the Museum when he presented her with the little marvel. Several of his friends, also scholars supported by the Museum, stood by to enjoy her reaction.

Now, as she had done all those years ago, Sophia dropped the marble into the top chute of the piece. The marble rolled down the chute, dropped to another, fell onto a tiny platform that lifted a lever, in turn releasing the marble to travel farther. Back and forth it crossed the inner workings of the mechanism, until it set in motion a tiny pendulum that clicked in rhythm between two blocks of granite.

The marble rolled to a stop in its trough again. The pendulum continued its clicking swing. Sophia touched one granite square with her fingertip, then closed her eyes and felt the beating of the pendulum under her. When it slowed, she again dropped the marble into the chute.

She lost count of how many times she set the marble in motion. The beat of the pendulum against the granite had become the beat of Kallias's heart to her, and she could not bear to let it stop. The oil in the lamp burned down until the flame was a mere speck.

In time, she laid her head on her arm at the desk, but still she kept the pendulum swinging in its tiny pool of golden lamplight. Tears fell to her unfinished letter and glistened there a moment before bleeding into the papyrus.

Kallias.

He was gone. The fickle gods she no longer trusted had taken him from her. She alone carried his dream, his legacy. What would he say to this present threat?

She wiped her face and retrieved her reed. *I will not fail you, Kallias. I will find a way to keep them safe.*

FIVE

The morning sun climbed above the city, spilled its warmth down the paved streets, and drifted through the palace window to the shrouded bed where Cleopatra stirred, fleeing her dreams for the day's reality. She stretched her arms above her head, eyes closed, then rolled to her side. With one eye open, she saw that she was alone in the massive bed.

She swept the sheets away and swung her legs over the side. Her *chitôn* lay nearby, draped over a chair. She wrapped herself and left the solitude of the bedchamber for the front room.

Caesar was dressed in his armor already, strips of iron held together with hinges and leather straps that hung to his waist. He was seated at her father's desk, scribbling upon a wooden tablet, and looked up briefly at her entrance. He smiled, like one who is confident of his possessions, and returned to his tablet. Cleopatra hardened her emotions against the casual treatment.

You may be assured of me now, Caesar. For it suits my purpose.

She did not have long to prepare, she knew. And though they had spoken of many things through the night, there was still more to be said to the Roman general who scratched dispatches at the desk.

She crossed to the door, yanked it inward, and leaned her head into the corridor. A soldier jerked away from the wall.

"I am hungry," she said.

Apollodorus was there in a moment. "Clean clothes," she said to him. "From my chambers."

Both men bowed, and for an instant she felt like a queen once more. The long months in Syria had nearly erased the memory.

The two were back shortly, and while the soldier resumed his post, she took the clothes from Apollodorus and retreated to the bedchamber to bathe and dress. She arranged a white chitôn around herself, its edges stitched in blood red, and smiled at the pieces Apollodorus had been wise enough to bring. With practiced fingers, she arranged the heavy black braids of the royal wig on her head. In true Egyptian style she fastened the *uraeus*, the rearing golden cobra, with its wide throat spread across her forehead.

When she emerged from the bedchamber, a meal of maza bread and seasoned lentils had been placed on the low table beside the white couches.

"Will you break your fast with me?" she called to Caesar, and reclined on the couch she had claimed last night.

He seemed to notice the food for the first time and paused for only a moment before abandoning the desk and coming to her. He eyed the rearing cobra, her black hairpiece. "And here is Egypt."

She smiled and held out the bread. "Ptolemy will respond to your summons soon. Pothinus will be anxious to gain your approval."

Caesar scooped lentils with a hunk of bread, then chewed slowly.

Speak, Roman. Do not make me beg.

The silence lengthened. "What will you tell him?" she finally asked.

Caesar shrugged. He understood her desperation, she knew. And would take full advantage of it. She would not underestimate him.

"If Ptolemy XIII and his advisors are expecting to find me sympathetic to their side of this rivalry, they will be unpleasantly surprised."

Cleopatra looked to him, and silent understanding passed between them, the acknowledgment that treaties are made in all manner of ways.

When the time arrived, Caesar was seated at his desk, and Cleopatra was surveying the city from the window behind him. One knock on the door, and the soldier on guard appeared, announcing the arrival of King Ptolemy XIII and his minister of finance, Pothinus. Cleopatra inhaled, steadied her heart, and turned. Standing behind Caesar, she placed cool hands on his shoulders. He looked up from his dispatches toward the door and did not pull away from her possessive touch.

Pothinus did not wait to be invited. He was elegantly dressed as usual but shoved the soldier aside and pushed into the room, the boy king in tow and a complaint already in progress.

"The king does not appreciate being called to his own—"

Pothinus stopped in the center of the room and drew up his considerable height. His eyes lifted from Caesar to Cleopatra and back again, lingering on her hands still resting on the general's shoulders. His speech hung mid-syllable, and now his lips formed a wide *O,* opening and closing, much like one of the harbor's red mullet fish.

Her brother appeared beside Pothinus, fat and unkempt as always, and his lips puckered into a pout, as though someone had gotten to his cakes before he and eaten them all.

Cleopatra's chest filled with a satisfaction so enjoyable she could not contain it. It spilled to her face and she felt herself smiling in spite of her efforts. A bubble of laughter erupted within her.

Do not appear a giggling child now, Cleo.

The delightful moment of shock broke, and Pothinus stuttered out a muddied series of single-word questions. "What—? When—? Who?"

Cleopatra covered the urge to laugh with an incline of her head and a greeting. "Good morning, Pothinus. Ptolemy. It has been too long."

Her slovenly brother looked to Pothinus, as though unsure how large a disaster they faced. The boy was still too short, with greasy hair grown too long, dirty fingernails, and a brown stain of unknown origin in the center of his *himation. How it must gall the fussy Pothinus to serve such a charge.* Like a nobleman waiting upon a street beggar.

Ptolemy placed pudgy hands on his hips. "What are *you* doing here?" The question came on a thin whine. "We thought you were in Syria."

Pothinus recovered and stepped in front of her brother. "It is a pleasure to see you again, Cleopatra. Perhaps we can finally end the strife."

She came from behind Caesar, letting her hand glide along his muscular shoulders. "Perhaps." She moved slowly away from the Roman, and circled Pothinus. He straightened and did not meet her eyes, but she could sense the usual discomfiture she caused him. She gave her brother a cold-eyed stare, then returned to Caesar's side.

Pothinus looked down his thin nose at her. "It seems you are— acquainted—with the Roman general already."

Caesar stood. "Cleopatra came to see me last night." He lifted a few of her braids and let them slide through his fingers. "I found we had much to speak of, and much in common."

Her brother shook a finger at Caesar, and his himation slipped from his shoulder. "Caesar, remember who it was that removed your great enemy Pompey."

Cleopatra hid her amusement at her brother's foolishness. Pothinus tried to smooth over the boy idiot's comment, but Caesar's face had already gone dark. "You treat a great man like a criminal and you expect me to reward you?"

Pothinus jerked the boy's himation straight and turned to Cleopatra, scowling. It was clear he had read the situation accurately, even if the brat was a fool. "Caesar," he began with a bow to the Roman, "you have come to collect on a debt, and the king has every desire to repay it. Do not let others convince you—"

"I do not need anyone to make my decisions for me, Pothinus." Caesar looked to her, then to her brother. "This civil war must end. It divides the country and wastes resources that could be used to produce revenue."

Cleopatra watched him carefully. Where was he going? Would he bring his legion to bear upon Ptolemy's troops, and reestablish her as the rightful ruler of Egypt, as she desired?

He looked to her with that disturbingly possessive light in his eye. "You must rule together, as your father wished. It is the only way to unite the country."

"No!" Ptolemy stomped a heavy foot. His full face reddened. "I will be king alone! Tell him, Pothinus! Tell him I want to be king!"

Pothinus licked his lips and eyed Cleopatra. She slid closer to Caesar and ran a light hand up his arm. "He is a boy, Caesar. Not ready to rule. And his advisors—"

Caesar held up a hand. "You have my decision. Rome's presence in your city has been one of peace to this point." He turned to Cleopatra and she felt a chill between them. "If you wish this peace to continue, you will end this rift, reunite your country, and repay the ten million denarii you owe Rome."

"That's not fair!" Ptolemy whined. "Egypt doesn't need a queen! One Pharaoh, that's all this land has ever needed!"

Pothinus wrapped long fingers around the boy's arm, and with the other hand he smoothed back his graying hair. "Come, my king. We have much to discuss." He dragged the boy from the room, and Cleopatra half-expected her brother to fly at her with a kick in the shins as he used to do when they were younger.

When the door clanked shut behind them, she turned to Caesar, her questions playing across her face.

Amusement danced in his dark eyes. "You are a powerful and brilliant woman, Cleopatra. You have more than proven yourself to me since you rolled out of that carpet at my feet last night. But you cannot rule Egypt alone. The people will not have it, and without the people, you have nothing."

She frowned and studied a tapestry that hung on the wall. The truth galled her, but it was the truth nonetheless. She must have a co-regent, even in name only, if she wanted to be queen.

She lifted her eyes to Caesar, willed them to turn soft and flattering. "I can see why every land you touch falls into your hands, General. But remember that Ptolemy and his advisors hold no affection for the Romans."

In two steps he closed the gap between them and swept her into his arms. "And you, Queen of Egypt? Do you hold affection for the Romans?"

She gave him her fullest smile. "One Roman, especially."

He met her lips with his own, but for only a moment. The peace of the chamber broke apart when a scream went up from outside the palace window.

Cleopatra ran from Caesar's side and leaned out the window to search the palace grounds below.

"What is it?"

"Ptolemy. He is running from the palace, crying like he's skinned his knee."

Caesar joined her and leaned through the open window.

Below them, Ptolemy lumbered across the courtyard, keening loudly. He passed the lotus-flower pool, ran under the squared-off stone entryway to the palace grounds where two sphinx sat guard, and into the street beyond. Cleopatra saw Pothinus amble toward the street, watching Ptolemy, his fingers intertwined at his waist.

"My sister has given Egypt to the Romans!" Ptolemy screamed to those who walked past. "This very moment she shares his bedchamber, and they plot against the people of Alexandria!" A crowd was forming, and Ptolemy pointed a fat finger toward the window where she and Caesar watched. She drew back, letting the window coverings conceal her.

The people will recognize petty jealousy.

But still, her palms felt slick. She gripped the fabric of her chitôn.

Caesar turned to her, eyes narrowed. "I have heard about the Alexandrians. They have a tendency to"—he seemed to grope for an inoffensive term—"assert their opinions most forcefully, do they not?"

She tried to smile. "Alexandria is filled with Greeks who live at the crossroads of foreign cultures. Their philosophy and their experience of the world gives them rightful cause to be opinionated. Their freedom gives them confidence to voice those thoughts."

The crowd outside the palace was growing vocal. Caesar wrapped a hand around her upper arm and drew her from the window. She pulled from his grip. "They will remember that I am still Queen of Egypt."

"Let us hope so." Caesar went to the door, leaned out, and barked a command to the legionary that stood guard. When he returned, his jaw was set in a hard line.

Now this is Caesar the Conqueror. The nervous twitch in her stomach settled a bit.

He crossed to the desk, his attention there, but his words were for her. "I hope that I have not made a mistake in backing you, Cleopatra."

She rubbed at the back of her neck. "My brother and his leeches will destroy Egypt. Better to rid the land of them now, no matter how difficult." She hardened her voice and played the moment well. "It is the only way to give Rome what she deserves."

Caesar glanced up at her, a shrewd look of knowing on his features. But his only comment was, "Hmmm."

Cleopatra spent most of the morning at the window, half-hidden by the gold silks, her eye on her city. Her father's chamber window was only three stories above the gardens, but even from here, she could see southward across the uniform grid of streets, each cell having its front on the street, with the privacy of gardens and fountains within.

From her perch she could see the dazzling white marble colonnades of the Street of the Soma, where Alexander's body lay along with other Ptolemaic kings. The street led southward, from the Gate of the Moon at the Great Harbor behind her to the Gate of the Sun at the south of the city. And beyond that, the flashing waters of Lake Mareotis winked in the sunlight, where shiploads of grain sailed northward to the Great Harbor, and returned with their hulls full of foreign treasures.

But it was not Lake Mareotis, or even the beauty of the city, that captured her attention today. It was the growing horde of Alexandrians that formed along the Canopic Way, the east-west thoroughfare that was the heart of the city, where merchants and philosophers both plied their wares and their ideas. It was here that Ptolemy's screams of betrayal were taken up and passed along, until the street was clogged with people, and the daily sounds of the market replaced with the noisy shouts of protestors.

"My soldiers are trained to quell unrest," Caesar said when the sun grew high and her skin damp. "You have nothing to fear."

She did not turn. "I am never afraid. I am only thinking on how best to sway the people. With proper rhetoric, any situation, no matter how uncivil, can be turned on its head."

He chuckled. "Spoken like a true Greek."

At that, she did turn and let her anger find its way into her voice. "But I am Egyptian as well. Do not forget that, Gaius Julius Caesar. I am a daughter of Isis."

He bowed his head. "A philosopher for the Greeks, a goddess for the Egyptians."

"And an ally for Rome."

His eyes found hers, and again, an awareness passed between them. In less than a day, she had found that they understood each other perfectly.

A mighty pounding at the door startled them both, and a soldier pushed into the room. "General! The mob has organized."

Caesar reached for his leather and mail body armor and slid it over his head. "How long?"

"Minutes."

"The First Cohort?"

"In place, and given instructions."

Cleopatra hurried to Caesar's side, but stepped back again when he brandished his dagger. "What is happening?"

He sheathed the dagger. "It begins. Your brother's eunuch has convinced the mob to storm the palace."

She swallowed and looked to the window. "They are coming for me?"

Caesar tightened the straps at his ankles. "For you. For me. For anyone whom Pothinus has accused." He straightened. "Stay here. My legion will have the situation under control within minutes."

She snorted. "Stay here? Who do you think I am?"

Caesar gave her a look—from the black wig with the rearing cobra affixed to her head, to the jeweled sandals beneath her chitôn. The question hung in the air between them, the question of who held control. With a slight smile, he turned his back to her and stalked from the chamber.

Cleopatra inclined her ear to the window once more, listened to the rising chant of her city, and then followed the Roman.

It begins.

SIX

Sophia awoke in her own bed, unsure of how she came to be there after falling asleep at her letter last night.

She burrowed deeper into the plush bedcoverings, unwilling to face the day. Cleopatra's visit had left her restless and discontent with her life. *Where are you this morning, Cleo?*

But the plight of the scholars finally drove her from her bed. She rinsed her face with water from an engraved bronze basin beside her bed and paused to breathe in the scent of a jar of cut roses. When she had dressed, she called Ares. He appeared in moments.

The letter was there, rolled and sealed, upon her desk. Ready to deliver to Pothinus, to beg the aid of Ptolemy XIII in rescuing the scholars from Roman interference.

"Here"—she said, pressing the sealed papyrus scroll into his hand—"deliver it to Pothinus. No one else."

He frowned and tapped the scroll against his bottom lip. "And where do you suppose I will find him?"

Sophia clenched a fist at her side. "Do you expect me to take care of all your other tasks, too? He will be about the palace somewhere. Find him!"

Ares nodded. "I will try."

He slipped from the room, but she called after him. "No one but Pothinus! Do not come back without delivering it!" She slammed the door and turned to the room. She should pray for Pothinus to help her.

She crossed to her wall niche shrine to Isis, bent the knee, and forced her eyes closed before the marble alcove that housed a small statue of the goddess. Isis loomed over her, with her headdress of cow's horns and solar disc.

Isis, speed Ares to Pothinus.

She lifted the small terra-cotta lamp she kept burning in the niche and touched the tip of a stick of incense to the wick that floated in olive oil. The incense smoked and caught, then burned off to a powdery yellow. The spicy scent overwhelmed the niche, and she pulled away.

Aloud she intoned a familiar prayer, then added her own. "Isis, protect the best minds of Alexandria, the future of Egypt, the future of the world."

Her voice came back to her from the rounded recess, hollow and dead, reminding her of the echo when one spoke in the empty chambers of the lighthouse's Base.

Is it only an illusion of emptiness? Does the goddess hear my prayer? Sosigenes was always speaking to her of his One God. She tried to push away the doubts he had planted.

The incense flickered and extinguished. She held the tiny piece to the flame again, too close. The flame licked her finger, and she jerked away. The incense fell to her tunic and left a scorched hole. She licked her finger, then took a small alabaster jar from the wall and poured a tiny drop of wine over her burned fingertip.

A burn is a small sacrifice if it will please the goddess. And yet, the action felt as empty as her voice.

A swoosh behind her startled her from her cramped position. "Ares! Must I whip you to secure your obedience?"

He was out of breath. "I have left to deliver your message and been turned back, mistress."

She stood, tightening her fingers into her tunic. "The whole city has fallen?"

Ares held out her message, still panting. "Not fallen, no. But there is much commotion, and the Roman soldiers are barring entrance into the city from our island."

"A riot?"

He swallowed. "They are saying it is because of Cleopatra."

She crossed the room and gripped his arm, ignoring the scroll. "Speak! What has happened to her?"

"She is in the palace. She has secured the Roman's support."

Sophia breathed and released Ares.

"Ptolemy is screaming of betrayal, and the city is forming a mob to attack the palace and rid us of the Romans."

Sophia turned away. "Fools. All of them. They would put a child on the throne, with those who care only for their own wealth sitting behind him. When they could have a true queen."

"What shall I do with the message, Abbas?"

She snatched it from him. "Perhaps it shall not be necessary. Cleopatra's influence may be all the help we need. We shall wait."

Ares left her. She returned to her desk, to yesterday's labor charts shoved aside so long ago, and tried to concentrate. But the charts were to be interrupted again.

Ares startled her with his knock, and she yelled her permission to enter. "Can you not give me a moment's peace?" she mumbled, still bent over the charts.

"News from the city, mistress."

She whirled on him. "From the queen?"

He shrugged. "I would not know."

She squinted her annoyance and took the scroll he held out. She broke the seal and unrolled it quickly.

Sophia, I was unable to make good on my escape, I am afraid. I have only a moment here before they confiscate my books and writing instruments. The Romans will set me aside, to rot in one of our city's own prisons. Do what you can. A discovery of momentous import is at hand, and we cannot allow it to be lost. Your faithful Sosigenes.

Sophia thrust the scroll from her, letting it drop to the table. A moment later she was digging her formal himation from a chest and thrusting it over her head.

"You are leaving?" Ares's shock rippled through his voice.

"I will go to see Cleopatra."

Ares slipped to the table and picked up Sosigenes's message. Sophia felt a flicker of annoyance at his presumption, supplanted by a glow of pride. Only in Alexandria were even the servants educated in language and writing. It was truly the center of learning.

She threw the himation's corner over her shoulder and shoved a pin through the fabric. It was for Alexandria that she now fought.

"He is an old man," she said to Ares. "With weak lungs. He will not last a week in a cell."

"Can you not wait until the mob returns to their homes?"

"No, idiot. I cannot wait. Who knows what these Romans might do, especially if they feel the city is rising up in defiance."

Ares smiled in suppressed amusement. "It is good to see you take care for someone."

Sophia grabbed her letter to Pothinus and secured it beneath her cloak. "I thought you were taught to read. Did you not see in Sosigenes's message that he has some new discovery? That is all I care about!"

"Take some kind of protection, Abbas. I will find you a dagger, a short sword—"

"I have all the protection I need, Ares. My voice and my reputation." She slipped her sandals on and ran a hand over her clipped hair.

Ares scratched the back of his neck. "If anyone could wound with her voice and her reputation, it would be you, mistress."

She raised her eyebrows. "What does that mean?"

He bowed and extended his hand toward the door. "Only that I am glad to see you well protected."

She took to the lighthouse ramp with speed and descended to the Base with Ares at her heels.

Out the lighthouse's arched entrance, she stopped only a moment before the two towering statues of Ptolemy II, each dressed as a striding Egyptian Pharaoh with a short skirt and striped nemes on his head. She tried to take some strength from the lighthouse's patron, then fled down the flight of steps to the bottom of the Base. The causeway that led from Pharos Island through the two harbors was seven stadia long, and so named the *heptastadion*. It was a stadia wide as well, with a bridged pass-through at its top and another at the bottom to allow ships to sail from one harbor to the other. It would take fifteen minutes to walk it. She could have taken a chariot, but it had been years since she had done so, and she knew it would take precious time to ready the vehicle.

She reached the far end of the heptastadion, her heart pounding at her pace already. The warehouses that stretched along the docks seemed empty of workers today, as though the heart of the city had sucked them all into itself, before the soldiers had massed to block entrance. They roamed the streets in seeming chaos, but Sophia quickly saw the pattern in their formation.

They are ready to take the city by force.

She pushed through the line of uniforms, ignoring their shouts. She must get to Cleopatra, get her to release Sosigenes.

"You there, man!"

She blinked at the voice and paused, but then pushed on. The city beyond boiled like a stew of angry Greeks and Egyptians, Romans and Jews.

"I said stop!" A soldier was in front of her then, *pilum* across his chest, barring her way. He was young. A boy really, with the barest sign of stubble on his chin. He wore full battle armor, from his helmet to his metal apron strapped with dagger and pugio. He lacked only a shield to be ready to wage war on innocent citizens. "No one enters the city until Julius Caesar gives admittance." His words faltered at the end as he took in her gender.

She stared him down, using the surprise. "I am a personal friend of the queen, and she has called for me at the palace. Let me pass."

He snorted. "A personal friend of the queen, you say?" His voice rose.

Another soldier drew close and her soldier turned to him. "The old woman here says she's the queen's best friend. Shall we let her through?"

Old woman. She was barely old enough to be the boy's mother! Was she such an old woman already?

"Of course!" The other soldier laughed. "Perhaps we should escort her there ourselves!"

Sophia opened her mouth to call down curses on their heads, but she was saved the trouble by the sudden escalation of shouts in the street beyond. Both soldiers turned, then ignored her to run to the fray.

She followed them.

Hundreds of Alexandrians thronged the Canopic Way through the Beta district. The granite-paved street was wide enough for two chariots, but today was filled with shouting and shoving citizens, fists raised in angry protest. Rows of Roman soldiers marched in furious succession, shouting orders and obscenities in turn.

Sophia followed in the wake of one centurion, toward the royal Alpha district. Ptolemy XII's massive palace loomed ahead, with its two enormous sphinxes on granite platforms, guarding the entrance.

She could move no faster than the mass of people who smelled of cooking spices and sweat. The odor mingled itself with the sun reflected from the white marble buildings, and a sharp pain knifed at her temples.

The chaos took her breath away and made her long for the quiet isolation of her lighthouse. The blurring white of himations, the bobbing dark heads of the city's Greek and Egyptian residents, the shiny metal and brown leather of the Roman soldiers, the shouts in Greek and Latin and Egyptian and Hebrew—all swirled and buzzed around her until she felt dizzy and sick. She bounced from one person to the next, stumbling and struggling to keep her balance.

Like a goose in the crowded harbor, tossed around in the wake of a dozen ships.

She raised her eyes and looked northward, to her lighthouse watching over the city. Unlike the goose, she could not take flight. She moved ever closer to the palace. Not much longer.

And then a pinch of her elbow and a harsh whisper drew her up short.

"Is this Sophia, descended from her dark tower?"

She half-turned her head, though she recognized the spiteful voice. "Pothinus." Her hand went to her waist, where the message she'd written him hid under her clothing. "I did not expect to see you in the city."

He bowed. "Nor I, you. But of course you have heard that your student has returned." He still spoke into to her ear, pressed close by the crowd. "I did not realize your affection ran so deep. To risk this violence . . ."

"I have come for the good of Egypt." She pulled the scroll from her waist. They were nearly touching now, and she tried to pull away. "Here, you must read this. The Romans—"

"Any harm the Romans cause is well aided by your young queen." Pothinus looked over her head, distracted by the mob.

"Pothinus, I ask you to put former animosities aside, for the good of the city."

He smiled down on her, and the expression seemed strange on his face, as though it creased the skin in unfamiliar ways. "Why Sophia, I have no animosity toward you. In fact, your husband and I were the closest of friends."

Someone fell against her and cursed. "Then for the sake of my husband, you must do something for the Museum." She pressed the scroll into his hand and he nodded once. The crowd shifted, carrying him away from her. She watched him go, watched him speak to many he passed, and realized that he was helping to incite the violence, not quash it.

She could not tell if it was his words, or simply a shift in the mood of a fickle crowd, but the tension seemed to tighten around her. There was a momentary hush to the random shouts, as though the people held their breath for something far more dangerous. Sophia held her breath as well and looked to the sphinxes.

Accusations erupted into swinging fists. A collective yell went up from the crowd, and they moved as one toward the palace. Sophia was caught up in the swell, like a piece of sea grass carried on the tide toward the shore.

The soldiers responded. Pila were lifted high above heads, smashed down on the worst offenders. Screams of pain and fury shredded the air. Men dropped at her feet.

Ahead, Sophia saw a centurion barking orders to his legionaries. He held the short *vitis*, the grapevine staff that signaled his authority. It was Bellus, the Roman who had invaded the sanctity of her lighthouse.

His eyes darted left and right, with the watchful awareness of an able commander. He yelled to several soldiers, who snapped to the troublemakers he indicated, and directed his men from an island of complete control. Not one movement or word was wasted.

Sophia fought the wave of people and stayed rooted to the ground, struggling to watch.

All around her violence surged. An elbow shot out from the crowd, caught Sophia on the lip, and knocked her head back. She righted herself, licked her lip, and tasted blood. For the first time she felt fear. Why had she come to the city?

The mob parted again and she saw Bellus, as through a tunnel. He turned toward her in that moment, and she imagined that he saw her too. That he recognized her. That the slight but sudden tilt of his head came from surprise.

And then both Bellus and the sun were blocked out by the towering presence of two Roman soldiers. One of them poked at her shoulder with the tip of his pilum. Sweat ran from his forehead. "Move along, fool!"

Sophia swatted the shaft away like an irritating gnat, and the other soldier tried to grab her.

"Keep your savage hands off me!"

The riot seemed to fall away then, and Sophia saw the pilum rise slowly above her, saw its wooden shaft and iron point bisect the cloudless blue sky, watched as it swung toward her in a beautiful, fluid arc.

She closed her eyes to wait for the blow.

SEVEN

As the mood of the Alexandrians grew taut and snapped, Lucius Aurelius Bellus cursed the soldier who had commanded this centuria before him. The man must have had a lust for blood that he ingrained in his men, a passion to crush the opposition with brutality, unthinking of strategy that might prevent losses on both sides.

Bellus shouted orders to his men to surround and subdue with as little bloodshed as possible. This they interpreted to mean they should batter every vocal citizen to the ground.

It should never have come to this.

"Close up! Tighten left!" The ranks turned and reformed.

But it was too far gone. The streets swelled with the frenzied mob, and his men had tasted blood. One young soldier swept alongside him, the red-smeared blade of his *gladius* swinging in wide, chopping strokes.

Bellus yelled, the boy turned, and Bellus saw the battle rage in his eye, a look he knew well from both sides. In a flash, he was back in the fields of Gaul, thick in the fray. Blood and sweat and spittle flying. Gladius thrusting, thrusting. Distinguishing himself, achieving rank.

He shook himself back to the present, fighting the same fury that devoured the young soldier. Alexandria was not Gaul, and these citizens were not enemy soldiers.

"First Sixth! Hold only!" His voice barely rose above the din. He swept his own pilum in front of him, clearing a space from which to survey the actions of the ranks.

A channel opened up, and he bore down into it. Ahead, one figure refused to submit to the soldier telling him to move. Bellus lifted his eyes to the man's face, then caught his breath.

Her again.

Dressed as a man, as she had been when they met in that cursed lighthouse. With her hair clipped in the fashion of men, it was an easy mistake.

The soldier beside her yelled once more, but her eyes were on Bellus and she seemed not to hear. He saw the soldier's pilum heft above the woman's head.

Bellus rushed forward, yelled at the soldier to stay his thrust.

The shaft sliced the air. The woman closed her eyes. Bellus jabbed his leather-covered arm above her head and took the weight of it against his forearm.

He heard the crack. Years of experience told him the bone had not broken. He hissed at his soldier. "Use your weapons on danger-ous men, not harmless women!"

The soldier's eyes widened at his centurion's chastisement. He backed away, into the mob.

Bellus stepped close to the woman, shielded her with his body, and let the battle storm around them. "You should not be here."

She turned her face up to his. She was not beautiful, not at all. She wore only a white himation, and her short, dark hair was threaded with white. He guessed they were roughly the same age. *And you have seen your share of battles, too, I can see.*

No, she was not beautiful. But she had the most intense eyes he had ever seen, eyes like polished black granite, with flecks of light that hinted at depth. The sounds of the fighting faded for a moment as he looked at those eyes. "Go back to your lighthouse . . ." What was her name? "Sophia."

She spoke to him then. Her voice low and strong, carrying to him in spite of the battle din. "I do not take orders from Romans."

Impulsively he slipped an arm around her waist and pulled her through the crowd. It took her only a few moments to loosen his grip and flash those dark eyes. "How *dare* you!" Her lips curled into a snarl. "This is not your city, and I am not your subject."

"You are going to be a dead free woman in a few minutes if you do not get out!"

She bore down on him with her steely glare. "I thought the Romans were famous for their warfare. And yet you cannot control a small crowd of angry citizens?"

Bellus huffed his frustration and shook a fist. "You Greeks have too many opinions. Go home, Sophia!"

And then a cluster of men with sticks came between them, and she was gone.

Bellus turned his attention to his command again. He had been distracted too long.

The mob had pushed as far as the palace gardens. Bellus fought a spark of panic. He had not thought it possible that they could storm the palace.

He gestured to his *signifer*, who carried the spear shaft of his standard, decorated with medallions and the open hand of soldier loyalty. The signifer crossed toward the palace, and Bellus nodded to the *cornicen* to blow the lion-headed horn that curled around his body, to alert the troops to a change of position. The trumpet blared.

Under his command, his centuria redoubled their efforts to push the people back.

The second cohort arrived, summoned from the south of the city. They advanced from behind the mob in the *testudo*, their shields locked to form a roof and wall as they marched to a steady drumbeat.

In the palace garden, the boy-king Ptolemy stood atop a stone sphinx and shouted. "Kill the Roman savages! Cleopatra has allied with the Roman savages!"

But with the two cohorts behind and Bellus's centuria blocking the entrance, the violence began to abate.

Ptolemy's senseless rant continued. He yelled from his perch, instructing all to strike down the soldiers, who were better armed and better trained than they.

Before the sun had reached its zenith in the sky, the two Roman cohorts had formed ranks before the palace, and the streets were empty of citizens, except those who lay dead or moaning at their feet. Ptolemy was removed to the palace interior, under guard.

Bellus stalked along his ranks, alternately praising and criticizing his men. A shout went up from them, and he turned to see Caesar at an open palace window, one hand raised in triumph. He called something, but Bellus was too far to hear.

A twinge of anxiety stirred in his gut. Though they had prevailed, the riot should never have occurred. As the centurion tasked with keeping the peace on palace grounds, he bore the responsibility—as he would bear the condemnation.

He did not have long to wait. Before he had finished dismissing part of his men and assigning others to stand guard around the palace, a messenger came with a summons to the palace. He finished barking orders, then crossed through the courtyard garden to the city-side entrance of the palace. He stopped to right a large terra-cotta planter that had fallen and spilled dirt and yellow flowers to the paved stones.

One of Caesar's personal guards led him to the chamber where the general waited. Bellus entered the room to find Caesar pacing. Not a good sign. Behind him stood a regally commanding woman.

This could be none other than Cleopatra, Queen of Egypt.

"Eighteen years we have fought together in the fields of Gaul, beaten the warring Belgae, crossed the Rubicon," Caesar said. "We've won battles, subdued kingdoms. And now an unruly bunch of wealthy booklovers manages to nearly assassinate me!"

"I am—"

Caesar raised a hand and stopped pacing. He turned flashing eyes on Bellus. "This is not the work of a Pilus Prior. You disappoint me."

Bellus held his tongue, a stray memory of his father intruding.

Caesar yanked downward on his chain mail and swore. "I have done all I can to ensure the cooperation of these people." He eyed the queen behind him. "I expect my legion to do their part."

Bellus's stomach felt like lead, weighted by the justified charge of incompetence.

Caesar resumed his pacing. "You have served me well, Bellus, in spite of your propensity to spend too much time in your books. The men respect you."

Thank you for that.

"But I cannot allow common citizens to appear equally matched with the Roman legion. You understand?"

"I understand, General."

Cleopatra drew alongside the general and wrapped a hand around his arm. He glanced at her, then waved Bellus away.

"Leave me now, comrade. But you will hear from me again, and I shall decide how best to deal with your failure."

Bellus saluted, pivoted, and marched from the chamber. In the hall, he closed his eyes and dropped his shoulders, relieved that the confrontation was past.

It was one of the great paradoxes of his life that as a Roman centurion, he hated conflict above all else.

Well, perhaps not all. Failure was worse.

EIGHT

The centurion marched from her father's chambers, and Cleopatra tried to exhale the tension of the past hour. The worst was over.

She had allied herself with Caesar, the city had reacted as she suspected, and they had been put down. She did not share Caesar's anger at the centurion. A little violence was never a bad thing. A few dead Alexandrians would only deter future uprisings.

Caesar pulled from her grasp and called for a messenger. A young clerk slipped in and saluted. "Get word through the city. I will address the citizens in the theater at dusk."

Cleopatra spoke to his back. "They will resent the very sight of you."

He spun to face her, then flexed his shoulders against his armor. "This situation is not under control. It is time for the people to hear what Rome expects from Egypt."

Cleopatra pressed her lips together, tightening her jaw. He raised an eyebrow, as if inviting her challenge.

"You are right," she finally said. "But they are my people. And I will speak as well."

By the time the sun descended over the Eunostos Harbor, the stone-seated amphitheater in the heart of the royal quarter had filled with thousands of unsettled Alexandrians, and Cleopatra stood beside Caesar in the cool recesses of the *parados*, the off-stage corridor, unseen by those who sat in the half circle of seats. She smoothed the white silk of her chitôn, tucked a stray hair behind her ear, and fingered the emeralds at her throat. The restless buzz of the crowd reached into the half light of the parados, leaving her ill at ease.

Caesar flaunted his military superiority by summoning Alexandria's citizens to one place so soon after the riot. His tight-lipped legionaries surrounded the theater, from the lowest level of the orchestra circle to the top row of seats high above them, with hands ready at their swords.

Caesar's attention was not on her. He stepped out of the corridor, into the orchestra circle, to the upraised roar of the people. He wore the fringed-sleeve toga of a Roman senator this evening, not a general's armor. The purple hem mirrored the jewel-colored sunset in the sky above the theater.

He held one hand aloft, the other gripped the robe at his middle. The noise lessened.

She watched him there a moment, hand upraised to the sky.

By the gods, he was a powerful man! Confident to the point of brutality, yet charming enough to win the affection of any man or woman he chose. She breathed deeply, remembering their time together, confident that she alone held him under sway.

"Citizens of Alexandria," he called, and the people hushed.

Cleopatra strode from the parados to join Caesar. She raised her head to the mass of people, their white tunics lit to an orange glow in the setting sun. The roar lifted again. She smiled and bowed, as though the shouts were those of acclamation, though she had doubts.

She stood beside the Roman general, but not too close. Better to appear set apart, though she longed to grasp his hand and present the people with a united leadership that could encompass all the world. Before her, the people's faces merged into a sameness. Her people, like a flock of sheep in the Nile fields, waiting to be led.

Caesar pulled a papyrus from his belt and unrolled it. "People of Alexandria, the Republic of Rome is not your enemy. We have come to restore peace." An angry murmur rippled through the crowd. "Listen. Listen to the last words of Ptolemy XII, who so recently ruled you."

Cleopatra licked her lips. Caesar had her father's will? She had forgotten that a copy had been sent to Rome. What did he hope to accomplish?

He read the opening statements, a reiteration of the public works erected by Ptolemy XII, the good years of agriculture for which he took credit as though he controlled the Nile's yearly inundation.

The people had called him Ptolemy Auletes—Ptolemy the Flute Player—a slur aimed at his penchant for leisure rather than politics. When the citizens had exiled him years earlier, and Cleopatra's older sister Berenike claimed the throne, it had taken the might and money of Rome to restore him. Her sister was executed immediately, joining her cousin-husband whom she had ordered strangled the week after their wedding.

Caesar continued the reading, reaching the passage that outlined Ptolemy XII's wishes for the future of his kingdom. "'My daughter Cleopatra and my son Ptolemy XIII shall rule after me, co-regents over this great land. Together they will continue the strength of Egypt, they will expand her wealth, they will care for her people.'"

It went on. Father had always been verbose. Cleopatra ground her sandal into the granite stones of the orchestra circle, rolling a pebble under her toe. Caesar's intent was clear. Her father had known that Cleopatra alone was fit to rule, but that the people would demand a king. Likewise, Caesar would not back her as sole ruler of Egypt. She must be content to have the brat on a throne beside her, as though he were her equal. The thought was like a bitter taste in her mouth. But so be it.

Caesar dropped the will to his side and addressed the people. "Rome desires to see the civil war end, to see the brother and sister rule in peace. We do not intend to conquer this land, only to help her be strong, and to request that the debt owed to Rome be repaid."

He paused and scanned the crowd as though he met the eye of every citizen. Cleopatra silently praised his oratory skills. He had them hanging on each word.

"As a gesture of goodwill," he continued, "Rome offers the island of Cyprus to be returned to Egypt's rule as it once was. It shall be governed by Arsinôe and the younger Ptolemy XIV."

The crowd cheered like they had each been given a personal gift by the man they so recently wanted to murder. *Ah, politics.*

It was a strategic move, giving back Cyprus, and at the same time removing her younger sister and one of her younger brothers from Alexandria, to a place they were less likely to cause future problems.

She readied herself to speak to the people, as Caesar had promised she could.

"And here in Alexandria," Caesar yelled above the din, "another brother and sister on the throne. But not brother and sister only. In the manner of true Egypt, you shall have a husband and wife on the throne. Ptolemy and Cleopatra will marry immediately!"

Cleopatra's stomach twisted and then surged. She stared at Caesar, who had turned a smile on her. He held out a hand and stepped aside, giving her the center of the orchestra. She swallowed, struggling to control the furious anger that churned in her chest.

Marry the brat? Yes, it was often done in Egypt's past. But what of Caesar? Were they not destined to rule the world side-by-side? She would not believe that he had so soon cast her off.

But hers was not the only objection. While the people cheered Caesar's announcement, her brother Ptolemy leaped to the circle from where he stood near the bottom of the rows of seats.

"A king needs no co-regent!" he yelled.

Roman soldiers jumped to his side and dragged him from the circle.

That was when she saw it. The wisdom of it all. The boy's advisors had trained him well, and Ptolemy would never accept her as Egypt's ruler. If she and Caesar hoped to retain power, they must do all they could to solidify her reign over the people. A royal marriage would bring the support of both the many thousands of Egyptians who still held to the old ways, and the Greeks who favored Ptolemy.

A plan both brilliant and odious, and she loved Caesar as a strategist, even as she hated him as a man. She turned to face the crowd.

"My people! You can see that Rome has nothing but Egypt's good at heart. You can see that Gaius Julius Caesar is Egypt's friend. While my brother's advisors have been making the foolish decisions to assassinate the Roman Pompey and to rebel against Rome's presence, I have been securing the friendship of this great leader." She held a hand to Caesar, and he grasped it. Together they lifted their hands above their heads. A smattering of applause went up from the people.

More. More is needed.

"You have before you a true Ptolemy, from a long line of great rulers. I will rule from my royal heart, not from the whisperings of eunuchs and teachers. And my brother will grow into his role as king at my side."

From below the orchestra, Ptolemy struggled in the grasp of two soldiers but was wise enough to hold his tongue.

"The Romans are here, citizens of Alexandria! They are a mighty people, and the world must take note. Will we make ourselves the enemy of Rome, to be trampled? Or will we work with this new power, and together build an even greater and wealthier new Egypt?"

She turned to the general at her side, whose admiration as he watched her, warmed her to her depths. She raised an arm in salute, and called out in a strong and full voice. "Hail, Caesar!"

There was only a moment's pause, and then the people responded, as she knew they would.

"Hail, Caesar!"

Triumph curled into a small smile, and she held her arm still upraised.

But in the roar of approval that followed, the voice that hounded her through all of her decisions would not cease its dark whispering: *You are committed now. For better or worse. And when it is all over, will Egypt still be yours? Or have you just sold yourself to Rome?*

NINE

It was dark when Sophia decided that the rotating Roman guard that paced across the palace courtyard had sufficiently thinned. They were watchful for angry mobs, but one woman who knew every inch of the palace could easily go unseen.

From the steps that led from the harbor, she crept along the garden wall until she reached the juncture where the wall met the palace. Here, a small door provided a quick exit for gardeners tending to the plants and flowers outside the official gardens. She had to bend to enter, so small was the opening. In the cobwebby darkness beyond, she squeaked the door closed, then eased upright. Silent as a tomb and just as dark. But Sophia and Cleopatra had often come this way when the queen was a child. Now Sophia moved forward, grateful to be on sure footing.

The corridor shot straight through the lowest level of the palace, and within minutes she emerged into the inner courtyard garden.

The sun had dropped below the palace walls, leaving her in blessed shadow. Only one soldier seemed about, beside the main entrance. He rolled his shoulders as though he had stood too long.

Sophia slipped along the inner wall, into another corridor that branched through the palace. A few yards down, and stone steps brought her to the throne room level.

Where are you, Cleopatra?

Would she find the queen alone, where she could entreat her to secure the release of Sosigenes? Or would Cleo be with *him*, the Roman who had imprisoned the scholar so unjustly?

She slipped along the chambered hall, peering into each room she passed.

She thought again of her rooms in the lighthouse. She would be lighting the lamps now if she were there. Settling down for the evening with some scrolls of Plato, or perhaps Zeno of Citium. A wave of anger at those who had forced her from comfort pulsed through her chest.

She heard chanting from the throne room ahead. Though it had only a modest squared entryway, the room opened into a grand columned hall, with carved reliefs and painted frescoes in the classic Egyptian style. The Greeks had always acted so in Egypt. Part flattery of imitation and part diplomacy and placating, they continued the styles of architecture and even religion that they had found when Alexander first arrived in Egypt three hundred years earlier.

The throne room had no windows. Cleopatra's father had built it to control the amount of light at any time of day.

With the night spreading up the corridor behind her and only a few lamps lit in the hall ahead, Sophia at first saw nothing but the dancing flames when she approached the doorway.

Several figures soon revealed themselves in the darkness. Cleopatra and her brother stood at the front of the hall, on the floor level below the raised platform that held two carved thrones with lion-head armrests. Before the two royals, a tiny bald priest lifted a sistrum in one hand, and an amulet on a cord in the other. Braziers on either side of the hall afforded the only light in the huge chamber, creating eerie shadows above the fluted columns, their middles bulging in the Egyptian style. To the left, a tall man with a squared jaw and steady eyes stood watching. He was dressed in the Roman fashion, with a toga that was simply a plainer version of the Greek himation swept about his shoulders, and his left hand held at his rib cage in the Roman way. She had seen him only from the distance of the top row of theater seats.

A few others stood about, but she ignored them, drawn instead to the center of the room.

She had stumbled into Cleopatra and Ptolemy's wedding ceremony.

Her foot scraped the granite floor, and the two in front turned to her.

Cleopatra let a smile play on her lips when she saw Sophia, then held out a hand. "Of course you should be here. Come and stand beside me."

Sophia crossed the room, mindful of Caesar's eyes on her. Even without speaking, he had a presence, a raw power about him that made one self-conscious. She found herself wishing she had dressed differently.

Cleopatra squeezed her hand and pulled her close.

"Are you certain about this?" Sophia whispered into her ear.

Cleopatra smiled, but her answer was spoken through clenched teeth. "What choice do I have?"

The priest eyed them both with narrowed eyes, as though affronted by the interruption. Cleopatra nodded to the little man, and he continued the chanting Sophia had heard from the corridor, swinging the amulet and rattling the sistrum before them all. His bare torso was all bony, protruding ribs and sharp shoulders.

The room was hot, the oil lamps smoked, and Sophia's skin grew damp in the still air. Two slave women fanned Cleo with flat palm leaves on poles, but she shifted on her feet, as though impatient for the end of the chant. She still held Sophia's hand, and her white chitôn drifted lazily across Sophia's arm, trailing its gold trim.

With the sing-songing of the priest, the warm night felt like Cleo's robes on her skin, like black and gold silk from the east, caressing with the lightest touch of luxury. Sophia closed her eyes and succumbed to the spell of the night.

But then the priest was whispering questions, and Ptolemy's adolescent squeak grated against the silkiness of the night. The boy had been cleaned up at least, but nothing could improve his personality.

Sophia ran a hand over the back of her neck and looked away. Across the room, a soldier watched her. She started and pulled her hand from Cleopatra's grasp. Again, that Roman! Four thousand Roman soldiers in Alexandria, and she saw this one everywhere! He lowered his head in recognition, and she wrapped her arms about her waist, remembering his own arm around her body.

The ceremony ended at last, with the priest shaking the sistrum too near her face. Its clatter of beads echoed from the carved walls and pillars of the hall. The priest slipped away, and Caesar faced the new husband and wife. "That is done, then. Let peace reign in Egypt."

Sophia looked to Cleopatra, who only offered her enigmatic smile and watched the Roman general. Sophia leaned toward her one-time student. "Cleopatra, I must speak to you."

Caesar turned on the boy. "It seems your advisors have left you to yourself, King. Achillas still heads your troops in Pelusium, Theodotus has fled from my wrath over his assassination of Pompey, and Pothinus—well, where is Pothinus, King?" Caesar's glance took in the Roman soldier at the side of the room, the one who had invaded her lighthouse.

"I—I do not know," the boy said. "He disappeared during the riot this afternoon."

"Hmmm." Caesar nodded. "I do hope he has not been hurt."

Ptolemy's eyes widened. The boy would be lost without his eunuch.

"Well, perhaps you can find your own bedchamber without assistance?"

Ptolemy's lips and chin took on a pout at the sarcasm. "Good night, then." With that, he took his leave.

"Cleopatra, will you not introduce me to the woman who managed to get past my guards and join us for the ceremony?"

Cleopatra pulled her forward. "Caesar, this is Sophia, my language tutor from the time I was very young."

Sophia lifted her chin to the Roman.

"Ah, language. Cleopatra has impressed me utterly with her command of Latin, Greek, and Egyptian."

Pride in her student coursed through her. "She knows Hebrew and Syriac as well."

"Then I must assume you are a supreme teacher. I thank you for your contribution to this astounding woman." His hand went possessively to the small of Cleopatra's back, and Sophia felt a spark of something like anger. She leaned her head to the queen. "May I speak to you in private, Cleopatra?"

Caesar waved away the centurions at the side of the hall. "We have no secrets, the queen and I. Speak."

Sophia hardened her voice and turned on the Roman. "You have come to our land to reap the best of it, no doubt. But already you have harmed the best and put it in chains."

Caesar's eyes narrowed. "I have dispatched no orders in regard to Egypt's grain."

Sophia laughed, not caring it rang with harsh disdain. "Grain nourishes a man for a mere day. Philosophy, mathematics, science—the academic disciplines will sustain the world for eternity."

The smoky oil lamps, the carved hieroglyphs of the columns, even Cleopatra beside her seemed to fade, and Sophia saw only Caesar's hard eyes, taking her in, measuring her.

"You speak of your Museum's scholars?"

"One in particular. A dear friend of mine, Sosigenes. You have imprisoned him. He is an old man and cannot survive it." She lowered her head. "I ask you, for the sake of Cleopatra's devotion to me, to release this man."

Caesar laughed. "One old man? He must be very learned."

She frowned. "He has much to offer the world, if you will but let him."

"Oh, but I do intend to let him." Caesar tugged at the folds of his toga and straightened. "That is why I have him here. To diagram and construct a great siege works."

Cleopatra intervened, moving to stand in front of Caesar. "But you will need no siege works here, Gaius."

He smiled down on her and traced her cheekbone with a finger. "Do not be so confident, my Egyptian queen. We have not heard the last of Pothinus, I am certain."

Sophia leaned into their conversation. "To force a man to create something that destroys when his whole life has been dedicated to progress is a great evil!"

Caesar pushed Cleopatra to the side and faced Sophia. "Not even my detractors in Rome have accused me of evil. Have you no idea of the power at my command?"

Sophia inhaled and squeezed her fingers into a fist. Her words hissed through clenched teeth. "*There is strength even in the union of very sorry men.*"

Caesar took a step backward, then broke into a laugh. "Who is this woman, Cleopatra? Quoting Homer, if I'm not mistaken? More than a palace servant, surely!"

"She is Keeper of the lighthouse," Cleopatra said. "Her family has controlled it and gathered the harbor taxes since the tower was first built."

"The lighthouse. Yes, the lighthouse." Caesar pivoted on his heel and strode from the smoky throne room, leaving Sophia to raise her eyebrows at Cleopatra and then to follow.

Caesar took to the steps she had ascended, crossed through the inner garden, and then down the wide marble steps to the palace harbor. Sophia and Cleopatra hurried behind, until all three stood at the dark water's edge, eyes lifted to the lighthouse above them.

Sophia felt another surge of pride. The polished bronze in the beacon chamber had been swiveled to reflect the firelight toward the east tonight, giving Caesar a magnificent view of its power. The structure poked at the night sky, so far above the city that even at this distance across the mighty harbor, one had to tilt his head back to take it in. It was a wonder of engineering, with its three tiers reaching forty stories above the vast platform. Sailors from lands as far as India and Lebanon knew that only the Pharos could guide them safely through the shallow reefs and narrow harbor entrance, to reach the wealth of Alexandria. Without her lighthouse, many a ship would have foundered on the rocks.

A familiar knife of memory sliced through her. The emotion threatened to steal her composure and she dug her fingers into her thigh. This was her reason for coming. Her husband's work must continue.

"It is quite a fortress, is it not?" Caesar said.

My fortress.

He rubbed at his chin. "The most strategic location in the city, actually."

Sophia pulled her gaze from the light and scowled at Caesar. "The lighthouse stands at the harbor to save lives, not to destroy them."

He still gazed upward, saying nothing.

"Your heavy-footed legion has already left carnage in the Museum and Library. Leave the rest of Alexandria as you found it!"

Caesar smiled again, and turned on her. "You women of Alexandria"—he took in Cleopatra with his glance—"part brilliant Greece and part passionate Egypt, but both more spirited than a dozen Roman women. Including my wife."

Sophia watched Cleopatra's eyes go dark at the mention of her rival, but she was unconcerned at the moment with the queen's jealousy. Something far more important had just been threatened.

For Caesar had turned away again and set his eyes on her lighthouse.

TEN

Astadia away from the harbor below the royal palace, Pothinus stalked the docks in long strides. His personal slave, Plebo, ran along behind with Pothinus's wooden case bouncing against his thigh.

Pothinus swore. "Where are they, Plebo?"

"Master, I—"

"Time is short. I told you to have them here by nightfall." Pothinus halted and Plebo stumbled into him. "Get away from me, you incompetent peasant!" He shoved the younger man backward with his shoulder.

"Master, I am sure the men will be here very soon. No doubt they are readying the ship—"

"I do not need the ship *readied*. I need the ship *gone!*" Pothinus inspected the shadowy harbor, hands on his hips. The night breeze had kicked up and it stirred the water and slapped small craft against the harbor wall. He studied the moon's ascent and cursed again.

How long until the Roman dog closes the harbor?

Pothinus had always prided himself on his ability to take accurate measure of the enemy. But he had underestimated Julius Caesar. And Cleopatra as well.

And the fools of this city could be swayed as easily as a papyrus reed at the water's edge.

"If that ship does not arrive soon, Plebo, it will be your carcass under a Roman blade!"

Plebo's lip quivered, and his weak chin wobbled. He was a Greek-Egyptian mutt, Pothinus's slave, whose favorite pastime was groveling. But Pothinus found him useful on occasion. The slave thrived on gossip and often brought him nuggets. This afternoon it had been Plebo he had sent into the crowds to whisper to Greek and Egyptian alike of the betrayal of Cleopatra.

The riot had escalated beyond his hopes, yet still Caesar and his new mistress had managed to calm the people, convince them that peace between brother and sister was best, and dupe them into believing Rome meant only good for Egypt.

And now the idiot-king and Cleopatra would marry, and Pothinus's life would be forfeit. *I must get away, rally Ptolemy's army. Achillas will know what to do.*

"There!" Plebo shouted beside him and pointed a crooked finger toward the water.

Pothinus followed the finger and saw an Egyptian, bare-chested and bald, lift a meaty arm. He stood astride the prow of a small boat, with a dozen or so oarsmen behind him. The boat skimmed into an open slot at the quay, and the Egyptian jumped ashore.

Plebo trotted to the sailor and jutted his chin toward the ship. "Where have you been? The master had need of you immediately." His nasal voice had the echo of Pothinus's own stridency.

The Egyptian pushed him aside. "We are ready, master. The ship is fit and ready to sail to Pelusium this night."

Pothinus crossed to the edge of the dock where the boat had been secured. He gathered his himation about his legs and stepped across. The boat dipped, giving him a moment of panic. He thrust out a steadying arm, then jumped.

The craft was frighteningly small, with ten beefy oarsmen, five at each side. The dark wood was aged with seawater and sun, and splintered in places. In the center of the deck a cabin stood open, but Pothinus was not yet ready to sequester himself. "Well, what is the delay? Shove *off!*"

Plebo swayed at the prow, one hand gripping the side, his face white.

"Come now, Plebo. Don't tell me you've lived your life in the trading capital of the world, and do not like to sail?"

"I—I have never tried it, master, so I cannot say whether I like it or not."

Pothinus covered his own concern with a harsh laugh. "The sea is our greatest ally, Plebo." *Or our greatest enemy.*

The boat shoved away from the dock, sails lowered to avoid notice. The men at each side began their rhythmic sweeps to guide her past the other craft clogging the harbor. But Pothinus's attention was not on the water. He lifted his eyes to the lighthouse jutting above them. It stood in mute testimony to the rocky shoals rising from the sea bottom across the harbor entrance, waiting eagerly to rip out the underbelly of any ship fool enough to not heed the light. Even from here he could make out the sea tritons that perched halfway up, on the corners of the first platform. The monstrous structure dwarfed the harbor, the ships, Pothinus himself. He inhaled the salt-tinged air and expanded his chest to deflect the ominous weight of that brooding beast. It was like an angry master, peering over the harbor with an acacia switch, ready to bring the lash down on disobedient ships. Pothinus shuddered.

Plebo staggered to where Pothinus stood in the center of the ship. He set the wooden case down and followed his master's gaze upward. "It is a fearsome thing."

Pothinus pulled his attention downward, to the brown splintered wood of the ship, the dark churning of the seawater.

Already white limestone reefs poked through the surface. They sailed past a gull perched on a rocky outcrop. The bird seemed to follow them with its eyes, waiting for their downfall.

"Do you think we will come back?" Plebo's voice carried a note of nostalgia.

Pothinus nearly slapped him. "We will come back. With all of Ptolemy's army at our heels, and victory before us!" He grabbed an amphorae of wine from a stand beside the cabin, unplugged it, and swigged at its contents. The wine was soured and went down like a slashing at his throat. He wiped his mouth with the back of his hand. "Alexandria has not seen the last of Pothinus."

"But Caesar has Ptolemy in his clutches. And Cleopatra rules from behind Caesar. The people have switched their allegiance—"

Pothinus did slap him then. The slave raised a hesitant hand to his lip.

"All of that can change in an instant, Plebo. Do not be a fool. There are many ways to incite a people to take up the cause of one ruler and destroy that of another."

"But the people of Alexandria want peace. They want to go on with their philosophy of the Museum, with their theater and their sciences."

Pothinus took a deep breath again and scowled at the sweaty odor of the men who dragged on the oars. For twenty years talk of the Museum had sickened him, since the day he had been ostracized by men who were by far his intellectual inferiors.

Plebo was still whining. "Perhaps if you had control of the new discovery from the Museum—"

"What discovery?" Pothinus plugged the amphorae.

Plebo smiled, as though he had stumbled upon a treasure and was the only one to know where it lay.

"Come on, fool, what whisperings have you heard?"

Plebo shrugged. "Something Sosigenes has been working on."

"Sosigenes." Pothinus turned away. It was the second time today he'd heard that name. Years ago, before Ptolemy XIII had been born and Pothinus had become the minister of finance, there had been a group of them. Hot-headed scholars, ready to change the world. *And we would have. Could have.* "What has Sosigenes discovered?"

Plebo shrugged again. "No one seems sure, but it is rumored that he has been reconstructing the mechanism once lost—"

Pothinus held up a hand to silence the slave. He inclined his head toward the ship's captain and the oarsmen. "No need to give everything away, Plebo," he muttered.

Sosigenes. The *Proginosko* mechanism. Could it be?

He thought of Sophia in the streets during the riot, pleading for the scholar's release.

His stomach curdled, partly in response to the sour wine and the swaying boat, and partly with a rancid ambition that had found a handle with which to turn the world. Yes, if it were true, it would change everything. Power had always been married to knowledge. With the right technology, even a eunuch could rule the world.

Pothinus turned on Plebo. "You must find out."

"Find out?"

"Exactly what Sosigenes is doing. Get word to me immediately at Pelusium."

"But how—"

Pothinus grabbed Plebo's arm. "I don't care how, just do it!" He pulled the slave toward the prow of the ship.

"But, I thought I was sailing—"

"Not anymore."

It took little effort. One arm around the scrawny man's waist, and one good heave, and he was over the side.

Pothinus leaned over, watched the slave come up sputtering and yelling.

"Careful of the pirates!" Pothinus pointed to the Pharos island, home to men who preyed on stranded ships. "And hurry!"

They had cleared the harbor entrance now, and Pothinus turned to the Great Sea. Though the way ahead was as dark as a tomb, Pothinus felt as though a torch had been lit solely for him, guiding him to what he should do.

Yes, I will return, Plebo. Backed with military strength and with a discovery for which the world would kill.

ELEVEN

Bellus was reading from a borrowed copy of Epicurus and finishing his morning bread and feta beside the palace harbor when Caesar's summons came. An Egyptian slave brought it. Bellus chewed the last bit of bread, now dry as dust. He slid the papyrus beneath his chain mail and followed the slave.

I must find a way to regain Caesar's approval.

They crossed through the tangle of sweet-smelling color in the gardens, past the lotus-filled reflecting pool, and under the square stone lintel. The slave led him upward, to the private chambers Caesar had claimed for his own.

The general sat with his back to the door, a Roman in the center of Ptolemy XII's sumptuous chamber. A barber stood behind Caesar, combing and snipping.

"Who is that?" Caesar called.

"Lucius Aurelius Bellus, General." He tried to keep his voice steady and stood with shoulders back.

"Ah, Bellus. My Pilus Prior who would rather study dead men's scrolls than defend Rome. What would your father have said?"

Bellus winced, remembering Caesar's words of the night before. *You disappoint me.* He straightened. "The events of yesterday should never have happened, General. I regret—"

Caesar pushed away the barber, who cowered at his touch, and swiveled in his chair. "You regret? Bellus, where is that weasel, the eunuch Pothinus?"

Bellus stood at attention under Caesar's gaze. His iron felt weighty against his chest. "We have not yet been able to locate—"

"I will tell you where he is. For it seems all of Alexandria knows. At least that is what I hear from Falah here." He stood and slapped the barber on the back. The Egyptian lowered his eyes to his blade. "He has sailed for Pelusium in the night. To join Achillas, and Ptolemy's troops, and no doubt lead them back here to attack me."

Bellus inhaled and inwardly cursed this land. He had not seen such failures in all of his military career as he had since landing here.

"It is strange to me"—Caesar brushed tiny hairs from his shoulders—"that Pothinus should have sailed from Alexandria. Because I thought I remembered giving you clear orders yesterday to find him and put him in custody."

From the bedchamber to his right, Bellus heard the low laughter of a woman. His hand went to his pugio.

A tray of olives and garlic, with lentils covered in a *gáron* sauce, was brought by a slave. The fish sauce was a delicacy not often seen in Rome. Cleopatra emerged from the bedchamber, dressed in flowing white robes tied at her shoulders, with gold armbands wrapped around each upper arm. Her long hair swung when she walked.

Bellus shifted his weight, shuffling his battle-worn sandals against the marble floor. He felt more like a boorish peasant than the Sextus Pilus Prior. "I will go after him, Caesar. He cannot have gotten too far ahead. I will bring the centuria and we will—"

"You have done all I have need of in this matter, Bellus. I have often noted your propensity to be slow to act."

"I am careful not to shed blood without cause, General. As you know, my centuria has suffered fewer losses than any other."

Cleopatra brushed past him and Bellus stepped backward. She drifted to a couch and stretched herself on it.

Caesar cleared his throat, and Bellus jerked his attention back to the general. "And yet I believe you are a bit too 'careful,' as you say, to shed the blood of the enemy as well." Caesar waved a hand. "In any case, I have decided to place you elsewhere."

"Elsewhere, General?" Bellus felt a ridiculous desire for his shield to stand behind. Caesar's accusations were like enemy darts.

"It has occurred to me that the lighthouse is our most strategic location on this island. The lighthouse controls the harbor, and the harbor supplies the city. We must retain control of the harbor." He joined Cleopatra on another couch.

Bellus saluted. "We will post ten legionaries at each of the—"

Caesar was shaking his head. Bellus let his plan go unfinished.

"No, there is no need of that yet." He reached for an olive. "Pothinus will be some time raising the troops. No, for now I simply want you to take the lighthouse."

"There is no enemy occupation in the lighthouse, General."

Caesar laughed and looked to Cleopatra. "You would be surprised." The queen smiled, but it was a smile tinged with annoyance. "But you are correct, there is no need to take it by force. I simply want you and your centuria to station yourselves there, until I have need of you."

Bellus opened his mouth, then closed it again. *Station ourselves there?* He shifted, and the metal discs of the *sporran* that hung from the front of his belt clinked discordantly.

Caesar's attention had moved to the food and the queen.

"Sir," Bellus finally said, "surely you have a better use for an entire centuria than watching over a lighthouse?"

"Think of it as some time off, Bellus." Caesar leaned his head against the red cushions. "You could do more of that reading you're so fond of. And perhaps the next time I have need of you, you will remember what it means to fight."

Bellus remained fixed before Caesar, searching for a way to refuse the shameful duty without insubordination.

"That is all, Bellus." Caesar turned his eyes to Cleopatra, who smiled and touched his hand. "You are dismissed."

Bellus saluted, pivoted, and stalked to the door.

"Oh, and Bellus?"

He turned.

"Watch out for that beast who runs the lighthouse. She may be the fiercest enemy you've yet faced!"

Caesar laughed at his own joke, but Bellus simply nodded and left the chamber. He marched through the palace, heedless of his surroundings.

Lighthouse duty! He may as well been asked to tend the palace gardens. He had fought the Belgic army, led a centuria through Gaul. And now he was expected to sit in that ghastly woman's tower and wait for Caesar to call him back from the dead?

He found himself at the palace entrance and blinked at the morning sun that shot across the city and into the courtyard. He scanned the three-tiered wonder from bottom to top, taking in the base level that must house hundreds of rooms, the tall bottom tier with its glass windows on every side. Above the first section was a shorter, octagonal tier. He wondered what was on the platform where the second tier began. Above the octagon, the third tier was circular, and housed the apparatus that directed light outward, day and night. He had to admit a certain curiosity about how it was accomplished. From this distance he could barely make out the figure of Poseidon atop the lighthouse, his trident stretched toward the water as though he alone commanded the harbor.

It's a fascinating thing, to be sure. But his curiosity could be satisfied with an afternoon visit. He did not need to camp there with eighty able soldiers!

There must be another way.

A palace slave scurried by, water pot in hand, and he roused himself, realizing he must look strange loitering about in the gardens. Besides, there was work to be done.

He crossed back through the palace and out to the city streets. This entire quarter of Alexandria was taken up by the line of Ptolemaic palaces that each successive Pharaoh-king had built for himself along the water.

These kings had too much time on their hands. Egypt's natural defenses of sea in the north and desert to the east and west had left her fat and rich, with little to do but wallow in her luxury.

Bellus's own centuria was housed in one of the smaller palaces, and he headed there now to raise his men. He marched through the cool marble hall to the series of chambers allocated to the soldiers.

The men hailed him as he entered the room. "Pilus Prior Bellus!" Soldiers scrambled from mats, buckling and lacing as they found their lines. There was a solemnity among them this morning. They felt yesterday's failures as well and desired an opportunity to make amends.

"We have been given new orders, men." They looked at him, expectant. He paused, his gaze taking in the faces of these men who trusted him not only in battle, but who came to him with their joys and heartaches as well. How many of them had he talked through the news of a wife who had married someone else while her soldier husband marched through foreign lands? He had slapped their backs upon the births of their sons, gripped their arms at the deaths of their parents.

"Our new assignment—"he hesitated on the edge of decision, knowing that professional death overhung his every choice—"Our new assignment is to take the harbor." Across the chamber chins lifted, chests expanded.

Once committed, his words came in a rush. "By midday today, we will have set up a perimeter guard around both the Great Harbor and the Eunostos. We will take ships to the narrow entrances and drop anchor, there to examine every craft that enters and exits Alexandria. No one will get in or out without our knowledge. You may have heard that pirates infest the Pharos Island on the western side. We will need to establish immediate superiority over these thieves and beggars as well."

It was done. And, he knew, so was he.

Bellus called for a meeting of the eight men of his first *contubernium* and sketched out his plan to them. Within the hour the centuria marched from the palace, intent on its new orders.

Bellus watched them go, not yet ready. The heaviness in his chest would not abate. He had dared to defy Caesar the Conqueror.

Not defy. Exercise my judgment in how best to accomplish Caesar's goal.

But Caesar's reference to his father ate at him. The military hero would have never suffered yesterday's loss, nor today's humiliation. He prayed to the gods that his plan would restore him to Caesar's favor.

In his tunic lay a letter, slipped to him minutes earlier by a messenger. He pulled it out and broke the seal.

From Valeria, back in Rome. He sighed and read, hoping she would say something to lift the weight. He read as he walked, in the direction of the harbor.

My dearest Lucius. How I long to have you back in Rome. I have found the most beautiful fabric with which to make my wedding robes . . .

He finished the letter. It would be unkind to leave it unread. But her words did nothing. She spoke of her clothes, of her pets, of her silly games. All the while the pressing assumption that he would marry her when he returned.

She is young. She will grow in knowledge and in spirit in the years to come.

He told himself these things often, reminded himself a wife need not be his equal in things of the mind. A man could get his fill of discourse and study in the Forum. No need for it at home.

He slid the letter back into his tunic and lifted his eyes to the harbor—to the lighthouse at its outer reaches.

No more of letters or of Epicurus's philosophy.

It was time for action. It was time to take the harbor, just as Caesar had ordered.

Well, almost.

TWELVE

Sophia paced the front hall of the lighthouse's Base, twisting her fingers together, then prying them apart and wiping her hands down the sides of her tunic.

What was taking so long?

She had sent Ares into the city long ago. He knew the back roads and alleys, and the people who frequented them. He could find someone for the task she required.

Last night's plan to have Cleopatra use her influence with Caesar had failed. Sosigenes would not be released, and if anything, Sophia had drawn more attention to the scholars and to her lighthouse than she would have wished.

And so it was left to her to find another solution.

She put her plan into action as soon as the sun rose, filling a sack with enough money to purchase the help of disreputable characters and passing it to Ares with whispered instructions.

Do what you must to free him from prison. Bring him to me. Take care that no one sees you come here.

After that she had no plan. Only to hear Sosigenes's important news and find a way to keep him safe. She stood now at the entrance, looking over the island.

The Base, the platform level of the lighthouse, housed over two hundred rooms in the corridors that formed a huge square at the tip of Pharos Island. In the center of the courtyard formed by the four corridors, the lighthouse itself began its ascent, with the ramp that spiraled upward. On this south side of the Base, the entrance led out to the heptastadion, and paths branched off in eastern and western directions to the small village that had been part of this island since before the time of Alexander.

Sophia had a clear view across the island and the causeway, but she saw no sign of Ares or Sosigenes. She returned to her pacing of the South Wing. She ran her hand along the stone corridor and trailed her fingers over a wooden door that led to an unused storage room. The dim light of the front hall did not reach into the shadowy corners of the doorway.

Back to the entrance, to squint into the sunlight, searching the heptastadion again. Villagers came and went. Some on foot, some in two-wheeled carts pulled by mangy horses. She could hear the far-off shouts of the village below her, the village that teemed with a community of people living together and loving each other.

To her left, the Great Harbor was fully into its business of the day. Across the blue water a golden sun-path sparkled, like a road inviting her to join the city. It seemed there were people in every direction she looked from her isolated position on the island.

And then she saw him. Ares, cracking a whip over the back of a horse, from his place at the front of a large wooden wagon.

Why a wagon?

She used her hand to shield her eyes and waited for them to reach the end of the heptastadion. Her heel beat an impatient rhythm against the stones.

Sosigenes was not with him. She prayed to the gods that he was in the wagon.

Ares jumped from the rickety vehicle, the switch still in his hands. The horse pawed at the ground and snorted. A canvas had been stretched and tacked over the back of the vehicle, making its load a mystery. Ares searched the area around the lighthouse entrance.

"Where is he? Did you get him out?"

Ares nodded once. "He is here." He inclined his head to the wagon and smiled. "And I have a surprise for you."

Sophia frowned and hurried to the back of the wagon. "You know I hate surprises."

"Not this one." He joined her. "You'll want to kiss me for this one, Abbas."

"We shall see about that."

A crude nail poked through the canvas into the wagon's splintered side. She yanked the canvas away and revealed part of the wagon's load.

It was enough.

Four white-haired men lay on their backs, grinning up at her.

"Sosigenes! Archippos! Ares, what—how many of you are there?" She attempted to pull the canvas farther.

Sosigenes propped himself on his bony elbows. "All of us, Sophia. The whole Council. All twelve."

"What are you doing here?"

"Where else would we go?"

Ares appeared smiling at her elbow, but she felt more inclined to slap him than kiss him. "What am I supposed to do with them?"

Sosigenes peered over her shoulder, toward the bustling village. "For now, I should think you would get us out of this wagon, and somewhere unseen."

Sophia snorted and yanked the canvas to cover again its ludicrous cargo. "Circle it to the lighthouse entrance," she said to Ares. "And be quick about it!"

Within a few minutes, the twelve top scholars in all of Greece stood in the front hall of the Base.

"You have more than enough room here, Sophia," Sosigenes said. "We can continue our studies—"

"You cannot stay here!" Sophia laughed, but the older man did not appear amused. "It is impossible. I live here alone, except for the servants. That is how it must remain. Besides, Caesar would certainly come here to find you first, when he learns that I am your biggest patron."

The other men murmured together at the side of the corridor. It was clear that none of them wished Caesar to know their whereabouts.

"Sophia"—Sosigenes gripped her arm—"I must speak with you."

Finally. "Yes. Ares, take the Council to the kitchen, find them something to eat. Bring the noon meal to my chambers for Sosigenes and myself."

Sosigenes followed her through the courtyard to the lighthouse, then up the ramp to her private chambers. He was huffing by the time they reached her door, and she remembered his weak lungs.

"You can rest here awhile, Sosigenes. Ares will bring food and wine, and you can tell me of this important news that you spoke of with such urgency."

She led the older man in and settled him on one of her couches. He was as lean as the day she had met him, but the effort of the climb seemed to show itself in the creases of his face. He stretched his long legs over the couch, reclined against a sand-colored cushion and sighed.

Sophia patted his arm and waited. Sosigenes loved to present his ideas dramatically. He would need to catch his breath first.

A lock of his white hair fell down across his eye, and Sophia pushed it aside.

The old scholar had been her husband's mentor, all those years ago, when she had been young and in love and thought the world would always treat her gently. Sosigenes had stood at Kallias's side, marveling over the younger man's calculations, cheering him as he developed the most extraordinary mechanism the world had yet seen. It had all been done in secrecy, with the knowledge that there were some who would go to great lengths to obtain his findings. Even Sophia, when she would bring Kallias his lunch of bread and cheese in the Museum, would have to stand on her toes and peer over Kallias's shoulder to get a glimpse of his work.

Then came the day when Kallias rushed home, swept her off her feet, and twirled her in circles, shouting, "It works! It truly works, my love!"

Sophia closed her eyes, tasting the memory of that day. It had been the beginning of the end, but she had not known it then.

Sosigenes gripped her arm and she opened her eyes.

"I have rebuilt it." His eyes held steady on hers.

She shook her head. "Don't speak to me in riddles, Sosigenes."

"I speak plainly. I have rebuilt it. Kallias's mechanism. The Proginosko."

"Impossible!"

He laughed. "Kallias had a brilliant mind, Sophia. But did you think he was the only one in all the world capable of such a feat?"

She stood, unwilling to remain still. "Perhaps not, but you—"

He smiled up at her. "You forget I was there, for the years that he worked on it."

"But you always said that you never could have built it. And when we lost him—"

"We lost everything. It is true. But always, all these years, I have worked on the idea when there was time. Hopeful that someday I would find the key . . ."

Sophia was pacing now. "And you have?"

"Almost. I was almost finished when those barbarians rounded us up and chased us from the Museum. The next thing I knew, I was in a cell simply because I refused to concoct a better way for them to attack us."

"And the Proginosko? Where is it?"

He laughed. "Your concern for my well-being is touching, Sophia."

"Don't be a fool, Sosigenes. Who do you think paid to break you out of there?"

He lowered his eyes. "My apologies."

Sophia bent to the couch and squeezed his hand. "No, no. I am sorry. It is just—I cannot believe—"

"It is well-hidden, Sophia. Kallias's legacy." He laughed. "Unless the Romans develop a deep appreciation of Lucretius's lesser works buried in the Library. No one will find it."

"You said that it was almost finished?"

"It is still in need of testing and perhaps some small adjusting. But in essence, it is complete."

"How much longer?"

"Two months. I must get enough readings from the various moon phases to be sure."

Ares's knuckle-beating on the door caused Sophia to jump. He didn't wait to be invited but pushed the door open and entered with a tray overflowing with meats and cheeses. "Those old men can eat!" he said, shaking his head. "It was all I could do to tear this much away for the two of you."

Sosigenes laughed and lifted his head. "Much sustenance is needed to fuel the mind, my boy."

Sophia took the tray from Ares and set it on her desk. She waved him out of the room with a flick of her hand and crossed to close the door behind him. She turned and leaned her back against it and frowned at Sosigenes. "It is too long."

"Since I have eaten?" He pulled himself to his feet. "I would agree."

"Two months. Too long for you to stay in Alexandria. Not with Caesar looking for you."

Sosigenes went to the food on her desk. "The One God has long had His hand on me, Sophia. He will protect me still."

Sophia snorted. "You talk of your 'One God' as though he cares for people personally."

Sosigenes lifted his eyebrows. "Yes, and He even cares for you, Sophia." He tore a piece of bread from a small loaf. "But the Roman cares only about warfare, I am afraid. I doubt he would even see the value of the Proginosko."

"We must get you out of Alexandria. Today. Before he thinks to look for you here."

"How?" The scholar popped a grilled chestnut into his mouth and chewed it slowly.

Sophia went to the wall of windows and studied the harbor. "You must sail to Athens."

"And what of my colleagues? Shall I leave them behind to be conscripted into building siege works that violate every bit of conscience they have?"

Sophia pressed her forehead against the blurry glass. "No. You must all go." She turned to him. "I will pay for passage for all of you. Do not worry." She crossed to the door, yanked it open and yelled for Ares, who was still on the ramp.

"You must give Ares instructions on how to find the Proginosko, Sosigenes. He can retrieve it and bring it here. Meanwhile, I will secure passage to Athens for you."

The man nodded, and Ares showed up at the door. "Take Sosigenes to the others," she told him. "Then do as he says. I will be back."

Ares's mouth dropped open slightly. "You are going out? Again?"

She scowled. "You make me sound like some kind of mad recluse, Ares." He said nothing. Sophia kissed Sosigenes on the cheek, grabbed a pouch, and hurried to the ramp. On the way down, she tied the pouch under her tunic.

At the bottom of the lighthouse, she found one of the servants charged with keeping the light functioning and told him to fetch a horse and cart for her. His eyebrows lifted in the same manner as Ares's.

Yes, I know. Twice in two days I have entered the city.

"Go!" She thrust her arm toward the stable.

She waited, using the time to run through possibilities. It would need to be a larger ship, already bound for Athens, to avoid suspicion. A captain who was unsavory enough to ask no questions about his new cargo, but trustworthy enough to place twelve invaluable men and the Proginosko in his care.

A twinge of panic grabbed at her heart at the thought of placing the Proginosko on a ship. The last time she had done that . . .

But she would not think of that. Athens was the only place safe for their secret.

The servant brought the horse and cart and offered to drive her, but she took the whip from his hand and climbed onto the two-wheeled black and gold vehicle alone.

It took only minutes to cross the white heptastadion. Besides providing access to the island, the causeway also carried water to the Pharos through the aqueduct that ran from the Nile canal to the hundreds of vaulted underground cisterns through the city. Another marvelous feat of engineering. Sophia entered the colorful chaos of the city and kept her eyes trained straight ahead, refusing to be panicked again by the press of people so unlike her lonely perch in the lighthouse.

She wheeled along the edge of the quay, the smell of rotted fish and seaweed in her nostrils and the variable breeze, so particular to the sea, blowing against her. In the mighty harbor, ships docked and sailed away, their white masts snapping in the wind. The dock warehouses bustled with activity. She eyed one long building, a special facility for the Ptolemies' questionable practice of seizing all the books that sailed into the city for mandatory copying. It was often the copies that were returned to the ships, with the originals bolstering the Library's ever-increasing collection.

There were people everywhere, more numerous than the ships. Sophia pushed away that same oppressive feeling she had felt in the riot yesterday.

A double line of Roman soldiers marched along the quay, and their feet slammed a beat on the stones that sounded like the drumbeat of battle. Sophia's hands tightened on the reins until her fingernails dug into her palms.

She circled half the harbor before she found what she sought. A mid-size ship, clearly preparing to set off, and flying the blue flag of Athens. She pulled in the horse, found a young boy whom she paid an *obol* to watch the chariot, and hurried to the ship.

Two slaves carried crates of supplies aboard. She asked for the captain and received only a vague arm waving.

The ship's heavy ropes still clung to the iron cleat on the dock, but she would have to jump to make it across. She measured the distance with her eye, looked both ways, then leaped across the water and landed with a jarring thump on the deck. Several pairs of slave eyes glanced her way.

A bulky man in a himation that had long ago gone from white to tan hailed her from the top of steps. "No more need of sailors, today, man."

She drew herself up. His face reddened.

"Pardon me. We do not often have the female sex aboard. I am unaccustomed—"

"You are sailing for Athens soon?"

"Aye. Fully loaded with Alexandrian glass we are, and ready to share the wealth with the rich folks of Athens."

"I have another bit of cargo for you. A delivery. And I will pay."

His left eye twitched, as though it sensed a mystery, and a profitable one. "Something you would rather not hand over to Roman swine, I take it?"

She half-smiled. "They would not have the capacity to appreciate it, I am afraid."

He extended a hand to the steps. "Come. Let us talk below." Sophia gladly left the bright hustle of the harbor for the inviting darkness of the hull.

A short time later the deal was struck. Erebos, the ship's captain, gripped her arm in farewell, and she disembarked, confident that the scholars and their valuable secret would be safe with him.

The Roman presence in the harbor district seemed to have doubled while she had been below deck. Sophia worried that she would have trouble getting the men to the boat. She cracked the whip over the back of the horse and took to the streets with speed.

Back at the lighthouse, Ares had returned safely with the Proginosko, and Sosigenes had wrapped the piece in cotton, secured it with rope, and placed it into a wooden crate that Ares had given him. The twelve men were assembled in the front hall, speaking in low tones. A general mood of adventure pervaded the group, and Sophia hoped that nothing would happen to sour it.

She and Ares loaded the men back into the wagon, and this time Sophia climbed aboard the front, alongside Ares. He turned to her with a grin and opened his mouth to speak. She put up a hand. "Keep it to yourself. Just drive."

Again, when they reached the harbor, Sophia had the sense that the Roman soldiers were spreading through the area like a plague. What was happening?

It took some time to navigate to the halfway point of the huge harbor. The heat was oppressive, and Sophia worried about the old men crammed under the canvas.

Finally they reached the boat, and Erebos's sailors jumped from the deck to help.

In the press of the crowd, few seemed to notice that the canvas pulled back from the wagon revealed men and not crates of wares for trade. The men slipped out one by one and were helped across to the prow of the ship. Sophia and Ares kept watch for Romans. Boats bobbed on the water up and down the quay, but the odd presence of the Roman legion hung over the harbor. Though the everyday shipping activity belied the violence of yesterday, Sophia felt the threat of war in the air, like an unfamiliar storm cloud building out at sea. She urged the scholars along.

And then there was only Sosigenes on the dock, the wooden crate in his arms. A sailor took it from him and jumped to the boat. Sosigenes wrapped his arms around Sophia. She returned his embrace stiffly.

"I don't like to think of you alone in that lighthouse, in this city, Sophia."

She smiled. "I have my books."

"'*It is not good for man to be alone,*' the Torah says. The Holy One gives us each what we long for—purpose and relationship. You will never be at peace until you accept both."

Sophia pushed him gently toward the boat. "Your One God is a mystery to me, Sosigenes. But now is not the time to explain him. You must go."

He hugged her again. "I will send word as soon as it is complete."

"Two months. I will be watching the moon." She pressed a bulging pouch into his hands. "The captain has been paid. Do not let him convince you that any more is owed. This is for the twelve of you, to keep you well in Athens."

He kissed her cheek. "You are like one of the Muses, my Sophia. May the One God bless you for your contribution to the world."

Sophia blinked away the tears of farewell and pushed Sosigenes toward the boat. "You must go."

He smiled a last time, then let a sailor hold his arm as he crossed to the ship.

When he was safely below deck, Sophia turned back to the wagon—and slammed into the chest of a Roman soldier.

No, not a soldier. The Pilus Prior of the Sixth Cohort.

"Bellus!" she said, unthinking.

He lifted an eyebrow—and the corner of his mouth—at her mention of his name. "The reports I hear of your reclusive habits seem to be exaggerated. You are the most visible woman in Alexandria, I believe."

Sophia bristled. "These are dangerous days, and I am simply a concerned citizen." She nodded in the direction of his double-line of soldiers. "We must do what we can to keep ignorance from overrunning our city."

His face darkened. "It seems to me the city's greatest ignorance lies in those who speak without knowledge of their subject."

His eyes were steady on her, but she refused to look away. Sophia felt the muscles between her shoulders tighten. Something about this man truly infuriated her. "I can only assume that a legion unable to control a boy and his eunuch does not act out of sound strategy or informed thought." She wondered if the boat behind her had cast off yet. *Stay below, Sosigenes.*

Bellus scratched at his stubbled chin. "It is you who are uninformed. We have the situation in hand."

"Oh? And where is Pothinus?"

Bellus's eyes strayed to Erebos's ship.

Sophia shifted her position in front of him. "Was it your task to keep him from leaving the city?"

He scowled. "Who told you that?"

Sophia smiled. "I assumed. What was that title you said you carried? Pilus—something?"

"Pilus Prior."

"Yes. Strange, I thought my Latin was quite good, but that does not seem to be the phrase for 'incompetent failure.'"

Bellus inhaled deeply. She watched his chest expand under the chain mail, and it seemed to her that the fingers of his right hand twitched at his side.

"I do not need lessons in leadership skills from a woman who spends her days locked in a lighthouse."

"Better alone in a lighthouse than leading men into disaster."

"Do you have some task in the harbor, woman? Because you had best get to it. Before long the harbor will not be a place to wander aimlessly."

Sophia glanced to the ship, its ropes still tied to the cleat. "Will you trample the harbor as you have already done to the Museum and the Library?"

"My men have orders to *secure* the harbor. We will see that no ships come or go without my knowledge and approval."

Sophia's stomach fluttered. "And when will this feat be accomplished?"

Bellus extended a hand across the harbor. Sophia followed his hand and could see now that the spreading stain of Roman military was an organized action throughout the harbor, and that Roman ships sailed toward the entrance, where the reefs narrowed the exit.

"Your men seem willing to follow you. That is at least a small credit to your leadership." She turned to face him. "Perhaps, in time, you will develop into an able commander."

Bellus clamped his generous lips together. Why did she continue to anger him when she much preferred to see him smile?

She indicated the harbor entrance with her chin. "Your ships, what are they doing out there?"

"They will drop anchor at the narrowest point. Every ship that attempts to enter or exit will need to be inspected and approved."

Sophia felt her breath rise and fall in her chest, which grew ever tighter. "I see."

"What did you say was your business here?" Bellus took a step toward her, forcing her attention back to himself.

She straightened. "I didn't say. I am procuring supplies for the lighthouse."

He nodded slowly.

"I suppose you think that the lighthouse is nothing but a fire and a mirror. You could have no idea what is involved in maintaining the safety of the incoming ships."

"I am certain you are most capable of handling the challenges you face."

Sophia narrowed her eyes, trying to determine if there was sarcasm in his tone. "You think me a tyrant of a woman, then?"

Bellus lowered his head, but then raised his eyes to hers. He was silent a moment, as though reading her thoughts. When he spoke, his voice was low. "I think you are lonely and bitter and angry, and you prefer that the world around you also feel the pain of it."

Sophia swallowed, but still she would not look away from his eyes. His words were an injury, to be sure. But not knife-sharp, not fatal. More like a large stone tied round her neck. A heavy sinking that made it hard to breathe. "I—I must go. As I said, I have critical business to attend."

Bellus saluted her, a mock sort of salute intended, she knew, as ridicule. "I will leave you to it, then."

With a glance at the Roman fleet now nearing the harbor entrance, Sophia left Bellus on the dock and jumped across to the ship. The ship carrying cargo that would never be allowed to pass.

On the deck she glanced back, but Bellus had moved on. "We must change our plans," she said to Erebos. He nodded, as though expecting the news and folded his hands across his wide belly.

"Bring the ship through the heptastadion channel to the Eunostos Harbor. Dock on the west side of the lighthouse."

Erebos snorted. "They have left the eastern harbor unguarded?"

Sophia looked across the water, sparkling in the afternoon sun. "I am afraid not. You will not reach Athens with this cargo."

"I must get to Athens—"

"I know." Sophia let her eyes travel to the lighthouse on the tip of the island ahead.

She depended upon her solitude there. Needed it. But her life was worth nothing if she did not preserve her husband's legacy, especially now that the Proginosko again promised hope for the future.

"We will bring them to the lighthouse," she said, as much to herself as to Erebos. "There is no other way."

THIRTEEN

Bellus shielded his eyes and calculated the time before the two ships had the Eunostos harbor. An army clerk neared at his right and saluted. "A message, centurion," he said, extending his hand. Bellus took the rolled papyrus absently and nodded.

The mission had proceeded better than he had hoped. His centuria had spread through the harbor in their ten contubernia, to take the mainland docks on either side of the heptastadion that stretched out to the Pharos Island. They had blocked the entrance into the Great Harbor. The Eunostos Harbor in the west should be guarded within the hour.

Bellus fingered the scroll in his hand. Had Caesar heard already about his success in taking the harbor? He unrolled the stiff papyrus and turned his body to shade the missive from the lowering orange sun.

Gaius Julius Caesar, General of Rome, to Lucius Aurelius Bellus, Pilus Prior. I have word that your centuria is securing the harbor. I was not aware that command of my legion had been given over to you! Your orders were to occupy the lighthouse. Have your troops there by nightfall or you will be dismissed back to Rome to till your fields or shovel dung or whatever it was you did before Rome called you to be a soldier.

The general's seal had been heavily stamped into wax at the bottom of the letter, and Bellus could almost see the animosity that bore down on that glob of red. He crumpled the roll in his right hand and stared over the water. Word had reached the general too soon. Bellus had intended to send troops to the lighthouse, then inform Caesar that both the lighthouse and the harbor had been secured. Instead, his plan to redeem his earlier failure appeared to be insubordination.

To his left, the lighthouse keeper still stood on the deck of her supply ship.

Better to arrive on that cursed island before she does.

"Quintus!" Bellus yelled toward the contingent that stood guard at the edge of the quay. One of them, his gangly young *optio*, turned and marched to him.

"Send word 'round the harbor. We regroup at the base of the heptastadion and march across to the island. Now!" Quintus saluted and ran.

But it was not to be so immediate. It took the better part of an hour to reassemble the centuria that had spread through the harbor at his command. When the men were lined before him at the head of the causeway to the island, four deep and twenty wide, Bellus paced before them, yelling orders.

"Be on your guard, men! The far side of the island is renowned for its pirates. These are men that wait upon the ill luck of merchant ships on the reefs, and then prey upon them. They are lawless, they are mercenary, and they are no doubt violent. They will not be pleased that Rome brings order and light to their dark endeavors." Men's chins lifted, chests expanded with the pride of Rome. "But remember, also, we are not at war. We have come to Egypt as ambassadors of Rome, to collect on a debt, not to conquer. Avoid unnecessary bloodshed."

He raised an arm, turned to the heptastadion, and let his

eyes linger on the massive lighthouse at the tip of the island. He breathed in the salt air, then swung his arm downward.

The men marched.

The causeway was wide enough for the men to march across in formation, shields locked. Bellus led them, feeling stripped bare without his horse. What kind of centurion led his men on foot? But the horses had been stabled in the south of the city when they had arrived here. Caesar had insisted that soldiers on horses would seem a greater threat to the people of the city. The general still wished to appear peaceful.

And yesterday's riot proved your success.

The two bridges that cut through the causeway, allowing ships to pass from the Great Harbor to the Eunostos Harbor, had not been raised today. Bellus had ordered that no ships pass through until both harbor entrances had been secured.

Seawater lapped at the rocky edges of the heptastadion, forming a counter rhythm to the beat of the heavily studded sandals of the eighty men at his back.

The causeway angled slightly west into the setting sun. Bellus's eyes ached from squinting across the island. Hazy shapes and rising puffs of dust in the distance caused concern.

By the three-quarter point of the causeway, his concern had heightened. A crowd awaited their arrival on the island. With the sun behind the island's inhabitants, they were only a silhouette of unknown threat. To their left, the island's Temple of Isis, with its twenty-cubit statue of the goddess, seemed to give sacred weight to their cause.

Bellus halted his troops, called a few more instructions down the lines, then turned and led them onward.

Within minutes, the shadow became individuals, yelling and brandishing farming tools.

Villagers, not pirates.

Bellus urged his men forward, pushing into the crowd of people. Just as the city had its Greek, Jewish, and Egyptian districts, the village was largely segregated to Egyptians. Shouted curses rained down on the soldiers, though mostly in Greek.

"Go back to Rome, dogs!"

Something hurtled through the air. Bellus raised an arm to block it. A half-rotted fish, its eyeballs still intact, splattered against his leather-wrapped forearm and sprayed his face with foul liquid.

The insult seemed to loose the crowd. They flew forward, heedless that they ran unarmed into the most elite army in the world.

"Forward, men!" Bellus shouted. They knew enough to avoid engagement. They marched in double-time, leaving the village to their left as they moved eastward to the tip of the island and the lighthouse.

Bellus ran to the side of the centuria. He let the lines pass and surveyed the villagers' attack.

Dark-skinned men, bare-chested and with white skirts in the old Egyptian style, wove through the centuria, fists raised and faces hate-twisted. There were even women and children among them. The centuria lost its rigid pattern as soldiers stepped out of formation to avoid trampling villagers. The setting sun seemed to melt the soldier's armor to gold and turn the sea beyond to silver, until the whole mass of men seemed like molten metal flowing around the dark chests and white skirts.

The smell of rotted fish and vegetables turned his stomach. Where did the people get their ample supply? Had they stored it for just such a time?

They were nearly to the second causeway, the narrower and shorter land bridge that would deposit them at the base of the lighthouse. As yet, there had been nothing more than foul-smelling garbage thrown. No soldier had drawn a dagger or lowered a pilum.

But in that moment there came a mighty roar, and Bellus knew immediately that the worst lay ahead.

A swarm came up and over the rocks that lined the small cove known as the Port of Pirates. Fifty men, Bellus guessed. Swords held aloft, and the indignation of violated territory in their upraised voices. "Hold!" Bellus shouted to his men. The command spread immediately across the line.

The villagers sensed their peril and kept moving, tripping through the centuria to get free. For a few moments, the entire village seemed trapped between the incoming wave of soldiers and the rushing river of pirates. Bellus feared a wholesale slaughter. He ran back and forth in front of the troops, gladius drawn.

"Disengage from the peasants!" he shouted to his men. And to the townspeople, "Get back to your homes!"

Finally the glut of innocents cleared, and Bellus lowered his right fist, signaling to the men that they were to move forward and take the lighthouse, by whatever means necessary.

They marched. The pirates ran. Undisciplined and untrained, they hurtled screaming into the perfect lines of soldiers and their shields.

The clang of sword on sword, the hoarse grunts of attack and the screams of injury all lifted from the stones of the island. Bellus lunged and slashed with his own sword. The stubbled and dirty face of a pirate rose before him, and he thrust with his short dagger, without thought. He had not been on the ground in battle in some time. It was terrible and wonderful at once, this freedom to give oneself to the fight.

But it could not last long.

FOURTEEN

Below the island, where the lowered heptastadion bridge blocked their passage from the Great Harbor to the Eunostos Harbor, Sophia stood on the deck of the ship she'd hired, yelling curses down on the head of the Egyptian bridge keeper who moved slower than a mid-winter canal to get the bridge cranked open.

"The soldiers," he had said when they first approached, pointing to the line of Romans disappearing across the dust of the heptastadion. "They did not want the bridge—"

"The soldiers are not here now!" Sophia rocked forward on her toes. "And they do not command the island!"

The Egyptian's shrugged shoulders spoke what they both were thinking: *It looks as though they soon will.*

Why had the Romans abandoned their positions around the harbor and begun marching to Pharos? Could it be in response to her telling Bellus she would bring the supply ship there? Did they somehow know that she carried something of far more worth than food and fuel?

If the Romans went all the way to the tip of the island, she had no idea how she'd land this ship and hide the twelve men away.

But why would they go there? Certainly they would cross and then head west, away from the lighthouse, to the Eunostos Harbor entrance. Perhaps they would board ships there and drop anchor to examine outgoing ships.

But I need to sail through there to circle around to the lighthouse.

"Faster, you lazy pack of slaves!" she called to the dozen bare-backed men who turned the crank that would raise the bridge.

The sun seemed weighted, rolling downward to the horizon at twice its normal pace, threatening to leave them passing through the Port of Pirates in darkness.

Finally the wooden platform creaked to a halt above their heads, and the ship's captain signaled the oarsmen to take them through. Sophia gripped the rail to still her trembling hands and kept her eyes set to the west, willing the ship to slice through the water with speed.

With her face raised to the spray of saltwater, she watched the mass of gleaming armor and snapping red pennants advance across the heptastadion and felt like a contender in one of the stadium's chariot races.

She glanced at the steps that led down to the inside hull of the ship and thought of the Proginosko. This prize was worth far more than any race.

Now that she had made the decision to allow the scholars to invade her peace, to hide away in the only place she could escape from the world, she simply wanted to get them there.

The race continued, with her ship sailing round to the far side of the island, where they could dock immediately below the lighthouse, and the Roman's centuria marching across the heptastadion. She watched their measured steps, though her ship had sailed too far now to hear the beat of their sandals.

The ship's captain joined her at the rail and watched the soldiers

in silence for a moment. The sun turned the water to diamonds.
"I am a trader, mistress. Not a warrior."

"I only ask you to sail, Erebos."

He jutted his chin toward the marching soldiers. "And if they
are on the other side to greet us when we put in?"

"I will handle it."

He laughed. "One woman against a hundred Romans?"

Sophia wiped seawater from her eyes, blinking away the sting.
"You might be surprised."

Sosigenes stumbled from the steps. "Sophia?" He came to stand
beside her.

She shook her head. "You need to stay below. We cannot take
any chances."

He placed a hand over hers on the rail. "You are sailing to
Athens with us?"

Sophia sighed and inclined her head to the heptastadion. "Not
Athens yet, I am afraid. I am taking you back to the lighthouse."

He followed her indication and scowled at the soldiers marching toward Pharos. "These Romans are like grasshoppers, eating
away at the health of Egypt." He wrinkled his nose. "But why back
to Pharos when the Romans are crossing to the island?"

"They want the harbor entrance. They will remain on the
western end of the island, I am certain." Sophia grasped his hand.
"Please, now, my friend, stay below."

He smiled. "All will be well, Sophia," he said, in that tone of an
oracle he sometimes used. She thought of Homer's Iliad: *"He knew
the things that were and the things that would be and the things that
had been before."* Sosigenes patted her cheek, nodded, and returned
to the steps.

They soon rounded the end of Pharos and headed back toward
the east on the other side. The soldiers were no longer visible, but
Sophia kept her attention on the main road out of the village,

expecting the red standards on poles and the marching lines to appear at any moment.

The sun threw the long shadow of the boat before them, as though they chased a phantom ship they could never catch.

When they rounded into the Port of Pirates, even Sophia prepared to go below deck. There was no use inviting trouble. This port was not regulated by the royal family, and it reeked of rotted fish and brackish water. But the port appeared deserted, so Sophia stayed on deck. They sailed across the bowl-shaped harbor toward the base of the lighthouse.

Sophia breathed out her relief that they had somehow missed the soldiers in their march toward the Eunostos Harbor entrance.

Erebos shouted commands at his oarsmen. "There!" He pointed to the small dock set up for lighthouse deliveries.

The captain's shout seemed to echo over the island and come back to them, louder than it had gone out. Sophia frowned and lifted her head. Erebos halted in mid-command. His glance turned sharply to her.

Another shout, and another.

The boat glided toward land, with all hands stilled.

And then on the raised strip of rock above them, as sudden as a sandstorm whips out of the desert, a mass of confusion swelled.

Sophia sucked in her breath. Roman soldiers! Covering the island, they slashed with swords, thrust with spears. And pirates, driving through the mass of soldiers with their crude weapons.

The ship went unnoticed. They simply floated there, suspended by the shock of the battle that raged above them.

She had never seen trained soldiers fight. Not like this. It was like a dance, slow and beautiful and tragic. She traced the line of a sun-kissed sword as it sliced the air and found its mark on the neck of a pirate who would have put his tapered pike into the soldier's gut. The red plumes of the Roman's helmets were like sprays of blood fanning through the dusky air.

Bellus. Was he there, among them? Safe?

She gripped the ship's rail and pulled her gaze from the glowing armor, to the dark hulk of the lighthouse that hung over them, watching in silent detachment. "We must put in!"

The captain roused and nodded once, then shouted a command to the oarsmen. Within moments a sailor jumped from the prow to the dock and secured the ship. Sophia did not wait.

"Come," she called down into the hull. "Quickly!"

The twelve elderly men began their ascent, blinking in the sun that seemed a horizontal beam across the sea now.

She touched each as they passed her, urging them forward, all the while her attention on the fighting not far to their right. She wished for a sword of her own.

Hold them a little longer, my island pirates. Never before had she been grateful for the parasites that gave her island a bad name. And yet, even as she wished them success, she thought of one Roman whom she did not care to see harmed.

"Go, go!" she hissed to the scholars. Each gingerly stepped from the prow to the dock, which swayed beneath their feet with the pitch of high tide. Seawater surged upward around the white limestone rocks that lined the island, leaving them darkened and coated with slippery green algae.

Sophia jumped to the dock, her eyes still trained on the fighting, which held.

"Follow!" Only the one word, and then she scrambled up the hill to the entrance to the lighthouse.

What were the Romans doing on her side of the island?

It was the finish of the race now, begun on the other side of the island when Bellus first told her the harbor had been sealed.

The final leg, with each of them bearing down on their horse to reach the finish line before the other.

The white of the scholar's himations as they picked their way up the rocky hillside seemed to glow with purity. Sophia was certain they would draw the eye of every soldier on the stony plateau. But still the soldiers fought, without regard to the procession that scurried to the building above them.

Sophia reached the entrance of the Base and shoved the first man through, then each after. The pirates seemed to be giving way now. She saw several turn and run toward the port. It would not be long.

Ares met them inside. "What? I thought—" His gaze traveled the group of men and came back to Sophia.

"No time, Ares. The Romans have blocked the harbor entrance. We must hide them here."

Ares ran a hand through his hair. "Here? Where will we put them?"

The men huddled in the front hall. "We have two hundred rooms, Ares. I think you can find a place."

"Storage rooms! You cannot put them in storage rooms! No beds, no baths—"

"No *time!*" Sophia grabbed his arm and pulled him to the entrance. She pointed to the battle below. "Do you see them?"

Ares's eyes went wide. "They are coming here?"

"I have no idea. But we must get these men hidden!"

Ares snapped to attention and turned to the men. "Come, gentlemen. We will find a temporary place for you, where you will be safe. Just temporary." He cast a withering glance at Sophia. "Until something that suits your position can be arranged."

The men followed Ares, like stray chicks followed anyone who fed them. Sophia watched them disappear down the corridor, and inhaled deeply for what seemed the first time in hours. She straightened, smoothed her tunic, and turned to the lighthouse entrance.

Somehow she felt no surprise to see Bellus framed in the doorway. A strange tremor of relief, perhaps, that he had not been slain by pirates. But not surprise. He gripped a sword in his right hand and held his helmet under the other arm. His hair had been ruffled by wind and exertion.

Sophia's hand strayed to her lips. "First the harbor, and now the island. Your general certainly keeps you busy."

He sheathed the sword and used the back of his arm to wipe sweat from his brow. "A simple day in the life of a Roman soldier." He stepped forward.

She moved to the doorway, to keep him in place. "Yes, *simple* is a word I would use to describe you Romans."

She waited for his customary comeback but saw instead the flicker of amusement. She bit her lip. "Pharos Island has nothing of worth to you. No grain to speak of. No treasure. What do you want with us?"

Behind him, lines of soldiers appeared. They had regained their symmetry after the squabble with the pirates.

"Nothing of value?" Bellus smiled. "You underestimate your own fine structure." He stepped out of the doorway and leaned his head back, though she knew he could not lean far enough to take in the entire height of the lighthouse. "It is truly a wonder"—he lowered his gaze to hers—"and of great interest to Caesar."

She felt her lips twitch. "You may tell your general that I would be happy to pay him a visit in the palace and explain to him the history and the function of our wonderful lighthouse."

Bellus tilted his head. "I am afraid Caesar has little interest in history or technology, unless they aid him in battle. I am not here for a lesson, Sophia of Pharos. I am here to stay."

Sophia swallowed, then flicked her gaze over his shoulder to the soldiers amassing behind him. "Stay?"

Bellus saluted. "General Gaius Julius Caesar and the legion of Rome are most grateful for your hospitality. I hope that we will not prove to be too much of a burden."

With that, he motioned to his troops to move forward.

Sophia, in an unaccustomed silence, could think of nothing to do but stand aside and watch as the First Centuria of the Sixth Cohort of Rome filed into her lighthouse.

Across from her, on the other side of the entrance, their Pilus Prior stood watching. Between each soldier that passed, their eyes met.

And Sophia had the feeling that it would not be these eighty battle-ready soldiers, nor the twelve elderly scholars hiding in the storage rooms, who would destroy the peace of her lighthouse life.

No, it would be this one sarcastic centurion with the stunning smile.

FIFTEEN

The soldiers settled into the darkening lighthouse like a horde of locusts descending onto a field of wheat. Sophia stalked through the South Wing of the Base, barking orders and scowling to no effect. By the time the moon rose over the night sea, the centuria had doused their torches and bedded down. Sophia intersected Ares in the front hall.

"No matter what, they must be kept apart," she said.

He chewed his lip. "I have given the old men instructions to stay only in the North Wing. But they have less fear than I would like and may simply do as they please."

Sophia eyed the sandy courtyard and considered crossing, to give her own instructions to the scholars.

"Go to bed, Abbas," Ares said. She raised her eyebrows and he bowed his head. "Mistress. It grows late, and you have had a long day. The old men are sleeping." He inclined his head toward the first storage room in the stone hall, where the snoring of soldiers could already be heard. "There is no danger for the moment."

She closed her eyes briefly, swayed on her feet, and agreed.

The night was all too short, however, and morning brought no assurances that this day would be better than the last. Sophia awoke in her immense bed, rolled to her back, and studied the white silks that hung from the four posts.

Even from here, sixty-five cubits above the ground, the sounds of a pack of soldiers disturbed her sleep. Her bedcoverings twisted between her fingers, and she felt her stomach harden. Soldiers in her lighthouse.

She threw off the bedcoverings and swung her legs over the side. She might not be able to command Caesar to remove his troops, but they were in *her* lighthouse now, and she was its Keeper.

Sophia dressed quickly in her customary tunic and tied her sandals. She poured water into a basin, splashed her face, and ran wet hands through her short hair to tame it. With no more preparation, she strode from her chambers, descended the ramp to the Base and crossed into the South Wing.

She was unprepared.

The hall of the South Wing looked as though a military garrison had exploded. Weaponry, armor, and crates of unknown contents lay scattered in the hall. Soldiers in various states of partial dress milled the area, talking and laughing, and peasant traders clustered at the entrance, yelling about deliveries or bartering with soldiers. And the smell. The smell of a hundred men the morning after a battle.

Sophia raised her voice above the din. "What is this?"

A few heads turned her way. Not many. Even those men that looked at her dismissed her quickly.

Sophia's earlier annoyance built in her chest, hot and tight. She shoved through the men, kicking shields and sandals out of her way. *Like a herd of undisciplined goats.*

And where was their supposed shepherd?

The first storage room she and Ares had shoved the intruders into last night looked much the same as the hall. She skimmed the heads of the men quickly, looking for one in particular. Nothing.

She marched to the second storage room with no success, and then to the third. Still outside the door, she noted the quiet voices within and slowed her angry rush.

"I do not know," Bellus was saying. Sophia hovered at the rough wooden door frame and pulled back, unseen. "The lighthouse is obviously a strategic point from which to command the harbor, and from here we can stave off an attack by sea."

Another voice spoke, too quietly for Sophia to make it out.

"Don't look at it as a punishment, Quintus," Bellus answered. "We have been given a new assignment and we will prove our worth here."

A third voice spoke. "How can we prove our worth when all we are to do is sit in this dungeon all day and play at dice?"

Bellus chuckled. "What would you have traded for a few warm days of dice, back when we tramped the muddy fields of Gaul for the winter?"

"At least in Gaul we did not suffer under the hand of a tyrant disguised as a woman!"

The room full of men laughed. Sophia could not tell how many. She pulled back farther and pressed into the wall.

"I did not say she was a tyrant," Bellus answered.

"But did you say she was a woman?"

More laughter.

"She is harsh, I will admit. But think of your wives, men. How many of them would welcome the lot of us into their homes with a ready smile? Eh?"

There was some teasing of one of the men and some talk of his nagging wife. Sophia leaned her forehead against the doorframe.

"Still," Bellus said, cutting off the jesting, "stay clear of the lighthouse keeper. She is an angry and unforgiving woman, with a tongue sharper than a gladius. None of you are well-trained enough to do battle with that kind of enemy."

Sophia brushed her head against the rough wood. A still and quiet coldness crept through her body.

The meeting was adjourning. Sophia jerked upright and turned to flee down the corridor. She took three steps, remembered her previous anger, and whirled again. She stood in the hall when Bellus emerged from the room, followed by four officers.

He drew up when he saw her, then waved his men past. "We are making the best of it," he said. "Getting organized. I assure you—"

Sophia huffed. "I want none of your assurances. If you are to stay here, I have certain requirements." She intended to give her orders, but felt a catch in her throat and coughed to clear it. "Find Ares and have him bring you to my private chambers in an hour. We have much to speak on." With that, she fled back down the South Wing and into the courtyard.

She had intended to retreat upward, but after a backward glance to be sure no soldiers watched, she chose instead to cross to the North Wing and check on Sosigenes and the others.

Inside the North Wing, her footsteps echoed in the heavy silence. Where were they?

She peeked into several rooms and finally found them in a smallish storage room toward the corner of the Base. It was empty of all but cobwebs and thick dust.

If the glut of soldiers had been like ships bumping and jockeying for position in the harbor, the scholars were more like a litter of frightened kittens in an alley. They huddled together miserably in one corner, conversing in hushed whispers. At the sound of Sophia's entrance they seemed to turn and shrink into themselves.

Sophia held out her hands. "All is well. At least for now. They are occupied with getting settled."

Sosigenes struggled to his feet, always the spokesman for the group. "When do we leave for Athens?"

Sophia approached him, clasped his hand, and lifted it to her heart. "It is not possible. The Romans are preparing for Ptolemy's troops to attack. They won't allow any ships in or out of the harbor without inspection. And if Caesar learns of your whereabouts—"

One of the men on the floor, Hesiod, finished her sentence. "We will be building catapults rather than models of the planets."

A general grumbling rippled through the group.

"So what are we to do?" Sosigenes asked.

"Stay here. Work here." Sophia looked into his eyes. "Finish the project."

"Here?" Sosigenes spread his hand to the empty storage room. "For two cycles of the moon?"

"I will bring what you need. Don't worry. I know it is not what you are accustomed to—"

Sosigenes smiled. "I have lived in many places over my many years, dear. Some much more primitive than this. The One True God can see me wherever I hide. It is not the accommodations, but our fellow guests that cause me concern."

Sophia tugged a hand through her hair. "And I as well. But we will find a way." She kissed Sosigenes lightly and promised them an improvement in their conditions, then went to find Ares and give him further instructions.

When she finally reached the door to her chambers, she paused, following the curve of the ramp further upward with her eyes. She felt a twinge of longing to escape to the special place she'd created for herself on the first platform above her chambers, but there was no time.

The hour until Bellus came passed quickly in her chambers, as she mapped out a plan to furnish the scholars with all they needed, and to keep the soldiers from discovering them. Ares brought her breakfast, thin slices of cheese and fresh grapes on a gold plate, but she only picked at it. She sat at her desk, facing the door, and scribbling on her charts.

Ares's knock came again, and still bent over her papyrus, she yelled, "Come."

The servant led Bellus into the room. Sophia forced her attention to remain on the chart in front of her.

Ares cleared his throat gently. "I have the Pilus Prior you requested, mistress." She heard the humor in his voice as he presented the Roman like a delivery of supplies.

She waved a hand distractedly in the direction of her couches. "Yes, yes, just put him over there somewhere, Ares."

Moments later, when Ares was gone and Sophia looked up, she was rewarded for her rudeness with a vicious scowl.

"I have much to attend to, if you are too busy to speak with me as you demanded." He had not lowered himself to her couches, but stood with legs slightly apart as though facing an enemy.

"No, no. This is fine. We can speak now. Sit, please." She indicated the white cushions, but he did not move.

"Ah. Now, you see, I am trying to be courteous"—she leaned back in her chair—"but you will not have it. I cannot seem to win with you, Roman."

"I was not aware that you were trying to win me."

She laughed and ran her fingers lightly over the surface of her desk. "You like to twist words, soldier."

"And you like to use them as weapons."

She licked her lips. "Yes, what was it you said? 'A tongue sharper than a gladius.' Was that it?"

She studied his face. He blinked twice, and the air seemed to go out of his chest.

"I—the men—I wanted them to leave you alone. You do not want us here, and I thought it best that they keep their distance—"

Sophia stood and turned to one of the windows, draped in a rich red. She let the fabric flow across her palm. "And so you thought to scare them, was that it? Keep them away from the monster in the tower?"

He did not reply.

She watched the harbor below for some moments, and when she turned back to Bellus, she found him surveying her chambers. The heavy sycamore tables and chairs, the expensive sculptures of Isis and Serapis, the wall niches crowded with her books.

"You think me a wealthy woman, no doubt. You are envious?"

Bellus jutted his chin toward the stacks of scrolls, her histories, philosophy, poems, and plays. "There is where your wealth lies, and the only thing you possess that I would want."

She sat heavily, flattened her palm on her desk again, and closed her eyes. She did not need this Roman to tell her she had nothing but books to offer. Yet still, it hurt. "Am I so terrible?" she said softly and lifted her face to his. "Do you suppose there is no hope for me, then?"

She saw the bewilderment pass over his face like a shadow, then clear and leave a small smile in its passing. "*The unexamined life is not worth living.*"

A Roman soldier who quoted Socrates? Sophia felt his smile as though it had reached across and stroked her cheek. She stood and pointed to the charts on her desk. "If you and your barbarians are to remain for any time in my lighthouse, there will need to be specific plans."

Bellus crossed the room to her desk. "Someday," he said quietly, "I will tell you of Rome. And you will see that we are not all the barbarians you would like to believe."

"Then prove it." She jabbed a finger at the papyrus. "Show me that your men can behave according to standards."

They leaned together over the lists and charts she had created, and Sophia issued her orders as though she were Pilus Prior. Bellus said little but nodded occasionally. When she had finished, she rolled the papyrus and handed it to him. "You understand that I must be made aware of anything that goes on here, and the men are restricted to only those areas which I have sanctioned?"

Bellus took it from her hand but kept his attention on her eyes, and spoke more softly still. "I believe I understand you perfectly."

Sophia swallowed, rubbed the back of her neck, and nodded. "Then you may go."

Bellus saluted her, that same mocking salute he'd given her on the docks, and turned to leave. At the door he called back to her, where she had collapsed onto her chair. "Let me know when you are ready to hear of Rome. I will come at once."

He had only been gone a few moments when Ares appeared. "I like him," he announced, as though she had asked his opinion.

Sophia looked out the window but could see only the blue sky at this angle. "Because he's the only other human besides you who doesn't seem to fear me."

Ares laughed. "Perhaps. But perhaps because I think there is a chance, only a chance, that you have met your match. And that the Pilus Prior is exactly what you are lacking."

"Did you come for a reason, Ares?"

He grew serious. "I do not see how we can make this work. Already the soldiers are tramping about the lighthouse. I am trying to bring in supplies for the scholars, but the servants keep bumping into the soldiers, who are, of course, too stupid to ask questions, but eventually one of them—"

"Stop, Ares." She rubbed her eyes. "I know it is impossible." She thought of Bellus. Of his quick mind and quicker smile. A warmth rose through her neck and face. "Yes, Ares. I am sure it is impossible."

SIXTEEN

Bellus didn't sleep well the first night in the lighthouse, nor the second. The oppressive presence of the Keeper seemed to hover about the place, making him irritable and jumpy.

In the makeshift garrison they forced from the storage rooms in the South and East Wings, Bellus claimed one room for his own. To furnish it, he commandeered a narrow bed, a wooden desk, and a chair. But they were small comforts, and even the privacy was not enough to ease him into sleep at the end of a maddeningly inactive day.

When the sun woke him on the third day, he lay still for several minutes, contemplating the useless hours ahead. He would run the men through drills in the central courtyard to maintain the illusion that they were active and needed. It would fool no one, but it was better than idleness.

Bellus had expected Sophia to haunt his steps these past few days, to make sure that her orders were obeyed. But she remained hidden, no doubt in her lair high above the dark rooms to which she had banished the soldiers.

He rolled over in his bed, pounded the cushions into a mound, and rested his chin on his arms. His small window looked over the courtyard, and in the center the lighthouse proper rose, dark and solid. He lifted his eyes as far as he could see. Was she up there, even now, brooding over her violated fortress? What lay above the level where she had her private chambers? He guessed that more than two-thirds of the building lay above her rooms.

What a view there must be from the top.

The pull of exploration roused him from his bed, and within minutes he was bathed and dressed and prowling the early morning corridors of the Base.

A familiar surge of pulse-pounding, like the excitement that accompanied a scouting mission, reminded him that he was still a soldier, even if currently consigned to playing nursemaid to a lighthouse.

The long stone corridors lay mostly in half light, with all doors that led to soldiers' quarters still closed. Bellus tread lightly, taking care that his sandals did not echo off the mildewed stone.

Down the South Wing, past the soldiers' barracks to where the Base turned, and another corridor headed north, along the western Eunostos Harbor. Several rooms lay open here, with sunlight streaming through salt-encrusted windows like flames turning grains of sand to glass. The rooms into which he poked his head smelled musty with disuse, and cobwebs clung to the corners.

He moved down the corridor, toward the North Wing, which Sophia had emphatically told him was forbidden. On soundless feet and with measured breaths, he slipped toward the corner of the Base, fighting a smile.

Through a window in a room to his right, he saw the movement of slaves hauling a wagonload of fuel through the central courtyard. Again, he felt the stir of curiosity to see the upper workings of the lighthouse.

But not now.

Ahead, movement at the corner of the West and North Wings gave him pause.

Ares held a tray and moved with purpose toward him, head down. Bellus side-stepped into the open room, but Ares had already lifted his head. He stopped at the doorway, his forehead creased into a scowl.

"Pilus Prior Bellus? Can I help you?"

"Just a bit of exploring, Ares. A good centurion always gets the lay of the land, you know." He leaned against the door frame and folded his arms.

The young man pursed his lips. "I wouldn't know at all. Has the mistress given you permission to 'explore,' as you say?"

"A good centurion doesn't wait for permission from the hostile natives, either, Ares," he said with a bit of a smile.

Ares looked him up and down. "Hmm. Let me accompany you back to the soldiers' wing."

"I can find my way."

The two men eyed each other in silent challenge, and Bellus was not surprised when the younger man backed down. He was a peace-loving Greek, a peasant, and probably twenty years Bellus' junior. He did not stand a chance.

Ares bit his lip, glanced toward the North Wing, and then continued down the murky corridor.

I don't have much longer now.

He hurried toward the wing that now held even more mystery. Rounding the corner with some speed, he was shocked to smack into another person.

Both men grunted and took a step backward.

"Excuse me," the other man said gently in Greek. Bellus dropped his head in apology, then studied the older man before him. Tall and rather thin, the man's dark and deeply creased face seemed to tell the story of centuries, with eyes that held answers to questions Bellus had not asked.

An oracle?

He wore a pure-white tunic that set off his unusually dark skin even further. He smelled of smoky oil lamps, as though he had been too long in a closed room.

"You are a long way from Rome," the ancient man said, switching now to Latin. His accent was peculiar, like someone who had lived in many places in his lifetime and accumulated the dialects of each.

"I beg your pardon. I did not hurt you, I hope?"

The man smiled. "I only appear fragile."

"You live here? With Sophia?"

The man's lips twitched in a partial smile. "In a sense."

Father? Lover? Bellus felt a twist of something in his stomach.

There was no more time for questioning, however. He felt the storm sweeping up from behind him. The old man's eyes lifted above Bellus's shoulder—and twinkled.

Bellus turned in time to see Sophia's furious charge. Her full lips were tight and the light flecks in her dark eyes flashed like a squall at sea. She wore something different than he had seen before— a white robe of the Greek fashion, with a softer fabric and gold pins fastened at her shoulders.

She looked for all the world like a goddess of fury sweeping across the Great Sea, and though he held his ground, Bellus half-expected to be blown asunder like a flimsy ship in angry waves.

"What did I tell you? Was I not clear enough for even a Roman farmer to understand? Did you need me to write it down for you?" She circled him and stood in front of the old man, as though her presence would render him no longer visible.

Bellus did not miss the wrinkled hand that grasped her elbow in quiet comfort. He raised his chin. "My orders are to secure this lighthouse for Caesar and for Rome. The *entire* lighthouse." He let his eyes travel from her head to her toes, communicating his disdain. "And I do not take orders from you."

"My lighthouse." She took a step toward him. "*Mine.* It is my understanding that Egypt is still an independent land, and Rome a tolerated guest. I expect you and your loutish soldiers to conduct yourselves as guests, not as conquerors." Her nostrils flared like an unbroken horse fighting the saddle.

He felt his own face flush and edged closer to her. "Your *understanding* is exactly the problem. You are ignorant of such matters and should occupy yourself with the business of keeping your little fire burning on top of your tower. Apparently that has been more than enough to keep you busy for years."

Her eyes narrowed to slits. "I am not accustomed to being insulted in my own home."

"*Think not those faithful who praise all thy words and actions, but kindly reprove thy faults.*"

"There is nothing of kindness in you, centurion. Despite your knowledge of Socrates, you are of a much more savage sort."

"Do not let yourself become distracted by military affairs that you are not competent to understand."

"Ha!" She poked a finger into his chest. "You wish to speak of incompetence? I am not so cut off here that I do not hear what they are saying about Lucius Aurelius Bellus, the centurion who let average citizens overrun the palace and the eunuch Pothinus escape to raise an army. You are here as punishment for your ineptitude, and your men are laughing at you behind your back!"

Bellus swallowed. He tried to breathe, to break the sudden constriction in his chest. The back of his neck prickled with sweat and the battle-twitch began in his fingers.

His hesitation cost him. She seemed to sense she had found a vulnerable spot in his armor and thrust for the kill. "You wear your title like a shield, 'Pilus Prior.' Very proud of it, aren't you? Caesar's favorite, perhaps?" She laughed. "But no longer. He has you penned up here like a disobedient dog, waiting for him to toss you scraps from his table again."

Bellus stepped to the woman, close enough to touch, close enough to feel her breath on his face. "If I am punished like a dog, then your precious lighthouse is the foul cage where I have been thrown, and you are the unfortunate warden forced to clean up after us ill-favored curs."

He thought she might attack him. The unbridled fury that swept her features brought back images of Athena the storm goddess again, and her hands formed fists at her sides. But the old man behind her had grasped both her arms now, and he folded her back against his own chest. Stiff at first, a moment later she relaxed against him. He whispered to her and she closed her eyes.

When she again fixed her gaze on Bellus, it was with a fearsome anger, made more frightening in its calm. "Stay out of the North Wing," she said through clenched teeth. "Do not test me again."

Though he was never one to retreat, Bellus thought it best to leave her while the old man still held her captive. For some reason he drew his pugio and held it at his side, not missing the widening of her eyes, and feeling somehow better for it. He turned and stalked down the corridor, back to the south end of the Base.

Test her? As though she were his master? Though he did not run, his breathing was as labored as after a battle, and the beads of sweat that had begun on his neck now formed rivulets down the inside of his tunic.

This is impossible. We cannot occupy this lighthouse as though there are no enemy forces here.

They were soldiers, and Bellus intended that they should act as such. Within minutes of reaching his room, he had scribbled out a dispatch to Caesar. It read simply and clearly: *Lighthouse Keeper uncooperative. Permission requested to treat as hostile and secure the lighthouse through whatever force necessary.*

He rolled the papyrus, tied it with a bit of leather cord, then opened his door and yelled for a soldier.

Caesar would have his request within minutes, and by the end of the morning, Bellus should be free to act as he wished. Caesar would see that he took every duty as sacred. And so would she.

He ran a hand over the sheathed pugio that hung at his side and remembered the woman's flashing eyes, the way they had flickered with a bit of fear when he had drawn his weapon.

She was not a goddess after all. And she could be subdued.

SEVENTEEN

In the marshy fields of Pelusium on the eastern extreme of the Egyptian Delta, Ptolemy XIII's army encamped, robbed of their boy-king, who was still in Caesar's clutches in Alexandria. But the real power behind Ptolemy was here, reclining on silk cushions within a massive three-roomed tent central to the encampment.

Pothinus stretched his neck, stiff from reading the pile of scrolls beside him, and reached for his cup of wine on a side table. The wine was the finest Lesbos could send and had reached the encampment only a day before he had sailed in from Alexandria.

From all reports, the soldiers here had grown first restless and then complacent. As the days without action lengthened, they had settled into a miserable routine of games of chance and brawls over real and imagined insults.

Pothinus leaned his head back against the cushions and studied the series of low torches that lined the back of the king's tent. He had felt no compunction at claiming the quarters for himself when he had arrived. Ptolemy was not here.

The tent had been set up to resemble the king's palace quarters as closely as was possible on the field of battle. Rich fabrics in red and gold covered a large bed with cedar posts, and braziers burned bright around a raised bath area with a marble tub. Even the gods had been represented, with marble busts of Serapis and Zeus on columns at the tent's entrance.

But one could not sit in luxury, nor command a standing army, for days on end without a plan.

Fortunately Pothinus had a plan.

He had read the battle histories of leaders gone before, had consulted with advisors. Within six weeks he could have Ptolemy's army inside Alexandria to oust Caesar's legion, slit the throat of Egypt's traitorous queen, and reclaim the throne for Ptolemy. With Ptolemy on the throne, Pothinus would never be far from power.

Outside the tent he heard the men moving about, making preparations for the night. In the distance he could make out singing, the vulgar songs of half-drunk soldiers. He finished the pomegranate he had begun earlier, pulling out its red seeds, then wiped carefully at the dripping juice and rinsed his fingers in a bowl of perfumed water that sat atop the table.

The large flap of the tent's forefront lifted, and the torches flared. Pothinus squinted past the flames. "Plebo?"

The servant he'd left in Alexandria entered on silent feet, head down.

"What took you so long?" Pothinus swung his feet to the ground. "I expected you within a day of my own arrival."

Plebo lifted bleary eyes to his master. "The sea was rough, my lord. We were blown off-course. I came as quickly—"

Pothinus waved away his excuses. "Tell me of the old man."

Plebo eyed the couch opposite the one where Pothinus sat and seemed to sway on his feet.

"Still on sea legs, are you, boy?" Pothinus jabbed a finger at the couch. "Sit if you must. But speak!"

Plebo sank into the cushions and closed his eyes. "Sosigenes was freed from the prison."

"Cleopatra went against Caesar's wishes?"

Plebo shook his head. "Someone paid well to get him out. He and all the Museum's scholars disappeared."

Pothinus creased a wrinkle into the white cushion beneath him. "But I am certain you located them?"

Plebo swallowed and blinked heavily. Pothinus thought perhaps the man looked a bit green. "No one knows where they have hidden."

Pothinus jumped to his feet and paced the tent. The torches seemed to respond as well. One of them smoked and sent curling black fingers toward the roof. A servant appeared to tend to it.

"There are rumors," Plebo said, "that it was Sophia of Pharos who paid for their escape."

Pothinos halted and held out his hands. "That's it then. If she is protecting them, Sosigenes *must* be working on the Proginosko. Did you see it, Plebo? Tell me you saw it."

"I saw nothing. There is also a centuria posted in her lighthouse."

"Caesar is protecting the scholars? I thought he wanted—"

"I believe the soldiers know nothing of any old men. Caesar wants the lighthouse only."

Pothinus laughed, feeling it in his stomach. "Poor Sophia. From recluse to host, and not of her choice." He ran a hand through his full hair. "But she must know where it is."

"Why is this thing so important?"

The arrival of three others cut short Pothinus's reply. His generals filed into the tent behind a servant, their faces appropriately somber. Pothinus turned from Plebo and waved them in.

"Come, men. We have every reason to attack Alexandria soon, and it is time to plan the movement of the troops."

He joined them at a large wooden table spread with a map that covered the Great Sea to the Nubian cataracts, and from the Western Desert to Sinai. An oil lamp beside the map created a circle of light. Pothinus tapped a long finger on Pelusium and looked up at the general, Marwan. "How long will it take to march to Alexandria?"

Marwan's glance went from Pothinus, to the map, to his fellow generals. Pothinus turned to the others, and their eyes also shifted away like guilty children.

"What is it?" he asked, with a growing dread.

Marwan answered. "The men, they are not convinced."

The wine in his stomach seemed to sour. "Not convinced of what?"

Marwan sniffed and scratched his neck. His fellow general, Razin, cleared his throat. "With Ptolemy not here—"

"He is a child!" Pothinus rapped his knuckles against the table. "Everyone knows that I am his advisor."

"The people favor a ruler, even a child. Not a eunuch my lord."

"Whom do they expect to recover their king, then? Shall we sit in the fields until Ptolemy becomes man enough to fight his own way out of Caesar's hands?"

Again the generals looked everywhere but to him. He raised his voice, and it sounded even to him like the desperate roar of a wounded animal. "Who?"

"Arsinôe arrived several days ago."

"Arsinôe! She is barely older than her brother Ptolemy, and younger than her sister who already holds Alexandria!"

Razin nodded. "Still, she is noble-born."

"And a woman!"

"Ganymedes accompanies her."

Pothinus spat. "He is nothing more than a tutor. Not even a politician. I was once a scholar in the Museum! Did you know that? Surely you have told the men that it is in their best interest to remain loyal to the ruler who has recruited them, paid them . . ." The guilty expressions of the men before him stilled his tongue. The generals were silent. The tent grew hot.

Pothinus turned from them, blinking away the anger that threatened to show as weakness. "And what does the girl Arsinôe propose?"

After a pause Marwan answered. "She proposes nothing as yet. Simply moves about the men, speaking to them, encouraging them."

"Of course," Pothinus turned back to study the map. "There is nothing that wins the loyalty of battle-weary soldiers like a pretty woman in their midst."

"She speaks like a true Ptolemy—"

Pothinus slammed the wooden table, and the oil lamp jumped. "I care nothing for what she says." He put his fingers to his temples. "The people are fools. Here, and in Alexandria. They would ignore intelligent leadership in favor of seductive charm. Fools. Leave me. I will call you later."

The generals glanced at each other, then backed away and fled the tent. Pothinus stared at the tent flap, still fluttering in the night air.

"What will you do now, master?"

Pothinus started, having forgotten Plebo's presence. The room beyond lay in shadows now, and Pothinus crossed his arms, aware that others could lurk unseen in the darkness. "Win them back, of course. Win them back."

Outside the sounds of the men and their singing had hushed, and Pothinus imagined that they whispered among themselves of the eunuch who had settled himself in the king's tent as though he commanded the army.

The Ptolemaic family had a long and bloody history of removing rivals in the simplest way possible. A knife between the ribs as one slept, a trickle of deadly poison in the bottom of a cup. With Arsinôe and Ganymedes here, Pothinus felt his mortality as surely as if the time and place of his death had been named.

He turned to Plebo, still reclining on the couch with the strange greenish cast to his skin. "The Proginosko. I must have it."

Plebo opened one eye.

"It is a wonder, Plebo. You cannot imagine. With this piece that Sosigenes is resurrecting, one can track the movements of the heavens—the stars and their orbits, the path of the sun and the earth. Time itself becomes the servant of the one who owns the mechanism. He can number the days and seasons with unheard-of precision, the eclipses of the moon and the sun, the tides and floods." He sank to the cushions. "In all the history of man, Plebo, we have struggled to master time and have only succeeded in making guesses. Even now, the calendar has drifted so far from the correct date, that summer is called autumn. But with the Proginosko . . . Master of time."

Plebo sat up. "But the army? What of the troops? Do they care if it is Metageitnion or Pyanepsion?"

"Perhaps they are heedless of the date. But this one piece of knowledge will set its owner apart as master of the heavens, Plebo. To the Egyptians, such a spiritual and superstitious people, the Proginosko will make him a god. And to the knowledge-lusting Greeks, he will hold the key to time itself." Pothinus closed his eyes, imagined the Proginosko in his hand. "Can you not see it? This one invention will unite the country under the man who holds it. With it, Ptolemy will become feared, loved, revered. And followed.

Caesar, with all his brutish soldiers, could never compete. Nor could the little girls who think to rule the country."

He reached a leg across to Plebo and kicked at the servant's arm. "I must have it, Plebo. Immediately."

The man's eyes narrowed. "How—"

"You must go back at once to Alexandria."

Plebo raised himself to sitting, his mouth open. "My lord, I cannot."

"Of course you can." Pothinus stood, the decision made. He went to the table, pulled out a blank papyrus scroll and ink from a small box there. "I will give you instructions for Dhakwan, whom you should find somewhere about the palace. He is always available to me for whatever unpleasant tasks I have." He began scribbling a message, while estimating the drachmas it would take to complete the task.

When he turned back to Plebo, the man was horizontal upon the couch again, whether asleep or unconscious, he could not tell.

Pothinus sighed. Why did it seem that he alone cared for the best interest of Alexandria and of Egypt? Cleopatra would sell all of Egypt to Rome. She cared nothing for the people as he did, only the power.

No matter. Within days he would have the Proginosko in his hand, the country would be his, and Sophia and Sosigenes would no longer be a problem.

EIGHTEEN

The platform atop the first and tallest tier of the lighthouse's three divisions stood more than a hundred cubits above the Alexandrian harbor, affording a view of the city and the sea that few had ever witnessed.

Here, beside the chest-high walls, Sophia stood and let the robust wind buffet her, let it try to sweep her from her feet. She leaned forward into it and felt a hint of moisture in the air, blown in from the solid clouds that hovered below the lowered sun in the west.

When the coolness had revived her flagging energy, she dropped to a cushioned bench and welcomed the shelter of the walls.

It had been a week since the Romans invaded her peace. Thankfully they had confined themselves to the Base and not breached her sanctuary on this platform. Still, the lighthouse felt no longer her own. Her hands balled at her sides to think of the soldiers tramping the lower levels, giving orders to her servants and expecting to be treated like guests. The scholars had been more appreciative guests, though Sosigenes's continual whisperings about the love of his One God continued to disturb her spirit.

This platform was her special place, accessed by no one other than herself. It circled the second tier of the lighthouse, through the center of which servants endlessly hauled fuel upward for the fire. Those who tended the fire and the mirror ascended to this height, but they knew to keep moving, past Sophia's platform, upward to the beacon chamber.

From the ground, no one would have suspected the delights the platform held, placed by and cultivated for Sophia alone. No less than seven species of roses grew here, crowded into raised wooden planting beds that lined the walls.

Sophia had used the fuel-lift to haul Egypt's richest soil to the platform, then carefully selected the finest canes for grafting. Years of careful pruning, combined with abundant sunshine and a lack of insects at this height, had overflowed her planters with a profusion of the soft red and pink beauties, nestled in glossy green foliage. Every morning four amphorae of water were hauled up in the lift and placed beside the platform entrance for her to dole out.

But late afternoon was not the time to tend or water. It was the time to enjoy. She lay back, closed her eyes, and sank into the softness of the cushions she had placed on the couch. The mingled fragrance of each variety, protected beneath the surrounding wall, seemed to hover just below the breezes. It formed a cocoon of scents and wrapped her in its pleasures.

She had seen Bellus five or six times in the few days since he had tried to explore the North Wing. Each time they passed with ill-hidden loathing, and then she escaped to solitude to recover from the distaste she saw on his face. Twice they had spoken, but it had been civil and polite. That must have been an effort for him. And how did such a man know Socrates?

Still, he had apparently abided by her wishes, keeping his men contained and under control, and staying away from the North Wing. She owed him some gratitude for that at least. She was aware

she retained little power here, with Caesar holding the city and
Cleopatra notably sequestered in the palace with him.

Yes, gratitude. Perhaps she should mention to him that she did
appreciate his diligence.

Roses forgotten, she ducked through the doorway and turned
downward, to follow the central ramp to her chambers. When she
reached her door, she leaned over the short wall, and peered down
through the cylinder to the distant floor.

"Ares!" Her voice bounced from the stone walls and dropped
downward.

Ares was never far. His upturned face appeared.

"Summon the Roman to my quarters. Tell him I want to speak
to him."

Ares massaged the back of his neck as though the angle both-
ered him. "And what Roman would that be, Abbas? General Caesar,
perhaps?"

"No, idiot. You know perfectly well who I mean. The centurion. Bellus, or whatever his name is."

"Hmm. Yes, I think it is Bellus. Something like that."

"Just go, Ares."

She turned back to her chamber. *Someday I am going to replace
that boy with someone who knows how to show respect.*

Bellus arrived within minutes, barely enough time for Sophia
to prepare. He stood at the door, clearly uneasy. He wore no armor,
only a brown tunic, and no weapons strapped to his belt. His dark
curls were a bit unruly today. He looked altogether ordinary, like a
farmer or a merchant. Sophia nodded to him from the large chair
placed at her desk. "Please, come in."

He took a hesitant step, turned and closed the door, then
advanced only a little farther into the room.

"Will you sit?" Sophia motioned to her pair of couches.

"Was there something you needed from me?"

"I need you to sit."

He turned to the couch, and she thought she detected a rolling of the eyes.

When he had reclined, she turned her chair slightly to face him, aware that their relative positions put him at a disadvantage. After the rushing wind of the platform, the chamber seemed still and quiet with waiting.

"I wanted to thank you for the—restraint—of the past few days. I had not thought eighty soldiers capable of anything nearing civil behavior, but I see I was wrong."

Bellus dipped his head. "The men have strict orders. I had hoped you would not be overly inconvenienced."

"Oh, do not misunderstand me. You are an inconvenience of the highest sort."

He turned a smile away from her.

"You are amused by me?"

Bellus studied her eyes. "Amused, at times, yes. More often, confused."

"I am a mystery to you?"

"Not a mystery so much as a muddle."

Sophia licked her lips and twisted her fingers together in her lap.

"You demand respect, yet do little to earn it," Bellus said. "You insist on solitude, yet cannot seem to stay away from the Base where nearly a hundred men prowl."

"I am making certain your men do not stray where they ought not! Making sure they do not steal or cause damage."

Bellus said nothing, only pulled himself from the couch and went to the wall of windows, where the afternoon waned and yellow light pooled on the floor beside him. Sophia studied the broadness of his shoulders and wondered how many battles he had waged.

"I have been longing to see the city from here." He gazed out for awhile, then turned to her. "But you cannot see much of the city on this side, can you? Only the sea." He regarded her, with the golden light behind him, and she watched his expression turn subtly from curiosity to pity. "Is there nothing you miss, secluded up in this place?"

Sophia's eyes strayed to the stringed lyre that hung on the wall. A small wave of emotion rippled through her. "Music. I sometimes miss the music."

He followed her gaze to the lyre and was silent a moment. "Do you never grow lonely?"

Sophia looked away and cleared her throat. "I have lived here in the lighthouse most of my life. My family has been its Keeper for generations." She extended a hand to the room. "The wealth you see is a result of that heritage."

He smiled, as though amused at her evasion of his question. "'*Without friends no one would choose to live, though he had all other goods,*'" he said.

Sophia raised her eyebrows. "First Socrates, now Aristotle. I may soon have to revise my opinion of Romans."

Bellus laughed. "I do not believe all the quotations at my disposal could accomplish that."

"Come now, Pilus Prior Bellus, tell me how it is that a man so obviously learned has a place among those who seek to rule by force and not by reason."

Bellus crossed his arms and leaned back against the wall. "'*We make war that we may live in peace.*'"

Sophia bit the inside of her cheek. "Will you continue to hide behind Aristotle, or will you speak your own mind? Or perhaps you have nothing in your mind but the thoughts of others?"

The dark light she was coming to recognize as anger shadowed his eyes.

"Do you truly believe," she said, "that a sword is the way to leave the world better than you found it?"

"Sometimes it is the duty of man to follow the orders he is given."

"Then you admit that you choose not to think for yourself, and only to rely upon the opinions of others?"

"Better that than to care nothing of what others think."

Sophia rubbed at her lips, then gripped the arms of her chair. "I need nothing from others—neither their opinions nor their good will."

"Well, that is certainly a fortunate thing, since you will not listen to the first and have none of the second!"

"Do not pretend to know me, Roman. A few words of gossip in the city do not paint an accurate picture of me."

Bellus had left his position at the wall and now stood towering over her. Sophia pushed herself to her feet and thought for a moment to climb upon the chair, if only to gain a few inches on him. She stood close to him, too close, and he backed up.

"I do not need gossip to tell me who you are. I have witnessed it for myself. You have your servants scurrying around the Base like ants, with you as their queen sitting high above them, immersed in your books. Do you even know what goes on down there?" He pushed away a curl of hair that had fallen before his eye.

"You dare to criticize my administration of the lighthouse? Do you know how many ships safely navigate into these harbors because of me? Your own ship included, I might remind you. And if I remember correctly, you were the one who said that my books were my real wealth." Sophia fought to control her breathing, but still stood with her lips slightly open and teeth clenched, unable to get enough air into her chest.

Outside the window the sun slid beneath a heavy cloud on the horizon, and the room darkened as though a pail of dirty water had been thrown on a warm fire.

Bellus took a step backward and lowered his head. "'*Wisdom outweighs any wealth,*' your playwright Sophocles said. But I fear that all your books may not have brought you wisdom of the sort that brings happiness, wisdom that seeks company."

Sophia sat again and rubbed her hands across her thighs. "You do not seem so happy yourself, centurion, even with all of your men and their loyalty. At least I do not have the condemnation of Caesar to contend with. Perhaps I am better off."

Bellus dropped his gaze, sighed, then looked around the room. Slowly he crossed to a niche in the wall and retrieved a small oil lamp. Shielding the flame with one hand, he crossed to a larger lamp mounted on a marble column at the wall and lit the second lamp. She watched his steady hand at the wick, the flex of the muscle in his arm. The simple act of courtesy shook her more than his words. He replaced the smaller lamp and turned to her, his expression composed.

"My men have need of me below, Sophia, and I must go. But I will leave you with the words of Aristotle once more: '*He who is unable to live in society, or who has no need because he is sufficient for himself, must be either a beast or a god.*'"

He lifted his chin to her, his eyes dark. "And you, Sophia of Alexandria, are no god."

NINETEEN

Cleopatra twisted her fingers through her long curls, secured them atop her head with a gold comb, and turned to get a glimpse of her profile in the bronze mirror in the bedchamber. She was dressed as a Greek, with a red mantle draped over a chitôn of pure white. Layers of jewels fell in heavy cascades around her neck, wrapped her wrists and dangled from her ears.

But is it enough?

The mood of the city increasingly concerned her. Today she would win them back.

She reached to arrange the red fabric around her shoulders, and saw in the mirror a glimmer of white behind her. Hands lifted the mantle and straightened it, then caressed her neck.

She turned to smile up at him. "You are ready for this day?"

Caesar shrugged one shoulder. "I am always ready."

Cleopatra felt her smile fade. "It is important, Gaius. Crucial that we win their favor."

Caesar ran a finger down her jawline. "Has anyone ever failed to fall under your spell once you have set your mind to gain their favor?"

Cleopatra heard the door swish open at her back. Caesar's eyes lifted above her shoulder, then followed the newcomer's path across the room. Cleopatra did not move. She waited for the intruder to become visible. Caesar's eyes were still on her pretty young maidservant when the girl looked up from where she placed clean clothing into a basket beside the wall. The girl blushed scarlet at Caesar's frank gaze.

Cleopatra watched them both, willing her expression to remain as light as a cloudless sky. The girl glanced at Cleopatra then fled the room.

Caesar's attention returned to her, but she pulled away, leaving him grasping at her robes.

She crossed the room to retrieve several gold armbands and took her time adjusting them on her upper arms.

"You are nervous." Caesar was clearly amused.

She lifted a leather pouch from its hook on the wall and set things aside that she would later require, all the while cursing her swirl of conflicting emotions.

She sought to control him, to use him. And yet at every turn she felt herself more at his mercy. Why should she be jealous of his eyes on a servant girl when his reputation as Rome's notorious womanizer had been the thing that gave her confidence to first roll herself up in a carpet to be deposited at his feet?

"The loyalty of my people is my chief concern," she said, as much to herself as to him. She finished packing the bag and straightened. "We should depart."

He half-smiled, a look of condescension she had seen bestowed on men of lesser rank, and again she felt the tormenting mix of the intent to rule him and the desire to fall at his feet and beg him to love her.

She paused, letting her resolve harden, then lifted her chin and exited the chamber. She snaked through the palace, down the wide, sun-warmed marble steps to her waiting chariot, without a glance backward to see if he followed.

He can stay in the palace with all the maids he wants. What is it to me?

The two-wheeled horse-drawn cart that awaited her in the street beyond the courtyard was driven by a beautiful slave, an Egyptian man who looked as young as she. She climbed up behind him, and Caesar joined her a moment later. She placed a warm hand on the slave's arm, smiled at him, and leaned close. "To the Paneium, Namir."

She had no idea of the slave's name. He knew enough not to correct her. She glanced at Caesar, but his eyes were on the city.

They started off, trailed by the Roman soldiers who seemed ever-present around Caesar. The general breathed deeply beside her, as though the city itself invigorated him.

"None of Rome is so fine as this, Cleopatra. You will see, if you visit someday. We are always building, always improving, but this . . ." He stretched a hand south through the Gate of the Moon at the harbor's edge, toward the granite-paved Street of the Soma, lined with the marble colonnades of the royal quarter. "Perhaps someday."

They turned west toward the Paneium, down the Canopic Way, and made their way through the noisy heart of the city to the *agora* filled with merchants and philosophers, all spouting opinions.

They drew attention, as Cleopatra had calculated they would. She held out a hand to women and children and smiled at the men.

A royal outing was uncommon, and with Caesar at her side, Cleopatra knew the citizens would follow. They passed down to the Soma, where they slowed to a stop, so the two could pay respects at the tomb of Alexander and former Ptolemies.

Inside the stone building Caesar ran a reverent hand along the translucent stone sarcophagus that held the body of the greatest conqueror the world had known. His body, blurry through the stone, seemed to float inside its burial place.

"He was so young," Caesar whispered. "Only thirty-three." He placed another palm on the stone. "I am fifty-two."

Cleopatra hooked an arm around his and brought her lips to his ear. "But I am not. And together . . ."

He turned to kiss her, but the gesture was halfhearted, distracted.

She tugged on his arm. "Come. The people are waiting."

The Paneium in the south of the city was a wonder, a man-made hill shaped as a fir cone, with a path that spiraled upward to the temple of Pan on its summit. Beside the temple they alighted, and Caesar enjoyed an uninterrupted view of the crossroad of the world. The entire city lay beneath them, all the way to the harbor. From here one felt almost equal with the lighthouse.

Cleopatra led Caesar into the temple. In the dark coolness of the stone, she prepared her mind to speak to her people with all the passion she felt in her heart. They waited for the crowd trickling up the hill to gather in the temple courtyard.

When she and Caesar emerged minutes later, blinking in the sunlight, with hands clasped and upraised, the reaction of the people was a mix of hails and jeers.

But Cleopatra had lived and breathed the political life since birth. She had seen her father woo and placate the people, had seen him rule them fiercely, and knew how to play the game.

She spoke her heart to them now, letting her voice rise and fall and weave a spell of words that hushed the protestors and delighted her supporters. She felt them ride along on the words with her, all the way to its triumphant conclusion.

"Egypt will again be great," she finished. "With all the power of Rome behind her, she will flourish here, with the Nile to feed her and the Great Sea to bring her wealth. And in the palace, one who knows you, who understands you, who is one of you!"

And then they escaped, through the crowd to the waiting chariot, amid the screaming cheers of the Alexandrians.

Caesar was laughing as they jumped into the chariot. "Magnificent!" He grabbed her around the waist and pulled her to him. Cleopatra laughed with him, still feeling the breathless exhilaration of her speech. "You are a marvel!"

There it was again, that dangerous happiness his words could bring her. She hardened herself against it, pulled his arms from her, and set her face forward. "We are not finished yet."

The city of Alexandria had divided itself into five districts, with three ethnic divisions. The royal Alpha, Beta, and Gamma districts, called the Brucheum, were home to both Greek rulers and Greek immigrants. The Jewish Delta district lay in the east of the city and the Egyptians' Epsilon district, Rhakotis, lay in the west. Their chariot sped them northwest through the Alpha now, to the other side of the Museum and Library on the waterfront, where they stopped and alighted.

In the street beside the massive twin buildings of the Museum and the Library, four Egyptian slaves waited with a gold litter on four poles.

Cleopatra hurried to the Egyptian-style litter, leaving Caesar behind to gaze at the gleaming marble steps that soared up to the columned Library entrance. It was a gorgeous structure, with at least ten interconnecting halls, each set aside for a different academic pursuit, with alcoves stuffed with papyrus scrolls and smaller study rooms for the scholars. Linked to the Library by a white marble colonnade was the Museum, with its private dining areas, gardens, and even exotic animals in small zoos where the scholars could further study. The complex rose like a temple to the gods of learning, and Cleopatra watched Caesar gawk at it with the eyes of a foreigner.

"You see now"—she climbed into the litter—"why you Romans copy our philosophy, our religion, even our architecture?"

Caesar looked away from the buildings. "*Rome est constructum in crepidoinis of Aegina.*" Rome is built on the foundations of Greece.

Cleopatra sank into the cushions of the litter and tugged at the curtains. Her Roman watched her and nodded. Whether he would follow on foot or return to the palace, she did not know.

The canopied sedan chair was carved with hieroglyphs and hung with the blue and white striped fabric of Egyptian royalty, and she molded her attitude to her new role even as the slaves lifted the poles to their shoulders and moved forward.

Inside, she slid out of the Greek chitôn, and removed the jewelry from her neck and hair. The leather pouch she had packed earlier rested in the corner of the litter. She pulled a new robe from it—the white sheath dress, close-fitting and filmy, of Egyptian royalty—and shimmied into it with some difficulty.

"Stop the jolting!" she called to the slaves. "You walk like a pack of Syrian camels!"

Her pouch gave up the rest of its contents. A wig of straight, shoulder-length black hair with bangs cut evenly across her brow. A pectoral neck piece of gold links that wrapped around her neck and lay heavy on her upper chest. Lastly the double-crown of Upper and Lower Egypt with its rearing snake at the forehead, a symbol of the Pharaoh since time began.

She felt the litter moving upward and knew they had reached the hill that dominated the city. She finished arranging the head-piece as the litter slowed to a stop and lowered to the ground. A beefy, bare-chested slave reached a hand through the curtain and she emerged, every bit the Egyptian queen.

She gazed around the outer court of the Serapeum and felt she might have been Hatshepsut, that ancient ruler who had been Egypt's only female Pharaoh.

Cleopatra loved the Serapeum Temple. Like a mirror of herself, it was a blend of the ancient Egyptian worship and the Greeks who had brought their religion with them. People came to the immense temple complex to seek advice from the god, to pray for healing.

The sandy courtyard was filled with pious Egyptians leading goats for sacrifices and shaved-headed priests in white skirts. Here the wealthy and the peasants mingled, made equal before the gods. And here Cleopatra would win her second audience of the day.

The crowd parted at her entrance, as it should. Her name whispered through the courtyard, and all eyes turned toward her. She carried herself with regal authority and was rewarded with the bent knees of many. They stretched dark arms in front of them, heads down, in the age-old mark of deference to a Pharaoh. She let a slight, pleased smile play upon her lips, and moved between the wide-slanted pylons and the two colossal statues of the Apis Bull. When she reached the square entry, she turned to the crowd and paused, waiting for all to return to their feet and pay her heed.

"My people, these are difficult days for Egypt. Grain has been short since last year's meager inundation. But we await the new season with hope. And in our hope for a stronger Egypt, we seek the assistance of our strong and friendly neighbor, Rome."

There was some stirring of discontent, and she hastened on. "You have heard, no doubt, that Rome's general, Julius Caesar, has brought his legion and settled into the royal quarter. You have also heard, I know, that I have not declared him our enemy, but instead have welcomed him into the palace." She breathed deeply, smiled at them all, and lifted a hand. "This is for Egypt, my friends. This is for Egypt. By Isis and Osiris, I will restore Egypt to her former glory." She pointed to the mighty carved reliefs of the Pharaohs that crossed the temple's wall in solar boats to receive gifts from the hands of the gods. "Like a true daughter of Isis, I seek only the glory of Egypt!"

The Egyptians did not cheer. She did not expect them to. They were not a robust and buoyant people like the Greeks. Instead, they bowed their heads in reverent approval as Cleopatra turned slowly and entered the temple to make her obeisance to the gods of Egypt.

Would he have said magnificent *here?* It mattered not. She had accomplished her goal. For the Greeks, rhetoric. For the Egyptians, religion.

She thought briefly of visiting the splendid Jewish synagogue in the Delta district but knew there was little use. The Jews, while many, took no ownership of Egypt. Their hearts were always for their own dusty land, even when displaced.

When she emerged from the temple, a wave of exhaustion swept through her limbs. The sense of impending war hanging over the city drained her energy. She accepted the arm of the slave who offered, let him lead her to the litter once more, and whispered instructions. She had need of something tonight, and it was not the puzzling affections of a Roman, nor the whining complaints of her brother-husband Ptolemy. She longed for companionship more steady, more trustworthy.

Sighing, she leaned once more into the cushions of the litter and let the slaves carry her to Sophia.

It was not until her slaves helped her from the litter in the entryway of the lighthouse that Cleopatra remembered the centuria of Romans stationed there. As she crossed through the Base to the lighthouse ramp, she smiled at the deference offered her by the soldiers she passed.

It pays to be the consort of General Caesar.

Ares met her at the entrance to the tower, but she waved him away. She wanted to surprise Sophia. It had been too long.

She found her former tutor on her couch, huddled over her books, as usual. Sophia jerked her head up at the interruption, then smiled slowly. Cleopatra watched the lines in the woman's forehead smooth away.

Sophia swept a few scrolls to the floor, making room beside her. Cleopatra hurried to the couch, embraced her, and dropped to the cushions.

"You have been too long gone, my dear," Sophia said. "Almost I have been thinking that your Roman has convinced you to abandon me."

She squeezed Sophia's arm. "Never. Where would I go to hear the truth, if not to you?"

Sophia touched the gold pectoral at Cleopatra's chest. "You have need of truth today?"

She sighed and leaned her head against the cushion. "I am trying to win them back, Sophia. The city. But it is not easy."

"You will win them only when you give them what they want."

Cleopatra smiled. "Ah, but this is why you will never be a politician, Sophia. You do not give the people what they want. You convince them that they *want* what you are *giving* them."

The corner of Sophia's mouth turned upward. "How is it you are so wise, when you are still so young?"

"You forget where I grew up. At my father's knee." She drew closer to Sophia and rested her head on the woman's shoulder. "And at yours."

Sophia patted her head.

"Do you think he loves me?" Cleopatra couldn't hold back the question. "Or is he only using me to gain Egypt?"

"What does your heart tell you?"

Cleopatra laughed. "Is this my Sophia, telling me to listen to my heart?"

Her tutor was silent, and Cleopatra lifted her head to study Sophia's face. She was surprised by the emotion there. "What is this?"

Sophia shrugged. "I am weary of others believing I have no heart of my own."

Cleopatra took Sophia's face in her hands. "No one has loved me better than you, Sophia. Show me the one who thinks you have no heart, and I will run a sword through his."

Sophia's eyes filled and she smiled.

"It is only that you do not pay attention to your heart, to the great capacity for love that lies there." She wiped at Sophia's tears and then embraced her. "I am not sure I have that same capacity."

Sophia pulled away. "Do you love him?"

"I do not want to. It is not wise."

"I am sure it is not."

Cleopatra laughed. "You see, I knew you would tell me the truth." She faced Sophia. "Now you must tell me, do you think he could love me? Do you think I am worth loving?" Even as she asked it, she knew the answer, because she had voiced the question so many times before. Why did it seem she needed to be told so often?

"I have seen you with him only once, Cleo. But it was clear on that night that he was much taken with you. I saw the way he watched your movements, smiled at every word you spoke."

Cleopatra closed her eyes against the cushions again. "You must come again, you must tell me what you think."

"I should rather avoid all Romans, I think."

Cleopatra laughed. "Then you must be spending all your time up here, as they are difficult to avoid below."

Sophia stood and scooped up the scrolls she had pushed to the floor. "A pack of arrogant, unruly dogs." She crossed to her desk and stacked the rolls of papyrus neatly.

Cleopatra stretched across the couch. "Come now, they are not all so bad?"

Sophia turned on her. "You do realize what they are doing to the Library? To the Museum? Can't you use your influence with Caesar to make them stop?"

"Ah, yes, your precious men of the Museum. Where have they all fled to, Sophia?"

The woman turned back to her desk and rearranged the scrolls. "They were forced to flee before Caesar had them spending their time on projects that would only bring Egypt to harm."

Cleopatra watched Sophia's back. "There are rumors that Sosigenes was working on something very important."

"Everything they do is important, Cleo."

"He worked closely with Kallias, did he not?"

"He was a good friend to my husband. And to me."

"But could he be trying to recreate the Proginosko that Kallias lost?"

Sophia whirled again, her eyes flashing. "He did not lose it!"

Cleopatra lifted herself from the cushions. "I misspoke, Sophia. Forgive me. It was lost with him. I know."

Sophia ran a hand through her short hair, and Cleopatra resisted a smile. When would she convince Sophia to let it grow?

"Persuade Caesar that Alexandria is the jewel of the world because it is the center of learning, Cleo. Convince him that he only weakens Egypt when he attacks what makes her great."

"I will tell him."

Sophia sank into the chair beside her desk, and Cleopatra watched her.

Where was Sosigenes? Sophia's evasiveness aroused her curiosity. Could he have completed the Proginosko? She let her mind toy with the possibility and its effects.

What would it mean for Egypt, and for her, to have the knowledge the Proginosko promised?

Sophia's attention had moved to the window now, to the sky beyond. Cleopatra inclined her head and studied her tutor. If the choice came, would she betray Sophia to gain the power the Proginosko could afford?

Her own words echoed back to her . . .

I am not sure I have the capacity to love.

TWENTY

I must escape this place.

Another week had passed since the Roman soldiers had infested her lighthouse, and Sophia thought she might be losing her mind, trapped as she was in her chambers and her garden. Though they had long been her only places of refuge and solace, she found that being confined there against her will plagued her in a way that hiding there by her own choice never did. She was loathe to descend to the Base, with all those men milling about with nothing to do but make coarse jokes and wrestle with each other.

But when she woke one morning to an unusually gray sky and a freshening breeze, she decided she must get away. Or lose her sanity.

It was a market day, and with the sky threatening a rare storm, the crowds would be out early, anxious to complete their business. Though Alexandria received more rainfall than the rest of Egypt that lay south along the Nile, still the Egyptians felt it an ill omen. The Nile supplied all the rain that they needed. Why would they want it to fall from the sky? No good—only floods, muddy streets, and disrupted shipping—could come of it.

Sophia dressed hurriedly in her customary tan tunic, belted it, and descended to the Base. She found Ares in the kitchen, supervising the day's cooking. Two slaves kneeled at a small fire in the center of the room, cooking a goose, and several others worked at tables, chopping cabbage. Sophia grabbed some maza bread before informing him of her plan.

"I was going to send Capaneus," Ares said, "as soon as he finished with serving breakfast."

Sophia chewed the bread and swallowed. "I haven't been to the agora in some time. I'd like to make the choices for this week's purchases myself."

Ares shrugged. "I will send Capaneus with you."

"No need. I will arrange to have my selections brought back."

Ares narrowed his eyes and pulled her to the doorway, away from the servants. "You are escaping. Is there a problem?"

Sophia eyed the servants, whose attention on them was barely concealed. "I have no need to escape, Ares. I am simply taking an active role in the running of my lighthouse."

Ares didn't nod. "As you wish. I will watch over things here."

In the end, she consented to have Capaneus drive her to the agora in a two-wheeled cart, as the sky still hung heavy with gray clouds and she had no wish to walk through rain. She dismissed him in the street, however, and entered the agora alone. She stood before the teeming square, divided into streets and smaller squares, and strangely felt the freedom of solitude for the first time in weeks.

She breathed deeply and plunged into the square. There were immediate looks of recognition, elbow jabs and points, comments whispered into others' ears at her presence. Smiling, hands fisted at her sides, she made the decision to ignore and simply enjoy the time outside the lighthouse.

Before the Romans came, I would never have believed I could find comfort in a crowd.

The agora of Alexandria was the finest in the world. Hundreds, perhaps thousands of stalls lined the streets, with a central square reserved for philosophers and teachers to expound their theories.

She pushed through the first thronged street and lingered at tables of golden olive oils, bleached white linens, and delicate blown glassware in a rainbow of colors. The scent of Arabian perfumes and spices from India tickled her nose and drew her on. She stopped to argue with a fat salt merchant, whose valuable store had come all the way across the Western Desert from the mines of Mali. She directed him to send a *mina* weight to the lighthouse, then pulled two drachmas from a pouch and thrust the money at him.

He laughed. "Do you think I drag the salt across the desert on my own back, mistress? There are many others to pay along the way!"

"That is no excuse to rob me."

"Rob you! It is you who robs my children. My five small children who will have nothing to eat!"

She pointed at his gut, bulging beneath his himation. "Perhaps you should share."

"Oh!" He threw his hands into the air. "Now you will insult me? Is this how you think to find a fair price?"

She pulled a few more obols from her pouch. "There. Buy a goat for your five hungry children."

He waved both hands and shook his head. "I cannot do it to them. Not at such a price."

Sophia shrugged and looked over his head toward the next street. "Fine. I think there is another salt merchant who does not have so many children." She edged away from the table.

"Mistress! You leave me a poorer man than you found me, but I must sell all of this today before I leave on a long journey. It is your good fortune that I am forced to do this. Three drachmas."

Sophia pulled the remaining coins from her pouch and dropped them in his palm. "Delivered to the lighthouse by the end of the day." The fat man lowered his head, as though she had beaten the salt from him rather than paid him a handsome price.

She moved on, into the small section reserved for the thriving Alexandrian gem trade. Emeralds, amethysts, topaz and onyx—they were all mined here in Egypt and then transformed into gorgeous cameos, carved ornaments and jewelry. Sophia slowed at the table of one merchant and ran her fingers over a stunning necklace of finely worked gold and tiny purple amethysts. She touched her own neck with the other hand and briefly wondered. But then her eyes drifted to her brown tunic and she drew her fingers away from the piece.

Behind her, a man much taller than she jostled close and bumped her. She turned a scathing look on him, and he quickly looked away.

It was time to move on.

She repeated the scene with the salt merchant several more times, arguing over a box of Indian cinnamon that she knew Sosigenes would appreciate sprinkled on his fruit, and insisting on the finest cut of goose at a reasonable price.

Twice more she turned to find the tall Greek nearby, and she studied his features, searching for recognition. Had Ares sent a servant to watch her? But he was not dressed as a servant, and she was certain he was unknown to her.

The crowd was thickening now. The tumult of merchants haggling with customers, the bleats and snorts of animals, and even the random singing that erupted from various quarters in the agora, mingled to create a chaos that pressed against her. It was as though the Great Harbor had tipped all its many merchant ships on end, pouring their luxuries into the agora for all of Alexandria to paw over. She put her fingers to her temples and tried to take a fresh breath, free of the jumble of scents. The uncommon moisture in the air seemed to hold the odors down with a heavy hand.

In the next street, Sophia passed by the stacks of fragrant cedarwood from Lebanon and stopped on a whim beside a table draped with leopard skins.

He is still there.

The lanky Greek. He had not anticipated her sudden stop beside the skins. When she turned to face him, he darted between a table laid with colorful silk from the Far East, and one with Indian cotton.

A prick of fear needled her. If Ares had sent the man, would he have worked so hard to remain unnoticed? She ran a hand absently over the leopard skin, her eyes still trained toward the adjoining tables. He seemed to be watching her from the edge of his vision.

Enough purchases for today.

She smiled at the skins merchant, shook her head, and moved away, ignoring his calls of protest. She forced her way through the crush of people, cringing at the touch of those she brushed against. *I should never have left the lighthouse.*

The agora gave way, finally, and she was free. But in the lonely street beyond she felt vulnerable and exposed. She hurried down the granite way, keeping close to the columned porticos and open shops.

At the entrance of a narrow alley, an arm swept around her waist, and a voice rasped at her ear. "Not so fast."

She tried to pry the arm from her body. She twisted her head, though she knew exactly who held her. His chin was unshaven, his hair longish and greasy. Wrapped in his embrace, she smelled the sea and fish and an odor she couldn't identify.

"Let me go!" She tried to wriggle from his grasp.

Her attacker laughed, a quiet growl, then yanked her sideways off her feet and dragged her into the alley.

Only the kitchen doors of estates opened to the narrow space. Garbage lined the buildings. Sophia tried to catch her breath. She felt her neck grow damp with fear. "What do you want?"

He pushed her against one of the stone walls. He released his grip on her waist, then used the arm to brace against her throat, and leaned in close. His breath stank, and he grazed her cheek with his lips. She slapped at his face.

So many young and beautiful women about. Why would he choose me?

She clawed at the arm that pressed her throat, then tried to bite it.

He pushed her chin backward. "Do you know how long I've been waiting for you, Keeper?"

She stopped struggling, stunned.

"Days outside that lighthouse. I was beginning to think you would never show your face."

Sophia reached for his arm again, tried to ease the pressure. The stone at her back felt cold, unrelenting. "What do you want?" she asked again. His arm seemed made of the ebony she'd seen in the market.

"Yes, I want something. Something you can tell me where to find."

"I have only a small amount of money." She fumbled at her waist to uncover her pouch.

He pressed her throat harder, and she cried out. She tried to turn her head, to see if anyone else walked the alley. "Release me!" But the words were only a croak with his arm against her voice, and she knew no one inside the homes would hear.

"Keep your money. I want the scholar."

If she hadn't been terrified, Sophia would have laughed. "What could you want—"

He used his free hand to grip her side, digging sharp fingers. "Just tell me where the old man is. Sosigenes."

Sophia blinked away the pain and lifted her chin. "He can be of no interest to you. He has no money of his own and he has not yet invented a way to make peasants smell like something other than dead fish." Her voice shook at the end of the sarcasm, but she did not flinch.

His eyes flashed and he bent to place his cheek against hers. His body pressed against the length of her own. She felt the scratch of his beard, coarse sand rubbed on tender skin. His fingers disappeared from her side but were back again in a moment, this time at her throat. She caught the flash of silver.

"He gave me leave to kill you if I must. 'At all cost, bring the scholar.'" A knife point tickled just under her chin. "If you will not help me, I have no use for you."

The fear she had felt first spark in the agora bloomed into terror. She had nothing more than words to defend herself, and they would not protect her against a knife. She kicked at his shins and tried to scream. He pressed the cold blade closer.

"Who wants him?" she whispered. "You must tell me that before I give you anything." *Does he know I merely stall?*

The sharp point traced circles under her chin, and something like regret passed over the man's features. "That is none of your concern. And I will not listen to any demands from you. Tell me where he is. Now!"

She had always suspected that her patronage of the Museum and its scholars would one day make her a target of someone's ill-will. Wherever there was progress, there would be those who oppose it, who fear it.

But this is not about fear. This is about power.

Someone had discovered what Sosigenes was creating, had discovered Kallias's legacy, and had come to seize the power for himself.

She could not protect Sosigenes if she were dead. But she could not tell this brute the truth. She floundered, with growing panic, for a suitable lie.

And the tip of the knife began a slow slice along her jawline.

TWENTY-ONE

In the grayness of the day, Bellus longed for Rome. Though his days in the countryside of Italy were most often sun-kissed, there were still drizzly days when the fire beckoned one to draw close and spend the time with books, with staring into the flames in contemplation.

But the lighthouse afforded no such luxury to him, and so the heavy clouds and dim corridors weighed on his spirit and eventually drove him outdoors.

He walked, wandering toward the city, uncaring if he was caught in a downpour. Eventually he found the agora and enjoyed a walk through. When he came upon Capaneus, a slave he recognized from the lighthouse, lounging beside an empty horse-drawn cart at the edge of the agora, he inquired as to his errand.

Capaneus jabbed a thumb toward the center of the agora. "She is shopping today."

Bellus raised his eyebrows and followed the man's thumb. "I did not realize she came to the agora herself."

Capaneus barked a laugh. "Never does." He pointed upward. "Ill-favored sky. It drives people mad."

Bellus smiled his agreement and waved farewell.

What kind of merchant would draw Sophia?

He wandered back through the stalls, searching for a short-haired woman among the mix of peasants and nobility.

He soon gave up. The agora churned with people, making his task impossible. He escaped from the central crowd and edged along the street, where vendors stayed in their shops, hoping to capitalize on the traffic to and from the market.

Bellus marveled again at the grid-like plan of the city, laid out so precisely by Alexander's men three hundred years earlier. Did he have any idea what he began?

Even the alleys ran straight from the streets, and Bellus glanced down each he passed, idle curiosity urging him on.

A woman's cry halfway down one alley arrested his progress.

A Greek, peasant from his dress, held someone against the wall. He assumed it was the woman whom he had heard. He hesitated, unwilling to get involved in a domestic argument.

But something about the conflict drew him farther into the alley.

The woman turned her head to him.

On the heels of startled recognition, blood rushed to his head and pounded in his ears.

Sophia!

She turned back to her attacker quickly, without a flicker to betray his presence.

Good woman.

Years of training took over. He moved forward on soundless feet, and his arms hardened as though iron flowed into them. His pugio found its way into his hand, an extension of his arm.

He was behind the Greek in a moment. He snaked an arm between them and gripped the man's forehead with his palm. The Greek's hair was greasy under his hand. Sophia's eyes were on Bellus, dark and wide with a vulnerable fear he had never seen.

A surge of anger flowed through him. The Greek stabbed blindly backward with a knife, trying to strike Bellus. In one quick motion he pulled the man's head backward, saw the target vein pound perfectly in the villain's knobby throat, and brought his dagger across it in a soundless, smooth slice.

The man stiffened. A gurgle sounded in his throat, mingled with Sophia's cry. And then he fell at Bellus's feet with a satisfactory thud, like a poor man's skinny goat offered for sacrifice.

Sophia's knees buckled, and Bellus reached to catch her, dropping the pugio to avoid another injury. A scrawny cat ran through the alley past their feet.

And then he saw the blood. At first he thought her attacker's blood had sprayed on her, but it ran too heavy down her throat, and spread across the neckline of her tunic like a petal-torn red rose.

"Sophia!"

Her eyes were open, but she was silent.

He bent and retrieved his pugio, then lifted her into his arms and strode from the alley. He found Capaneus where he had left him, picking meat off the leg of some bird.

The slave jumped up, eyes wide.

Bellus climbed onto the cart, placed Sophia on the floor at his feet, and grabbed the reins. He said nothing to Capaneus, who stood open-mouthed, simply yelled to the horse, which took off at a trot.

The reins were tight and coarse against his hand. When he had navigated through the worst of the crowds, he glanced down at Sophia. Her throat still bled. He did not think it was fatal, but his chest felt constricted nonetheless. "Can you press your chitôn against the wound, Sophia?"

She was silent still, but unwrapped the fabric from her shoulder and held it against her chin.

The sky opened then, sending the first heavy drops like scattered arrows, then a curtain of water that drenched them in moments. The entire city seemed sheeted in gray, and they swam alone through the fog.

Another glance at Sophia. She had lifted her face to the rain, as though to let it wash away the attack. Her chitôn grew pink with watered blood, and she blinked away the rain that assaulted her eyes.

He snapped the reins against the horse's flank and took a corner so sharply they nearly toppled.

Across the heptastadion, empty of all travelers and beaten with angry waves, and then past the Pharos village and the short causeway that led to the lighthouse. He steered carefully around ruts and stones and drew the cart up close to the entryway.

A moment later she was in his arms again, in the front hall of the Base.

Ares rushed to them. "What have you done?" He reached for Sophia. Bellus turned away, putting himself between the servant and Sophia.

"She has been attacked. Light a fire in her chambers and bring bandages."

A look of resentment flashed in Ares's eyes and he glanced at Sophia, as if to get different instructions. But the woman was silent in Bellus's arms, huddled against his own pounding chest.

Ares hurried ahead of them, through the inner courtyard and up the ramp.

Halfway to her chambers, Sophia stirred in his arms. "I can walk," she whispered. "Put me down."

"I will not."

"It is too far."

"I have carried armor heavier than you for miles across the battlefield. Be quiet."

Amazingly, she was.

By the time they reached Sophia's private chamber, a fire surged at the side of the room and Ares had brought a basin of water and clean rags.

Bellus tried to lay her on the white-cushioned couches, but she resisted. "On the floor," she said. "By the fire."

He glanced at Ares, who then flew to the bed in the adjoining chamber, ripped a covering from it, and returned. With a flick of his wrists, he snapped the royal blue fabric taut and let it float to the floor beside the fire. Bellus kneeled and laid Sophia on it, and she exhaled as though relieved, though whether to be in her room or out of his arms, he wasn't sure.

Ares hovered.

"We are fine, Ares," Bellus said, still kneeling at her side. "That will be all."

The servant's feet didn't move. Bellus looked upward into his eyes and saw a mix of anger and something more. Jealousy?

Their eyes connected for only a moment, then Ares apparently remembered his place and backed from the room.

"The boy cares for you very much," Bellus said to Sophia as he reached for one of the rags Ares had left.

Her voice was low. "He hasn't known a mother for many years."

She lay on her back, and Bellus knew the bedcovering gave little relief from the hard floor. "Let me move you to the couch." He glanced to the next chamber. "Or the bed."

"No." The word was sharp. "No, this is fine."

Bellus left her for a moment to retrieve small cushions from the bedchamber. He was there only a moment, but the femininity of the room, with its rich fabrics enveloping the bed and ornately carved furniture, surprised him.

He propped a cushion under Sophia's head and then dipped the rag into the basin of clear water and wrung it out. "What happened? Who was that?"

Sophia swallowed. "I don't know. He wanted money, I suppose. I am often recognized when I go out."

Bellus stroked the cloth across her throat, taking care not to get near the wound until he could assess it. The rag left a wet streak across her bloody throat. He wiped again, gently. The rag turned pink in his hand as he washed the blood from her neck and then her upper chest. She stilled beneath his hand, her eyes on him. He could see her pulse, pounding in her neck. Oddly, he was aware of his own beating heart as well, which seemed to speed faster here than it had in the street with her attacker.

Battles I know. Women, I do not.

The fire snapped beside them, and she jumped. Bellus touched her arm with his free hand. "Lie still."

He bent closer and leaned his head to the side until it nearly rested on her belly, to examine the cut. With a clean rag, he washed the blood from it. It had stopped bleeding, and he was careful not to reopen it. She trembled a little as he cleaned it, and he thought again of the petals of a flower, bruised and crushed.

Her teeth began to chatter.

"You are soaking wet," he said.

"So are you."

He shrugged. "I am accustomed to harsh weather." He went to the bedchamber once more and came back with another covering, but then changed his mind. "You should change your clothes."

Her eyes widened.

"The cut has ceased its bleeding. With careful tending it should heal without a problem. But you need to get dry."

"And you think to stand there and watch me?" A little of the old fire had come back into her voice.

He straightened. "Why should I want to do that?"

She pulled herself to sitting. "I have no further need of you. You may go."

He scowled, staring her down. "I will stay out here while you dress in dry clothes."

She stood. "You said yourself that the wound is nothing."

"I didn't say it was nothing. I said it should heal. I want to be certain you do not reopen it."

"Tell Ares to send for the physician when you see him in the Base."

"I have treated more wounds on the field than any physician has ever seen." He met her stare for some moments, and then she shrugged.

"Do as you like." She brushed past him, bumping his shoulder with her own. He didn't turn, but the place where she had touched him seemed to spark with heat.

He quoted Homer to himself, uncaring if she heard. *"Do thou restrain the haughty spirit in thy breast, for better far is gentle courtesy."* He lowered himself to the bedcovering beside the fire and waited with his back to her bedchamber. She returned in a few moments. He could feel her standing behind him, as though deciding what to do. And then she circled and kneeled. He grabbed at the extra covering he had brought and wrapped it around her shoulders. She relaxed before the fire.

They stared into its flames for some minutes, wordless. And then he felt her shift and knew she would speak. He did not turn.

"Thank you," she whispered. "Thank you for rescuing me."

He dared not look at her. "I was pleased to be of service to you. But Sophia . . ." He paused, then forged on. "That was no beggar looking to rob you. What did he want?"

She was silent, and for a moment he thought she might tell him the truth. "I suppose you do not believe he could have been preying on my womanhood."

"I never said that! I only want to know if you are in danger." His face felt hot, from the fire no doubt. "It is my duty to secure the lighthouse, and that means its inhabitants as well."

"So we are your prisoners, now?" She turned to him. "Should I have asked your permission before going to the agora, centurion?"

He drew his shoulders back. "Perhaps if you had, you wouldn't have come back wet and bleeding!"

"And perhaps if you savages hadn't invaded our city, it wouldn't have turned into a nest of violence!" She gripped the edges of the fabric wrapped around her in tight fists.

Bellus shook his head. "That was no Roman whose throat I cut today."

"Ah, so only we Greeks are violent? Is that what you propose?"

He snorted and faced the fire. "You are impossible, woman. I do you a kind deed, and somehow you find a way to blame me for its necessity."

She shrugged. "There is little these days that is not the fault of you and your legionaries."

He bore holes into the smoldering wood with his eyes. "You should stop talking. You'll reopen your wound."

She laughed. "Is that the way you win an argument? I thought you were of a stronger intellect."

Bellus stretched his legs in front of him until his sandals nearly touched the fire, then leaned on one elbow on his side and faced her. He said nothing. She looked down on him, swallowed, and turned her face away.

He hated conflict. In spite of all the battles, all the scrambling for position in the Roman army, he was not his father, and at his core he wanted only peace. Sometimes that meant walking away from a fight.

Today he was not walking away. But he would not be drawn in.

He plucked at the threads on the fabric beneath them, up close to her thigh. He felt her tension, like reins on a horse that strained at the bit to run free. The air seemed charged, as though the storm had not yet broken. He lifted a hand, meaning to trace a line down her thigh.

I have lost my mind.

He let his hand drop and closed his eyes.

In his mind, he saw again the Soma, the crystal sarcophagus of Alexander the Great, installed in the city far below them. The conqueror's lifeless body, close enough to touch but shrouded in stone.

But no, she was not cold and lifeless. She was more like the fire that burned every night atop the lighthouse. Fiercely hot—and completely out of reach. A single flame, isolated, yet dutiful.

"You do not need to stay," she finally said, her voice low.

He sighed. "You have no further need of me, I know."

He pulled himself to his feet. She kept her eyes on the fire. Again, a desire to reach out to her washed over him, but he stayed his hand, and frustration replaced the desire. "Should you find that you do have need of another human being, you can always send for me."

She was silent a moment, then turned her face to him. "Should I ever find I have need of someone, you would not be the one for whom I send."

They locked eyes for one angry moment, and then he turned and left her sitting beside her fire. Alone.

TWENTY-TWO

Four days passed, and the cut on her throat was healing. Sophia sat on the edge of her bed and angled a small polished bronze beneath her chin to catch sight of the wound. The slice was neat and the edges had come together correctly, though there would certainly be a scar. She had a flash of the throat of her attacker, opened and gushing. She shuddered and laid the bronze on her bed.

It had been too long since a visit to the temple, and she felt the need this morning to pay respect to the gods.

It was still early when she slipped from the lighthouse. No soldiers nor servants impeded her, and she chose to walk. She tried to enjoy the sounds of the morning and the sunshine, still too hazy to build the heat. But thoughts of her attacker plagued her, and she kept her eyes up as she walked. *"To him who is in fear, everything rustles."* Sophocles did not help her today.

The sun could not penetrate the heavy shroud she felt within. Since the attack and Bellus's rescue, she had been restless, yet inactive. She had spent too many hours gazing out to sea from her chamber windows or sleeping on her couches.

The Temple of Serapis had been built by the Greeks, but unlike the palaces and public buildings, it was thoroughly Egyptian in architecture, with square-cut doorways and flat walls that leaned slightly inward. An attempt by Ptolemy Soter to convince the Egyptians that this new god was actually one of theirs.

She tried to shake off the doubts that were becoming pervasive of late. How could this manufactured Greek-Egyptian god claim her worship? How could he be a god, when he had not existed a few centuries earlier?

Sophia crossed through the sun-washed courtyard, passed the mighty statues of the Apis Bull, and entered the darkness of the temple.

Inside, the thickly columned hall, with its carved reliefs spread on every wall, was still dim, with only one fire burning in a low brazier on the side. She found herself the only worshipper, and the heaviness of the dark interior descended on her at once. She felt sealed up, as if she had been brought to one of the underground tombs of the ancient kings and left there to await the afterlife.

She moved slowly across the hall to the altar at the front.

A priest appeared, his white skirt gleaming in the darkness and his shaved head catching the firelight. She kneeled before him, and he touched her forehead with his finger. She felt the residue of oil that remained.

He began a chant over her, and she fumbled for the coins she had brought. They were smooth and heavy in her hand, and she pressed them into his. He accepted the sacrifice without breaking the rhythm of his chant.

Sophia's eyes grew heavy. She blinked several times and let them close. She waited for the peace that had often descended on her in the temple, but it did not come.

Too many questions now. Sosigenes had done that to her with his frequent talk of One God. *Yes, One God.* Oh, to put aside the ever-changing pantheon of Egyptian, Greek, and now Roman gods. To know only one to worship. She felt the pull of it on her soul, felt the truth of it whisper to her heart.

Her chest felt weighted; it grew difficult to breathe.

The priest paused in his singing over her, and she rose and fled. Past the red and gold painted columns with Isis and Horus presiding over the world, to the wide-open brightness of the courtyard. It had been foolish to come.

She crossed the city from the Serapeum again, moving north toward Pharos, through the commercial district. Vendors were beginning their day, opening shop doors, sweeping garbage into the street. Sophia was noted, though not hailed, by many. She made a few stops, arranging for purchases to be delivered.

Back in the lighthouse, she avoided contact with the few soldiers who were stirring. Bellus was not about. She crept to the North Wing, then down the cool stone corridor to the room she had set up for the scholars to do their work. Would they be awake yet? She pushed the heavy wooden door open slowly, and it squeaked on its hinge.

Twelve gray-haired men in pure white himations raised their heads to her.

"Sophia!"

Here it was different. Not like the street vendors. Here she was welcomed, appreciated. She belonged.

She had given the scholars each a desk of their own, and they hovered over scrolls, with more books tumbled in piles around them. The room smelled of lamp smoke, ink, and men confined.

Sosigenes pushed away from the table where he worked and crossed the room to her, his hands extended. "Finally," he said, smiling, "a woman to break the tedium of a dozen old men!" He gripped her hands and pulled her to himself. She leaned into his embrace and felt her eyes water.

"How goes the work?" she said over his shoulder.

He patted her cheek. "Come and see."

The Proginosko sat upon a low table along the wall. Unassuming, it might have been taken for a rich man's toy. It was a bronze slab, less than a cubit long, with one large dial on the front and two on the back. It had more than thirty gears, with teeth formed by triangles, and the dials were marked by degrees in both Greek and Egyptian. Hands revealed the relative positions of the sun, the lunar phases, and all five planets.

"Look here." Sosigenes turned the Proginosko to show her the back. "I've been able to reconstruct the spiral dial for the Metonic tropical cycle and the subsidiary dial for the Chaldean cycle, to calculate the eclipses." The pride in his voice brought a smile to Sophia's lips.

"And this?" She pointed to a lower dial, also a spiral.

His eyes twinkled. "You know how I love the games. It is for the Olympiad, to calculate the cycle of the games."

"Then you are finished?"

Sosigenes drew her close. "Nearly. Only the testing, and the moon wanes. But there is more."

She studied the creases in his thin face, like a map of ages.

"I am working on some calculations." His voice dropped to a whisper, and she realized that even among the academic pursuits of the Museum, rivalry existed. She leaned in to hear better. "I believe I have found an even more accurate way to construct the calendar."

"More accurate than the Romans?"

Sosigenes waved a hand, dismissing her joke.

"The Romans don't know Ianuarius from Februarius. No, Sophia"—he gripped her arm with one hand and nodded toward the Proginosko—"more accurate than the Chaldean, than the Callippic. Based on Meton's work, but my calendar would not see a drift of a day for over a hundred years, and even then would be adjusted!"

Sophia smiled. "The Sosigenes Cycle."

The older man dropped his head. "It can be named for anyone, I suppose. The important thing is the accuracy of it."

Sophia sighed, pleased with his progress, but a bit envious of his dedication to something. Anything. She gazed over the other scholars, who had returned to their cramped positions at their desks, reeds scratching over papyrus with lovely purpose, as though their minds had run ahead and their reeds struggled to keep pace.

Sosigenes wrapped an arm around her waist. "All this is because of you, Sophia. You are indeed wisdom, as your name. Without you I cannot imagine what would have come of us." He squeezed her to himself. "Kallias, he would have been so proud of you, to see this."

She nodded but did not trust herself to speak.

"Did you come so early for a reason, Sophia?"

She swallowed and pulled away. "I wanted to see your progress. I fear we may not have long to hide. I was out early to visit the Serapeum, praying for our cause."

"Ah." Sosigenes moved away, toward his desk.

"I know you do not approve."

He sat heavily in the chair and looked up at her. "Do not seek my approval, Sophia. I am not the one who determines your destiny."

"I just do not understand how you have come to embrace this Jewish God—"

"God is not Jewish, Sophia. He is God."

Sophia sighed. Sosigenes had spoken often to her of the One True God of the Jews. It was difficult to accept that a primitive country such as Judea, or its thousands of captive peoples here in Alexandria, had discovered the only god, and that all other peoples were somehow mistaken. "I think perhaps we each worship in our own way, and whatever gods exist, they are pleased."

Sosigenes smiled, a sad smile she knew well. "Ah, but I could tell you stories, my dear. So many people who have believed that to their peril." He leaned heavily on the desk beside them. "The One God has existed from the beginning, before we toiled in the desert to build the Great Pyramid. He watched as we went our own way, ignored Him to set up idols of stone and wood. But He was not content to let us go. He reached down and chose one of us, Abraham, to set apart, one through whom He would reveal Himself. But still, He is God of all."

Sophia drew close, unwilling for all the room to hear her questions. "And the Jews, they came from this Abraham?"

"A mighty nation once. They grew up and multiplied in Egypt, until the One God called them out of that land and into their own. He went before them all the way, showing Himself strong in the face of the false gods of the Egyptians and the Canaanites. He spoke through fire and wind, earthquakes and floods, and put His message in the mouths of many prophets. Throughout all these years, as cultures have risen and fallen, He has remained."

Sophia watched the other white-haired men, busy about their work through the room. "You speak as though you were there for all of it."

Beside her Sosigenes was silent for a moment, then smiled. "It is my calling, Sophia. To testify to the hand of the One God through the ages."

"You would have me believe that all the Egyptian gods, all the Greek deities . . . they are all false?"

"There is only One God, Sophia. And only one way to be reconciled to Him. Only the way He makes for us."

"This Messiah you await?"

He lifted his head to the air above them and closed his eyes. "I know that my Redeemer comes."

Sophia plucked at her chitôn. "It is hard—"

"Yes, Sophia. It is always hard to turn away from what your culture deems to be truth."

She traced a circle on the desk with her fingertip. "And what does this One God offer that is so much better than those I have worshipped all my life?"

"If He is the One God, Sophia, then He is the only one who offers anything."

She made a face at the older man. "I don't mean to argue philosophy with you, Sosigenes. I want to know what makes your One God different?"

"Love."

"Love? That is all?"

Sosigenes smiled. "'*One word frees us of all the weight and pain of life: that word is love.*'"

It must be the day for Sophocles.

Sosigenes patted her hand. "Love is everything, my dear. As old as you are, you have yet to learn this."

She drew her hand away. "Then this is the best reason to disbelieve you. Why would any god ever choose to love me?"

He was silent a moment, then whispered, "Or any of us?"

Sophia desired to escape. She sniffed and looked to the door. "I purchased some things for you. I will see if they have arrived yet."

He smiled, and she knew she had only postponed the rest of the conversation.

In the South Wing, several servants sent by merchants delivered goods to the front entryway of the Base. Sophia had to weave through soldiers who milled about in their ever-present way. Still Bellus was not among them.

"Here"—she called to a boy with a small cart of crates—"bring them with me." She led the boy back toward the North Wing. The wheels of his wooden cart clacked painfully along the stone corridor in a rhythm, and Sophia wondered if they would reach the back of the Base before the rickety thing fell to pieces.

She had the boy set the two crates on the floor at the door of the scholars' makeshift Museum, gave him some money, and sent him back around the corner before opening the door. Three men closest to the door hurried forward to help her with her load.

"What is this, Sophia?" Hesiod asked. "We have need of nothing more than our books here."

She pulled at the lid, then lifted it to reveal the contents. Nestled in a bed of straw were two dozen plump oranges.

The intake of breath from the men around her was reward enough.

"I have not had an orange since—I don't know when!" Hesiod said.

They were surrounded by the others at once, and within a minute the fine spray of citrus perfumed the air. Sophia laughed to see the men pop bits of the juicy flesh into their mouths and chew greedily. She was embraced more than once.

A movement from the side of the room caught her attention and she turned.

The door slid open to reveal the figure of a man who did not belong. The Roman Bellus.

Sophia felt the smile erode from her face. The centurion's eyes roamed the room, taking in the desks, the piled books, the white-robed men holding oranges. She felt unable to move, and the room grew quickly silent, each man's actions suspended.

Bellus moved forward into the room with slow steps, then closed the door behind himself. His eyes found Sophia and his lips parted. "How could I have been so stupid?" He shook his head.

"I knew you were hiding something of importance back here. What else would it be?" He gazed across the room again, his eyes wide.

Sophia pulled away from the center of the group of old men and crossed the room. She grabbed Bellus by the arm, yanked open the door, and dragged him into the corridor. With the door firmly shut behind her, she said only one word. "Come."

She knew he followed. Along the corridor to a doorway that opened onto the central courtyard.

In the hot sand of mid-morning, she whirled to face him. "So now you know."

Bellus's eyes still held that far-off look. "All of them? You have all of them here?"

"What else could I do, with your general breathing threats if they didn't give up their noble pursuits to build your war toys?" She paced before him, and the scratch of her sandals in the sand was like an irritation under her skin. Little puffs of dust floated at her feet each time she turned in her pacing.

"Can I talk to them?" Bellus's attention went to the door they had come through. "Can I sit with them awhile? Hear about their work?"

Sophia stopped her relentless movement and stared at him. That light in his eye. She knew it well. It was the light of inquiry, of wonderment, of curiosity. Like a child who has stumbled upon the door to another world.

The impact of this insight hit her like a weight to the chest. *Ah, Bellus, you have no idea how much we are alike.*

He turned back to her, saw her watching him with suspended breath, and smiled, a smile that was both amiable and conspiratorial. "You are amazing, Sophia. To have them here, with all of us"—he pointed to the South Wing where his centuria was stationed—"all this time."

She moved toward him, wrapped shaky fingers around his forearm. In spite of the heat that built in the sandy courtyard, his skin was cool to her touch. She searched the light still sparking in his eyes. "You will keep my secret."

She spoke the words as a command, though they both knew he had the right and the power to destroy her and the scholars. And even as she loathed the truth that she was at his mercy, a tiny part of her heart welcomed it.

He covered her hand, still on his arm, with his own. They stood that way for a long moment, close together and breathing in unison. She sensed the mighty wrestling that went on within him.

"I will keep your secret, Sophia," he finally said. "I will keep your secret."

TWENTY-THREE

Pothinus strode past the tents and fires in the dark marshes of Pelusium, greeting soldiers with a regal nod or a partial bow. The darkness hid their expressions, leaving only the whites of their eyes glowing around the fires for him to decipher whether each was loyal to him and the boy-king or had let his allegiance be bought by the scheming sister Arsinôe and her hulking idiot tutor, Ganymedes. The army's general, Achillas, slipped beside him in the night, and Pothinus jumped.

"You have nothing to fear from me, my lord," Achillas whispered.

"The shadows hide both friend and foe."

"More friends than foes, I believe."

"Tell me."

Achillas rubbed at a stubbled chin with grimy fingers. He was shorter than Pothinus, as were most Greeks, but with a thickness of body that few would want to face on the battlefield. They walked through the tents and sidestepped the orange fires with their embers twirling into the night. The smell of roasting meat mingled with the usual tang of soldiers encamped far from home and luxury.

Achillas lifted his chin toward the reedy plain, dotted with fires like stars in the black night. "The girl still sends whispers through the troops, promises of wealth and time away from battles."

"She offers what she does not have."

Achillas shrugged. "She may soon have all she could desire."

Pothinus slowed and studied Achillas. "You said the troops were still loyal."

The general scratched at a place under his leather. "They still believe that Ptolemy should be on the throne, as his father desired, perhaps with Cleopatra. But few of them believe a woman should be co-regent. Not Cleopatra nor Arsinôe."

A soldier approached with a metal plate of roasted goose and offered it to Pothinus. He took the plate and bowed his thanks. The soldier did not move. Pothinus obligingly lifted a slab of the meat to his mouth and tore off a smoky bite. He chewed and swallowed the tough flesh quickly. "Good man," he said to the soldier.

Now be gone.

The young man disappeared back into the night, and Pothinus shoved the plate at Achillas. "So the troops will follow my orders?"

"Arsinôe is telling them that she desires to restore Ptolemy as well. She says that while you sit on your hands in your tents here, she will send to Alexandria to have Ptolemy rescued from the Roman."

Pothinus drew up his full height and scowled into the darkness. "Then we shall have to find a better way."

Achillas punched him lightly on the upper arm. Pothinus pulled away.

"May the gods be with you on that one, Pothinus," Achillas said and pointed upward. "Because I am beginning to believe they favor Rome."

Pothinus gazed again over the starry plain. How many of them would he sacrifice to gain the throne for Ptolemy?

How many would I not?

The night had chilled, and Pothinus retreated through the tents to the royal enclosure that he had assumed for himself. He had barely washed the dirt of the fields from his feet and reclined on one of the low couches when the tent flap lifted and two figures slipped in, unannounced. Pothinus lifted his upper body from the couch, then forced himself to relax when the faces of Arsinôe and Ganymedes appeared in the bright light of the tent's torches.

Achillas followed quickly. No doubt he had been watching and feared that treachery was in the air.

Arsinôe glided forward and stretched herself upon the opposite couch, as though she were an invited guest. She was a striking girl, younger than Cleopatra by only a few years, and hovering between the innocence of youth and the hard edge that came early with Ptolemaic rule. She raised her black eyes to him, and Pothinus smoothed his hair back with a hesitant hand.

"It is good to have the nobility among us." Pothinus eyed the lumbering Ganymedes who had come to stand behind the girl's couch.

"Hmm," she said. "I will say 'thank you,' though I am quite certain you are not sincere."

Ah, I was wrong. The innocence has already fled.

Pothinus reached for a cup and raised it to her. He drank alone, and the small slight of not offering her any wine did not go unnoticed. Her lips drew together and Ganymedes seemed to tense and puff out his chest.

"Will you join us, Achillas?" Pothinus gestured to the couch that sat at a right angle to his and the girl's. His general came forward and lowered himself slowly.

Arsinôe wore a strong perfume, floral and heady, and as the inside of the tent grew warm with the abundance of lit torches and braziers, the air took on a torpid, sleepy feel. Pothinus struggled to keep his wits sharp. "I hear that you intend to rescue the boy. Most ambitious, and likely to bring the wrath of the entire Roman legion down upon you. And those few you command."

A flicker of challenge sparked in the girl's eyes, and Pothinus thought them sharp, as though daggers could shoot from them if she so wished it.

She reached for a platter of figs on the table between them and waved away the flies that hovered there. "We shall see." She lifted a fig to her mouth. "There may be more soldiers who wish to see the boy free than you think."

"Ah, but we all wish to see him free, Arsinôe." Pothinus eyed Ganymedes behind her. "Though some of us have the benefit of wisdom guiding our actions." His hand went to his gray head again, this time with the confidence borne of age.

Arsinôe looked over her shoulder at Ganymedes, and something passed between them that Pothinus could not see. Ganymedes nodded slightly, as though he understood her silent request. Arsinôe returned to watching Pothinus. "Let us not talk of battles and politics," she said with the voice of a little girl. "Such boring matters." She shrugged prettily and leaned to the table to pour herself some wine.

Pothinus studied her movements. *What has happened?*

He played her game, passing the time with conversation about philosophy, nature, and history. Achillas removed himself from the conversation after some minutes, claiming that his duties called to him. Ganymedes followed not long after. Apparently the lout had no interest in their conversation.

The night wore on, Pothinus' eyes grew heavy, and he sought for a way to end the girl's visit. When Ganymedes returned, he felt almost relieved. No doubt he had come to return Arsinôe to her tent.

But the girl's eyes shifted to her tutor, again sharp and cunning. The huge man bowed once.

She sighed and turned a smile to Pothinus. "We talk of history, my friend. Of those who came before us and seized what they wanted through the power of their will."

"Some of them had the right of birth to do so, and some of them did not."

"Ah, but in the end that did not matter, did it?" Arsinôe drew herself up and stood before him. "You speak of wisdom, you claim worthiness by virtue of your age. And yet, it is really *power* that matters, Pothinus. And power can be wielded at any age."

She turned and left, Ganymedes at her side.

What has the whelp done?

He was left alone only a moment. Plebo, his personal slave sent to get rid of the dreadful Sophia and bring back the scholar Sosigenes, appeared inside the tent's entrance, his eyes wide.

"Yes, Plebo. That was indeed Arsinôe. Much has happened since you departed. Now tell me—"

"You have not heard!"

"Of course I have not heard, you fool! You have just arrived." Pothinus swung his legs over the side of the couch and flexed his fingers, knuckles popping.

"Achillas is dead!" Plebo's lower lip seemed to tremble.

Pothinus frowned. "No, it was Sophia you were sent to take care of. And bring Sosigenes and the Proginosko."

"My lord." Plebo's voice slowed as though he were the tutor. "I have just arrived, and the camp is abuzz. Achillas has been found at the edge of the encampment, a blade between his ribs. Arsinôe is moving among the troops, assuring them that she is in control, that Ganymedes will serve as their new general, that they have nothing to fear. The incompetence they have served under will not be tolerated . . ." Plebo grew silent, as though he feared his master's reaction.

But he need not have feared, for everything inside Pothinus seemed to grow still, as though he had turned to marble, an unyielding sculpture of the man he had been. Within the stillness, his mind grasped at only one thought: *I must win them back. There is only one way.*

He pounded the table. "Where is he?"

"They are bringing his body—"

"Not Achillas. *Sosigenes.* Where have you put him?"

Plebo swallowed, the knob in his throat bobbing twice. "There was some difficulty."

Pothinus closed his eyes. "It was a simple task. Did you not find the man I sent you to?"

"I found him, paid him, sent him on his way. But he was slain by a Roman."

Pothinus's eyes snapped open. "A Roman? Why would a Roman care—"

"You forget there are a hundred of them in the lighthouse."

Pothinus stood and lifted his head to the gods. "This can mean only one thing. The Proginosko is there, and Caesar thinks to use it for himself. He has surrounded one old man and his patroness with a hundred trained soldiers for protection."

He thought of his comment to Achillas earlier. *We must find a better way.*

The gods had given him his answer.

He fixed his gaze on Plebo again. "It is time to move. Time to gather those still loyal to the king and take back what is ours." He reached for his cup of wine and tossed it back in one gulp.

"We will attack the lighthouse."

TWENTY-FOUR

Sophia paced before the fire in her private chambers. Three days since Bellus discovered her secret—the cache of intellectual giants hidden away in the storage rooms of the North Wing.

Three days, during which he had kept his word and not told Caesar. This she knew because the scholars were not seized. And because every time she saw Bellus, whether passing him quite unexpectedly in the South Wing of the Base or seeing him by chance when he gave his requests to the kitchen staff, he would whisper reassurances to her, or catch her eye and wink.

But it was late afternoon and he would not be about his morning errand in the kitchen, nor his midday stroll through the South Wing to inspect the troops, nor even his occasional early afternoon nap in the central courtyard's sunny sand. All the places she might happen upon him. Unexpectedly.

And so she paced.

When her feet grew tired, she climbed to her garden and searched for distraction. A cutting she'd been nurturing cried out for her attention. The little plant was fighting for life, struggling to reach for the sun, and for reasons she did not fully understand,

Sophia felt a deep and desperate longing to see the flower succeed and flourish. She pruned a bit of its growth and aerated the soil at its roots and found herself whispering a prayer that it would somehow grow in beauty.

But even her roses could not hold her today, and finally, with an exasperated sigh, she left the platform and hurried down the ramp.

The front corridor of the Base, where the soldiers were housed, lay in stillness. It was the hour when the men were required to do little in the way of drills, and not yet time for the rowdier entertainment of the evening. The sun through the windows of the South Wing fell in squares in the corridor and warmed the stone. Sophia passed from one yellow pool to the next, her head down but ears trained to distinguish voices in each separate barracks room.

She found the room she sought, passed it slowly, then stopped on the other side of the door and retraced her steps to stand outside. In the room Bellus was speaking to his men. She held her breath, remembering the painful words that had once drifted to her in this hall.

But this was a history lesson.

She stood, fascinated, as Bellus related the history of Alexandria to the men. He told of Alexander's visit to this north coast of Egypt, of his affection for the spot as a place to build his greatest namesake city.

"Ordered his men to map out the future streets with barley flour, he did." Bellus's voice rang with admiration. "They say the birds came and pecked at the grain, and Alexander's soothsayer declared that Alexandria would one day feed the world."

Sophia turned her back to the wall and leaned her shoulders and head against the warm stone beside the doorway.

"From the beginning it was a thoroughly Greek city in a foreign land. When Alexander died and his kingdom was sliced up between his three generals, Ptolemy took Egypt for himself and showed great wisdom, for the Nile has given Egypt more grain than she could ever use."

"And the lighthouse?" one of the men asked. "Did he build that, too?"

"His son, the second Ptolemy, was responsible for this magnificent structure." Bellus's voice changed direction, and Sophia imagined him looking through the windows to the courtyard, where the lighthouse rose above them.

"The city was located in such a strategic location, it was destined to become a great trading center. But only if ships could find it in the flat coastline and then navigate the waters, broken by sandbanks and shallow reefs. Only in a city of great minds, where mathematicians like Archimedes and Euclid had already been expanding the body of knowledge for years, could a structure of this scale ever have been completed."

"What is it like up there, Bellus? How far can you see?"

"Perhaps he does not look out the window when he is up there," another soldier joked, his meaning clear. The men laughed.

Ares chose that moment to round the corner and ask Sophia in a voice that would have carried halfway to Memphis, "Can I help you with something, Abbas?"

Sophia flushed and shook her head, but Bellus was already at the doorway. "Sophia." His small smile said he knew she had been eavesdropping. "I was just about to tell my men what an amazing view you have graciously permitted me to see from the upper levels of your lighthouse." He extended a hand into the room. "Will you join us?"

Sophia bit her lip and glanced to Ares, who raised an eyebrow and said nothing.

She ducked into the room, refusing her second thoughts. Bellus followed.

About two dozen soldiers lounged in various positions. She scanned their faces, saw the amusement there. She swallowed and felt her face flush.

"Men!" Bellus's voice was sharp, a tone much different than that of his history lesson. The soldiers knew it well and jumped to their feet as one, straightening tunics, sporran, and spines. Their eyes fixed, unseeing, on some point behind her, they snapped into two horizontal lines.

Bellus walked back and forth in front of them, inspecting each in turn. "Have you forgotten that the lady is our host?"

"No, Pilus Prior!" Their voices barked out the response in unison.

"Then show respect!"

"Yes, Pilus Prior!"

How did he command both their respect and their affection? She had never been able to accomplish this balance with her own staff of servants and slaves.

"Did you need something, my lady?" Bellus asked. "Have the men trespassed where they ought not?" His eyes twinkled with their shared secret, and he turned his back to his men so that only she could see his smile.

"No, no. I was only passing by and heard you so eloquently explaining the history of Alexandria and the lighthouse. I was not aware you had become so learned about our city."

Bellus shrugged and stopped before her. "I have had too much time on my hands since my arrival, I fear."

She nodded, and the silence grew until she sensed the suppressed amusement flickering across the faces of the men again.

"I should like to learn more, however." Bellus drew close. "To broaden the education of my men. But some things cannot be learned so well in books." He was only a breath away from her now. "One must see and touch the thing to know it."

She feared for a moment that he might touch her and took a step backward.

"Perhaps you would show me the city?"

Sophia felt the flush creep upward from her chest. *Must he do this here, in front of his men?* "I can arrange for a servant to show you the points of interest—"

"I do not want a servant." His eyes steadied on hers, holding her captive. "I want you."

One of the soldiers did succumb then. A quiet snort of amusement, quickly muffled. Bellus did not turn his head, but instead placed himself between his men and Sophia, close enough to block her from their view. Regret shone in those eyes. "I have embarrassed you," he said quietly. "I apologize."

She shook her head and lowered her gaze to the floor. "It is nothing. I care not what your men think." She looked up to him. "I will take you through the city."

"Now?"

"If you wish."

"I do."

Within minutes, they were perched in a two-wheeled cart, with the horse's reins in Bellus's callused hands. Sophia stood beside him this time, unlike the last when she had huddled on the floor, bleeding and stunned. The memory seemed to also come back to Bellus. He reached a hand to her chin and tipped her head. "How is that cut?"

She stilled under his touch, inhaling slightly as he ran a gentle finger over the injury.

"You heal well," he said, then frowned. "I have been insensitive to ask you to return to the city. Would you rather remain in the lighthouse?"

"No." Sophia looked across the heptastadion. "No, I think a centurion should be protection enough. Besides, I know of no one who wishes me harm." *Except Caesar, who wants my scholars. And whomever sent the killer in the alley. And half the city who hates me for one reason or another.*

The air was cooling as they set off, bumping over the rutted road to the causeway. A cloudless sky shone over the two harbors and the water was calm today. But when Sophia glanced back at the lighthouse, her ever-present fortress, she felt like a sand crab pulled from its protective shell.

Once they reached the paved heptastadion, the ride grew smooth and Sophia was able to let go of the side of the cart, no longer afraid of being knocked into Bellus.

He clucked the horse into a trot, and the warm salt air tried to tangle her hair. She closed her eyes to the sting of it, and when she opened them again she found Bellus watching her, smiling. The contented smile she liked best.

She raked her fingers through her hair, smoothing it against the wind, then gripped the front of the cart. Her arm rested near Bellus's lean and tanned one, where he held the reins. He shifted slightly and his arm brushed hers and remained there.

Sophia fought the tightness in her chest and took a deep breath. *How long since I stood this close to a man?*

Dangerous. And yet she did not move away.

"Have you been to Athens?" she asked, to break the tension that seemed to build between their arms. "To any of the Greek islands?"

"I am afraid my battles have taken me farther west than east of Rome."

"Alexandria is more Greece than Egypt, as you told your men. Someday, if you are able, you should sail up the Nile and see the rest of the country to the South."

"The ancient pyramids?" he asked, as they bumped over the

final bridge of the heptastadion and passed the warehouse that held the scrolls for the Library.

"Yes, magnificent. In Giza, Saqqara, Meidum, Dahshur. And farther south, the temples in Luxor and the desert valley where so many ancient kings tried to hide their tombs."

"They are all robbed, I hear."

She smiled. "Perhaps. Perhaps there are more to be found."

"I shall try to visit."

"The Nile itself is a wonder," she said. "Flooding its banks every year, swamping the country and leaving precious soil when it departs months later. All that green and fertile land, with the scorching sand of the desert at its edges."

"You love Egypt."

She tucked windblown hair behind her ears. "Alexandria is the future, with its academics and its economics. But the rest of Egypt," she pointed southward through the city, "that is the past." Her voice dropped to a whisper. "And the past should never be forgotten."

Bellus slowed the horse and gave him his head. He pressed his arm against hers with clear intention now. It was warm and strong, and Sophia could not take her eyes from their two arms together. "Tell me of your past, Sophia," Bellus said softly. "The past you will not forget."

The story seemed like a solid thing in her chest, all the truth of which she never spoke. She wanted to bring it out, open it up like the box with Kallias's invention on her desk in the lighthouse. Bring it all out to show to Bellus.

She shook her head, then looked to the city. "What would you like to see first?"

Bellus pulled his arm away and lifted the reins again. "Take me to your favorite place. Show me the best of Alexandria."

She smiled. "That is an easy task." She pointed to their right. "To the Library."

They rode through the central royal quarter in silence, Bellus watching the great palaces slide by, their columned porticoes and marble sculptures gleaming. Past the sphinxes and obelisks that reminded the visitor that this was Egypt after all, and the statues of Pharaohs, left foot striding forward and arms stiff at their sides. Sophia directed him along the coastline, past the amphitheater built into a hill and the Forum where the scholars would often meet with students.

She sighed as the conjoined Museum and Library came into view, and Bellus laughed. "I am surprised you have not holed yourself up here instead of that lighthouse."

"If there were anywhere else I could live, it would be here."

A young boy with curly hair and a dirty tunic bounded from the Museum steps to take the reins of the horse. Bellus gave him a coin and promised two more when they returned.

They alighted and Sophia led the climb up to the portico of the Museum. They turned when they reached the columns and looked over the city. From under the shaded roof, they could observe the sea to the left, the Soma Mausoleum where Alexander's body lay ahead of them, and even the vast gymnasium to their right. The Brucheum quarter of the city seemed filled to overflowing with marble and granite, and with the sun behind them, it took Sophia's breath away.

Beside her, Bellus quoted, *"Far ahead of all the rest in elegance and extent and riches and luxury."*

She gave him a quizzical look.

"Diodorus Siculus," he said. "One of your Greek historians who spoke of Alexandria." He turned to the Museum entrance. "I thought we were to see the Library first."

She led him to the arched entrance of the building. "To understand the Library, you must first see the Museum."

Bellus followed her through the halls of the city's Temple of
the Muses, designed to nourish the fertile minds of those who lived
there. Various young men passed them as they traversed the main
floor, bowing at the waist in recognition of Sophia.

"Who are these men?" Bellus asked.

"Apprentice scholars. Not the main council of twelve." She
smiled. "They are not here. These young men are only beginning
their studies. It takes many years to understand the complexities of
their chosen discipline, be it mathematics, geography, philosophy,
or any other."

She led him upward first. They climbed a staircase to the upper
mosaic terrace of the Museum, where scholars watched the night
sky, to chart the movement of the stars and planets. Back to the
main floor, and then Sophia led Bellus down another flight of wide
steps, twin to those in front, and into a central courtyard laid out
in a grid of teeming gardens.

"The scholars enjoy their plants, I see," Bellus said.

Sophia strode to the center of the courtyard and Bellus followed. Here one stood in the center of a cultivated riot of color,
undergirded with green. Sophia trailed a finger over a silky leaf. "It
is not merely a matter of enjoyment. Some are horticulturists. They
cultivate and cross-breed plants for their beauty, their medicinal
uses, for food. This is their laboratory."

She wandered to a section of rose bushes where she knew
Archippos kept his special cuttings and was gratified to see that
someone had been pruning and tending in his absence. His protégé,
no doubt.

Bellus joined her, once again close enough that their shoulders
brushed.

"This one here"—Sophia touched the crimson-edged petals of a white rose—"this is Archippos's special project. He hybridized a Lotus Pink with a Lily White to breed this beauty."

"It is lovely. Does he call it the *Archippos*?"

She smiled and turned away. "It is called the *Sophia*."

She wandered to the other side of the courtyard, aware that Bellus followed closely. They ducked into the back of the building, then skirted toward the Library, past private chambers and dining halls. Outside again they arrived at the exotic zoo kept by the scholars. Cages filled with various types of boar lined a small garden enclosure, and monkeys roamed free in the space. Another young scholar knelt in the center, scribbling notes on a papyrus. They approached and saw that he knelt beside a spiny-tailed lizard.

When he saw Sophia hovering, he scrambled to his feet, scrolls in his arms. "My lady!" He bowed quickly and dropped his papyrus. Bellus retrieved it for him, and he nodded in distraction. "I did not expect to see you—with the others gone—I did not know—"

Sophia touched his arm. "Be at peace, Diodoros. I am only showing our Roman guest here why our Temple is so important."

The man's gaze flitted to Bellus, then back to Sophia in confusion, though whether from her friendliness toward the Roman or her kindness toward himself, she could not tell.

The young scholar excused himself, bowing several times too many on his way out of the zoo.

Bellus watched him go, his face set. "I did not realize."

"What?"

"How much you are respected in this city."

Sophia shrugged. "Among the scholars, perhaps. And the nobility, I suppose."

Bellus laughed. "Then it seems you must only win the peasants and you will rule Alexandria."

She smiled. "Well, there is not much chance of that."

Bellus turned to her. "Perhaps you should put away the pretense of harshness and let them see what I do."

There it was again. That pressure in her chest. "It is no pretense, I am afraid. I would need to become a different woman before I deserved their affection."

"The greatest love is the love we do not deserve."

Sophia looked to one of the monkeys, hanging from a tree limb. "One of your Roman philosophers?"

He laughed. "Yes. Lucius Aurelius Bellus."

She couldn't raise her eyes to his. "And how does one gain this love he does not deserve?"

Bellus was silent a moment behind her. "It is not gained," he said quietly. "Only accepted."

Sophia led him forward, not trusting herself to respond. It was time to move on. "Let me show you the Library."

TWENTY-FIVE

They left the private zoo and crossed to the covered colonnade that led from the Museum to the Library. Two dozen columns lined the walkway, throwing shadows across its marble floor.

Though the Museum was so called because it was the unofficial Temple of the Muses, for Sophia the entrance to the Library of Alexandria was like a portal to the gods. They crossed under the mighty door frame into the first hall dedicated to astronomy. The center of the room contained a series of tables, and the walls were covered with charts. Each wall was broken by a honeycomb of alcoves, stuffed with scrolls of papyrus, and even of leather.

Bellus stood in the center of the room, and Sophia watched him try to take it in. He crossed to a star chart and ran his fingers over the markings. Then to the next chart, and the next, as though he wanted to soak in each drop of what others had learned. He peeked into the alcoves and tried to count the scrolls in one. "So many books? I had no idea there were so many."

She laughed. "This is only the Astronomy Hall. There are nine more halls."

His eyes went wide. "Nine more! How do they even remember what books they have?"

"There has always been a Librarian. He catalogs the books as they are brought. Even the scrolls that contain the lists of books take up an immense amount of space."

"All in one place." Bellus shook his head.

"Yes, Alexandria has benefited from the questionable collection practices of the Ptolemies, I am afraid. Let us just say, if a Ptolemy asks to borrow scrolls from Rome, do not rely upon getting the originals returned. This is how we have created the greatest Library in the world."

Bellus turned a circle in the center of the hall, his eyes turned upward to the lofty ceiling. When he looked again to her, he said simply, "Show me the rest."

She led him through the Poetry Hall, then Mathematics, each of them silent and echoing with their steps. Bellus studied every chart, every room. They passed no one here in the Library, and in the vast silence Sophia felt as though they walked the earth as the first man and first woman.

They reached the central gallery with its branching lecture rooms that altogether could have held the entire Roman legion stationed in Alexandria. Bellus read aloud the words carved high on the wall of the Great Hall: "The Place of the Cure of the Mind."

Sophia showed Bellus the remaining halls, but he was clearly overwhelmed by what he had seen and grew silent long before they circled back to the main entrance and emerged into the sun. She stopped him on the Library's portico and gripped his arm. "Do you see," she said, her eyes pleading with him, "why Rome must not be allowed to overrun Alexandria?"

He covered her hand with his own. "What will be, will be. But I have also seen a thirst for knowledge in Rome, Sophia. What the

Greeks have accomplished will not be forgotten. It will be built upon and expanded, I am certain."

She looked over the marble city and exhaled. "Would that I could be as certain."

"Come. I am hungry." He took her hand and pulled her down the Library's grand steps, then down the street to their waiting horse and cart. Two obols to the boy, and they were on their way again, side-by-side through the city.

Sophia let him take the lead now, and soon saw that they would enter the agora.

After the sacred hush of the Library, the noise and heat and color of the market was like an assault. They left the cart once again and Bellus led her through the agora, as though he knew his destination. Fabric dealers called out to Sophia, their reds and yellows and oranges heavy and inviting. She and Bellus crossed the perfume section, then through the spices. Sophia's head swam, and still Bellus led her forward.

But when a jewelry dealer hailed Bellus and suggested he take home a bit of gold to his wife, he finally slowed.

The merchant saw his invitation and bustled forward, bony fingers draped with delicate chains. "You and your friend will find good deals here for your ladies," he said, then flicked a glance at Sophia. She looked away, not needing to see the usual surprise, followed by distress. "Begging your pardon, my lady." He bowed, bending his ropy neck toward the dirt. "I did not—"

"How much for this one?" Bellus said, and Sophia eyed the beautiful piece, beaded with lapis lazuli on links of gold. She wondered whose neck it would adorn and moved away to study the wares at the next table.

"Sophia, come and try it on."

She turned back to Bellus. "I am not a fitting subject on which to test its beauty. You should find someone young and pretty to see how it looks."

Bellus frowned. "But it is for you."

Sophia jerked her head toward the next merchant. "That is not amusing."

Bellus returned the necklace to the dealer and drew close to her. "I was not trying to amuse you. I was trying to buy you a gift."

She studied his face. *Is he in earnest?* "Look at me, Bellus." She indicated her tunic, her hair, everything. "I cannot wear that."

He reached a hand to her throat and traced a line where the necklace would lay. "I think you would look beautiful with those beads around your neck."

She wanted him to take his hand away before he felt the frantic pounding in her throat. She licked her suddenly dry lips and swallowed. "Even so"—the words came out in a raspy croak—"I cannot accept it."

He dropped his hand and nodded, as though he knew it had been a foolish idea. "Come, it grows late."

Indeed, the sun had begun to dip below the marble façade of the city, and the merchants they passed were packing their treasures into crates to await the next market day. Bellus hailed a meat merchant as though he were an old friend. The man's stained apron stretched over his ample belly, and he swayed as he walked toward them.

"You are late today, centurion." The big man grinned, a partially toothless smile that brought to Sophia's mind one of the monkeys they had seen in the Museum's zoo.

"On a tour of your great city." Bellus gripped the man's arm. "Couldn't pull myself away."

"Ah"—the merchant bowed to Sophia—"and you have a most knowledgeable guide, I see."

Sophia nodded a greeting.

"Any pheasant still left?" Bellus peered over the merchant's shoulder.

"For you, I will find something." He retreated to an iron pot suspended over a smoldering fire, dug out some brownish stew and ladled it onto a stone plate. He tossed some flat bread on the plate, then brought it to Bellus and glanced at Sophia. "For the lady, as well?"

Sophia shook her head. She had never eaten in the agora, nor eaten standing on her feet.

Bellus scooped a piece of pheasant with the bread and held it out to her. "Oh, but you must try Barakah's stew, Sophia. He is a magician with meat."

Nor had she ever eaten food from someone's hand. She hesitated only a moment, then let Bellus place the meat and bread into her mouth. The pheasant was tender, with a mild spice she did not expect.

"You see?" Bellus nodded and winked at Barakah. "She will be down here next market day, I know it."

"Come early!" Barakah said, laughing. He wiped his hands on his apron and returned to packing up his stall.

They wandered away, strolling through the stalls that were being broken down as they passed. The crowds had gone, and a quiet serenity spread through the agora, replacing the usual chaos.

It is good to walk here this late in the day.

They reached the edge of the open market, where an old Egyptian sat cross-legged. He struggled painfully to his feet at their appearance and hobbled forward to Sophia. He was dirty and unshaven, and reeked of too many days without a home.

Bellus stepped in front of her and held out an arm.

"All is well, Bellus," she said. "He is here often."

Bellus lowered his arm, but still kept a scowl on his face for the beggar's benefit.

The old man bobbed his head. "Thank you, mistress. The gods bless you, mistress." He grabbed her hand and pressed something into it. She glanced at the flash of turquoise, closed her fingers around it, then fished out a few obols from her pouch, and dropped them into his hungry palm. "May the gods bless you as well," she said.

He seemed surprised at her generosity, and a wide smile split his face.

Do not expect as much the next time.

They walked on, finding the horse and cart guarded by yet another Egyptian, this one much younger, like the boy at the Library. Bellus paid the lad, then helped Sophia onto the cart.

"What did the beggar give you?" he asked, turning the horse toward the lighthouse.

"Give me?" Sophia turned innocent eyes to Bellus and slipped her left hand between the folds of her himation.

Bellus gave her a sly look. "Don't try to fool me. He gave you something. Pressed it into your hand. What was it?"

Sophia held up her right hand and wiggled the fingers. "I have nothing in my hand."

Bellus laughed. "The other hand!"

She grinned and brought out the stone. It was no wider than an obol, though heavier, and the color of the sea.

Bellus peered at it. "Turquoise?" he asked, surprise in his voice.

"Look again."

"It is only painted!"

Sophia used her finger to roll the stone in her palm. "Pretty though, don't you agree?"

"He gave you a bit of painted rock and you paid him for it?"

The cart wheeled through the streets, now darkening where the setting sun could not penetrate. Ahead, the lighthouse stabbed at the sky, but Sophia did not look at it. "Ah, I see your Egyptian history is not as good as you think."

Bellus's forehead creased, then cleared. "It represents a scarab beetle!"

He reminded her in that instant of the young Ptolemies she had tutored years ago, when they discovered the answer to a sticky verb conjugation. She laughed. "Yes, it brings good fortune to its owner."

The cart sped on, and Sophia held the stone out to Bellus. "For you," she said lightly. "You need it more than I."

Bellus switched the reins to one hand and plucked the stone from her palm with the other. His eyes lifted from her hand to her face, and he closed his fingers around the stone. "I will treasure it."

Sophia straightened and looked toward the lighthouse. "It is only a piece of stone." She could feel his eyes still on her.

"It is a gift. From a friend."

She turned back to find him smiling, the open, joyful smile that had been the first thing she noticed about him. For a moment she thought to touch his lips, to discover what made that smile possible. She gripped the front edge of their cart and turned her face toward home.

The lighthouse swelled ahead, dark and foreboding as a tomb. Was it only a few hours ago she had feared to leave it?

They rode in silence now, but Sophia was acutely conscious of the air between them, though something invisible pulled at both of them, drawing them together, wearing down her resistance.

She felt some relief when they rolled to a stop outside the entryway. A servant hurried out to relieve Bellus of the reins.

Inside the lighthouse Bellus took her hand with his own cool one and gripped it firmly. "Thank you, Sophia, for the most enjoyable afternoon I've had since arriving here."

She nodded, too quickly. "I thought it time that you understand our city better."

He smiled a little and released her hand. "Good evening, my
friend." With that, he turned and slipped into the first storage room
she'd allowed the soldiers.

Later, when darkness had fallen completely and her restlessness
had abated, Sophia lay still on her bed and relived the afternoon in
her thoughts. She came to several conclusions.

I am a fool.

I must stay away from the Roman.

And I fear I cannot.

TWENTY-SIX

For Bellus the day in the city with Sophia marked a change. No longer could he see her as simply the angry, bitter Keeper of the lighthouse. She had shown him a human side, and in spite of himself, he was drawn to that humanity. A day or two later she invited him up the ramp to see a particular work of Aeschylus's they had been discussing. He stayed the evening, poring over the book by lamplight, and then another and another of her collection, with Sophia at times watching, at times leaning over his shoulder where he sat at her desk, to point out some part of the text.

Soon their evenings settled into this pattern. After the soldiers finished their last meal of the day and Bellus inspected the ranks, he would collect an amphorae of wine from the servants in the kitchen, ascend to Sophia's luxurious private chambers, and spend the next few hours in exhilarating discussion about history, philosophy, anything their minds found to probe. They conversed in Greek, then wandered delightfully to Latin, to Egyptian, and back to Greek.

This evening, a hint of the coming autumn chilled the air. Bellus had drawn a chair to the fire, a scroll of Arcesilaus on his lap. Sophia had burned some incense in the room before he came, and the spicy scent still lingered, making him think of Rome in late summer.

Sophia looked up from where she reclined on the couch across the room. She, too, pored over a scroll—the Septuagint, she called it. The Greek translation of the Jew's holy books, created here in Alexandria by seventy Jewish scholars two hundred years ago. "You know Arcesilaus?" She pointed at his work.

Bellus yawned. "No. And I am struggling, I am afraid."

"Is that the Arcesilaus or the wine?"

He laughed and looked to her. One of her rare smiles played about her lips. "Are you accusing me of having too much to drink?"

She shrugged, still smiling. "I noticed you brought the wine from Kos tonight."

"Hmm." Bellus lifted his cup from a table at his side. "I suppose I was feeling indulgent. But it is not the wine, I assure you. I find Arcesilaus's arguments a bit—"

"Circular?"

"Exactly!"

Sophia rose from the couch and crossed to him. "Show me."

He straightened and smoothed the crisp scroll, the papyrus unyielding. Sophia rested her hand on the back of his chair and looked over his shoulder.

Outside the wind rose and whistled a melancholy tune through the windows. Bellus looked up at Sophia and smiled. It felt as though they were alone in the world.

"Here," he pointed to the book.

They spent some minutes arguing over Arcesilaus's work. Finally, Sophia said, "*It is the mark of an educated mind to be able to entertain a thought without accepting it.*"

"Plato?"

She smiled and returned to her Septuagint. "Aristotle."

Bellus went to the window.

In the Eunostos Harbor below, a few ships burned small fires, creating pinpricks of light in the inky sea. But beyond, there was only darkness, and Bellus again had the notion that they were at the edge of the world, the last remnant of humanity. All that darkness out there, all that isolation.

He turned back to the light and warmth of the room and found Sophia watching him, her expression relaxed. Perhaps even happy. She saw him differently now, too, he could sense. It was all quite surprising.

Less than an hour later, a timid knock sounded at Sophia's chamber door. Sophia frowned her puzzlement, then crossed to open it. A man stood at the door, and Bellus invited the young Egyptian to enter.

"Who is this?" Sophia's voice faded as she saw the lyre in his hands.

"I found him in the agora," Bellus said. "I asked him to play for you."

Sophia's eyes found his own and remained there for a long moment until the musician began to play. She sank to her couch and closed her eyes.

Bellus had only half-expected the emotion the music evoked in her. The mute lyre on the wall had testified to a lost musician, but the sweet sadness on her face, the tears left unchecked, caused him to fear he had made a mistake.

When the Egyptian finished, Bellus paid him and sent him on his way. Bellus stood at the door, waiting for Sophia to meet his glance. When she did, still misty-eyed, there was nevertheless gratitude in her shy smile. He nodded, then returned to his musing over another work, leaving her to regain composure.

Later, after fighting the heaviness of his eyes for some minutes, a furious pounding at the door of the chamber nearly knocked him from his chair.

He jumped to his feet. Was it an attack?

Sophia shook her head. "It is only Ares. Come!"

Ares entered and bowed his head to Sophia. "It grows late and I plan to go to my bed." He glanced at Bellus. "I came to see if there is anything else you need of me."

"No," Sophia said. "No, I think we are fine here. Good night."

Another look was shot at Bellus, then back to Sophia. "You will also be retiring shortly, Abbas?"

Bellus saw a twitch of amusement cross her face. "Yes. You can be assured of that, Ares. Thank you for your concern."

He bowed and backed from the room, and again his look was for Bellus, and not completely friendly.

When the door closed, Bellus laughed. "What was that?"

Sophia rubbed her neck as though her studies had tightened it. "He is protective."

"This is his first evening appearance, however." Bellus set the scroll aside.

Sophia leaned her head against the cushions. "I do not know what sparked his wariness tonight."

"Sophia . . ." Bellus was hesitant with the next words. "He is more than protective. He is insolent and sometimes almost authoritative with you. Why do you allow it?"

She sighed and her eyes fluttered shut.

The long silence worried Bellus. "You do not need—"

"He was born here. The child of a maidservant who hid her pregnancy. I might have cast her out, but it was a . . . difficult time in my life, and somehow having the boy here softened it."

"And the father?"

"I never knew him. He came the night of the birth, I believe. I was still ignorant of the situation at the time and didn't know who he was. Later, when she presented the baby, I assumed it was the father I saw. Though what Eleni saw in him, I cannot imagine. He was a horribly disfigured man. He never appeared again."

Bellus leaned forward, elbows on his knees. "So he is the illegitimate son of a lying maidservant. This does not explain your tolerance."

Sophia smiled slightly and raised her head from the couch. "His mother died a few years later, when he was still a small thing, running through the lighthouse as though it were his private playroom, irritating the rest of the staff with his curiosity. I had grown fond of him by that time. He was the same—" She left off, again sealing up her past. "I let him stay. Perhaps my indulgence over the years has led to his familiar way with me, but it does not trouble me."

"Because you care for him, very much."

She lifted her chin. "I did not say that."

"You did not have to."

"He is a servant."

"And I am a Roman and those scholars down there are old men and the beggar in the agora was only a beggar."

She frowned. "You speak in riddles."

"Then I will be plain. Sophia, you play the part of a tyrant, but there is something inside you that wants to love and to be loved."

He sat back in his chair, his breathing a bit uneven, certain he had pushed too far. But Sophia dropped her head, and he could see she was not angry.

"You speak like Sosigenes," she said. "He is trying to convince me that there is only one true God, and that this God has a heart of love for me."

Bellus looked back to the emptiness of the window where he had stood some time before. "Would that it were true." He smiled at Sophia. "When are you going to let me spend time with them?"

"Why should you want to?"

Bellus flexed his hands, knuckles popping. "Why should I want to? Are you jesting? The finest minds in the world reside beneath my feet. An hour in their presence would be an honor like none I've received in battle."

Sophia studied him and he raised his eyebrows.

"Then you shall have your hour. Tomorrow morning."

He grinned and stood. "Then I should get my rest. I would not want my mind fuzzy and dull."

Sophia walked him to the door. He clasped her hand before leaving. "Thank you." He leaned in to kiss her lightly on the cheek.

She did not pull away or even look away. Instead her eyes found his, unblinking. Quietly she said, "You are welcome, my friend."

Bellus still pondered those words the next morning as he finished drilling the troops. His shouted commands echoed off the stone walls, but it was an inner monologue that occupied him. A debate with himself over the wisdom of continuing this friendship with Sophia.

He marched past the lines, poking the hilt of his pilum at those whose posture showed the slightest bit of slouch, wondering what Caesar would say if he learned of the unusual way his orders to "take the lighthouse" were being carried out.

And Caesar would learn of it, Bellus had no doubt. There were too many eyes about.

"Dismissed!" he yelled, and the men had sense enough of his mood to slink away.

Sophia knew his schedule and would be down before long to fulfill her promise. He leaned back against the front wall of the Base, crossed his arms, and prepared to wait, still lost in the turbulent thoughts that criss-crossed in his head.

He heard footsteps approach and turned to greet Sophia, but

found Ares. The boy carried a tray with the leftover bits of a break-fast of maza and olive paste. Presumably Sophia's. He slowed when he saw Bellus.

"She is well this morning?"

Ares stopped before him, his face a slight scowl. "She has no need of a guardian."

Bellus grinned. "No, I learned that the first time I met her."

Ares seemed to relax a little, his shoulders dropping an inch. "She is not as strong as she appears, either."

Bellus eyed the boy seriously now. "And I am learning that as well." He gripped the servant's arm. "I only want to be her friend, Ares. I have no desire to bring her pain."

"But pain sometimes comes without intent."

Bellus dropped his hand. "You speak wisely. And I will confess that you echo my own thoughts this morning."

Ares swallowed, suddenly seeming much younger. "But if there is a chance—"

"A chance?"

"That you could break this curse . . ."

Bellus tilted his head and studied the boy, but the scrape of sandal on stone interrupted them. They both turned to see Sophia walking toward them through the corridor, and Ares hurried off.

Sophia drew alongside Bellus, and he forced himself not to stare at the string of red beads she wore uncharacteristically around her neck.

"You were not chastising Ares for his behavior last night, I hope," she said.

"On the contrary, we were sharing our mutual respect for you."

Sophia actually blushed, and Bellus was struck again, as though by a physical blow to his chest, what a dangerous game he played. So many insurmountable barriers stood between them. Race, class, geography, occupation. Ares was right. Pain sometimes comes without intent. But a man can be wise and walk away before such a thing occurs.

"You are ready to meet the scholars?"

He smiled. "More than ready."

They reached the South Wing, with Sophia looking over her shoulder multiple times along the way. She pulled a key from under her chitôn and unlocked the door, then led the way into the room.

They were all in there again, as they had been when he first discovered them more than a week ago. Bellus slid into the room, awed and silent. The buzz of the scholar's quiet conversation faded, and a dozen pairs of eyes turned on him. He straightened his shoulders.

Sophia locked the door. "A friend, men. One who values learning over subjugation."

The old men still held their positions, scattered around the crowded room, its tables overflowing with scrolls, charts, instruments, and inventions. Bellus swallowed. "Sophia has graciously allowed me to glimpse your work. It is a great honor."

Sophia crossed to the side of the room, where a small table at the wall held cups and a stone pitcher. She poured a cup of water and brought it to him. Her hospitality seemed to convince the men, and they nodded in his direction before returning to their studies. Bellus exhaled.

Afraid of a group of old men, Bellus? What would Caesar say?

But thoughts of Caesar led him to remember that his general anxiously searched for this treasury of wisdom he had discovered. Better not to think of Caesar.

She took him from table to table, introducing him to each of the men in turn, explaining their special area of interest. He marveled over the tedious translation work of one, the intricate machinery of levers and dials created by another. In the corner, nearest the small window set high in the stone wall, one scholar worked over pots of cuttings.

"This is Archippos," Sophia said. "And his roses. He is creating a new species that will be more drought-resistant."

The old man patted her hand. "We could not continue the work without this fine woman."

They weaved through the white-robed gentlemen, and Bellus asked questions until he was certain he would annoy them with his interruptions. Finally they reached Sosigenes, of whom Sophia had spoken often during their evenings together.

The tall man was bent at the waist, peering into a metal box of some interest to Bellus, covered as it was with gears and dials and markings in both Greek and demotic Egyptian. Sophia touched his back lightly and he straightened and turned.

His weathered face was creased heavily with the lines of age, and though Bellus had assumed he was Greek, he was no longer certain.

"Sosigenes," Sophia was saying, "this is Lucius Aurelius Bellus, the Roman soldier of whom I spoke."

Sosigenes bowed. "Centurion." His eyes held suspicion, but no fear. "It is good to meet you. Again. Sophia assures me you are to be trusted with our room of secrets."

Bellus bowed. "She honors me with her trust, as you do with your time."

"How goes the work?" Sophia bent over the mechanism.

"Fine, fine." Sosigenes circled the front dial with thumb and forefinger and turned it a quarter-turn. "I was aligning it—" He looked again to Bellus, then back to Sophia.

"Speak freely, Sosigenes."

The two talked together of the mechanism's testing, and gradually Bellus came to understand the piece's intended use. Following on the heels of understanding came the realization of the power the thing could yield.

"This must not be allowed to fall into the wrong hands," he said, interrupting the two.

Sophia turned briefly to him and nodded, as though to recognize his impassioned warning, then returned to talking with Sosigenes.

Bellus watched her, her face animated and her hands fluttering as she spoke. They laughed together over some small error, and Sophia wrapped an arm around the older man's bony shoulders. Something akin to jealousy flared, building heat in Bellus's face and tightening the muscles of his arms. He shook his head to clear the feeling.

She noticed him there again and pulled him into the conversation, bringing him to the table to more closely examine the piece. Behind him, she spoke quietly in his ear. "The Proginosko will tell us more of the heavens than we have ever known and create a calendar without drift, at last. It is near to completion and requires only a few weeks more of testing, as the moon waxes." Her voice was low. "You see now, Bellus, why I had to keep them here, to safeguard them. The Proginosko is too important."

And you have trusted me with it.

Bellus again saw the flash of Caesar's face in his mind.

Trapped between Sophia and Sosigenes, he felt unable to breathe. He pulled away from Sophia's voice.

What have I done?

The older man seemed to sense his discomfort and moved aside. Bellus escaped to the table that held the water pitcher and refilled his cup. He drained it, still facing the wall.

The knowledge that Sophia had trusted him with something so precious, to her and to the world, sent his thoughts careening. He felt the clash of duty and friendship keen and sharp in his chest and wished that he could command his emotions as he would his men—marshalling them into line with none outside the boundaries he imposed. It made him angry that he could not.

"Bellus, what is wrong?" Sophia stood behind him.

"Nothing." He did not turn.

"You have seen enough?"

He could hear the confusion in her voice. "Too much."

A coldness seemed to grow between them. "Tell me," she said, "tell me that I have not endangered these men by bringing you here."

He turned on her. "I will keep your secret, Sophia, but you were foolish to share it. Who am I? I am a Roman centurion."

She shook her head. "That is not all you truly are. You know this."

"I know nothing but Rome and duty."

Her lips formed a line, a hard, straight edge without mercy. "Yes, it was foolish of me to forget. To think that you cared for anything more than war and conquest."

He reached for her without thought, then caught himself and lowered his arm. "We are here on a military assignment, and what is good for Rome is good for me." He lifted his chin, hating himself. "Keep your scholars to yourself, and I will tend to my men."

He set the cup on the table, too hard. The room quieted once more. Bellus looked into the faces of men for whom he had great respect, then pivoted sharply and let himself out of the room.

Behind him, he heard the door swing shut again and lock from the inside.

TWENTY-SEVEN

The days wore on, and Sophia chose to watch the city gird itself for war from the windows that pocked the face of the lighthouse from base to tip. There were rooms at every level as one ascended the spiral ramp, with glass panes that afforded every view of the city, yet kept Sophia remote from all that transpired below.

Including the centuria that marched and drilled and wasted their time.

This morning Sophia took her breakfast tray from Ares and pushed it across her desk.

"You are not hungry?"

Seated with labor charts before her, Sophia kept her back to Ares. "Later," she said.

"You have not been down in days."

"You bring me everything I need."

Ares's silence spoke much. She turned and frowned. "Yes?"

He shrugged. "I like him."

She went back to the charts and tore a piece of barley bread from the small loaf. "Who?"

"You know who. The Roman."

"Yes, you've mentioned that."

"You were going along well there for awhile, reading together in the evenings—"

"Ares!" She stood, arms crossed. "My evenings are of no concern—"

"I have been talking to the old man."

She sighed. "Now what?"

"He tells me that you were not always this way."

"You weary me, Ares." Sophia dropped to her chair again.

"He tells me that when you were young, you were carefree, happy. He said that you could always make him laugh."

Sophia scowled. "I'm sure you found this quite astounding."

"No. I asked him what would make you happy again."

Sophia brushed crumbs across her chart with careful fingers, amassing a tiny pile. "And what did he say?"

"He said that you must believe that you are loved, even if you do not deserve it."

"Ha!" She flicked the crumbs to the floor. "Sosigenes believes his god of love should spread his sentiments to everyone else. A pretty notion, but wholly untenable."

"He says that you have been under the curse of sorrow for so long, you have forgotten how to be happy."

Sophia eyed him narrowly. "Sosigenes should focus on his calculations and numbers and leave my heart to the physicians."

Ares shrugged. "He seems wise to me."

"He talks too much."

"Still," Ares said, and Sophia huffed. "Still, I see how the Roman speaks to you, how he watches you when you walk across the Base or attend to matters in the kitchen."

Sophia rubbed at an invisible spot on her chitôn. "Does he? Watch me, I mean?"

"Always." She could hear the smile in Ares's voice.

"Then the Roman should be instructed in appropriate behavior." She waved Ares away, then stared at the closed door when he had left.

They would be drilling in the courtyard. She waited until Ares would have reached the Base and moved on to other duties, then crept from her room and descended to the first south-facing room.

The small space was overfilled with old pots, many cracked and tipped. Sophia twisted through the mess to the blurry window and pressed her forehead hard against the pane.

Indeed, in the courtyard below, eighty soldiers formed ten tight lines of eight. A solid block of belonging, far below her lonely perch. And in front, one man whom she would have recognized even if he hadn't stood apart.

It had been days since he had left her with the scholars. They had passed each other, been courteous. That was all. Their camaraderie had been lost that day, and she did not understand the reason.

Enough.

She picked her way out of the room, ran lightly down the rest of the ramp, and emerged in the courtyard, blinking against the sun and panting. The troops stood in their formation with their backs to her. Bellus still commanded from the front, but too many bodies blocked her view of him.

The courtyard smelled of the peculiar soldiers' odor of leather and sweat, which she was coming to recognize, and seemed almost as familiar as the scent of sand and salt and fish she knew so well.

Bellus yelled out *"Incedo dextro!"* The men yelled *"Dextro!"* in response, and then the block swung right and marched, their sandals kicking up dry sand in the courtyard.

When the area before her had cleared, Sophia crossed to the other side. Bellus's back was to her as he marched along with his troops. She watched him march, and the *V* of muscles in his calves looked as solid as his shield. The centuria reached the other end of the courtyard, Bellus gave a shout of *"Incedo sinistro!"* and they pivoted and faced her.

Sophia lifted her chin to the oncoming horde, though she noticed no one but Bellus, whose face betrayed his surprise.

Still they marched.

Sophia held her ground. When he was only a few inches from her, Bellus shouted *"Desino!"* and the group took two more solid steps and ceased their movement as one.

"Did you come to witness the finest army in the world, mistress?" Bellus asked. "Or was there something else?"

Sophia smiled serenely, and hoped it communicated a certain haughtiness. "Your men spend much time in the sand. And then track it all over my lighthouse on the bottoms of their sandals. Unless you have servants of your own to clean up after them, I will thank you to have them clean their shoes before entering the Base."

It was a minor irritation, one she had settled on as she ran down the ramp. Her heart beat a little unevenly at the contrived complaint. "Or perhaps," she added, raising her voice, "you would like one of my servants to show *you* how to sweep out the corridors?"

The ripple of amusement that ran through the men did not go unnoticed by Bellus. His face darkened. "I apologize most sincerely for the carelessness of my men. In the future I will instruct them to leave every grain of sand in the courtyard where they found it."

Sophia rubbed the back of her neck, frustrated with his composure. "I would not want to tax the men unduly, knowing how accustomed to leisure you have allowed them to become."

Bellus's eyes went from dark to stormy then, and she silently congratulated herself. He grabbed her arm without a word and dragged her to the courtyard entrance.

She said nothing as he pulled her. His fingers were hot on her skin. He yanked her through the doorway, and several feet down the stone corridor, then spun and faced her.

"What do you think you are doing?" His voice was low and threatening, and a sheen of sweat had broken over his brow, dampening the curl that always teased at his right eye. He still held her, and his fingers dug into her arm like bands of iron. He stepped closer. "Not in front of my men, Sophia. Never in front of my men."

Sophia tried to pull away. He gripped her a moment longer, then shoved her from him. She smoothed her chitôn. "Why are you angry with me?"

"Why?" He paced before her. "You parade across our drills, accuse me—"

"Not today. Since—since I showed you—"

He held up a hand. "I have not been angry. But I am here with a mission, Sophia. It was foolish of me to get caught up in books and conversation."

"Conversation with me."

"Yes, with you! Who else?"

She turned away, wrapped her arms across her chest. "You would not feel that way if I were young and beautiful." The words spilled out, and then she hated herself for them.

Behind her, Bellus groaned. "What kind of madness is this?"

She did not turn.

"Women," he muttered, "I am through with you all." She heard the crispness of papyrus pulled from his tunic and faced him again.

He used the back of his hand to swipe the dark curl from his eye.

She would trim that curl if he asked.

"There," he said, and threw a flattened roll of papyrus to the stone between them. "Read that if you want to see how a beautiful woman behaves!"

He stared at her for one long moment, then brushed past her to the courtyard doorway.

"And then, by Jupiter, let me do what I came here to do!"

TWENTY-EIGHT

Sophia read his letter. She read it once, with a hasty desperation, then again with deliberate focus, scraping every bit of meaning from its loopy flourishes.

Hours later, the letter still rested on her desk in her darkening chambers. Sophia did not bother to dress the lamps around the room. A tiny wick in alabaster pooled light in a lonely circle on her desk, bleeding onto the edge of Bellus's letter. Sophia sat before it, no longer needing to study the words. They had burned across her mind hours ago.

She touched the papyrus with a fingertip.

See, I have written to you on your Egyptian papyrus, Lucius. Is this piece not lovely? You would laugh to hear the story of my finding it in the marketplace. I had gone that morning to search out the newest fabrics from the East . . .

Valeria. She talked of fine robes, of glittering jewelry, of feasting and dancing in the triclinium of her father's house.

A beautiful woman, Bellus had said. Yes, and it radiated from every line, written in her own hand, in large and confident letters.

The oil lamp sputtered and nearly died. The circle of light shrank, leaving the letter in darkness. And Sophia as well.

A pervasive and heavy silence weighted her chambers tonight. Though it was earlier than her usual time, she stirred, thinking to continue her worthless vigil in her bed, with the coverlet drawn over her head. The two months of the Proginosko's testing were beginning to seem a lifetime, and with the constant threat of Roman violence hanging above the city, even the air seemed weary with waiting.

But the door burst inward without warning.

Sophia swung in her chair, then stood. She could not mistake the figure outlined in the doorway, even in the darkness.

"Cleopatra!"

The queen of Egypt paused, panting.

"Why do you insist on keeping yourself so far above the city, Sophia? I am ready to collapse from merely reaching your door."

Sophia crossed the room and led the woman to her couches. When Cleopatra dropped herself heavily onto one of them, Sophia used a reed to light a low brazier near the wall. The bowl flamed to life and a hazy smoke wafted upward.

Cleopatra wore robes of scarlet tonight, and she lay like a red gash against Sophia's white couch. She had belted her robe with gold, and a string of gold pieces was woven through her abundant hair, in the Greek fashion. But around her neck she wore the royal pectoral of gold links that had graced the throats of Egyptian Pharaohs through the millennia.

Sophia was struck once again by the strength and beauty she exuded and glanced in the direction of Bellus's letter. Her own tunic seemed a dirty gray, and her hair too short to braid anything.

She dropped to her knees beside Cleo's couch and laid her head on the young woman's arm.

"Sophia," Cleopatra said, "are you ill?"

"In my spirit only."

Cleopatra sighed. "As am I. There has been word from the army."

Sophia lifted her head. "In Pelusium?"

"No longer, I am afraid. They march this way."

"Achillas will attack the city?"

Cleopatra laid her head onto the cushions and rested the back of her hand on her forehead. "Achillas is dead. My sister Arsinôe had him murdered and has placed her tutor Ganymedes as general. But Pothinus has convinced them to join with those loyal to my brother, and the whole army marches toward Alexandria to reinstate Ptolemy on the throne."

"And Caesar still holds Ptolemy?"

"Yes, the brat is being 'protected' in the palace, under guard." She closed her eyes. "Sophia, I am afraid."

Sophia stroked the girl's arm. "Caesar will not allow you any harm."

"I hope you are right." Her eyes flicked open and she caught Sophia's gaze. "I carry his child."

Sophia exhaled, as though the breath had been struck from her chest.

Cleopatra smiled. "Nothing to say, my teacher?"

"I am certain you act as you see best." Sophia moved to another couch and reclined.

Cleopatra swung her legs to the floor. "Yes, I do. My father's foolishness left Egypt too indebted to Rome to ignore, and too weak to fight her off. We must ally ourselves with the Romans. Caesar will be their ruler when he has finished his campaigns, I know it. And what better way to ally Egypt to Rome than to bear a child who will have one foot in each of the two great kingdoms?"

Sophia watched Cleo's eyes, could see the shrewd calculations that ran behind her expression. "You think this child will rule both?"

Cleo lay back again, licked her lips and smiled, like a satisfied cat. "Perhaps."

Sophia glanced at Bellus's letter on her desk, remembered the wedding plans that Valeria had detailed, gushing with the effusive silliness of youth. "Does Caesar not have a wife in Rome?"

Cleopatra waved her hand as if the truth were only a gnat buzzing about her head. "I will convince him to divorce her. She is nothing to him but a strategic alliance of two families."

Was Valeria merely a strategic alliance?

"I wish that I had your confidence." Sophia picked at a thread that frayed the cushion where she lay.

Cleo sniffed. "What need have you of confidence? You sit in your tower here, watching the deeds of the city from far above. No one has challenged Sophia of the Lighthouse for many years." Cleopatra ran a hand through her hair and loosened it from its gold combs. Sophia followed the long fingers that raked through curls. "Would that my life were so simple," Cleopatra said.

"Your Caesar has complicated my life."

"Your life? Ah yes, the centuria. I had forgotten."

Sophia shifted on the couch. In all these years, she had rarely spoken to Cleo of her own heart. They were both much too occupied with Cleopatra herself. She tried to keep her voice light. "Their leader does not think much of me, I fear."

Cleopatra laughed. "That much is quite clear. I was present in the palace hall when the centurion made his report to Caesar." She grinned at Sophia. "But he does have the most winning smile, does he not?"

You already have Caesar, Cleopatra.

"And you are correct," she continued. "He is quite passionate in his distaste for you. 'Beastly' I believe is the word he used. You must have made your mind clear to him, I daresay."

Sophia felt her eyes flutter and let them close.

"Take care not to be too harsh toward him, though, my Sophia. The centurion suggested to Caesar that you might need to be removed if you stood in their way. And I do not believe he implied relocation."

Sophia felt she could not breathe, so great was the pressure that fell upon her chest in that moment. She forced air into her lungs and found her voice.

"You believe he would have me killed? And yet you sent no word of warning to me?"

Cleopatra made a little pouting sound that Sophia well-recognized. "I have been quite occupied, Sophia. Do not forget that I am the ruler of an entire country. I cannot concern myself with every centurion that marches about."

The heavy tightness lessened, replaced by a numbing cold in her limbs that made Sophia feel almost sleepy. "Why do you suppose he hates me?"

"Caesar? He barely knows your name."

"Bellus."

"Who? Oh, the centurion." She paused, and Sophia thought she must be considering her answer. But when she spoke again, her voice was young and uncertain. "Do you think he loves me, Sophia?"

"You want Bellus to love you as well?"

"Caesar, Sophia! What silly games you play!"

The conversation had wearied Sophia greatly, and she turned away from Cleo, her face tucked against the back of the couch. Even with her eyes closed, she could see Cleopatra's full lips, her piercing eyes, her voluptuous body and creamy skin. "Of course he loves you," she whispered. "How could he not?"

"I pray to Isis you are right. Everything depends upon it, you understand."

"Yes." She felt her heartbeat slowing, felt the ache flowing out of her limbs.

"Do you think I am more beautiful than his wife in Rome? I know I am more intelligent than the little mouse. How could he return to her when I am here for him? And she has not given him a son. Did you know that, Sophia? That is right, no son. I know that Isis will favor me and deliver a boy into Caesar's arms."

Cleo's voice continued, surging like a flame that burned hotter and hotter, consuming everything, devouring all the air in the room.

And in that moment, as Sophia succumbed to the deadening sleep she could no longer fight, she knew that everything had changed. Cleo no longer belonged to her. Caesar had taken her, as surely as he had taken the city of Alexandria.

And Sophia was truly alone.

TWENTY-NINE

Only a day passed before the weight of guilt, together with the fascination he could not suppress, drove Bellus to seek out Sophia to apologize for his rough treatment.

He learned from Ares that she had not descended from her chambers since retreating there last night. He climbed the ramp, his fingers tightened around a small blue stone, a token lightly given at the beginning of this strange friendship.

Yes, he would apologize, as any civilized man would do. Nothing more.

He expected her imperial "Come!" and was surprised when she opened the door. He pushed the blue stone into the leather pouch at his waist.

Her eyes were dark, almost sunken, and her lips a tight slash. "What is it?" she said, her voice flat.

Bellus cleared his throat. "May I come in?"

"Do you not have a mission to command?"

"Sophia, let me in."

She shoved the door open, then turned and walked from him. Bellus entered and nudged the door closed.

The late afternoon sun poured through the western bank of windows and reminded him of the first time he had entered this room. She had been such a mystery to him then.

She still is.

The light fell in long streaks on the thickly carpeted floor, creating bars of shadow between, as though Sophia were caged here, high above the sea. She stood apart, her back to him, and ran her hand over a small box on her desk.

Bellus adjusted his tunic, feeling half-dressed without his armor. He took a deep breath. "Sophia, I treated you with disrespect yesterday. I came to offer you my apology."

She did not turn. "A strange manner of warfare, you Romans have. To apologize to those you conquer."

"I did not come to conquer you."

Her back stiffened. "No? And yet you tell your general that perhaps it would be best to have me executed, so that you may better secure the lighthouse."

Bellus's heart missed a beat. He reached to Sophia, then let his hand drop. "Who told you this?"

"Does it matter?" She faced him, betrayal etching deep lines around her eyes.

He moved toward her, took her hand. "Sophia, that was long ago! When first we came to the lighthouse. Before I—before I knew you."

She yanked her hand from his. "Do you think I care? It is who you are. You bring death with you."

"I follow orders. That is all."

"You cannot even do that! Is that not why you were banished here to the shores of Pharos? Because Caesar recognized that you could not manage the simplest of tasks?"

He took a step back. "And yet I have managed the lighthouse, and even its Keeper, haven't I?"

"Yes, conquest runs in your blood, I suppose. You should be quite proud."

Bellus slowed his breathing, tried to blink away the fury. She watched him, her chest rising and falling visibly. He shook his head. "You know me better, Sophia. You know this is not true."

She crossed her arms in front of her chest. "I know nothing of you, centurion. Just as you know nothing of me."

Anger sparked in his veins. "That is right, Sophia. I know nothing of you." He leaned closer. "But the gods know that I have tried! You are as closed as a sea oyster, and just as hard."

Her lips whitened and her eyes seemed to bore into his own.

Jupiter, she is beautiful.

The thought rode over him, like an army swelling over a battlefield, furious and undeniable. His gaze roamed over her ridiculously cropped hair, the angry eyes, her lips pale with emotion. And he wondered at the absurd idea.

She must have felt his thoughts. Her lips parted, her shoulders dropped, and she blinked several times.

Bellus noticed for the first time the strong scent of roses in the room.

"Let me in, Sophia," he whispered, ignoring the strange fear building somewhere deep inside. "Let me in."

She dropped her gaze to the floor, turned back to her desk, to the small box there. Beside it, a terra cotta pot spilled over with glossy-leafed stems of roses.

He moved to stand behind her, close enough to look over her shoulder, to reach around her body and touch the box's engraved lid with two fingers. "What is it?"

She exhaled and relaxed backward, not quite touching him, though it felt like an embrace.

She opened the box and removed a small mechanism. From a trough at the base, she took a tiny marble and set the device in motion.

"It is wondrous. Did Sosigenes make it?"

"Kallias," she whispered. "My husband."

He stilled. "Tell me."

"I was very young when we were married." Her voice was so quiet, he strained to hear it. "He was an inventor."

Bellus heard the pride in her voice. "You loved him."

"More than life."

Yes, as I knew you could.

"Sosigenes worked with him, in the Museum. Kallias was constructing the Proginosko."

Bellus held his breath, did not move. It was a fragile thing, he knew, this confession.

"He was done. There was only the testing month to complete, to wait as the phases of the moon passed over our heads and to be certain the gears were set correctly, that his calculations had been accurate. We were traveling through the islands, and then on to Rome, meeting with governmental leaders. Sosigenes was with us, and Pothinus, too."

Her voice shook, and from behind her, Bellus wrapped his hands around her upper arms to give her strength to tell it.

"There was a storm. It arose at night, when most were asleep. We scrambled to the deck to do our part. The sailors were frantic to shorten the sails. Running and yelling. The captain screaming 'The ship heels! The ship heels!'"

He felt her body tighten. Her head dropped.

"Seawater everywhere. Decks awash as though the angry hand of Poseidon fought to pluck us from our feet. I tried—" her voice broke. "I tried to hold him . . ."

"Kallias?"

She shook her head and tears dripped from her chin. "Leonidas," she whispered. "My baby."

Oh, God.

He pulled her back against his chest.

Her body shook with silent sobs. "I tried. But he was pulled from my arms. He was so small. He had only me."

"Sophia," he whispered into her ear. "It was not your fault. Not your fault."

"He had only me." The tension flowed from her then, as though she had been wrung out and tossed aside.

Bellus wrapped his arms around her from behind and laid his head on top of hers, rocking her gently.

"I awoke on Antikythera, that tiny island near Crete. I do not know how I got there. Sosigenes had survived with me and two sailors. Pothinus was on Crete, I later learned. The rest—my husband—even Leonidas—were . . ."

Bellus shushed her and turned her to himself. He used the back of his hand to dry her face. "It was long ago."

"It feels like yesterday."

His own eyes filled with tears. "I am so sorry, Sophia."

She bent her head. "It has taken all these years for Sosigenes to reproduce Kallias's calculations."

"It must be difficult for you. To see it again."

She pulled away. "What is difficult is to think that it could be lost again." Her eyes narrowed. "If you Romans have your way, all that makes Alexandria the center of the academic world will be destroyed."

Do not retreat from me now, Sophia.

He grasped her hands with his own, willing his warmth to penetrate her icy fingers. "Let us leave Caesar and his legion in the city tonight. Here I am only Lucius."

She blinked away the tears that still brimmed. Bellus pulled a stem from the pot of flowers on her desk, and with the pink bloom, traced a line along Sophia's jaw to her lips. She took the rose from him and tried to smile.

"Your scholars have sent you the work of their hands," he said, indicating the rose. "They care much for you."

She bent her head to the bloom and inhaled. "Not the scholars." She lifted her eyes to him. "Come."

He followed her, across the chamber and through the door. *She intends to lead me upward.*

The thought sparked his latent curiosity about what lay above, but it was overshadowed by the privilege he knew she extended.

The ramp that circled the inside of the first tier of the lighthouse spiraled past Sophia's private chamber and continued upward another sixty cubits or so. Bellus followed Sophia, and from her pace realized that she was far more accustomed to the climb than he.

They reached a wide doorway to the first platform as the sun touched the horizon, a great glob of orange on the edge of the dark blue sea.

The platform formed the base for the next tier of the lighthouse, but circling it was a wide space, walled to his chest, and enclosing the most riotous tangle of pink and red, white and green that he had ever seen. Bellus froze in the doorway, his eyes drinking in the display.

Not even the palace courtyard rivaled this feast. The scent of the roses hung like a shroud over the platform. Droplets of water shimmered on silken petals and dripped to emerald leaves. Bellus looked to Sophia and saw that she watched him. Her smile shone with the pleasure she took from his reaction.

"It is impossible!" was all he could think to say. "Up here. No rain. How—?"

She indicated the pulley system that ran upward through all three tiers of the lighthouse to feed the fire above.

"The servants send up water twice each day." She moved through the raised planters, around the central octagon and out of sight. Bellus followed, still transfixed by the wild chaos of it, so unlike the well-ordered Sophia he thought he knew.

The wind tugged at his hair, a cooling breeze as the sun descended.

On the west side of the platform, Sophia stood waiting beside a low couch the color of wine, buried in the midst of a cascade of white roses tinged with red.

And he saw that she was at home here, as much as she was below, in her room of luxury surrounded by her books. This garden was the rest of Sophia, the hidden fragment she had never uncovered.

Behind her the sun struggled to remain above the sea, then surrendered to its watery resting place for the night. A divine artist's brush striped the sky with bands of blue, blurring to orange and then to black.

"Do you like it?" She held out a hand to the roses. Her voice seemed to tremble on the breeze.

Bellus crossed to her, his legs like seawater, like the first day off the ship when he'd arrived in Alexandria.

He had never touched her face before. Though he'd thought of it often, he admitted to himself now. His fingers brushed her temples, her forehead, her cheeks and lips, as though he were a blind man discovering her for the first time. Her skin was as soft as the rose petals. Everything about her was soft now, and he tried in vain to steel himself against it. His heart beat with a fear he had never known in battle.

Her smile faltered at his first touch, replaced by a fearful knowing, one that he also felt. The knowing that things were changed forever.

He stroked her throat with one hand, felt her beating pulse rise to meet his fingers.

"I love it," he whispered.

When he buried his fingers in her hair and pulled her lips to his own, he felt the fear shout at him again, but it was far too late to listen.

He had said that he did not come to conquer. But as he took his first taste of her, he knew the battle within had long ago been lost.

THIRTY

S ophia closed her eyes as Bellus kissed her once, with gentle uncertainty, and then again. She felt as though she rode the crest of a wave of loneliness that had carried her for too long.

"Sophia," Bellus whispered over and over, as though her name were the very air he exhaled.

He pulled away to search her eyes. She did not know what he would read there, for passion and fear battled for control. She had brought him up here on an impulse, wanting to prove that she was not as tightly closed as he accused. She had not imagined he would see into her soul.

Bellus guided her to the couch, lowered them both to the soft cushions to sit with hands entwined and knees touching, sheltered from the wind and caressed by the scent of roses. Sophia felt unable to speak, struck mute by the tightness in her chest.

She reached a hand across to touch his chest. Did he also feel as though the world had ceased to breathe?

He caught her fingers and held her hand against his tunic between his own, the rough hands of a soldier. The gentle hands of a scholar.

The wind had loosed the errant lock of his dark hair, and it curled toward his eye. She used her fingertip to brush it aside, and then he was kissing her again, wrapping her up in his soldier's battle-ready arms.

"Lucius." She whispered the name between his kisses, giving herself to him, and he laughed and pulled her to his chest where she belonged.

No. No, she did not belong there.

She pushed away the thought, but it would not be ignored.

Even as his kisses grew more urgent, she felt herself withdrawing. As though the crest of the wave she rode had surged past him, rushing her forward to dash her against a rocky coastline.

He cannot love me. Not me. I cannot be loved. Too long on my own. Too long the fiend in her tower.

Like an angry beating drum, the words pounded at her. She thought of his beautiful Valeria. She would never be what he wanted. She pulled his hands from her face, moved outside his embrace.

He grasped at her, as though she had taken flight on the wind. "Sophia."

She shook her head. "No," she said, releasing him. She struggled to her feet and sought protection against the wall. "No, this cannot be."

He half-smiled. "I know that well. But it is."

She held up a hand, palm facing him. "I am not—you are not—" *How can I explain that he gives his love to one unworthy?* "I have done nothing to deserve this."

A shadow passed over his face. "You make it sound as though you have been punished."

She would have laughed, if her heart had not been shattering. But his misunderstanding gave her strength to push on.

"Not a punishment," she said, lifting her chin. "Do not be too hard on yourself. It is many years since a man has shown interest. But do not confuse my being flattered with something more."

Bellus stood and moved toward her. She held up her hands again, a wall of self-protection.

"Sophia, do not do this. Do not run away—"

"You are too familiar, centurion."

"Too familiar!" He pushed her hands aside and drew close, his forearms braced on the wall at her back, his face only inches from hers. "As if we did not share all those evenings over Plato and Arcesilaus."

Sophia forced a laugh from her throat, strangled and hoarse. "Arcesilaus. Did you truly not realize I was patronizing your supposed understanding of his work?"

He blinked. Pulled his head back a bit.

She tried to smile. "It was all I could do not to laugh in front of you as you struggled through the Greek texts in your ludicrous country accent."

He shook his head, only once, but was silent.

Sophia pushed on, smashing herself against that rocky shore now. "I do thank you for helping me to pass the time, though. It was most amusing, and for one who prefers to remain alone, I must admit that you were a pleasant diversion."

From the flash of his eyes, she knew that denial had flowed into anger now.

"Stop, Sophia." He shook her shoulders. "You speak foolishness and we both know it. You cannot convince me—"

"The only foolishness here is your own, Bellus. You shame yourself with your girlish emotions. Do not embarrass us both any further."

Like an arrow well-aimed, that last remark found its target and lodged deep. He backed away, dropped his hands, and stared at her. "You are more like the roses than I realized, Sophia."

She licked her dry lips, tried to swallow.

"I believed I had finally seen the truth of you." He reached into a pouch at his waist. "That I had found the hidden part of you that was like the petals of your glorious flowers." He held something in his hand, she knew not what. "But it seems you are made of thorns as well. Tempting and inviting and beautiful. Then sharp enough to shred a man to ribbons."

He rolled the thing in his palm until he held it between thumb and forefinger, then lifted it to catch the dying light.

The blue scarab stone she had given him in the agora. He closed his fist around it again and brushed past her to the platform's walled edge.

He will heave it into the sea. And then be done with me.

But he did not send the stone soaring over the wall. Instead, he placed it on the edge, as though inviting her to make the decision.

The sky was dark now, and the night wind seemed to rise to a shriek. It tangled her chitôn around her legs, as though lashing her in place.

He turned from the wall and crossed the platform, close enough to touch her as he passed. But he did not even look her way.

She saw his broad-shouldered form hesitate in the doorway of the second tier. And then he was gone, his head disappearing down the spiral ramp.

And Sophia crossed to her couch and threw herself upon it, too bruised to think and too weary to weep.

THIRTY-ONE

Cleopatra did not become the queen of Egypt by letting events pass her by.

The city grew increasingly hostile, and she dared not parade through its streets in her litter, but she must know what was transpiring out there, among the people.

She trusted no one. Not even Caesar.

This morning she lingered in the palace courtyard garden, near a spurting stone fountain encircled by red poppies. She picked a bloom from the poppy and tore it apart, one petal at a time. Her gaze roamed the garden and rested briefly on each Roman soldier scattered there—for her protection, of course.

Along the courtyard wall, under the tangled growth of safflower and mint, a linen pouch waited, placed there in the dark last night. When the soldiers' attention shifted to a changing of the watch, Cleopatra grabbed the pouch and hurried along a sycamore lined path, to a small iron gate in the stone wall.

Her fingers trembled at the latch.

Hurry.

She was not a prisoner. But with Caesar's growing affection for her, a subtle tug-of-war for control had also developed. He preferred she remain in the palace; she preferred to make her own decisions.

With the gate closed behind her, Cleopatra slipped along the palace wall until she reached the narrow alley between her father's royal building and her grandfather's. Tradition, that each Ptolemy add to the royal quarter by building his own new palace.

And when this business with Rome is concluded, I shall build my own.

In the cleft of the two palaces, Cleopatra stepped out of the linen dress she had donned upon rising this morning. She pulled an alternate robe from the pouch, one especially selected for her task today.

She had considered dressing as a slave but feared she would still be recognized. Better a Jew, for their women covered up more completely, with even their hair hidden. She adjusted the woolen head covering over her long waves and fixed the cord about her forehead. The tunic she had procured from one of the Jewish servants in the palace kitchen reached only to her calves, as she was a good deal taller than the old woman, but it would suffice.

The shoes.

She had not thought to bring other shoes, and with the shortened tunic her elegant jeweled sandals seemed to scream of her deception.

She shook her head and strapped the pouch, now stuffed with her dress, over her neck. No going back now.

The city smelled of fear. Fear and dust. She crossed through the royal quarter, using the narrower side streets to reach the center of the city, where she would better be able to take the pulse of the people. But long before she gained the square, she had seen more than she expected.

Makeshift workshops had been set up in storefronts, on corners, in every empty space. Slaves were employed there, bent over fires and tools, pounding out swords, sharpening arrowheads. Cleopatra drifted past, head down but eyes taking in every detail.

Who paid for all this labor?

It could only be the city's rich, certain that war was coming and finding ways to protect their own wealth.

A slave glanced up from his smoldering embers, then gave her a second look.

He recognizes me.

But then he smiled, gap-toothed, and winked. Cleopatra turned her head and hurried on.

Crowds thronged the streets, but it was not the busy glee of market day. On every face Cleopatra read a mix of fear and fury.

The army was coming. Of this she had no doubt. Pothinus, Arsinôe, Ganymedes. Her enemies were many and their forces imposing. And they would be greeted by a city who rejoiced to see them come and would rise up with the army to defeat the Romans among them.

She had sent word to her own army in Syria to recruit others from as far as Judea and to come at once. Meanwhile, Caesar told her, the Thirty-Seventh Roman legion sped across the Great Sea toward the Alexandrian coast.

Yes, war was coming. And those on foot raced those on ship for the first entrance into her beloved city.

On the street ahead, a tower she did not recognize rose above the shops. When had this new construction taken place?

The tower seemed to move. Cleopatra blinked and stopped in the street, letting the press of people flow around her. She was jostled from behind and shrank from the touch of the peasants that clogged the streets.

Yes, ahead, the tower rolled toward her, a siege tower, constructed of wood on a set of four wheels, pulled by a team of horses.

Cleopatra ducked into another alley and quickened her steps toward the central square of the city near the agora where the merchants hawked their wares several times each week. It was there that she would discover what Alexandria truly thought. The street grime clung to her feet, but she welcomed the disguise of her royal footwear.

Cleopatra had no more desire for Egypt to become a Roman province than any of her people. She would never be ruled by another. But in a war with the Romans, Alexandria could not win. Did they not see that?

The Egyptian army could perhaps rout Caesar's legion, and even the Thirty-Seventh, on its way here. But if all of Rome's military resources were brought to bear upon Egypt, they would be slaves within a season.

No, there was only one way to escape becoming yet another conquest under the mushrooming Roman republic. And it seemed that only Cleopatra could see that answer.

She hurried forward, her hand straying to her belly, still deceptively flat.

The alley ended, opening to the central square. Cleopatra strode out of the shadows, then stopped.

She had not expected the merchants today, but neither did she expect to see the center of the city crammed with soldiers.

Not Romans.

Her eyes darted left and right, making quick calculations. Cohorts of veterans, soldiers finished with their compulsory service in the Egyptian army, formed small groups within the square, evidently assembling themselves into an army of their own, ready to join the forces of Pothinus and Arsinôe when they reached the city.

Cleopatra started forward, her royal blood boiling, then stopped herself. It would do no good to declare herself here and order them all to stand down.

A horse and chariot sped past, the driver yelling to her to step away. A cloud of dust followed in its wake, leaving grit in her eyes and mouth. Cleopatra spit on the ground and rubbed at her eyes with the back of her hand.

My city.

Like a nest of angry snakes, Alexandria writhed and turned upon itself, unaware that it would be its own downfall.

She had seen enough. The suspicion that had been nagging at her for some time was confirmed. She needed something more than her Greek rhetoric and her Egyptian piety, more than the fickle affection of the Roman general or the ridiculous marriage to her brother. She needed something to guarantee loyalty. And from the rumors she heard, her Sophia might know where to find it.

No longer caring to remain unknown, she strode down the Canopic Way, back toward the royal quarter.

The air was filled with the expectation of violence, and people's tempers were short. Townspeople jostled, shoved and yelled, and fights erupted on street corners, like the first bubbles in a pot about to boil.

Cleopatra peered into shops and homes she passed, and into the tight and wary faces of her people.

And then the Canopic Way came to an end.

Not where it should have, at the west end of the city where the embalming houses lay beside the Necropolis, but abruptly, still on its way to the city of the dead.

A stone wall, mortar still wet and stones set haphazardly and ill-fitting, rose from the wide granite street.

Cleopatra lifted a hand to the wall, traced her fingertips along the jagged line of stones.

Somehow this barricade struck her in a way that all the arms-making and congregating veterans had not.

An image flashed before her. Her childhood self, riding proudly beside her father as his chariot glided along the Canopic Way, to the adulation, however forced, of his people. She had not known then that the waving arms and upraised faces hid an animosity for what Ptolemy XII had brought to Egypt. She had believed that they loved him. That they loved her. And she had been happy.

Hot tears stung her eyes now, and she wiped at them, then laid her wet fingertips upon the wall.

This should never have been.

"You'll have to go around it, woman."

She heard the derisive jeer behind her but ignored it. The wall before her seemed to also seal up something in her heart. But she would not allow this to be the end. She would not be ruled by Rome, and she would not be ruled by the Alexandrian mob.

Cleopatra slipped along the wall to a narrow side street where she could detour and reach the royal quarter. Her pace quickened as she went, resolve strengthening her legs.

The royal quarter had been taken over entirely by the Roman legion, and Cleopatra expected less activity when she reached it.

Instead, she found more.

Roman soldiers, their iron chain mail glistening in the sun, criss-crossed the streets, yelling to each other and forming clusters of angry concern.

What is happening?

She stopped a soldier. "Has the Egyptian army come?"

He shook off her hand. "Them we can fight! But we cannot fight nature!" He hurried on.

A slave neared, an old man who had probably given many years to the palace, bent and broken under a lifetime of servitude. At the corner, she grabbed his arm. "What is it? What is this disaster?"

He looked up at her with bleary eyes. For a moment they seemed to clear in recognition. "The water. Brackish and tainted."

Cleopatra looked across the streets, toward the nearest cistern. "How?"

The old man shrugged. "Salt water somehow. Started here, and the rest of the city said we were crazy. But now the lower parts are saying so, too."

She let him go and started toward the cistern.

"Be careful, my lady," the old slave called.

He has served too long at my table to be fooled by Jewish clothing.

Soldiers huddled around the cistern's lip, drawing water and taking turns in the tasting.

"Let me through." Cleopatra pushed one aside. She cared little for subterfuge now. She grabbed a cup from a young soldier, who objected, then lowered his head to her.

One sip convinced her. The cisterns, and therefore the canals, had been compromised.

And if the rest of the city were also complaining, it must be the entire web of underground cisterns.

For all their weapons and training, the Romans could be defeated by this one simple thing: dehydration.

And from the expressions she saw on each soldier's face, they knew it well.

THIRTY-TWO

When Pothinus formulated his plans in his tent on the plains of Pelusium, he had never imagined that the whole of the Egyptian army would be at his back. But in the blue-green of the Great Sea, twenty ships rode at anchor, fifteen stadia off the coast of Alexandria, waiting for their moment of glory.

Pothinus stood at the rail of a mid-sized quinquereme, one that held one hundred soldiers to man the oars, and Arsinôe and Ganymedes besides.

He had intended to summon part of the troops in secret, those loyal to him and Ptolemy, to take the lighthouse and secure the Proginosko. Before he could set his plan into motion, Ganymedes had declared that the entire army would move on the city. To reclaim Ptolemy as rightful king, Ganymedes said. Which everyone interpreted to mean *put Arsinôe on the throne*.

And so now they floated, an army of ships bobbing in the sea, and Pothinus paced the wooden rail, his eye on the distant lighthouse. They were near enough to see the black finger pointing upward from the coast, to see the sun's rays reflected back across the waves from its summit. But too far to reach out and pry the Proginosko from Sophia's greedy fingers.

Ah, but he would have it.

Pothinus wrapped his hands around the rail and studied the lighthouse, imagining the secrets it held. His memory slipped back to the night he had left, running from Caesar and his legion, sailing out under the lighthouse's ever-watchful eye.

The ship lifted over a swell and dropped again. Foamy water slapped at its hull. Pothinus filled his chest with the salty air and smiled. Perhaps he had left like a meek lamb. But he returned as a hungry lion, with the might of Egypt behind him.

Plebo appeared at his side.

"Did you tell him?" Pothinus asked, without turning his head to acknowledge his diminutive slave.

"He will come," Plebo said under his breath. Pothinus shook his head, amused at the little man's cloaked whisper.

Plebo enjoys the subterfuge of politics as much as any royal Ptolemy.

"This time we will do it right," Pothinus said.

Plebo sniffed. "I recruited the man whose name you gave me—"

Pothinus waved away his objection. "It is the mark of wisdom to make corrections midstream when they are warranted. You should have seen that he would not be effective."

"How could I know that—"

A lean soldier slid to the rail beside Pothinus, and Plebo's voice dropped away.

"Good," Pothinus said. "I see that you are a man who knows where his loyalty will best be rewarded." He watched the man from the corner of his eye.

The soldier, Shadin, shrugged one shoulder. Though his bones seemed to protrude in sharp angles, Pothinus could see that there was a wiry strength to him, one conditioned by many years in service. He had a reputation for extracting information from those unwilling to give it. "Your slave mentioned drachma. That is what I know."

Pothinus frowned. He had hired one simple mercenary before, without success. He needed something more this time. He turned on the soldier. "You are loyal to whomever pays?"

Shadin eyed him and hesitated, as if unsure what truth would best serve him. "I am loyal to Egypt, and I fight for her king. Though them that joins me is not always clear."

Pothinus allowed the soldier a tight smile of approval. "Then let me tell you how we are going to put Ptolemy back on the throne."

But a sharp-fingered jab in the side silenced him. He glared at Plebo, who jerked his head over his shoulder in the direction of the steps that led from the hull.

Arsinôe ascended, Ganymedes on her heels.

Shadin disappeared, confirming to Pothinus that the soldier understood much.

The two joined Pothinus at the rail. Arsinôe tossed her hair behind her, letting the wind catch it, and smiled. "It will not be long now, Pothinus. We will soon take my brother from the Roman dogs."

And then what?

"Reports are back." Ganymedes stared over the water, but his smug smile was too large to miss. "The cisterns are failing. The soldiers are in a panic."

Pothinus pressed his lips together, felt his jaw muscles tighten. "You are a fool, Ganymedes."

"We shall see."

Arsinôe laughed. "You two are much alike. Two old dogs fighting over the same scraps."

Pothinus bowed slightly to the naïve girl. "Alexandria is much more than a scrap, my lady. Perhaps in a few years you will better understand—"

The flash of hatred in her eyes stopped him.

"Do not underestimate me, Pothinus."

"It is you who overestimates your teacher, here," he said, thumbing Ganymedes. "He knows nothing of warfare and has only succeeded in weakening your greatest ally."

She frowned. "What ally?"

Pothinus laughed. "I see that he does not even inform you of any opinions contrary to his own. The people, my lady. The people of Alexandria are your greatest ally."

Arsinôe gazed out to the coastline. "The water."

"Yes, the water. In tainting the cisterns with salt Ganymedes weakens the Roman troops, it is true. But we could have defeated them, coming in from the sea, and with the army marching from the east and all of the city formed into volunteer militias at the Romans' backs. But now, as the soldiers dehydrate, so does the city."

Ganymedes put his hand on Arsinôe's arm. "We do not need them. The army is enough."

Pothinus snorted. "Perhaps. But when you subdue this one Roman legion, what people will you rule? And who will rise to your aid when the rest of Rome descends upon us? The people will not soon forget."

Ganymedes spoke only to Arsinôe. "Ignore him and his weak-willed fears, my lady. He has been a woman longer than he has been a man."

Pothinus locked his arms behind his back and tried to focus on a gull that circled the ship. He had long endured the insult of being a eunuch. He would not allow a man such as Ganymedes to bait him into useless scrabbling in the dirt. Not when the Proginosko was so close.

Arsinôe giggled at Ganymedes's joke. Pothinus swallowed and lifted his chin, following the flight of the gull.

The two were gone moments later. Pothinus reached to the case at his feet, lifted it to the rail, and rested it there. It was the size he remembered of Kallias's Proginosko. He held it between his hands, imagining the new device.

In the sea ahead, he watched the water stream alongside the rope that held the next ship at anchor. The ship strained at the rope, anxious to move forward just as he was.

Almost unconsciously he stroked the case in his hands, remembering the beauty of the Proginosko, its gears and dials whirring with the knowledge of the heavens.

Shadin was at his side again. Pothinus placed his case at his feet. "You will wait until nightfall. I will make certain those on watch are paid well enough to not raise an alarm. Take one of the smaller sloops and row with haste to the lighthouse."

Quickly Pothinus whispered to Shadin a description of the Proginosko he was to retrieve, and the old man who must come with it. He struggled to keep his voice even and low as the reality of having the Proginosko in his hands gripped him. With it, he would no longer suffer insults from Ganymedes or anyone.

"Do whatever you must to gain the box. I chose you because I am told you are skilled in such matters."

Shadin grinned. "Most know nothing but the sword to get what they want. They kill first and seek answers second." He waggled an eyebrow. "I have other ways. If there is people with answers, those answers will be mine."

Pothinus nodded, satisfied. He had engaged such services many times before. Though they bobbed in the water in a ship smaller than the palace's royal court, the ship was only a scaled-down version of the palace, filled with secret plotting, betrayal, and in-fighting, in which Pothinus was well-skilled.

"He must be kept alive," Pothinus said, hating the admittance. "The scholar, Sosigenes. I need him. But the woman—" He lifted his eyes to the lighthouse that he felt certain held his treasure. He felt almost a physical hunger for it now. Soon. Soon it would be his.

"If she gets in the way, kill her."

THIRTY-THREE

The afternoon dragged in the Base of the lighthouse. In his cramped quarters, Bellus tried to keep his eyes from blurring over the lines of ink on the papyrus before him.

High above him, he knew, Sophia hid in her chambers, unwilling to emerge.

So much the better. He did not need to see her now.

He rubbed his eyes and traced the scrawl again, but the words of the Jews' Septuagint were lost on him. He shoved the book to the side of his small table. Then shoved it again and watched it fall to the stone floor.

A soldier does not concern himself with religion and philosophy. Not a real soldier, at least. His father's words.

Many times since he had earned the rank of centurion he wished his soldier father would have lived to see it. But not today. What would he think of Bellus now, trapped in this lighthouse, with no other task but to study the history of an archaic people? Even if that history did whisper something to the part of him he had long denied.

He pushed away from the table and went to seek out more fitting company.

Hours later, he sprawled in the sand of the central courtyard, cup in hand, with some of his men, attempting to join in the coarse jokes and stories of blood and glory. They sat in the shade of the lighthouse, their backs against its granite wall.

When a messenger appeared beside him with a smart salute, Bellus barely looked up from his wine.

"Caesar requests your presence," the young soldier said.

Bellus snapped to his feet. "When?"

"Immediately." The boy peered down his nose at the rest of the soldiers who still lounged in the sand. "And you are to ready your troops. Without delay."

"Ready for what?" Around him, the men slowly lifted their attention to the news.

The soldier shrugged. "Ready to move. That is all I know. But Caesar wants Lucius Aurelius Bellus to appear in the palace."

Bellus swung to his men. "Spread the word. Pack up. We are at last getting out of this prison."

The men scrambled to their feet, then dispersed.

Bellus pivoted and nodded to the soldier. "I will dress and come at once."

Within minutes he had procured a horse from the lighthouse's small stable. It did not cross his mind to ask Sophia's permission. As the horse's hooves pounded across the heptastadion, Bellus did not look back.

With any luck, he would not have to. It appeared that his exile had ended. He kicked at the horse's flank, urging him to fly.

In the royal quarter of the city, soldiers congregated in tight groups in the hot streets, and the citizens were notably absent. Bellus slowed to a canter and scanned the clusters of men. There was a tension in the air. Something was happening.

The Egyptian army?

But it did not appear that the city was under attack. In the distance, the siege works built by the Alexandrians stood in place, and Bellus could see the makeshift stone barricades erected in the wide avenues. But no Egyptian soldiers flowed through the streets, and the Roman army had not formed for battle.

What is it?

Soon enough he was dismounting in the palace courtyard, with a nod to the young groom who relieved him of his horse. He slapped the boy's shoulder and crossed the garden to the wide steps of the palace, where a group of fellow centurions clustered.

Caesar appeared on the steps above them as Bellus reached the group. At his side was the enigmatic Cleopatra, and they looked down upon the soldiers like deities from on high.

"The soldiers are panicking!" one centurion called out from the flower-lined path, and others murmured about him.

Caesar held up a hand for silence.

Bellus leaned to Metellus, a centurion who had once fought beside him in the Nineteenth. "What is going on? Why the fear?"

Metellus raised his eyebrows, then smirked. "Ah, yes, you've been shut up in that cursed lighthouse, right?" He poked a thumb over his shoulder toward the city. "Egyptians have salted the canals somehow. All the cisterns are brackish, undrinkable."

Caesar spoke from the marble steps above them. "Men, this is not a time for weakness. We stand on the edge of victory here."

Bellus watched Cleopatra with interest. Her eyes strayed to Caesar and narrowed, as though she objected to the term *victory*.

"Thirsty men can't fight!" one of the centurions answered.

"Your men shame themselves, Portius. So the cisterns have gone bad. Yes. Does not every sea coast have fresh springs somewhere underneath? There is fresh water to be found, which we have only to locate." He lifted a hand toward the harbor beyond the palace.

"And should we not find it, we have only to board ships and sail down the coast, to either east or west, where water can be found in abundance. The enemy has no fleet."

Beside Bellus, Metellus spoke up. "The men criticize your delay here, General. They are saying that we should retreat, take to our ships."

Caesar laughed. "And that is why I am general, men. Look at the city." He pointed to the streets beyond the royal quarter. "If we come out from behind the defenses we have built here, we will never return. That mob of crazy Alexandrians will set upon us." With this he wrapped an arm around Cleopatra, as if to soften his words. "And though we are trained and we are strong, we are also sorely outnumbered, at least until the Thirty-Seventh Legion arrives." His voice was smooth, placating. "Let us not be foolish now, men."

Caesar examined the group, and his gaze seemed to rest on Bellus.

Yes, even I am here, General.

"Bellus," Caesar called, surprising him.

"General!" Bellus saluted and stood at attention.

"I am placing you in charge of the search for fresh water."

"Yes, General," Bellus kept his voice steady, in spite of the surging in his blood.

"Bring your centuria out of the lighthouse. Leave only a few to hold our position there. And the rest of you—all hands are to be devoted to the effort of digging fresh water. Bellus will tell you where to dig."

He turned again to Bellus. "Put all that learning to use today, centurion. You have been given my trust. Do not disappoint me."

"Yes, General."

And with that, the two seemingly divine ones disappeared back into the palace, and the group of centurions looked to Bellus for direction.

He spent the following hour in a ground level chamber of the palace, poring over maps of the city and peppering various soldiers with questions, those he had called in for their expertise in city planning and building. He sent word to the lighthouse and ordered his men to quit the place and march through the city to the royal quarter.

A decision was made as to location, and they were off. Three centuriae to three different locations, all two or three stadia from the sea and still in the royal quarter, where Bellus had made his best guess that water might be found. Bellus followed his own centuria to the first location.

The ground was rocky at first, but with a porous limestone that could be easily chipped away. Bellus strode through his troops, organized into work gangs that hacked at the ground with hoes and spades. They had shed their armor and worked in only their tunics like peasant farmers.

Sweat formed on the shoulders and necks of the soldiers who dug. Bellus watched their eyes, saw that they dug in fear, knowing that every swing of the spade sucked water from their pores, that everything depended on finding more. An army should never operate in fear.

"Courage, men!" he yelled through the troops. "Water in abundance is to be found. Before the morning is here we shall find it!"

Which may or may not be true.

He had brought the horse, and he mounted it now to oversee the digging in the second location along the coast.

Darkness fell as the animal carried him along the edge of the harbor with speed, and Bellus felt a familiar anger building in him with each hoof beat.

It was the anger that came before a battle. The rage that carried him through, that made him able to ride into the enemy and wield a bloody sword through the sons of mothers who waited at home for their soldiers to return, just as his did.

Yes, this was the part of him that he needed to strengthen, to recognize, to feed.

Bellus sensed the lighthouse's summit flame to life in the encroaching darkness, but he refused to pay it heed. There was nothing for him there.

He reached the second work site, dismounted, and yelled at the soldiers who seemed to be murmuring to each other more than they dug.

The hours passed in a haze of dirt. Dirt in his hair, in his nose, in his mouth. The anger swelled within him, too, and broke out onto the men as the night wore on, until they dug with a recklessness that comes of a commander who is harsh and unreasonable.

The flame of the lighthouse never wavered above them, and still Bellus refused to lift his eyes to it.

Instead, he dropped down into the deepening hole, feeling the dirt with his hands to assess its moisture.

"Almost there," he said to himself, and the promise was carried to the men who dug and the men who hauled dirt to the top of the hole.

Do not disappoint me. Caesar's words. Father's words. They echoed and urged him on with the promise of affirmation.

And then, just as clearly, there was Sophia's face in his mind.

She was as far from him as she could be, in her tower high above the harbor, and him in a hole beneath the city. He raised his eyes then, to catch a glimpse of the lighthouse fire.

But he was too deep.

He dropped the hand he had lifted to her without thought, just as a gush of fresh water burst from the ground and surged around his sandals.

A shout went up from the men, and greedy hands were cupped and dipped from water to lips. Ropes were tossed down to aid their climb and they began to evacuate the hole. Bellus let them have their moment of glee, without reminding them that all of this distraction about the water had made them forget what mattered— that the Egyptian army surely planned to weaken them because they were waiting in the marshy delta beyond to swoop in and pick them off.

Bellus remained in the hole until the end, as though the water there anchored him beneath the ground, far below the city. And the lighthouse.

Caesar will be pleased. And that is all that matters.

THIRTY-FOUR

One day had seeped into another, and Sophia remained in her chambers, relying on Ares to bring her all she required.

Beside the dying flame of her small oil lamp, she huddled over the lighthouse's accounts, adding and subtracting figures in her head.

She thought, perhaps, she should apologize to Bellus. But no, it was best to remain apart. To move on.

And so she gave her thoughts once again to the only purpose she had clung to for these many years since Kallias and her son were swept from her. The two places she gave herself for the protection of—the lighthouse, so that no ships would be lost on the shores of Alexandria, and the Museum, to press on with the legacy Kallias had left.

Something Sosigenes has said yesterday bubbled to the surface. "It is not the flame in the beacon chamber you guard with such vigilance, Sophia. It is the flame within you. But it is meant to be shared, and only God can keep it safe."

She tossed aside her reed and sat back in her chair.

She had tried to dissolve the doubts about the gods by keeping busy, tried to answer her misgivings with the rhetoric of Greek philosophers. But Sosigenes's words wore away at the barriers of her heart like gentle waves erode a stone wall. It seemed so clear now that the gods of the Egyptians and Greeks were man-made foolishness. But could she accept that there was One God . . . One alone who had existed since the beginning of time and who would love her just as she was?

Such thoughts were for another time. She needed to focus on the Proginosko and the Museum.

What would Sosigenes do with the Proginosko once he had finished the testing phase? Another tour of the centers of power, as they had undertaken twenty years ago? No, the sea was too dangerous a place for something so precious.

Those in power around the world would surely come to them, to see the Proginosko, to share in its knowledge, which should be available to all.

But she was not so naïve as that. The Proginosko must also be protected. And only royalty had the power to fully protect.

I will speak to Cleopatra.

But would she? The thought of entering the city made her neck damp with anxiety. Would Cleopatra come to her? She should write to her.

Sophia pushed aside the accounts and searched for a blank piece of papyrus on which to send a message. She looked in the writing case on her desk, on the floor where loose scrolls sometimes dropped, even on her shelves. She found none.

Sighing, she dropped back to her chair.

It was late. Tomorrow would be soon enough.

But an hour later she rolled from her bed and padded across the room to relight a lamp.

Her days had been too inactive to allow sleep to overtake her quickly. And her mind was more restless than her body, reliving moments in rose gardens that she would prefer to forget.

The night was too far gone to call down through the lighthouse for Ares to bring her more writing supplies. Besides, her stomach was also calling out for something. She'd wander to the kitchen, and then find more papyrus on her own.

In the South Wing, all was surprisingly quiet. The soldiers often continued their games and stories late into the night, but they seemed to have retired early.

She passed Ares's chamber, located near the front entrance of the lighthouse where he could keep track of those who came and went. She had not intended to stop, but a low moan came from under the door and arrested her steps. She tilted her head, listening.

Another moan, this one louder.

Sophia pressed her lips together and frowned. She did not approve of staff liaisons. And though his mother's morals had been questionable, Sophia had hoped that her own influence on the boy had been more effective than this.

She raised her hand to knock, then held her hand midair as the memory of Bellus's face, so close to hers, played in her mind. She dropped her hand and continued.

But it came again, the sound from Ares's room, and this time, it sounded more of pain than pleasure. She returned to his door, leaned her head against it.

Two voices. Both male.

She frowned again, wondering if she did not know Ares as well as she thought, but then the words filtered through the wooden door and she heard Ares cry out.

"I do not know anything!" The words came sharp and fearful.

Her hesitation fled. Sophia shoved the door open and pushed inside.

The room was dimly lit, long and narrow. She had never entered it before tonight. She took in the surprising clutter of books and the mural-painted walls, then focused on the two men at the far end of the chamber, who turned to her.

Ares sat in a chair, his arms lashed behind his back. Beside him, a gangly man dressed as a soldier of the Egyptian army held a knife.

And then she saw the blood. Pooling on the stone floor below Ares's bound hands, running down his left arm, dripping from his palm.

"Ares!"

"Get out, Sophia!" Ares's pain-laced voice thudded against her chest.

The soldier had another idea. Before Sophia could react, he leapt across the room, closed the door behind her, and leaned his back against it, a smug smile washing over his face.

He was all bones, like a skeleton thinly covered in flesh, but there was a lethal strength to him that sent a shudder down Sophia's back.

"What do you want? What are you doing to Ares?" Her voice was softer than she desired. She glanced back to Ares. His only injury appeared to be the parallel slashes running down the inside of his arm, as though the knife were making deliberate progress toward his wrist.

"Two of you, now, have I?" the soldier said. "And the second more valuable than the first, I wager." He circled around Sophia, bringing his face to hers, close enough to smell his foul breath. She closed her eyes.

"I'm wanting the contraption. And the old man with it."

Sophia sucked in her breath but did not respond.

"That's right," he said, running a dirty fingernail down her own arm. "You thought you were so secretive. But there is people that knows. And them people want what you've got."

"I have nothing here. I don't know what you have been told—"

"Hah!"

The word was a puff of odor in her face, and she blinked against it, the cold fingers of fear dancing across her spine now.

"He said you might be a problem. Said if you was any trouble, I was to kill you."

Sophia placed a hand against the cool stone of the wall, against the painted shoulder of a Egyptian treading corn that Ares must have created. "Who? Who told you to kill me?" She tried to draw strength from the stone.

"I don't cut women, though."

Sophia watched his eyes, which roamed over her and chilled her blood.

"I have other ways with the women."

Behind them, Ares yelled and bucked in his chair, trying to reach them.

The soldier's eyes flicked to Ares then back to Sophia, as though deciding which direction would be more effective.

"Leave her alone!" Ares roared. "Finish with me."

"No!" Sophia said. "He doesn't know anything. Haven't you proven that already?" She pointed to the blood circle, widening on the stone floor.

The skeletal monster smiled. "Maybe the painter-boy is stupid, but it looks to me like you would talk to save him."

He was beside Ares again in an instant, the blade on his arm. "Don't know exactly when I'll hit the spot where the blood starts to really spurt. But it goes quick then, don't you worry. His blood'll empty in no time."

Sophia stomach clenched and she tasted bile. "Wait!" She held both her palms outward, her eyes on the knife. Her hands twitched before her—rapid, shaky movements she could not control. "I will get it for you. The Proginosko. I will bring it. Do not cut him."

"Sophia—" Ares tried to object, but it ended in a yelp as the soldier pressed the blade to his skin.

"No, no, I will go!" Sophia turned to flee.

"Not just the box," he yelled behind her. "The old man, too!"

She was in the corridor a moment later, her feet rooted to the floor.

A wave of affection for Ares, feelings she had never known existed, surged through her heart. Ares, with his room full of books and paintings. She had never known that side of him. Ares, trussed up like a sacrificial sheep at the mercy of an executioner.

But Sosigenes. She could not trade his life for Ares, either.

Bellus.

With hardly a thought for their past encounter, she fled to Bellus's chamber and slapped her hand against the door, fighting to remain quiet so Ares's torturer would not hear.

"Bellus," she whispered through the door. "I need your help!"

No answer.

She pushed the door open, entered, and called him again. Moonlight trickled meagerly through the high window, but it was enough for her to pick her way across the room to the bed. Propriety aside, she meant to shake him awake.

The bed was empty.

She did not linger. Moments later she was in the large storage room that had been converted into a sleeping hall for many of Bellus's centuria.

Empty.

Frantic, Sophia turned circles in the center of the open space.

Why now? Why did they leave? After all these weeks of invading her privacy, now when she needed them.

Think, Sophia. His life depends on you.

She swept from the room and sprinted along the west corridor, to the opposite side of the Base, where the scholars were housed. The beat of her sandals echoed back to her like the frantic pounding of her heart.

She slowed and moved down the North Wing on silent feet, until she reached the room where Hesiod slept. A plan had sprung to her mind. Risky, but all she should think of before she feared Ares's life would be forfeit.

The room was unlocked. She slipped inside, closed the door quietly and tiptoed to Hesiod's bed.

He lay striped with the black and white of darkness and moonlight, his mouth open slightly with the gentle snore of the aged.

Sophia bent over him, touched his arm. "Hesiod," she whispered.

His eyes flew open, big and round as the moon that peered through the window. "Sophia!"

"Shh. Hesiod, I need your help."

He rose at once, grabbed his himation, and wrapped himself, then followed Sophia.

Three doors down she pulled a key from the pouch she wore and unlocked the latch that held the door to the scholars' work area. She bid Hesiod to follow her in, and shut them both inside.

"What is happening, Sophia? Have the Romans found us out?"

"Not the Romans, I fear. I believe it is Pothinus, acting on behalf of my brother."

Hesiod growled. "That scheming rat has been clawing his way to power since he realized he would never have the mind for true greatness."

"And now he thinks to achieve it through stealing what great men have accomplished."

Hesiod straightened his back and lifted his chin. "What can I do?"

"Your mechanism. I need it. As a ruse."

Hesiod blinked twice in seeming confusion, then his expression cleared. "I will get it."

He crossed the room, and she followed him. "I am sorry, Hesiod. I know you have been working long on it—"

He shook his white head and unlocked an iron chest about the size of the Proginosko. "It is a hobby, a diversion. Nothing more. Nothing like—" He glanced at the table where Sosigenes worked. "It will not change the world." He handed it to Sophia, who bore the heavy box in two hands. "This is perhaps its greatest purpose."

"Thank you, Hesiod. Tell no one. And stay behind closed doors."

"You are in danger, Sophia."

She tried to smile. "We are all in danger, I fear." She lifted the box slightly. "But let us pray this will save us all."

Hesiod held the box while Sophia locked the door behind them, then returned it to her, along with a quick kiss on the cheek. "Be careful, my dear."

She nodded and retraced her steps to the South Wing, more slowly this time, with the weight of the device in her arms.

At the door to Ares's room, she paused, tried to fill her fear-tightened chest with air, then kicked at the door to push it open.

Ares was still tied in the chair, but his chin had dropped to his chest.

No. No.

She nearly dropped Hesiod's mechanism.

But Ares looked up then and blinked through the sweat that ran from his forehead.

The soldier pushed himself away from the wall where he leaned and studied her.

"I am here." She held the device to him. "You have no idea what power you are giving to someone who should not wield it. It is not too late."

He laughed. "If I want to get paid, I need to deliver." He crossed the room and took the box from her, the knife still in his hand. "And the old man? Where is he?"

"Gone."

The soldier's eyes narrowed.

"He has long feared the coming violence in the city. Today, I learned, he decided to flee to Athens. He left on a ship early this morning."

The wiry man set the box on the floor and moved toward Ares, knife extended.

"No!" Sophia said, "I told you—"

He flicked the knife between Ares's wrists, and the rope that bound him fell to the bloody floor. Ares jumped to his feet and turned to his attacker, one hand covering the injuries to his arm.

"Go," the soldier said to Ares. "Go and tell the old man that if he is not here before I grow tired of waiting, then the lady is dead." He bared his teeth at Sophia. "I have no use for either of you. It is only the old man I want."

Ares hesitated, his eyes on Sophia, pleading for direction.

"Go!" the soldier said, poking at Ares from behind.

"I am telling you, Sosigenes is no longer here!"

She did not blame Ares. The boy did what anyone would have. With a last look at her, he fled from the room.

Their captor came to her now, wrapped a rough arm around her shoulders and dragged her to the chair that Ares had left behind. He forced her to sit but did not bind her.

Instead, he pulled the narrow bed closer to the chair and sat cross-legged upon it. He leaned his elbows on his knees, bent at the waist toward her, and watched her face in silence as though entertained by her fear.

And she did fear. For herself. For Ares. For Sosigenes. It came to her fleetingly that she did not fear for the Proginosko, and this seemed a strange thing to her.

The minutes ticked by. She searched for words to convince her captor to take the box and go.

She offered payment, more than he had received from Pothinus, she hoped.

She threatened, using her relationship with Cleopatra, and by extension, the Roman general Caesar.

And finally she begged.

He is old. Let him live out his final days in peace. You have the Proginosko.

But her words seemed to fall on deaf ears, and he only watched her, his amusement growing with her desperation.

And then they were back, as she had feared. If the books and the paintings in this room had come as a surprise, this did not. She knew Ares well enough that he would not leave her here at the mercy of a monster. And neither would Sosigenes.

"I am here," Sosigenes called from the doorway.

Sophia closed her eyes and dropped her head.

"Ah," the soldier said. "And you have brought a gift."

Sophia turned and saw that Sosigenes had brought the Proginosko with him, clutched in his arms like a bulky shield.

Her eyes filled. Memories flooded through her. A storm at sea. Angry waves and frightened cries. The first Proginosko, plucked from them along with her husband and child. And now it was lost again.

The soldier would not even take the Proginosko from Sosigenes. He made the elderly man carry it himself, prodding him forward at knifepoint.

Sophia followed them into the corridor, with Ares at her heels. The soldier growled at her. "Any further, and I kill all three of you."

And then the two disappeared through the lighthouse entrance, into the night.

Behind her, Ares shifted on his feet. "Abbas," he whispered.

Sophia turned to him, looked at his bleeding arm, then through the doorway again. She had lost something precious tonight. Someone. But there was another, still here, that needed her attention.

For now, that was all she could do.

THIRTY-FIVE

In the royal palace, the new day dawned with rejoicing over the fresh water sprung up from out of the limestone overnight, and consternation over the news that the Thirty-Seventh Legion, anchored off the coast of Chersonesus, suffered from adverse winds which kept them from entering Alexandria.

Cleopatra stood at an upper window overlooking the harbor, letting the sea breezes catch her robes and her hair and blow them backward. She closed her eyes to the breeze and imagined it bringing her everything she still fought for. Control. Of Alexandria. Of Egypt. Of Caesar.

Behind her Caesar swore mightily and slammed the table with his fist. The messenger sent from the dispatch sloop hurried from the room to the safety of the corridor.

"I need that legion, Cleopatra!"

She turned and nodded. "We do not have long before Ptolemy's army, with Arsinôe at its head, arrives."

Caesar joined her harbor-watch at the window. He nodded toward the lighthouse. "The device you suspect she hides is most intriguing, but the Thirty-Seventh brings arms, darts, military engines, provisions. And experience." He sighed. "They were

Pompey's men, before your brother's ill-timed assassination of that great man. And Pompey trained them well." He gripped the edge of the window. "I need them here, not stuck out there, dying of thirst."

"Always the water," Cleopatra said. "Ironic. By the edge of the sea, still we rely on the gift of the Nile as much as the deserts of Upper Egypt need her."

"I am going to them."

"With the Egyptian army on our border?"

"I will not be long. But the delay is too great. I must meet with Calvinus, general of the Thirty-Seventh."

Cleopatra pushed away from the window and crossed to the bedchamber. "I am going with you," she called over her shoulder, and pulled clothing from a basket on the floor.

In the outer room, Caesar was silent a moment. "I am flattered that your desire is to be by my side—"

She huffed to herself. She had no intention of giving him time to wonder if he could rule Egypt alone. "It is only fear that bids me go. With Ptolemy's army so near, I am surely a target. I will be safer with you."

Caesar stood in the doorway, his arm braced against the stone arch and his eyes on her, with that cunning look she had come to love.

"And Ptolemy," she said. "Certainly they will want to take him from the palace, to parade him as their figurehead, to rally the city to their aid. We cannot allow that."

"You would have me kill your husband?"

She dropped the dress to the bed and sighed. "What else can we do, Gaius? It is unfortunate, but it is the only way."

His lips tightened for a moment, then he shook his head and pushed away from the doorway. "I will double the guard around him." He disappeared into the outer chamber.

Because you are still playing both sides, waiting to see where the advantage lies.

The thought angered her. She stuffed a few clothes into a pouch and stomped out of the bedchamber. "I am carrying your child, Gaius!" she said to his back. "And still I do not have your loyalty!"

He whirled on her. "You have more of me than anyone ever has, Cleopatra!" He crossed the room and grabbed her arms, squeezing tightly. "Do not push me to give more!"

She twisted away from him. "I will expect more, when I place your son in your arms. Do not forget that."

His eyes narrowed for a moment, and then he gave her his approving smile, the one he reserved for her more ruthless moments. "We leave in an hour."

They sailed out under the late morning sun, under the lighthouse. Cleopatra glanced up at the dark tower. Did Sophia look down on them? Caesar ordered the standing fleet to follow, assured that the land forces he left in the city were sufficient to guard the siege works there.

The Thirty-Seventh Legion rode at anchor a little above Alexandria, with an easterly wind preventing the fleet from reaching the harbor safely.

Cleopatra stood at the rail of the small galley they had employed, watched the fleet grow larger as they approached, and realized again that the might of Rome was such that Egypt could not win. Here was only one additional legion, and, combined with Caesar's, it was easily sufficient to destroy the Egyptian army.

Yes, war was coming. And it was her people who would suffer. But she would be there after, to heal the broken pieces and smooth the way for Egypt and Rome to become partners in ruling the world.

They reached the fleet by early afternoon, and Caesar bid her stay where she was as he boarded the ship that carried Calvinus, their general.

She settled into some cushions in the center of the swaying deck. She ignored the stare of the sailors on board and tried to sleep in spite of her anxiety.

As the afternoon passed they pushed closer to the shore, until they were near the coast of Chersonesus. Caesar returned from his battle plans. "I have sent some of the sailors ashore to find water," he said, and dropped beside her. He flicked a look of disdain in the direction of the Thirty-Seventh. "It is all they can think about, apparently."

But as the sun began its descent, and the sailors had not returned, Caesar paced the deck. Cleopatra watched him from her place on the cushions.

"I do not like this." He scanned the coastline.

"Captured, you think?"

"If so, they may have reported our location. And even that I am present, without a contingent of trained soldiers large enough to protect me."

Cleopatra resisted the desire to repeat that they should have stayed in Alexandria. She had long ago learned that control is better achieved through support, not criticism.

"Back to Alexandria," he said, then repeated it loudly to the sailors. "We will wait no longer."

The sailors lifted the anchor, the oarsmen bent to their tasks, and the galley turned and began its journey home.

The wind seemed to have abated some, and the Thirty-Seventh made to follow Caesar, to his approval. But they were still three stadia out when his expression turned to concern. Cleopatra saw the change and followed his gaze out to sea.

"What is it?"

Caesar jutted his chin outward. "They are waiting for us."

Indeed, Cleopatra could make out ships on the horizon, but not whose flag they flew. "Roman?"

"You do not know your own army?"

She bristled. "The Egyptian army does not attack at sea."

"But they have enough ships to engage us. They hope to take out the great Julius Caesar, and thereby destroy the courage of the entire legion."

Cleopatra hid her amusement at the man's conceit. It was, after all, largely justified. "We will cut them down without effort." *Yes, my own people. It has come to this.*

"We are not equipped for sea battles, Cleopatra." Caesar turned on her, impatience in his eyes. "We have a fleet of foot soldiers being carried in ships, that is all."

She gripped his hand. "Then we must use what we have."

Caesar studied the horizon. "We will not engage them. Night will soon be upon us, and they will certainly have the advantage, knowing the coastline as they do."

He pulled away to give instructions to the sailors. "Pull closer to the coast. We will put in there."

But it was not to be.

One Rhodian galley, part of the Thirty-Seventh's fleet garnered from the waters of Rhodes, sailed ahead, heedless of the retreat. And when the Egyptian army engaged the Rhodians, Caesar had no choice but to advance to her relief, though it was amid much muttering that she deserved whatever fate she met. But perception was everything in war, and Caesar could not afford to lose even one ship at the start of this one.

It was the closest that Cleopatra had ever been to battle, though she had ordered that many be fought, and even commanded her own army.

She stood in the center of their small ship, the smooth metal of a sword in her hand, thrust there by one of the sailors. Around them, ships engaged, and the sounds of battle rose from the water. Yelling soldiers, the clang of sword on sword. Wooden boats cracked, bodies and crates splashed into the churning, darkening sea.

Two boats drew near each other, and soldiers streamed across in both directions, swords hacking, bodies flying upward and into the sea like the spray of water breaking on the reefs.

Cleopatra remained in the center of their ship, her feet planted but her back straight and her chin high. Whatever came, she would meet it with her sword.

Within the hour, the dead floated like fish in the water around them. Flames engulfed one of the four-decked ships the Egyptians had manned, another had already sunk, and a third had been taken by the Romans and all on board had been killed.

A Roman ship slid near Cleopatra's boat, and Caesar jumped across to join her, grinning.

"We could have taken them all, if not for the night falling," he said, brandishing his sword, then sheathing it.

She smiled in return, though the battle had cost her something she could not name.

They sailed in victory into Alexandria. The contrary winds had been defeated as well, and the Thirty-Seventh Legion floated past the lighthouse behind them.

Before they had disembarked, a message was delivered to Caesar. The Egyptian army was poised to attack, and the city ready to join their cause.

Caesar strode to the palace, and Cleopatra hurried to keep pace, one hand sweeping her hair from her eyes—and one hand on her belly.

THIRTY-SIX

While Alexandria slept, Pothinus had put off from the small galley that had brought him to the harbor and climbed aboard a sloop manned by two Egyptian sailors, with Plebo clutching the sides. They slipped along the coast to a lonely spot in the Eunostos Harbor, then hoisted him onto the rocky shore to gather his himation about his legs and climb into the wet sand.

Attempting to ignore the disgrace of it all, Pothinus trekked through the dark streets, followed by Plebo, until he reached the place he had chosen for his base during the battle to come: the Library of Alexandria.

It was fitting, he mused as he climbed the shadowed steps, that he return here to the halls where he had begun his career in the city, a young scholar hungry for knowledge and eager for advancement.

At the top of the steps, he turned to survey his city, lit with only occasional torches at this hour but still beautiful in the reflected glow of the moonlight.

And of course, the lighthouse.

He raised his eyes to the behemoth that towered above them always, to its magnified flame that led ships to safety.

There is no safety, is there, Sophia?

His mouth curled into a smile. Even now, Shadin would be gaining entrance and taking the last piece that Pothinus needed to establish supreme authority, that little piece of theatrics that would outshine all the superficial charisma of those in the royal palace.

But the dawn came and Shadin had not returned. Pothinus fidgeted over a light breakfast in the courtyard, then took to the streets to accomplish what he must.

What ships the Egyptians had would push in from the sea. The army would march from the east. And from the south, the citizens of Alexandria would be relied upon to provide defense. It was to the peasants that Pothinus went, to whip them into a battle frenzy and provide a plan by which they would jointly crush the Roman legions between them.

The gleaming white marble of the city, which blinded the eye and enchanted the visitor, gave way to shadows and filth as Pothinus ventured deeper into the Gamma quarter. Here, in narrow residential streets, there were no philosophers prating their rhetoric on street corners, nor politicians making and breaking personal alliances in gardens and courtyards.

Instead, young children, their tunics dirty and torn, kicked balls of hide and chased each other with sticks. Garbage piled and reeked in alleys, with flies buzzing and stray cats criss-crossing the streets.

But it is in the streets of poverty that the battle can be won.

These were the discontented people, the citizens who had nothing to lose by fighting for something promised.

Pothinus hurried through the district, breathing through his mouth to settle the revulsion of his stomach. He was anxious to gain the central square, conduct his business, and return to the Library, where surely Shadin would have returned with the Proginosko and Sosigenes.

But a man such as himself could not remain unnoticed, and by the time he emerged from the narrow streets of houses into the square, a following had sprung up and begun to press around him.

Pothinus cringed at the touch of dirty hands on him, yanked his arms from their grasp, ignored their questions.

"When will Ptolemy be restored?"

"Will we become yet another Roman province?"

He pushed forward, gaining the square where the veterans of Egyptian wars past had formed themselves into volunteer cohorts, ready for their orders.

His name spread like fire among them, and from a worn tent in the center of the square, a grizzled soldier emerged. His uniform fit too tightly around the middle, and he looked to have spent the years since his service in the company of too much wine and too many women.

This is how we will defeat the Romans?

But what he lacked in apparent fitness, Pothinus learned, the old soldier made up for in bitter acrimony toward the Romans.

They spent an hour bent over city maps, with Pothinus tracing routes over the papyrus, and Adrastos following with a dirty, callused finger.

"I am pleased with the works I have seen erected thus far," Pothinus said, straightening. "The people have done well."

Adrastos grunted. "We hear tell the Romans think we're so fast at building up defenses, they think it's them who copies us, instead of the other way 'round."

Pothinus nodded. "The Alexandrians, above all else, have a reputation for extreme cleverness."

"That's not all we've got," Adrastos growled. "Just let them Romans start with us, and they'll see what we can do."

Pothinus glanced through the tent flap to the veterans milling about the square. "These are all your numbers?"

"Hardly. These are the experienced ones, I'll grant you. But we've got a whole city full of men and boys ready to charge through the streets and hurl rocks from the rooftops when the call comes. We'll be ready."

Pothinus licked dry lips and nodded. "I will send word when you are needed. It won't be long. If you need to reach me, I can be found in the Library."

"Take care, General," Adrastos said, and Pothinus suppressed a smile at the title, which pleased him greatly. "There's Romans about everywhere, and all of them eager to put a dagger into a great man such as yourself."

Adrastos's warning repeated in his mind as Pothinus crossed out of the square, again to the pressure of the crowd. He glanced left and right, before and behind. Could one of these peasants be a Roman soldier who heard that Pothinus was in the city and feared the great effect that his strong leadership would have in the coming battle?

He shoved open a path before them and hurried back across the city.

The sun was rising beyond the royal quarter, and Shadin would be back with Sosigenes. A messenger greeted him at the steps to the Library with news.

"Ganymedes sends word. Rome's Thirty-Seventh Legion had nearly reached the city but is detained by adverse winds still off the coast."

Pothinus listened to the boy, his eyes on the harbor.

Not long now.

The wind tugged at his himation. He pulled it taut, spun to the Library entrance, and hurried in, exultation pounding in his chest.

In the Great Hall two men stood facing him.

Shadin, the bony soldier with the penchant for torture, and Sosigenes, the perpetually old man with a mind keen enough to pursue several disciplines in the course of one lifetime. And Sosigenes clutched something to his chest. A metal box.

A warmth spread through Pothinus's chest, flowed up his neck to his face, and ended with a smile that felt like the sun rising.

The Proginosko. At last.

"Any trouble?" he asked Shadin.

"Nothing I couldn't handle."

Sosigenes glared at Shadin. "You will pay for what you did to that servant."

Pothinus pretended to pout. "A servant only? I am disappointed, Shadin. I thought you would most certainly kill the woman." He watched in glee as Sosigenes's eyes flamed into anger. "Or did Sophia simply hand over the old man gladly, perhaps?"

"She put up a fight, she did. But she was smart enough to do what was best."

"Yes, I see." Pothinus circled around Sosigenes, his head bent to the old man's. The ancient scholar kept his gaze fixed straight ahead, his arms clenched around his precious Proginosko.

"And I see you have brought us a toy, Sosigenes." To Shadin, he waved a hand. "Find Plebo. He will pay you. Then return to your ship."

Shadin glanced at Sosigenes, then shot his hands out to the old man in a feigned attack. Sosigenes jumped backward and Shadin cackled.

When Shadin had gone, Pothinus stood face-to-face with Sosigenes, alone for the first time in many years.

"You think this will bring you what you seek, Pothinus, but you will never be content."

Pothinus laughed. "You have always been an expert with the numbers and the calculations, haven't you, Sosigenes? It was I who knew the history. So let me explain this moment in history to you, my old friend. This moment when everything I've planned comes together like the gears in that box of yours." He grabbed Sosigenes's elbow and swung him to face the Library entrance, to look out toward the sea.

"Out there are Egyptian ships, armed for battle. And down there"—he pointed into the city—"are the Egyptian people, itching to destroy. And marching toward us even now, an entire army. We are about to crush every Roman legionary, every centurion, and even their general, between us. The days will soon be bathed in blood. We will take the city, the palace, the harbor, even your Sophia's precious lighthouse."

He drew up close to Sosigenes's ear. "And at the end of the day, my friend, when you have given over the secrets of the Proginosko to me, I will destroy you as well. And that, old man, will content me very much."

THIRTY-SEVEN

The day was far spent when Sophia stirred from her place on the white cushions of the couch in her private chambers.

She lifted her head, disoriented, then let it drop again, her eyes blinking away the blurriness of sleep.

Ares slept across from her, on the opposite couch, his bandaged arm cradled to his side.

She watched him for a moment, his mouth opened slightly and his dark hair spread across the white cushion. The terror of the night flowed back through her, bringing with it the frightening ache that had gripped her when she saw Ares in that chair, blood dripping from his hands.

She pulled her gaze away, tried to busy her mind elsewhere.

Better to busy her hands. She rose from the couch slowly, her eyes on the sleeping Ares, but he did not awaken. On the table between them lay a basin of red-tinged water and bloody rags. She had brought Ares here last night to dress his wounds and keep watch. She would summon a physician today to be sure that no infection took hold.

The dawn had almost been upon them when she had finished, and they both collapsed on the couches and let sleep overwhelm.

Sophia took care of the rags and water, then washed and dressed in her bedchamber. When she emerged, Ares still slept. She slipped from the room and descended to the Base.

One of the servants charged with fueling the fire approached her in the South Wing, head down. She stopped him with a word. He cringed at her address, as though she would strike him. Sophia let the reaction only lightly brush her emotions.

"What has happened to the centuria quartered here?"

He raised his head, as though relieved that her interaction did not involve his service. "They have gone."

"All of them?"

"Nearly all, mistress. He—the centurion—left a handful behind to hold the lighthouse."

"But why?"

The servant shrugged. "There is a war coming, mistress. I suppose the Roman general needs all of his men."

Sophia inhaled and looked toward the lighthouse's entrance. "Indeed." She turned back to the servant. "Listen carefully, I have several tasks for you."

He straightened, as though the king himself had summoned.

"I need you to fetch a physician. Bring him to my private chambers. I also want you to arrange for news from the city to be brought to me each hour. I want to know if fighting breaks out, if armies are moving—anything at all of interest. You understand?"

"Yes, mistress." He bowed once.

"And then bring me papyrus. I have nothing to write on."

Back up the ramp, she found Ares standing at her window overlooking the western harbor. He did not turn when she entered. "The sun is past its summit."

"You needed to sleep." She closed the door softly.

He lifted his bandaged arm and held it with the other. "Thank you, for caring for my arm. For letting me sleep. For not throwing me into the street."

She crossed the room to stand beside him and looked out over the water, choppy today, as though it also feared what was coming to it.

"You have done nothing wrong, Ares. It is my fault that you were hurt."

His laugh was derisive, angry. "Because of me you have lost the thing you valued most."

Sophia pressed her forehead to the glass and watched a group of fishermen haul nets far below, so small they appeared like insects crawling over the coastline. *Have I truly valued a* thing *above all else?* "There is no one to blame but the man who took him."

"Pothinus?"

She turned away from the window, back to the room that had once been her haven and now felt like her prison. "It could be no one else. The Romans would not have sent an Egyptian soldier. And no one else would know enough to care about the Proginosko."

She wandered across the room, which seemed strangely silent when she considered the brutal activity that was beginning to churn in the city below.

"What will you do?"

She went to her desk, to the box that held the device her husband had crafted so many years ago. "Pothinus will have no use for Sosigenes once he learns how to operate the Proginosko."

"He will kill him." Ares's voice held the same sorrow she felt in her own chest, and she glanced to him, seeing something new.

"All those books in your room, and the paintings. They are all yours?"

He looked down, tugged on the bandage that covered his arm. "I will not be able to paint for some time, I fear."

"Nor pound on my door hard enough to break it down."

He lifted his head and smiled, the shy smile of one beginning to let himself be known.

Sophia felt a strange tightness in her throat and rubbed the back of her neck. "I did not know you enjoyed such studies. Nor that you had such talent for art."

He shrugged. "I have lived here all my life. It seemed only natural to pursue learning."

How could I have allowed harm to come to him? And to Sosigenes?

She dropped to the chair beside her desk and rested her forehead in her hands.

"You could ask the Roman for help," Ares said, his voice tentative and soft.

"They are gone. All but a few left to keep us in line."

"Perhaps you could find him—"

"He is gone!"

"The queen, then. Perhaps she knows where Pothinus is keeping himself."

Sophia lifted her head and nodded, and a timid knock sounded at the door. "You see," she said, unable to resist, "that is how it should sound." She opened the door to the servant she had engaged downstairs, who gave her a stack of flattened papyrus sheets.

"Stay. I will have a message for the palace. You can deliver it to the queen."

The servant cleared his throat and seemed to have something to say.

"Yes? What is it? Speak up!"

"It is the queen, mistress."

Sophia's heart lurched into her throat. "What has happened?"

He rocked from one foot to the other. "She is not in the city."

"Where, then?"

"She sailed out under Roman colors this morning with the legion's general. They are saying that they went to meet another of Rome's legions, caught by the winds off the coast."

Sophia exhaled heavily. She tossed the papyrus on her desk. "You have taken care of the other tasks I gave you?"

"Yes, mistress. The physician has been sent for, and word from the city will be brought as well."

"Good." She waved him away, but he did not move.

"Yes?"

He held out another papyrus. "A message."

She sighed and took it from him. "You are as forthcoming as a river stone!" The message was brief but deadly. Somehow Caesar had learned that she likely held the Proginosko. And he wanted it immediately, or he would have his soldiers remove her from the lighthouse.

"Get out," she said to the servant. "Get out!"

He bowed from the room, no doubt grateful to get back to hauling dung.

"You sent for the physician?" Ares said, recalling her thoughts.

She shrugged and pointed to the door, where the servant had disappeared. "You see what I would have to make use of, should an infection steal you from me. I am only protecting myself." But her voice faltered, and the casual words fell flat. She dared not look at the boy, lest he see the tears that pooled in spite of her best effort.

She fell to her chair again, into a brooding silence. Ares returned to the couches, and she regretted not telling the servant, whose name she could not remember, to bring food. Ordinarily, she would simply yell down the ramp and somehow, always, Ares would appear.

She should send him away, back to the Base where he belonged.

But she did not.

The sun began its slant through her western windows, and still she stared, blank-eyed, at nothing.

What was happening to her? She had worked hard to keep to herself here in the lighthouse. Over the years her fearsome reputation had spread, and those who had a choice avoided her. Those who did not have a choice bowed and scraped to please her.

Yes, she had been successful in building walls around herself. And now, when she needed help, she had no one.

And yet . . . in spite of the walls she had built, in spite of the tower she kept, some had broken through.

Ares. Sosigenes.

Bellus.

She swallowed the hot regret at the thought of him, and the memory of his touch, his kiss. It had been the first time she had felt like a woman in many years.

She wanted to sink into the memory, to let it wash over her with softness and warmth. Instead, something within rose up to fight it, to raise an angry sword and slash away.

This is what comes of getting attached. They cannot love you. You do not deserve their love.

The physician came and with him, a servant. Ares called him by name, sparing her from having to ask.

"News?" she said to Talal, directing the physician to Ares.

"The city is readying for battle," Talal said. "Pothinus directs them."

"Pothinus! Where?"

"He has set up headquarters in the Library, it would seem."

Sophia put her hands to her hips, anger at the man's audacity roiling in her stomach.

"And ships," Talal continued, "are sailing into the harbor."

Sophia hurried to the window, and indeed, the horizon was littered with the masts and hulls of a fleet of ships.

"They cannot be Egyptian. Not that many."

"Roman," Talal said behind her. "Cleopatra and Caesar return, with the strength of a second legion behind them."

So it begins.

Talal disappeared, the physician tended to Ares, mumbling that he had never seen accidental cuts so parallel, and Sophia watched the ships outlined against the setting sun.

They trembled on the brink of war, all of them. But for Sophia, only one truth held sway. Pothinus had Sosigenes and would surely kill him. And Pothinus was in the Library.

"I am going," she said, when the physician had left.

"You cannot go alone, Sophia."

She could hear Ares cross the room behind her. "I have no choice. There is no one else."

"Even with one arm, I am better than nothing."

"No. I will not endanger you further."

"Find the Roman, Sophia. He—he cares for you. He will help—"

She spun on him. "You forget yourself, Ares. Do not take advantage of my kindness. You are my servant, and I do not require or desire advice from a servant!"

Ares tilted his head, looked at her with pitying eyes, then dropped his gaze. His pity only angered her further.

"See about your duties, Ares. I expect you to do all you can, even with your injury, and to find others to finish what work you cannot. You have wasted an entire day here. Do not give me reason to regret it."

With that, she pushed past him, past the hurt in his eyes, out of the chamber.

The ramp blurred before her as she stomped down it, uncertain of where her feet took her, but with one thought uppermost in her mind: *It is time to come out of the tower and take to the streets.*

Pothinus would soon feel what a tyrant like Sophia could do.

THIRTY-EIGHT

Bellus waited on the docks along the waterfront that housed the dozens of warehouses, loaded with goods both coming and going from Alexandria, center of the trading world. One of them, Sophia had told him, housed perhaps thousands of scrolls being copied for the Library. But he would not think of Sophia or of books today.

In the harbor ahead, framed against the glorious sunset that splashed the sky with billows of smoky orange and royal purple, Caesar's ship navigated the reefs and sailed toward the dock, with a legion of reinforcements behind him.

Bellus did not stand alone. Hundreds of soldiers stood with him, lining the dock like a passel of fidgety children, waiting for the father's return.

Along the dock, he knew, stood at least twenty other centurions of his rank, also anxious for Caesar to hear their reports, to nod his approval, to pat their heads.

Though it had been the way of his life for many years, tonight something inside him rebelled at the familiar scene.

Caesar's ship bore down upon them all until Bellus could see the great general at its stern, his lean form, his patrician nose, his hair combed forward to cover his balding pate. He wore the glow of battle on his face. At his side stood the queen of Egypt, her chin lifted to the air, one arm entwined around Caesar's.

Bellus stood straighter, as though the general would be watching him alone. As though they all did not jostle and maneuver to catch his eye. Bellus kept his gaze fixed on Caesar, despite the push of soldiers from behind and the press from either side.

But Caesar's attention had shifted to Cleopatra, who leaned over to speak into his ear. He covered her hand on his arm with his own and smiled.

A stab of unreasonable jealousy caused Bellus to blink rapidly, though he could not name its origin, whether from a desire for Caesar's attention, or a desire for the attention of a woman who loved him.

He kept his eyes from the lighthouse.

The boat bumped against the dock, and the soldiers gave a shout of victory. Through the day word had spread of Caesar's victory at sea. The single quinquereme taken from the Egyptians sailed amidst the Thirty-Seventh, a beleaguered testimony to the military prowess of the Romans. Every soldier along the dock pounded his pilum onto the stone quay.

The ship was tied, a plank lowered, and Caesar and Cleopatra hurried from the deck, as though anxious for the sanctuary of the palace.

Bellus elbowed his way through the rank and file *milites* soldiers to reach the path cleared for the general, but Caesar ignored the well-wishers along the quay, his long-legged pace leaving Cleopatra to hurry behind.

As he passed Bellus, Caesar slowed and nodded. "I hear you saved us all from a thirsty death."

Bellus saluted.

"Come to me at the palace. I will have new orders for you. Something better fitted to an officer of your standing."

Bellus gave a quick nod. "Yes, General."

The mob swelled behind Caesar as he moved on, filling in the gap.

Bellus let the air escape from his chest and relaxed his fisted hands.

At last.

It had been two long months, since they had first arrived and found the Alexandrian mob to be more quarrelsome—and the machinations of the Ptolemies more brutal—than they imagined. He had been exiled to that lonesome lighthouse, to wait out his general's displeasure, to be given another chance to prove himself.

And now, at last, his punishment had ended, and he had gained what he most wanted. The approval of the Master of the Mediterranean.

Behind him, the sun faded away into the sea. He glanced back, still guided by his usual habit of checking the lighthouse flame.

Yes, there it was, as always. He slowed to watch the flame brighten and swell. No doubt servants worked to angle the mirror to send its messages over the sea.

His gaze slid down the darkened tower, past the circular top section, the octagonal middle, halfway down the tallest, bottom tier. Sophia's private chamber did not have windows on this side of the building.

She faced away from him even now.

The palace called to him, but he let the crowd flow around him, past the warehouses and into the royal quarter. He sat on a wall along the harbor until he was alone, and studied the lighthouse.

It seemed so remote, as though he had lived a different part of his life there.

And in a sense, he had. It was a different Bellus who had lived there. Bellus the centurion had been shed like an outworn skin. Something new and alive had been called forth, there in Sophia's chamber, with her books and her keen mind and her shy smile.

Which is the true Bellus?

She had uncovered the part of him he had endeavored to keep hidden. But instead of scoffing and derision, she had given him encouragement. Friendship.

He had wanted so much more for her. Freedom.

Why had she pushed him away?

The solitude of the harbor pressed upon him. Caesar would be waiting. He shook off the reverie and turned his steps to the palace.

Inside the palace hall, he heard voices ahead and turned to the main audience hall.

"Ah, Pilus Prior Bellus," Caesar held out a hand from the front of the columned room, and the eyes of a handful of senior officers turned toward him. "Restorer of the water."

Bellus crossed the hall to the back-slaps of several of his fellow centurions.

Restorer.

The name struck him, for it spoke of his hopes for Sophia, of what he might offer. But it was not simply what he could do for her that drew him, that pulled him back to the lighthouse as though a cord stretched between them.

". . . with the water," Caesar was saying, and Bellus tried to focus on him. "We must be ready to face the next threat, coming from all directions."

Would Sophia be in danger? A mighty battle was coming, that was certain. What would that mean for the lighthouse?

"Eh, Bellus?" Caesar said. "You understand?"

"I—I am sorry, General—"

Caesar laughed. "I think my centurion needs more sleep. Portius, explain Bellus's next assignment to him." The general waved them out, but then called to Bellus before they left the hall.

"You have proven yourself with the water, Bellus, so I have trusted you with much more. Do not disappoint me."

But Bellus was already planning what he would say to Sophia when he reached the lighthouse, and he barely heard his general's final words.

THIRTY-NINE

Sophia paced through the North Wing, counting her steps, counting the hours, counting everything that had gone wrong in her life of late. Sosigenes and the Proginosko were in the grasp of Pothinus, and after the full moon of this evening, Pothinus would have no more use for her friend. She could not leave Sosigenes or the Proginosko with Pothinus. But if she recovered them, would it only be to hand them over to Caesar? She fumed at the impossible situation. She could not protect the scholars, and she could not send them away.

The day had not been completely wasted, but it was much later than she had hoped, and still she was not ready to set out.

The corridor of the North Wing was strangely dark, due to the addition of a mighty hinged wooden door in the entrance of the lighthouse. She had never before felt the need for such a thing.

Outside, the city held its breath, ready for the storm that rumbled on the horizon.

Finally, finally, there came a pounding on the door and a shout she recognized. She lifted the iron latch and swung it open.

They seemed to swarm into the Base, these men she had hired. Down to the last of them, they were dirty, poor, and frightening.

They spent their days on the rocks of the Eunostos Harbor, waiting, hoping for ships to founder on the rocks and spill their luxuries into the sea. They were ever vigilant for such spoils, but also willing to be drawn away from their watch for the promise of easy and sure money. Sophia had sent word through a servant from the village that she had a task requiring a dozen men not afraid of a fight. She would pay well.

And here they were.

One of the pirates sallied alongside her and leaned close. "So this is the lady of the lighthouse." Some of his letters hissed curiously through a gap left by a missing tooth. "The fearsome Sophia who rules Pharos Island from up there." He jabbed a finger skyward and circled her, his face still close. "In need of a few good men, we hear."

Sophia addressed herself to this obvious leader, though she backed away a few steps. She resisted holding her hands as a barrier. "I need you to go to the Library."

Laughter erupted all around, loud cackles that reminded her of the seals that often barked off the western coast. "We don't get much call to visit the Library, mistress."

She shrugged. "You do not go to read books."

"Ah, good thing, then."

"You go to rescue someone in danger."

The laughter settled, though amusement still played about their faces.

"We see plenty of folks in danger, mistress. But rescue's not our usual way."

"Then today you will redeem yourself for many ills." She pushed through the lot of them toward the new door. "You will be well paid when we return."

"We?" More laughter.

She turned on them. "The city is readying for war. It is not safe to travel alone. I expect your protection. And when we reach the Library, there is someone we must extract. There may be violence. Any questions?"

The group stared blankly, and she wondered if she had made the right decision. After weeks of watching the well-trained Roman army live and drill beneath her, she knew not whether this rag-tag group could remove a bird from its nest.

Sophia lifted the iron latch once more, pushed the door open, and nodded to the men. They filled in around her, and then they were off.

She left it to Ares to close the door. He no doubt hovered somewhere, though she had not seen him since she had scolded his familiarity last night.

They crossed the causeway to the main part of the island, then walked en masse through the village, drawing the stares of towns-people and the frightened yelps of children. Even here on her island she could feel the people's fear.

Across the heptastadion, over the bridges that could be raised to allow ships to cross harbors. No boats passed now. There would be no trade today.

To her left, the Great Harbor was clogged with ships of a different sort. Roman galleys, filled with a new legion of soldiers to fortify the first and ensure Egypt's submission.

Sophia directed their steps from her place in the center of the dozen men. Along the outskirts of the royal quarter, to draw less attention. Through the Beta district with its narrow streets and tiny shops, closed against what was to come.

The streets were deserted, but the rooftops as crowded as the stadium during the games. Strange catcalls fell on them as they passed through homes and shops. Clearly the townspeople did not know what to make of twelve pirates and the lighthouse keeper crossing the city.

But then something shifted. Sophia was not sure if she felt it physically, in the wind, in the sounds of the city, or if it happened somewhere deep inside her, in the deeper part of her that was connected to Alexandria. But somehow, she knew.

The battle had begun.

She looked upward, to the flat rooftops of the city, and saw that the people there strained at the lips of their homes, their faces turned to the harbor. Her heartbeat seemed to slow.

And then came the sound.

The awful, wrenching sound of ships engaging, of a thousand military voices raised in battle cry, of a city manning its defenses. A chill shook Sophia's body as though she were a reed beside the Nile.

"We must hurry," she hissed to the men, and they responded, following her hasty steps toward the Library.

But it was too late to reach the magnificent building unaccosted. Peasants flowed through the city like water breaking through a dam. They rushed toward Sophia and her escorts, armed with clubs, with knives, with rocks and even swords. Her mouth went dry and she bit her lip to keep from crying out.

Self-protection pushed them all against the walls of the nearest shop, to wait out the first deluge of angry citizens.

When it had passed, they continued, and Sophia felt sweat build along her spine.

The Library and Museum emerged ahead, and Sophia urged them on, through the widening street, up the marble steps, under the portico.

They spread into the Great Hall of the Library like a stain bleeding onto the white floor. The sudden echoing silence of the Library sucked Sophia's breath away after the chaos of the street.

"Remember," she said to the men, "he is old. Take good care of him. The other one—do whatever must be done."

The twelve men dispersed into the ten halls, as though she had tossed a handful of grain to the birds. Sophia kept her place, as the Great Hall seemed the best place to supervise their mission.

She could hear their slapping sandals on the marble floors, an occasional shout as they searched the halls and alcoves. But none appeared with Sosigenes in tow, or with Pothinus in their grasp.

She feared she had been wrong.

What if he has killed him already? Too foolish to wait until the Proginosko was perfected?

Or perhaps Pothinus had taken Sosigenes elsewhere. The Library was an obvious place to station himself. Too clear a target for anyone who wished to assassinate him.

Stupid, Sophia. And the time grows short.

She turned to the wide doorway and peered across the city to the harbor. The Egyptians had waited until nightfall to attack, knowing they would have the advantage in their own harbor.

Wooden towers on wheels were being dragged through the streets by horses, and peasants clambered up them with quivers of arrows slung across their backs. All around the city, torches flamed to life and charged through the streets.

Pothinus would have heard all of this. Known that he was not safe.

Where would he have gone?

Years ago, when she had been a young woman and in love with a scholar who made the Library his second home, there had been a room, just a storage room, in the bowels of the Library. She had met Kallias there sometimes, when he could sneak away from his work.

Sophia found the small door to the steps as though it been only weeks ago that she had used it last. It opened easily, revealing shabby steps descending into darkness. But at the bottom . . . *there!* She could see some light. There was something down there. Someone.

She looked over her shoulder, hoping to find a few of her hired pirates. But the Great Hall was empty.

A sound drifted up from the lower level. A cry, perhaps?

And then again. Yes, a cry of pain.

Sophia felt a tingling in her fingers that spread up her arms, but she hesitated only a moment, then plunged downward, her eyes on the yellow glow that barely reached the base of the steps.

She hit the bottom on silent feet. The murmur of voices reached around the corner. She pressed her face against the stone, then slid enough to allow one eye to peer into the room.

In the tiny storage room that held many fond memories, Pothinus stood with a knife held to Sosigenes's throat and a wicked smile on his face.

FORTY

All the fight had gone out of Bellus. The day of battle was upon them, the day they had waited and prepared for since coming to this city on the sea. Caesar had given again his respect and new orders, and Bellus found that all he could think of was a woman and her books, closeted in a lighthouse high above the city.

But he had his orders, and no matter his emotions, he would not forsake his post. And so he marched his centuria to the Eunostos Harbor, west of the lighthouse, to secure the docks as he had been commanded.

In the Great Harbor to their right, past the heptastadion that led out to Sophia, the Roman fleet, including the ships of the newly arrived Thirty-Seventh Legion, floated in the bowl formed by the crescent-shaped harbor. Farther out, past the shallow reefs that endangered any passing into the harbor, the Egyptian ships blocked any escape, and certainly made ready to attack.

Somewhere to the east, the Egyptian army marched upon them as well.

In the smaller Eunostos Harbor, though, five more quiriremes floated, lashed to the docks. Egyptian ships, but they must not be allowed to join their fellows in the Great Sea.

Bellus had mounted his horse and now crossed back and forth behind his lines, the measured slap of their sandals carrying them forward to the docks.

Once the docks are secured, I will cross to the lighthouse and find her.

He glanced over his shoulder, to the royal quarter. Somewhere on the roof of Ptolemy XII's palace, Caesar surely watched the city, watched them all fall into position like pieces of a child's puzzle. What would he think if Bellus broke from his centuria to seek out the Keeper of the lighthouse?

I will do my duty. Nothing less. And nothing more.

But duty proved to be a burden greater than expected. They were met at the docks, not by a gaggle of fishermen mending nets after the night's take, nor even by the band of pirates that made the harbor famous. Instead, as they marched downward to the sea and then along the stone dock, they were set upon by a horde of furious sailors, both Greek and Egyptian.

The sailors charged, erupting from water, from warehouses, from ships like a swarm of screaming monkeys. They brandished weapons of iron and wood.

Bellus jerked his horse to the left and thrust through the centuria to its flank. The ranks broke immediately. The attack was unexpected.

He assessed with lightning speed. They were equally matched in number. But certainly not in skill.

The sailors rushed the centuria with a frenzy borne of rights perceived trampled, of national fear.

His soldiers weathered the first blow. Then pushed back, their training taking over.

But emotions can be a strong ally, and the Alexandrians had waged a war of propaganda long before today's battle began.

Without training, without armor, without the razor edged blades of the Romans, still they held the centuria.

Bellus found himself beside his horse, in the thick of the battle, regretting every sword thrust that found purchase in the gut of a sailor. He dodged wooden clubs, knocked daggers from tight-fisted grips, brought the flat side of his sword down on sun-browned necks.

The familiar slow motion of the battle came over him, with every parry and thrust seen in sharp detail against the blue sky, every groan of pain and grunt of effort like a single sound in a silent hall.

His leather-wrapped hands grew slick, and sweat flung from his brow, ran in rivers from his temples until he tasted the salt of it.

Men staggered and fell alongside him, sailors and soldiers alike. Still the Roman standard snapped in the wind, the gold and sapphire blue like jewels flung to the sky above them. Bellus's shoulders tightened like a bowstring, and a powerful thirst scraped at his throat.

He fought with his arms, his legs, his chest, and yet his mind functioned apart. It climbed the circular ramp to find Sophia. He could see her there, leaning over her books at her desk, turning as he entered, her slow smile breaking like an early dawn.

His breath rasped under his helmet. The sailors were falling back. Those who remained were taking to one of the ships.

"The quirireme!" Bellus yelled to his troops. The soldiers shifted and pushed. That ship could not be allowed to sail.

Three sailors worked frantically at the ropes lashed to the iron cleat.

Bellus kept one eye on the sailor who lunged at him, one eye on the contingent of men that broke off to take the sailors at the cleat.

There were enough sailors to take the boat out, but not enough to hold the centuria. The Roman troops broke through and rushed the ship.

Bellus pulled up, and a break in the fighting afforded him a brief glance at the lighthouse.

Focus, Lucius.

And then, there were more. Another mob of Alexandrians armed with nothing more than homemade weapons and pent-up fury.

Bellus located his horse, mounted, and rode back thirty paces to take stock of his own personal battle.

We need reinforcements.

He grabbed the first soldier to run past him. "To the second centuria, the other harbor. Bring them here."

The soldier gave him a quick nod, then sprinted eastward to the Great Harbor, where flames were beginning to consume ships.

Bellus crossed behind his troops again and recalled all but a few from the ship, now secured, to fight the new wave of Alexandrians, crazed and bloodthirsty.

The messenger he'd sent must have flown to the Great Harbor and back, for it seemed to Bellus only a few moments until he reappeared, breathless and soaked with sweat.

"The Second," he panted, looking up to Bellus on his mount. "They have moved."

Bellus stilled his fretful horse. "Where?"

"The lighthouse," the boy said, doubling over a bit.

Bellus jerked his eyes to Sophia's tower, outlined in black relief against the orange sky of the dying sun. "What goes on there?"

Three soldiers ran past and his messenger jumped closer to avoid them. "All our ships are in the harbor now. Caesar has given orders that the light up there be extinguished, to give no aid to Egyptian ships that might attack."

The news fell like a stone into Bellus's heart. His gaze shot again to the summit of the lighthouse, Poseidon with his trident atop the uppermost tier. Though the mirror was positioned away from him now, Bellus had no doubt that it caught the last rays of the sun and projected them outward, just as it had done every day without fail for all of Sophia's life.

And when the sun had dropped into the sea, the fires would be lit. She had never let it fail, for it was through the fire that she tried to earn her redemption. It was the fire that led ships and their passengers to safety. A safety not given to her family twenty years ago.

To extinguish the light would be to extinguish something within Sophia's soul. She would rather die than see it quenched.

This he knew with a certainty.

The second centuria, charged with storming the lighthouse and dousing its light, would have to go through Sophia to do it.

And he had no doubt they would.

FORTY-ONE

Sophia pressed herself against the stone wall at the bottom of the Library's steps and listened to the raspy breathing around the corner.

There came a small laugh, a sound of sick amusement that even after all the intervening years since they had worked together, Sophia recognized as Pothinus. She swallowed and closed her lips. Tried to control her labored breathing.

"Do not even think of trying that again, old man," Pothinus said beyond the wall where she stood. "They will not hear you down here anyway. You are buried in stone already. Do not give me reason to make it permanent yet."

"She will not give up."

Pothinus laughed again. "I fear you may be right. But we shall wait, all the same. And after all, we have only to wait until the moon rises this night, correct? Once the Proginosko proves itself this last night . . ."

"You think Sophia searches for me. But it is the Proginosko. And she will not let you have it."

Sophia bit her lip and closed her eyes.

"Hmm," Pothinus said. "She is a hard woman, that I know. Many women have lost husbands, but I have never known one to give herself so fully to her grief."

"She lost more than a husband in that storm."

"Yes, we all did, didn't we?"

Sosigenes cried out again, and Sophia held herself back, knowing that Pothinus had a painful grip on the man.

"But now," Pothinus said, "now we have it back again, thanks to you."

Sophia took a step backward, found the edge of the bottom step with her foot, and slid upward.

One careful step at a time, she retreated back to the main level. She was not foolish enough to confront Pothinus alone.

The door at the top of the steps creaked painfully, and she held it half-open, her body wedged between door and frame, breath caught in her throat. Below her all was silent, whether because they had heard something or because they were too far off, she could not tell.

In the Great Hall, Sophia stood with her hands on her hips, her feet apart, looking to the Rhetoric Hall, the Astronomy, the Mathematics.

Her pirates, wherever they were, had melted into the Library, like water over dry sand.

A movement in an alcove caught her eye. The leader, Biti, wiggled three fingers in her direction, a silent salute.

She crossed the Hall. "I have found them. Gather the others."

Within minutes the group massed at the cellar door. "He has a weapon," she whispered. "And Sosigenes must not be harmed."

Biti flexed his shoulders. "How will we know him?"

"Keep the older man safe. The arrogant one, my age, he is the one we have come to defeat."

Sophia realized a strategic error the moment she opened the door. Only one of them could fit in the stairwell at a time. They could not overwhelm Pothinus as a group, taking him down before he had a chance to react.

Nevertheless, they started down, and Sophia prayed that Pothinus's need for Sosigenes's intellect, and his need for something to bargain for his life, would keep her friend safe.

Six before and six behind. She slapped down the steps in the center of her pirates, comforted in part by the sense of safety they afforded, but still with wooden legs, stiff with fear.

She rounded the corner at the bottom, surrounded by her men.

They stood at a face-off with Pothinus. He held Sosigenes as a shield, with his arm around the older man's bony shoulders. A small dagger flashed in the torchlight, held at Sosigenes's throat.

"No farther!" Pothinus yelled, his voice strained and tight. He caught sight of Sophia and his eyes flashed. "I will kill him, Sophia, you know I will."

Sophia took stock of the small room, unchanged since the days she had stolen time here with Kallias. It had been hewn out of rock under the Library and smelled of musty decay. The group of them filled the dark room, with unmarked wooden crates stacked at its perimeter and a low stone shelf carved into the wall to her right. Her eye caught a flash of something metallic on the shelf and she looked again.

The Proginosko.

She glanced at Pothinus. He had followed her gaze to the shelf, and now his attention flicked back to her, a flash of uncertainty in his eyes. "Take it, and I will have no reason to keep him," Pothinus said, edging the knife closer to Sosigenes's neck.

Sophia looked to Sosigenes, unwilling to see the fear on his face, but unable to ignore him.

He smiled and nodded as much as the knife would allow, his expression filled with a peace that he seemed to want to pour into her.

Pothinus's face, in contrast, was twisted with a greedy hate that stretched across the years.

Sophia took a step toward Pothinus. "You have been jealous of him, even of Kallias, for all these years, haven't you?"

Pothinus chuckled. "It would seem that jealousy, when cultivated at length, gives a man all he desires."

He watched her, and she couldn't keep her eyes from straying to the Proginosko. She had only to take a few steps to her right, reach out, and she would hold it in her hands. True, she would not have Sosigenes. But could not Hesiod, or another of the twelve left back in the lighthouse, make any final adjustments if needed?

Untold benefits awaited the world with the advent of the Proginosko. In the hands of only one, however, great destruction could be wreaked. Would not Sosigenes be the first to say that the sacrifice of one man was a small price to pay for the safety of the knowledge?

Had Kallias been a small price to pay?

Her emotions warred within her, while the blood in her veins seemed to flow to her feet and root her to the floor.

She had worked so hard to never attach herself to someone again. It was too difficult to let people go, once they held part of your heart.

And yet, she had failed. She knew that now.

Sophia thought of Ares, his bleeding arm. Her choice to trick the sadistic soldier Pothinus had sent to retrieve the Proginosko. She had nearly cost Ares his life in her quest to preserve the technology of the Proginosko.

She would not make the same mistake again.

Around her, she felt the tension of the pirate mob she had brought. They held steady, like a quiver full of arrows nocked and aimed, ready to fly.

He will not kill Sosigenes. He cannot afford to.

She reached out slowly with both her hands, grasped the arms of the men on either side of her in a silent message she knew they would understand.

And then she shot her arm toward Pothinus, finger pointed, and gave the command, strong and clear. "Take him!"

They rushed as one. Flowed around her like a mighty wave.

She saw Pothinus's eyes widen. Saw the knife point prick Sosigenes's throat. Hesitate. He drew blood but could not finish it.

They were on him like a pack of wolves on a wounded rabbit.

The knife flew upward in a metallic arc, then clattered to the floor. Sosigenes fell away from Pothinus, bloody fingers held to his neck. Pothinus fell beneath the blows of three or four of the men.

"Do not kill him," Sophia said. "We will leave justice to others who have the right to wield it."

She pulled Sosigenes to her side. "Let me see," she said and peeled his fingers from his throat.

It was a deep cut, but it had not struck a vein. It bled, but slowly. "We are a matching pair now," he said with a weak smile.

Pothinus was jerked to his feet. One eye had already begun to swell shut. His lip was split and blood trickled down his chin. He tried to smile. "You surprise me, Sophia, I will admit."

"Because I care for more than power?"

"Because for all these years, since the loss of Kallias, you have not deigned to descend from your lighthouse, have not kept the company of any but your own family, and here you are beneath the city, for the sake of another."

Sophia pulled the Proginosko from the shelf and clutched it to her chest. "You give me too much credit, Pothinus. I have not kept the company of any but my memories, for the sea took all else."

Pothinus yanked an arm from one of his captors and tried to smooth his hair back. "Did your brat grow up to leave you then, too? As your husband did?"

Sophia swallowed the bitter anger that his harshness provoked. "You have no weapons but your words now, Pothinus, but I will not be hurt by them."

He laughed. "Ah, I see I must be close to the truth. Perhaps the half-eaten sailor that brought him to you found that his mother had no capacity for gentleness, for kindness."

Something pricked the edge of Sophia's memory, a thought she failed to take hold of, like an elusive scent on the breeze. Beside her, Sosigenes seemed to lose the strength of his legs, and leaned heavily against her.

"Come," she said to the group. "Bring him up." She turned to go, but then hesitated. The scent again, a thread of memory.

She looked back to Pothinus. "Half-eaten sailor? Of whom do you speak?"

He stuck out his split lip and tried to wriggle from the tight hold of the pirates. "Come now, you cannot have forgotten. I have never seen such a monster. Empty eye socket, ear torn from him along with half his face. A gruesome sight for even a baby."

Sophia felt her body go slack, her lips fall open. "Baby?"

"How long did it take him to bring the brat? Perhaps the thing had become an idiot by the time he was returned to you?"

Sophia looked to Sosigenes, whose face revealed the same swirl of conflicting thoughts in her own mind.

"My baby?" she whispered.

Pothinus seemed to grow aware of her confusion then and pulled himself upright. "Perhaps I know more than you about that time. Let me go and I will tell what I know."

The quivering in Sophia's heart hardened. "Bring him up."

They moved upward and gained the main level of the Library, finding that the sun had set while they were beneath the Hall and the underscholars had moved through the Library, lighting the lamps as was their duty.

The Great Hall flickered white and black as they moved through it, long shadows cast to the carved ceiling high above.

Sophia led the group, with Sosigenes at her side, through the Great Hall, past the alcoves of scrolls.

Her mind was not present in the Library, however.

It had traveled back, many years, to a stormy night and a stranger with a disfigured face and an illegitimate baby born to a servant . . .

And then a sharp cry behind her brought her back to the present.

She whirled and found her pirates backing away as one from Pothinus. He held a torch in two hands and waved it before him like a flaming sword. "If you give the Proginosko to Caesar, Sophia, I swear by the gods I will kill you."

She growled in frustration at the pirates' inattention. But they were not trained soldiers.

"Get behind me," she said to Sosigenes.

"The scrolls!" he said, pointing.

In the alcove nearest them, flames licked at the edges of a dozen papyrus rolled where they were stacked in tidy rows on stone shelves.

Her pirates had realized their mistake and were circling Pothinus.

"Fire!" Sophia pushed the nearest pirates toward the alcove. "Save the scrolls!"

Pothinus eyed his work, smiled greedily, and waved his torch. He seemed to sense his opportunity.

Her men scrambled over each other in confusion. She could read their thoughts. Should they flee the fire? Douse it? Move the scrolls? Hold Pothinus?

Pothinus dodged from the group and ran across the Great Hall, past the statue of Euclid in the center, to an alcove opposite them. He touched the torch to scrolls there, then ran back toward the Great Hall.

He is insane.

She must make a choice. Her mind sifted through options with haste.

She had the Proginosko. She had Sosigenes. She did not need Pothinus for anything but revenge. She could not sacrifice the knowledge of the Library to her own anger.

"Leave him! Douse the fires! We must not allow the Library to burn!"

They spread through the Halls, to each of the places where Pothinus had touched his insane torch. They pulled scrolls from shelves, stamped them out with smoking, melting sandals. Sophia did not let go of the Proginosko, only shifted it in her arms to pull burning papyrus to the floor.

Even Sosigenes fought the flames, his hand still at his bleeding throat.

And then it was over, the Library filled with smoke and the burnt remains of countless scrolls. Sophia's eyes stung with smoke and with the realization of the lost knowledge at their feet.

But they had saved the Library, and the bulk of the scrolls that still lay enshrined in its sacred halls.

Pothinus was gone.

They ran to the Library steps but pulled up as a group when they reached the portico.

In the darkness beyond, the harbor burned with dozens of small fires, like an echo of what they left behind. Flaming arrows arced through the night sky, some plummeting into the sea, some finding their targets of man and ship.

The city had erupted while they fought inside the Library.

The lighthouse.

"Come!" she called to them all and led the way down the steps with pirates and scholar streaming behind.

They fought their way across the royal quarter, dodging rolling siege towers, small skirmishes between townspeople and Romans, and clusters of Alexandrians that clotted the streets with angry fists raised and clubs in their hands.

They gained the heptastadion, and Sophia slowed, breathless. The Proginosko grew heavy in her arms, and Sosigenes leaned against her, his strength clearly ebbing.

"Can you make it?"

He did not answer.

Behind her, Biti appeared and braced an arm under the scholar's shoulders. "Come on, old man," he said. Sophia thanked him with a nod.

Small boats were engaged along the causeway, Roman soldiers fighting townspeople who had put out in any craft they could find. Others scrambled over the rocks that lined the bridge to the island, their crazed battle cries lifted into the harbor air.

An explosion rocked the ground. Sophia turned without thought.

A warehouse on the dock erupted in flame.

More books. Oh, not the books.

Sophia held back the tearful cry and pushed on. They must reach the lighthouse.

They gained the end of the heptastadion and ran through the village, picking up angry townspeople along the way. Ahead, the lighthouse beckoned, its solid and dark strength a comfort to her.

But before they reached the entrance, a boat bumped against the rocks behind them and disgorged its passengers, too many Romans to count.

They roared with battle-lust and fell upon the townspeople. She had learned enough of Roman warfare to recognize that it was a centuria. What did they want with the island? With the lighthouse?

Sophia pulled Sosigenes to the newly-set wooden door and pushed against it. Latched, as she expected. She slapped her hand on the splintered wood and yelled.

Inside the lighthouse, someone answered.

"Let us in," she screamed. "It is Sophia!"

Behind her, the pirates turned on the Romans, holding them off.

The door swung open only a crack, and Sophia pushed forward, leading with the Proginosko. Ares stood within. She thrust the box into his hands and yanked Sosigenes through the opening.

"Secure the door!" she said to Ares, then turned in time to catch Sosigenes as he fell against her.

Ares set the box on the floor, shoved the door closed, and dropped the latch in place.

Sophia held Sosigenes upright. "I will take him to the others. Hide the Proginosko. Watch from a window. Come to us when the lighthouse is secure."

Ares nodded and bent to the Proginosko.

Sophia ran her gaze over her young servant, and Pothinus's revelation built inside her chest, until she feared she might explode as the warehouse had. But there was no time. No time to think, to question, to believe.

She pulled a hand free from Sosigenes to grip Ares's arm. She waited until he lifted his eyes to hers. "Come to me. As soon as it is safe."

His eyes flickered in response to the intensity of her voice, but he nodded, lips tight and jaw set.

Sosigenes was fading. From exertion, from blood loss, even perhaps from fear.

Sophia held him as best she could and pulled him toward the North Wing. Toward safety, she hoped.

But with the city and the harbor burning around them, she did not know if any of them would survive the night.

FORTY-TWO

From the Eunostos Harbor where Bellus left his centuria in full control of the docks, the lighthouse seemed a distant thing, a far-off fortress on the tip of a remote island. The heptastadion, the village, and an encroaching second centuria stood between him and his impossible goal, to reach the lighthouse unharmed, and before any harm could come to Sophia.

He plunged to the task, the iron of his pilum cold comfort in his hand. He ran along the docks, avoiding citizens who would have engaged him in fruitless combat, keeping his head low when Roman soldiers passed.

He had not deserted. Not quite. His men had taken the docks as ordered, and now he went to secure the lighthouse, as only he could. Caesar would understand.

Though I care not whether he does.

The bridges were lowered to prevent ships crossing from one harbor to the other. Bellus ran along the edge of the causeway, prepared to climb down its rock wall if necessary.

Ahead, a mob of villagers clogged the end of the causeway, guarding the lighthouse.

Bellus glanced up as he ran, saw that the light still burned high atop the tower, a pinprick in the dark sky, a mirror of the flames that burned all around him in the harbor and on the docks behind.

Yes, the city burned. And Bellus feared for Sophia in spite of her stone fortress.

The smoke of flaming ships choked the causeway, a wall that stung his eyes and throat as he plowed through.

The lighthouse pulled him forward, calling to that buried part of him. He was a soldier, yes. *But that is not all I truly am.*

The smoke cleared and Bellus kept his feet churning over the ground while his eyes darted left and right, aware of everything at once.

The battle raged in the harbor. Screaming Egyptian soldiers, ordered and disciplined battle calls of the Romans. Burning and cracking and grating ships.

Bellus ran like a silent Odysseus, flying to rescue the endangered Penelope.

He neared the end of the causeway. He could not plow through the townspeople, not as a Roman soldier.

He sheathed his sword with reluctance and took to the slippery black rocks that braced either side of the causeway. Algae and seawater slicked his hands and resisted his feet. He went down on one leg, felt the rock bite his shin, and scrambled forward through the pain.

He kept low, willing the mob above to keep their eyes on the sea, on the causeway, anywhere but the rocks. And then he was at the end, curving around toward the lighthouse, in full view of any of the people who might look his way.

A loud crack against the rocks behind him stayed his feet. He glanced back and saw that a Roman ship had bumped the causeway, and now a hundred hungry soldiers poured onto the stone and gravel bridge to engage the townspeople. The second centuria, come for the lighthouse. But first they must deal with the villagers.

It was the distraction Bellus needed.

He leaped over the uppermost rocks, reached the sand of the island, and plunged toward the lighthouse, barely keeping himself upright in his haste.

Sweat burned his eyes. He ripped his helmet from his head and swiped at his face.

The battle hardness was on him fully now, but he did not fight for Rome, nor Caesar, nor even his father.

He fought for Sophia.

He reached the lighthouse and stopped in shock at the wooden door he had never seen. He shoved against it with a yell, but it would not budge. He pulled his sword from its sheath and pounded the hilt of it against the door. Behind him, the centuria and the mob had fully engaged. He could hear the screams of untrained fighters. It could not be long before the soldiers stormed the lighthouse.

He pounded the door again and yelled for Sophia, for Ares, for anyone.

A muffled shout returned to him from the other side.

Ares.

"Let me in, boy! It is Pilus Prior Bellus!"

"I cannot! She said to allow no one!"

Bellus slammed a palm against the door and then his forehead. "It is for her own safety, Ares. Please! You must trust me!"

A pause, too long, then a single word called back.

"Wait!"

Bellus turned and leaned his back against the door, panting, and watched the battle beneath him, the flaming ships in the harbor, the burning docks beyond. The strength in his legs threatened to give way, and the fear in his chest tried to assert itself. He braced his head against the door. The words of Sophocles ran ridiculously through his mind. *Men of ill judgment oft ignore the good that lies within their hands, 'til they have lost it.*

Let me in, Sophia. It is time to let me in.

FORTY-THREE

Sophia half-dragged the injured Sosigenes to the scholars' study room. She called out through the door while still a few paces off. The door was unlocked from the inside and pulled open only a crack.

Several pairs of dark eyes peered out on her, then swung the door wide.

"Sosigenes!"

Strong hands took him from her grasp, led him forward to a couch in the torchlit room, and pulled her in.

They spoke, all at once.

"What is happening in the city?"

"Who cut you?"

"How did you find him?"

"Ah, the Proginosko!"

Sophia found herself breathing too hard to answer. She pointed to Sosigenes, to his pale cheeks and sunken eyes. "See to him."

The scholars pressed around the two, blocking the torch's light and making it difficult for her to catch her breath. And then Ares was there, at the edge of the crowd, standing on his toes, peering around white heads to find her.

A chill broke over her, passing through like a tremor. She reached out for him, her mind still muddled but her heart telling her impossible things.

"Sophia!" he called through the chattering lot. "I must speak to you."

Yes, yes, I must speak to you as well!

He saw her hand extended to him, palm up, and reached past Archippos to grasp her fingers and pull her forward.

"Ares, Pothinus said—" Sophia began, looking up into his dark eyes, so unlike his mother, Eleni.

"Sophia, at the door," Ares bent to whisper in her ear. "It is Bellus, yelling to be admitted."

"Bellus!" She pulled back. "Why has he come?"

"He says it is for your protection. He says you must trust him."

Sophia eyed the cluster of old men who had sprung into action now, treating Sosigenes's cut and searching out clean rags. "The battle continues below the lighthouse?"

Ares ran his hand through his hair. "The Roman soldiers are being held off by the villagers, remarkably. I cannot say how long they will last."

"But Bellus is alone? Not with his men?"

"I believe he is alone. But I did not unlatch the door. The men that he had left here in the lighthouse joined the fray outside."

Sophia bit her lip and looked back to the scholars in the yellow pool of torchlight, the men whose lives she had sworn to protect. And Ares. She must protect him now. But it was not any Roman at the door. It was Bellus.

The floor seemed to ripple beneath her feet, and she covered her face with her hands. It was too much. Sosigenes hurt. Bellus returned. Ares—no time to even think of the possibilities. A long-unfamiliar swell of churning emotion broke like a wave over her heart, and her eyes burned with unshed tears.

Sosigenes called to her, as though he could read her heart. "You must believe that love overcomes, Sophia. Before it is too late."

"What shall I tell him, Abbas?" Ares said. "In truth, I fear for him there at the door. I do not think he acts with the approval of his general."

She could almost see Bellus, waiting at the door, his brow furrowed in frustration, entreating her to open her lighthouse.

She dropped her hands, blinked away the tears, and nodded to Ares.

"Let him in, Ares. Let the Roman in."

FORTY-FOUR

The battle outside the lighthouse raged on. Bellus huddled against the wooden door, trying to melt into its shadow. *The people fight for their lives.*

It was the only explanation for the way they held off the better-trained centuria.

At his back, the door trembled. He spun and heard the latch lift. When the door had opened hardly more than a handbreadth, Bellus squeezed through and pushed it shut.

Ares dropped the iron latch.

Bellus clapped the boy on the shoulder. "Thank you. You have saved her life, believe me."

Ares narrowed his eyes. "Do not betray her."

Bellus felt his stomach turn with what he was about to do. "I will always act in her best interest, Ares."

The boy nodded. "I will take you to her." He turned and started toward the East Wing.

Bellus hesitated only a moment, then sprinted the other direction. Through the arch that led to the central courtyard, across the sand, into the bottom tier of the lighthouse, to the ramp. He grabbed a torch from a wall socket at the bottom and started upward.

He heard Ares's shout behind him. He did not slow.

Bellus had run uphill in many a battle. The burning of the calves, the thighs, the breath sucking hard in his chest—it was all familiar. Yet he was not many cubits up the ramp before he was forced to slow, to admit that he had never climbed a hill like this one.

You will never make it at this pace, old man.

He steadied to an even march on the balls of his feet, switching the torch to the other hand and following the uneven glow it cast ahead.

He passed Sophia's private chamber without a pause. She was not there, he knew from Ares. But the sight of it was like a blow to his chest all the same. He climbed to quench a light that she had dedicated her life to keeping lit. She would never forgive him.

His breath came hard, chest heaving, throat burning. Still he climbed.

He reached the first platform, where her roses gleamed in the moonlight, tumbled together like pink and white shells on dark sand. He rested a moment there, let the memories, hot and painful, hurt him further.

Then upward, winding around the second tier on a narrow flight of wooden steps. He had never been this high.

The third tier, a circular structure half the height of the second, also had steps. He slowed and crept upward on silent feet. The fire was never left untended, Sophia had told him. How many would there be?

He paused, intending to draw his sword, then checked the impulse. These were Sophia's servants, not enemy soldiers.

The steps ended on a small platform, barely enough room to stand, with a doorway to the beacon chamber. Low conversation came from within.

At least two, unless one has gone crazy with solitude.

He stuffed the torch into another wall socket, and cringed at the scrape of it against the stone. He took a deep breath and breeched the doorway, arms tense and hands curled into fists.

Two indeed.

They straightened from their crouch beside the flames, eyes wide.

In a single glance, honed by years of training, he took in the age, the build, the attitude of each, along with the surroundings.

They were boys, afraid of the battle raging below, afraid of the Roman in their tower. The fire was smaller than he expected. There was little on the platform aside from the pile of fuel, some pots, and what was probably the boys' provisions for their shift.

All this he saw in the instant that the two boys backed away.

"We are taking the lighthouse!" he shouted, hoping to intimidate further. "If you value your lives, you will find a place to hide!" He shifted to his right, clearing a path to the doorway.

One boy, the younger of the two, darted around the fire and disappeared through the door. The other seemed caught between duty and fear.

"The light cannot go out," he said, his lip trembling.

Bellus stalked around the central flame, summoning up a murderous glare and drawing his sword.

The boy's eyes widened in terror. He ran around the other side of the fire and took to the steps.

Bellus sheathed his sword, greatly relieved that he had not been forced to use it. He took stock of the platform. The fire crackled over the charred pieces of wood that had been brought up on the lift, and turned the dung chips to glowing embers. The chamber smelled of the fuel and of the smoke that curled upward through a small opening in the roof. He followed it to where it obscured the stars. The entire chamber was walled with windows, and he allowed himself only a brief glimpse at the harbor so terrifyingly far below.

The boats, the water, even the fires, seemed to belong to another world. He turned back to his task.

Though Sophia had explained that the curved bronze mirror on a track around the fire was responsible for magnifying the flames, it still surprised him to see how small the fire was. To think that this whole mighty structure upon which he stood, a wonder among nations, existed solely to house a fire sufficient for cooking only a few pheasants at a time!

But it was a testimony to the ingenuity of man, to make much out of so little.

And now he must kill it.

He searched the platform for the means, and found, not surprisingly, two huge pots of water standing ready for an emergency. He dragged them both to the edge of the burnt-brick pit that housed the fire, then sat back on his haunches and took a deep breath.

Do it, Bellus. You must.

He put his hands to the pots, but then looked into the flames and saw Sophia's eyes, deep and angry, staring back. He felt physically sick.

And then he tipped them forward.

Water gushed from the clay, poured over the fire, pooled in the pit. The flames sizzled, trying angrily to consume the water. Were consumed themselves instead.

Only a few embers remained. They would not glow for long.

Bellus righted the pots clumsily. One tipped and fell. He slumped beside it, smoke and pain burning his eyes.

Had the fire glowed every night since before Sophia's birth?

He feared somehow that the death of the fire signaled a death for Sophia as well.

FORTY-FIVE

The color was returning to Sosigenes's cheeks. Sophia knelt beside him, her hand on his arm, while Diogenes finished tending his cut and twisted bandages around his neck. She glanced toward the door every few seconds, waiting.

"I must look the fool," Sosigenes croaked, eliciting a laugh of relief from his group of friends.

Ares slipped into the room and Sophia jumped to her feet and crossed to meet him at the door.

"He did not come with me," Ares said, shaking his head. "He climbed the tower."

Sophia looked upward, as though she could trace his path.

"I told Bellus I would take him to you." Ares's voice was strained. "I don't know why he didn't follow."

"He is here for the light, Ares. Not for me."

"He cares for you, Sophia—"

She smiled and drew him to the wall. "Leave Bellus to his work." Her breathing grew rapid and shallow, her throat tight. "We have other things to speak of."

She had kept her hand on his arm. He looked to it and then back to her face, his expression open but puzzled.

"Ares," she began, and her voice caught. "I—I have something to tell you." Tears rose, choked her throat, spilled to her cheeks.

"Sophia!" Ares held both her arms now. "What is it? Tell me."

She was sobbing now, trying to stop it, trying to speak, to unveil the truth, the impossible truth. "Pothinus," she managed to whisper.

Ares's grip on her arms tightened. "Did he harm you?"

She shook her head. "He told me something. Something I never knew."

"He would say anything to hurt you, Sophia. Do not—"

"No, no. He thought I knew. He—he didn't know—" She covered her mouth, felt the tears drip over her hand.

Ares was nearly crying now himself, and he pulled Sophia to his chest.

"Ares," she sobbed, her voice muffled against him. "Ares, you are my son."

He pulled back, looked down on her, wiped her face with his hand. "Sophia?" His voice was a whisper, as though he dared not take her words for their apparent meaning.

She blinked up at him and brushed tears from her chin. Her shoulders heaved. "I have never told you all of it. How I lost my baby and my husband in one night, to a storm at sea." She was stroking his arm now, unconscious of the gesture. "We were shipwrecked. My family, Sosigenes, Pothinus. All of us. I was washed up on Antikythera, along with some others. Pothinus found his way to Crete. My husband and my baby—I never knew where the sea had taken their bodies." The last words came with laughter, and Ares pulled her close again, as though certain she had lost her mind.

She pulled away, her heart racing. "Listen to me, Ares. My baby—he did not die as I thought. A sailor rescued him, one with a disfigured face. Weeks later, that same sailor, he came at night to the lighthouse."

Ares studied her eyes, falling into the spell of her story.

"I did not know why he came that night, but now I know. He came to bring my baby back to me." She gripped his arms.

"I do not understand. What became of your son?"

She smiled through the tears. "A servant woman claimed him as her own. Made me believe she had hidden her pregnancy. I thought the dreadful man I had seen that night was her lover."

Ares swallowed and took a step backward, his eyes dark and his own breathing shallow now.

Those eyes. How did I never see how like Kallias's they were?

"That servant's name was Eleni, Ares. She claimed you as her own. She—she took you from me, my own son. My own son." The tears fell afresh, matched this time by the tears of her baby boy who stood before her, tall and strong and so much alive.

And then he was in her arms at last, and the pain and the loneliness and the isolation fell away in an embrace that bore the sorrow of twenty years and the hope of the future.

Sosigenes was there beside them then, smiling in happy confusion at master and servant. Sophia laughed and cried at once and pulled him into their circle.

"Sosigenes," she said, taking his hand and the hand of Ares together, "I would like you to meet my son. Leonidas."

Ares's blinked at the unfamiliar name. She laughed again with the wondrous irony of the name's meaning. "Yes, *son of the lion.* But we will call you Ares, I think. *Warrior.* Your father would have liked that."

Sosigenes still smiled but glanced between the two. "I do not understand—"

"I barely understand it myself, my friend," she said, and then retold her story with more laughter than tears this time. When it was done they embraced again, all three.

And for one accustomed to isolation, Sophia found herself unable to let go of these two precious ones.

"Sophia," Ares finally said, pulling away, then laughed and shook his head. "Mother," he whispered, causing Sophia's tears to flow again. "What of the Romans? Of Bellus?"

She breathed deeply. "I told you, Ares. He is here because of the light, under Caesar's orders no doubt."

Ares shook his head. "I do not know his intent, but I can tell you that he is here for you."

She dismissed the thought with a shake of her head.

They stood huddled together, and now Ares and Sosigenes faced her, each with a hand on her arm.

"Sophia," Sosigenes said, "I do not know if the boy—if your son—is right about the Roman. But I do know that your heart has only begun to open here. There is more, much more."

She swallowed and tried to catch her breath.

"You can feel it, Sophia, I know you can. The lady of the lighthouse is beginning to know what it means to find a community with others. You must embrace it fully now."

Sophia tried to pull away, but the two would not allow it. Her mouth had gone dry and her hands trembled.

"Who else, Sophia? Who else is calling you to relationship?" Sosigenes eyes were twin fires, burning into her soul.

She thought of all he had taught her. "Your God," she whispered, a tiny bit of belief taking root.

"Yes, my dear girl." He touched her cheek. "And you must open your heart to His love, to His atonement, to His forgiveness."

She could barely speak the words, the foundation of all her doubt and fear. Her eyes shifted to the floor and she breathed out the awful truth, feeling its piercing pain. "I do not deserve to be loved."

Sosigenes smiled and pulled her to himself. "No, my dear Sophia. You do not deserve it. Not one of us does. And that is the glorious wonder of it all."

Something within her grew still and silent then, as though she had entered a holy place and found that it was her own heart. It had been filled with the words of the Jews' history and prophecies she had read, with the stories of Sosigenes, which had beaten back all the deadness of her own religion with a living light she saw in the old man's eyes and heard in his prayers. She nodded, unable to speak, but knowing this was the only way. Only a love that would love her first.

"And I believe," Sosigenes said, pointing upward, "that another calls you forward as well."

"He cannot," she said, too quickly, with a denial borne of instinct.

Ares smiled. "You must find out."

Sosigenes nodded his agreement. "It is time."

They each embraced her, as though commissioning her to battle. She felt herself grow numb with fear, stunned at what she contemplated.

"Go," Ares whispered. "You must go."

And she did. She crossed the room, opened the door. Slipped from the North Wing, through the courtyard. Found the ramp. Began the climb.

The numbness gave way, leaving every sense heightened. She felt each step, heard the battle that continued in the harbor. She smelled the musty stone of the tower, tasted the salt of her own tears.

And she climbed.

Past her private chamber where she had hidden for so long. Shedding her isolation with each painful step. *The keenest sorrow is to recognize ourselves as the sole cause of all our adversities.*

Yes, she felt that keen sorrow. Felt it swell in devastation through her heart, yet somehow give strength to her climb.

She was nearly to her roses when she heard the yelling.

It bubbled up from below, echoing through the central shaft. They had breached the Base, had entered the tower itself.

She slipped out to her garden platform. The roses were open to the moonlight tonight, their blooms spread wide, so vulnerable and so beautiful. The scent of them drowned all others, as though the city were not filled with smoke.

She stood at the doorway, listening.

The voices below were too muddied together to distinguish words. But they were moving upward. She waited, her heart pounding.

Their shouted conversation grew clear. Greek, with some Egyptian woven through. Not Latin. Not Romans.

But they would find a Roman when they reached the beacon chamber.

She strained to hear. How many?

Two, she thought. Or perhaps three.

She searched the platform for a weapon. An unlit torch. Several heavy terra cotta pots.

Should she yell to warn Bellus? Or remain silent, to attack in surprise? Her hands fluttered in indecision, then settled on the torch.

They would have two tiers to climb after her attack. That should be time enough for Bellus to ready himself.

She waited.

They pounded upward, heedless that she stood outside the door at the top of the ramp, the torch held out from her body like an oily club.

Slap, slap, slap. Their sandals beat an even rhythm. Sophia pictured them circling upward, measured their progress.

She took a deep breath, adjusted her grip on the torch. And then the first came into view.

She swung. And she yelled.

The Egyptian soldier dropped like a stone thrown into the sea.

But it was not a second Egyptian soldier who violated the purity of her rose garden.

The entrance filled with the tall figure and patrician face of Pothinus.

Sophia's torch dipped. She jerked it aloft again.

"Come, Sophia," Pothinus said. "We are not brutish soldiers, we are scholars. I have come for the Proginosko and nothing more. No one need be hurt."

Another soldier appeared behind Pothinus. Sophia raised the torch but he caught the end with both hands and wrenched it from her.

She scowled. "I would sooner let the Romans have it!"

Pothinus laughed. "Yes, one in particular, I hear. But I doubt even the Proginosko could purchase the affections of a Roman for you."

The truth of his words pierced the vulnerable place in her heart, but still she had hope for the scholars and the Proginosko. She could not defeat Pothinus herself.

But she had opened her lighthouse to another, one who might be their only salvation.

FORTY-SIX

Cleopatra stood on the roof of the royal palace with the harbor and the city burning beneath. Her eyes were not on the flaming ships, however. Nor the riots in the streets, nor even the lighthouse and its yellow flame.

Instead, she watched the man at her side, his chiseled profile fit for sculpture, his shoulders held back and his chest out.

"How goes the battle?" she asked, not taking her eyes from him.

His brow puckered. "We have them running."

She did not know whether his words were truth or mere bravado. With all the scheming and backstabbing and even royal assassinations she had witnessed in her privileged life, Cleopatra was still unfamiliar with war.

She shifted between overflowing flower pots to get closer to the wall. "The warehouses are burning."

"Hmm." Caesar's response told her nothing.

"So much fire."

He glanced at her. "Do not blame your burning city on me. Your crazed citizens are the ones shooting their flaming arrows as though they are nothing but children's toys."

Cleopatra held her tongue. His mood was dark.

Her mind played with possible outcomes.

If the Romans should fall to the incoming Egyptian army and the city's mob, would she be able to convince the people of her right to rule alongside her brother? Or would her father's wishes, his will, be disregarded?

Caesar crossed his arms over his chest and growled at some loss below.

If the Romans crushed the Egyptian army, would Caesar let her stand at his side? After all these weeks together, still she could not be certain of his feelings.

It is all waiting now. Between two armies, her fate hung suspended, uncertain.

She could do nothing now to sway the affections of the people. But she was not powerless. Not by far.

She sidled closer to Caesar, wrapped a warm hand around his upper arm, still crossed and tensed.

"We must finish this tonight," he said. "The army is close, too close."

"The Egyptian fleet was foolish to attack without their army in place."

Caesar laughed, a condescending sort of chuckle that made her shoulders tighten. "Silly girl."

She realized her mistake. Caesar had engineered the start of the battle early, to weaken the fleet and the city before the army's arrival. She tossed her hair back over her shoulder and studied the chaos below, breathing so hard she felt her nostrils flare.

From the palace roof the battle sounds were muffled, and a view of the entire harbor was afforded to her. She held her fingers aloft and formed a circle that encompassed all she could see.

Would that my fingers were a net I could draw around it all. A net drawn tight to secure her world, control it.

"Your friend is causing us some trouble." He jutted his chin toward the lighthouse.

She dropped her hands. A flower brushed at her side and she tore it from its stem. "The lighthouse has always been Sophia's duty to preserve."

"Sophia." He huffed out her name in derision. "You are young and naïve, Cleopatra. Too young to know when you have given too much power to someone who should not hold it."

Cleopatra shredded the red flower petals and let them float to the rooftop. "Or perhaps I have secured the loyalty of those who *already* hold power."

He looked sideways at her, his eyes narrowed. "No matter. She will not hold it long."

"What have you done?"

He shrugged. "The light needs to be extinguished tonight. Our ships are all in the harbor. We do not need to guide in our enemy's reinforcements."

Cleopatra followed his gaze out to the lighthouse. Would he have Sophia killed? She wavered between the need to remain at Caesar's side and the instinct to warn Sophia.

I need her. No one else loves me like she.

Caesar did not comment when she slipped from his side and crossed to the steps from the rooftop.

In her own chamber, Cleopatra lit an oil lamp and pulled out papyrus and ink. She leaned over the desk and scratched out a warning, then blew on the words to dry them. Some of the ink spread with the force of her breath. No matter. The message would be received.

She rolled the papyrus, tied it with a leather cord, and went to the door, intending to call for a servant to deliver it.

The door burst inward.

Cleopatra cried out, stumbled backward, dropped her missive.

They were Egyptian, that much she saw in the flash of dark skin and white skirts and angry eyes. She smelled the odor of sweat and battle, heard their exultant shout at finding her, and then their hands were on her arms like iron clamps.

They dragged her from the room. She did not go quietly.

In the hall outside her chamber she saw two guards in a pool of their mingled blood, throats slit.

Fear mixed with bile in her chest.

She dug her heels to the stone, pulled at their arms and yelled. They clawed at her, trying to keep their grip.

One of them let go to cut down another palace guard. But the guard hacked her attacker's arm, before the sword went through him, and left him unable to hold both sword and Cleopatra.

The other grabbed her around the waist and flung her over his shoulder.

She pounded his back with her fists and kicked her feet into his gut.

They ran through the palace hall, and the memory surged of Apollodorus, bringing her to Caesar, rolled in a carpet, and slung on his back.

So long ago.

Footsteps pounded behind them. She tried to lift her head.

A shout, a clash of swords, a thrashing of legs and clothes and hair.

She was on the ground. Eyes closed. Breath coming in gasps.

Unhurt.

She bolted upright, swept the hall with her gaze.

Her attackers lay dead. Three Roman legionaries wiped their swords.

And Caesar knelt before her and swept her up in his arms. She closed her eyes and leaned against him.

"Are you hurt?" He touched her arms, her legs, her belly.

"I am well. Thank you. For rescuing me."

He crushed her to himself. "I could not live if you had been taken from me."

She smiled in his embrace and closed her eyes, a warmth spreading through her.

The road ahead stretched out with some uncertainty, but there in the arms of Rome's most powerful man, Cleopatra knew her world was forever changed. She was learning new lessons in power now, and in the future she would wield the power with sure and steady hands.

She thought of the scribbled message to Sophia, still lying on the floor of her chamber. But it was only a fleeting thought, for in truth, she did not need Sophia any longer.

Caesar is mine.

FORTY-SEVEN

From his dark and smoky vigil beside the extinguished light-house flame, Bellus heard the cry below him.

He leaped to his feet, sword drawn in one fluid motion, ears strained to hear any approach.

But the fight was far below, and only the strange acoustics of the lighthouse had carried the sound to him, as through a huge, vertical tunnel.

He stood inside the doorway of the uppermost tier, ready to spin down the steps.

Had the two servants brought help?

He tightened his grip on his sword, his jaw clenched. If he allowed them to light the fire, more troops would come and every-one in the lighthouse would be slaughtered. Could he kill a few innocents to save many? To save Sophia?

But then another cry shot upward to him, and he knew the voice.

It was hers.

He took the steps in pairs, twisting downward through the circular tier, then through the next doorway and down the steps of the octagonal. He slowed. The angry words were close now.

In the rose garden.

The thought was incongruous, somehow.

He braced his feet on the bottom step of the second tier, his back to the wall. Slowed his breathing. Listened.

A cultured laugh, arrogant and condescending. A mocking comment about himself, he suspected, that hardened the muscles of his arms and tightened his jaw.

A moan came from the floor near Bellus's hiding place. Another voice joined the conversation, this one dulled with pain, near Bellus's feet. "Kill her, Pothinus. Be done with it."

Bellus flexed his fingers around the hilt of his gladius. He pivoted off the step, jumped over the figure that lay doubled on the floor. His blood surged, hot and fierce, in his veins.

Sophia saw him there behind Pothinus and another soldier. Her face was pale as the full moon, her eyes dark. A rush of desire to protect her filled his chest.

The Egyptian soldier whirled, in his hand an unlit torch. He swung it outward from his body. Bellus stepped to the side, out of range. He felt the thorns of blood-red roses prick his calves. Pothinus retreated to hide behind Sophia.

The Egyptian lifted the torch above his head, and Bellus felt a twinge of regret that it was not Pothinus whom he must kill.

The torch crashed down, but he dodged. Sophia cried out. Bellus spun an arc around the Egyptian and brought his sword between them, a sure and steady defense.

He saw Sophia move toward them, behind the Egyptian.

No, Sophia. Step back.

The Egyptian sensed his moment of fear, saw his distraction, knew the cause. He grinned, then swung the torch backward.

The heavy wood caught Sophia in the stomach. Bellus heard the air whoosh from her lungs, saw her crumple over the club.

Battle fury filled him.

Before the Egyptian could regroup for another thrust, Bellus ran at him. A scream tore from his throat. He drove the end of his sword into the Egyptian's middle. The man's eyes bulged and Bellus yanked the sword from his gut, breathing out his revenge.

Sophia lay on her side on the platform amid her roses, watching him with silent, smoky eyes.

His mind and heart churned with fear and with regret. *Sophia.*

He heard his sword clatter to the floor. He fell forward to Sophia, his eyes on hers.

But the emotions had made him foolish. Behind him, the scrape of sandals on wood. He turned only a moment before the second Egyptian fell upon him with a short dagger.

He scrambled for where his sword should have been sheathed. Not there.

The Egyptian's blade dug into his shoulder.

Other side. Pugio. Fingers closed around it.

Up from below, into the side of his attacker.

The blade was too short for death to be instant. The Egyptian's fury carried him past the pain and he raised his own knife again.

From deep within, a yell of rage raced through Bellus's chest, his throat. He brought his forearms against the man's chest and shoved.

Back, back across the platform. Through the doorway. Past the steps upward. Past the ramp downward.

To the center shaft. Still he pushed and the Egyptian scrambled backward, until they slammed against the low wall that formed the shaft. Bellus stared into the whites of the man's eyes until they tipped away with his head and shoulders, then were joined by his chest, his trunk, his legs. The Egyptian screamed as he fell, and the sound of it filled the shaft, as though he pitched straight into the Underworld itself.

Bellus fell against the wall, caught his breath. Replaced his pugio. Then stumbled back to the platform.

His shoulder bled, but the Egyptian's knife had glanced off the muscle there.

But Sophia. *Oh, Sophia.*

Pothinus jerked his head left and right, as though searching for another way off the platform. Below them, Bellus heard the second centuria crash through the wooden door. Bellus fought the conflict for a moment between revenge and concern for Sophia, then left Pothinus to the Roman legionaries that even now filled the Base.

He ran to where she lay, her breath shallow and eyes fluttering. Pothinus pushed past them both and took to the ramp.

"Where are you hurt?" Bellus ran his hands over her arms, her legs, searching for blood and finding none.

She swallowed. "I—I do not know. My stomach. My ch— chest." Her breath caught.

Bellus dared not turn her. He felt carefully for broken ribs, fearing a pierced lung. She did not cry out at his touch, which eased his concern.

But something was wrong. Her face seemed even more bloodless than before.

"The moon is full," she whispered. "He will finish tonight."

"Don't speak, Sophia." Bellus stood and rushed to the platform's wall. Beneath him, he could see the harbor battle beginning to slow but not yet won. He could see the island, the heptastadion. The pocket of fighting near the village was nothing to what he could see was coming. It looked as though Caesar had released several hundred soldiers to the island.

He returned to Sophia, knelt beside her, and gripped her hand. "There is no way to bring a physician yet. Rest now."

She lifted her free hand to touch his face, smiled, and tried to breathe deeply. "You came back," she whispered.

Bellus wrapped his own trembling hand around her fingers and held them to his cheek. "Where else would I go?"

The strength of her arm failed and he lowered her hand to her side. His eyes filled with tears borne of fear and of longing.

Sophia moistened her lips, tried to speak.

"Rest, my lady," he said, his voice thick in his throat.

She shook her head. "I must tell you." The words were soft, like a fragile silk thread spun through the night, like the petals of the flowers that surrounded them.

"Tell me," he said.

Her chest rose and fell with labored breaths. "I never thought . . ." Her face twisted in pain, and Bellus gripped her hand. Her words came in a rush then, as though she feared she would run out of time to say them. "I never thought I could love again." She smiled, full and sweet. "Lucius, you taught me to love again."

He kissed her fingers, tears blurring his vision of her.

She spoke again. "I know—I know you came for the light—"

He moaned, her hand still held to his lips. "I am so sorry, Sophia. I had to put it out. Caesar would have killed you all—"

She pressed her fingers weakly against his mouth. "I know. I cannot save everyone. That is the past."

Her own eyes filled and overflowed. He brushed away the tears that ran along her temples. "It was not your fault, Sophia. What happened to Kallias and your baby. It was not your fault."

She smiled. "So much to tell," she whispered. Then sucked in breath as though a fresh injury assailed her.

"Not now," Bellus said, though he knew it could be forever.

She nodded, and he knew she thought the same. "It is better this way."

"I cannot live without you, Sophia."

She smiled again, her lips white. "You will go back to Rome. A hero. Go back to your beautiful woman."

He frowned. "What woman?"

"Valeria. Your letter." Her eyes fluttered. "She is beautiful, you said."

Bellus lifted her head to cradle it in his hand. "No, Sophia! I never—When I threw that letter at you, it was to prove that outward beauty is nothing. She is vapid and selfish and stupid. You could not think that I would want—"

Sophia's eyes closed, but her face seemed to light from within and her smile came from a place of peace.

Bellus pulled her upper body to his lap, leaned over her precious face, growing still. "No, Sophia. No." He bent his head to hers, kissed her with all the longing in his heart. "Do not leave me. Not now."

Her body relaxed in his arms and his tears flowed over her like an anointing.

"I love you," he whispered. "Sophia, I love you."

He knew nothing then, except that when he looked upon her, he saw that she seemed transformed into the most lovely creature he had ever beheld. Like a goddess come to earth, come to enchant him, to steal his heart and capture his soul and leave him nothing more than a shell, aching for the beauty he had once known.

Above them, the moon poured its full face upon the open roses, and the sky sprinkled dew like tears.

FORTY-EIGHT

L ow voices. Muffled by Egyptian flax. Pinpricks of light. More darkness.

Sleep.

Hands probing. Whispering. Light and dark fluttering. Falling, falling. Darkness again.

Warmth. Sun-warmth on her face. Heavy, heavy lids struggling to open to the morning sun, to the night's torches, to the sun again.

And then a face sharpening into focus before her, a beloved face, smiling, smiling at her.

"Ares." Her voice was dry as the western desert, her tongue thick and her throat burning with a thousand suns.

"Drink," he said.

Watered wine moistened her lips, gentle as morning rain. She sucked at it greedily.

Time passed, she knew not how much. When she awoke again, the afternoon sun slanted through the windows of her private chamber.

Her wakening did not go unnoticed. Ares was beside her in a moment, kneeling at her couch, touching her hair. Sosigenes stood behind him. At the edge of her vision, Diogenes.

"How long?" she croaked.

Diogenes bustled forward. "You've been sleeping two days, Sophia." He laid a hand on her forehead. "We had some trouble with fever, but it seems past. Your injuries were all of the internal sort. Not much we could do but watch and wait." His eyes softened. "And pray."

She lifted her hand to weakly grip his. "Thank you."

He snorted. "Do not thank me. Thank these others." He extended a hand to Ares and Sosigenes. "And your Roman. They hauled me up to that the rose garden of yours like a pile of dung fuel on that cursed lift. Imagine!"

Sophia smiled.

"Do not laugh. They brought you down in the same manner, my lady!" He shook his head at the indignity, then turned his head to a noise at the door.

She tried to follow his gaze but did not have the strength. The men before her backed away.

And then he was there beside her, on his knees, her face in his hands.

"Speak to me, Sophia," he whispered. "Say my name."

She reached for him. "Lucius. Pilus Prior Lucius Aurelius Bellus."

He threw his head back and laughed, as though he had held the laughter in clay pots for many years.

Ares knelt beside them.

"Lucius," she said, but put her hand to her son's face.

"I know," he laughed again. "Your son. Back in your arms."

Tears sprang to her eyes. "Ares, bring me the engraved box on my desk."

He returned a moment later. She struggled to sit up, and the two men helped her. Ares laid the box in her lap. She lifted the lid, studied its contents.

"For you, Ares." She brought out the granite device and the little marble to place in his hands. "Your father made it. He was a good man." She found his eyes with her own. "I do not know how I never saw him in you."

Ares's eyes shown as he took the device.

Sophia reached into the box again and brought out a small object. She held it to Bellus, suddenly uncertain.

He smiled at the blue scarab stone in her hand, then closed his own fingers over it. "We do not need luck, Sophia. Someone greater than us watches over our affairs."

The door scraped open again, and more men poured into the room. Sophia smiled at each of the scholars who had made the climb to see her. She held out a hand as they clustered around her.

The room was so full. Overflowing with people. Full of color and light, laughter and life. Sophia fell back against her cushions, and contentment and belonging spread through her, warmed her.

The men talked among themselves, but Bellus's attention was all for her.

"What of the battle?" she asked him.

He nodded, his face grim. "The fighting has been fierce, with many losses on both sides. But when word of Roman reinforcements marching around the Delta came to the city, the people yielded. The Egyptian army still stands afar off. They cannot win."

Sophia nodded, her heart heavy for the people, but glad the battle had ended. "Any word of Cleopatra?"

"She presides at Caesar's side in the palace. Her brother Ptolemy has been sent to join his army."

"A death sentence," Sophia said.

"Perhaps. We must wait to see what becomes of Egypt in the hands of Cleopatra and Julius Caesar."

"Pothinus?"

"Executed. Yesterday."

Sophia sighed and laid her head back. "So much death."

Bellus smiled sadly but glanced at Ares and the camaraderie of the twelve men in the room, then smiled.

"And also life."

FORTY-NINE

Sophia was still thinking of life five days later, as she stood in the shade of the Museum's portico, surrounded by friends and by family, and with Bellus at her side, ready to recite the vows she never dreamed she would speak again. She wore a dress of finer silk than any she'd ever owned, and the female servants in the lighthouse had insisted on weaving flowers through her hair and layering jewels on her neck.

The city was damaged but healing, as she herself was. The Library fires had destroyed many scrolls, and the warehouse fires even more. No one would forget the night that Alexandria burned.

But as she looked across the harbor to the lighthouse, its beacon lit by the sun once again, she knew that as the city would never be the same, she was also forever changed.

She would return to the lighthouse, but it would not be to hide. Already she had plans to open the tower to visitors, to give others a chance to be awed by the breathtaking view. She had learned that if she did not open her heart to love, hate would take it by force.

On the street a few steps below, she watched Sosigenes speak with a dark-skinned man seated on a camel, with a pack of traders on camels behind him. Sosigenes patted the man's leg and nodded, then turned and climbed the steps toward her.

"They leave tonight and will be across to the East before the next full moon. It will be safe there."

Sophia watched the trader move away, a large pack secured to his camel. "Will they know how to use it?"

Sosigenes turned to watch the traders. "Do not fear. The magi there have ways to search the skies for knowledge, ways that even I do not understand."

Bellus wrapped an arm around Sophia's waist but spoke to Sosigenes. "What do they search for?"

The old man's smile held the riddles of the ages. "For the Long Awaited One. The consolation of Israel." He lifted his eyes to the sky. "I have waited for the Messiah for many years myself, but I believe, my friends, that I may not have much longer to wait."

Sophia barely noticed when another joined them, but Bellus turned her to face a man she had only met once. Julius Caesar stood on the portico, a confident smile on his thin lips, his hair combed forward over his forehead. "Your *corona vallaris*, Pilus Prior Bellus," he said, and held a gold crown to Bellus. "Well deserved. And I am certain you will honor Rome with your continuing duty here in Alexandria. For another year, at least. Until your discharge."

Bellus closed his hand around the crown and nodded.

Caesar turned to Sophia and to Sosigenes beside her. "It seems I have been imprudent in my attempt to waylay Alexandria's scholars," he said with a bow to Sosigenes. "Your citizens have made that clear. And someone else"—he looked to a chariot that awaited him in the street—"has assured me that this magical device of yours was nothing more than a ruse created by Pothinus as an excuse to attack the lighthouse."

Sophia looked to the chariot, to Cleopatra who lounged inside. The queen gave her a small wave, a tiny smile.

Sophia nodded to her former student and smiled in return.

"Still," Caesar said to Sosigenes, "I should like to speak with you soon about rectifying this ridiculous calendar of ours."

Sosigenes bowed, and then Caesar was gone, down the steps and into the chariot beside Cleopatra. It lurched forward, and Cleo was lost to Sophia's view.

She turned her attention back to those on the portico.

Bellus. Ares. Sosigenes. The scholars.

Husband. Son. Father. Community.

The mistaken belief that she must make herself worthy before she could be loved had been her curse for many years. But as Bellus lifted her hand to his lips and smiled, she knew that it was only the love that had the power to change her. The love of Bellus, of the One God, and of the Redeemer to come.

As the curse that had held her captive for so long fell away, she breathed deeply of the Alexandrian air and spread her arms wide to embrace them all, to share the flame within her, and to see herself reflected in their eyes.

Finally free.

Fully loved.

In a lofty tower set high above a teeming city,
There lived a solitary woman
Whose guilt and pain had long ago turned to ugliness.
And when the ugliness became its own prison,
And the pain of rejection too much to bear,
Loneliness seemed the only answer.

Until there came the whisper of Beauty
The promise of Love
In one so unlikely she nearly missed it.

He did not ask her to change first,
Before he would love her.
For in truth, she could not.

No, he loved her as she was,
Because he chose to.

And it was the loving
That transformed her.

Author's Note

The list of the Seven Wonders of the Ancient World evolved slowly, from their first mention by the Greek historian Herodotus in 450 BC, to the poet Antipater in the second century BC. Though only the oldest of the seven, the Great Pyramid of Giza, still stands, their mystique has endured, each a wonder of engineering and a testimony to the creativity of ancient peoples.

The Lighthouse of Alexandria was built by Sostratus the Cnidian around 250 BC, and was the first lighthouse in history. At about four hundred feet, it was among the tallest man-made structures in the world for millennia, second only to Khufu's and Khafre's pyramids. Currently the tallest lighthouse in the world is in Yokohama, Japan, and is only 348 feet tall. The Lighthouse of Alexandria stood until a series of earthquakes in the Middle Ages eroded its foundation. Its blocks were used to build the medieval fort that stands at the tip of the island even now.

The story of Beauty and the Beast has been often told through literature and film, and I hope you enjoyed my variation on this theme. It endures, I believe, because the frightening knowledge of our own unworthiness and the longing for a love that will transform is buried deep within each human heart.

And this is how God loves. Not based on our beauty or our achievements, but simply because He chooses to love. And it is His love that changes us and makes us beautiful.

Guardian of the Flame is a fictional story built around many historical facts. If you'd like to read more about Caesar and Cleopatra's relationship, the Proginosko, the Alexandrian War, and the harbor fires that burned the Library, please visit me at www.TLHigley.com. Experience the sights and sounds of my travels in Alexandria, learn what is fact and what is fiction within the book, and take a few moments to share your heart with me. I love to hear from readers about the adventure of their own lives!

T. L. Higley on the site of the Lighthouse of Alexandria, where a medieval fort stands today, using many of the blocks from the Lighthouse.

Another Exciting Title by
T.L. Higley

Nominated for a
2009 Christy Award

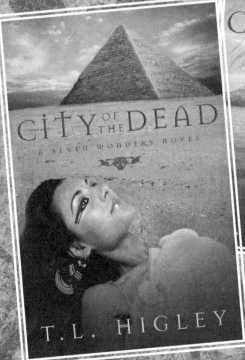

B&H
FICTION

Pure Enjoyment™

www.PureEnjoyment.com